Men of the Mountains

JESSE STUART

Men
of the
Mountains

With a Foreword by
H. Edward Richardson

THE UNIVERSITY PRESS OF KENTUCKY

To Martha and Whit
who published my first story

Cover illustration by Barbara McCord

Copyright 1941 by E. P. Dutton & Co., Inc.

ISBN: 0-8131-0143-3
Library of Congress Cataloging in Publication information on p. 351

Copyright © 1979 by The University Press of Kentucky

Scholarly publisher for the Commonwealth
serving Berea College, Centre College of Kentucky,
Eastern Kentucky University, The Filson Club,
Georgetown College, Kentucky Historical Society,
Kentucky State University, Morehead State University,
Murray State University, Northern Kentucky University,
Transylvania University, University of Kentucky,
University of Louisville, and Western Kentucky University.

Editorial and Sales Offices: Lexington, Kentucky 40506

CONTENTS

FOREWORD

LIFE, ANIMATE EXISTENCE, ABSORBS JESSE STUART. Never is it more
vital than when juxtaposed with death, hence the contrasting mo-
tifs of life and death permeating his work. The hills, he tells us in
the title story of *Men of the Mountains*, are where men *live*. They
"curse the mountains," but they love them too, as they fell the
timber, clear the land of stumps and rocks, and plow deep furrows
to the sound of popping roots. The crops may fail, but hillmen do
not fear the mountains, the molds in which their lives have been
cast. Always the hills have fed them. The intimate rapport existing
between man and earth is of greater significance than any single
lifetime. This kinship exists in all seasons, has existed through generations from the old people, whose revenants walk in the moon
shadows, to whatever transient present life may concern. Hence,
the hillman's life has been tinctured with family lore, mountain
customs, a storied and nearly palpable presence of old people long
gone, and persisting regional legends of which the briars and stones
and trees are enduring monuments.

Jesse Stuart's world exists in dimensions of real geography and
elaborate imagination. Not unlike Thomas Wolfe and William
Faulkner, Stuart moves easily between autobiography and fiction
and often does not bother to distinguish one from the other.
Greenup County blends into Greenwood County, and W-Hollow
in both fiction and fact is subject to the proprietorship of the bard
of Appalachia. His is always a real world where even the heat of a
July day is not left to generalities but "hot as a roasted potato," and
dust rises like "white soup-beans." It is a place of "sun-scorched
buff-colored clouds." Wind moves in "dry burning sheets," and

7

Nature has emotion as well as a voice when cornstalks are "crying for water . . . whispering—to the hot wind." In apt idiom Pa says, "A awful drouth."

Devotion to hard agrarian labor is the core of Thorny Kirk's philosophy of life in the story "For the Love of Brass," a core of meaning that finds expression in paternal love and loyalty toward a miracle-worker with a hoe, an itinerant laborer, who turns out to be a compulsive thief of brass. The thief takes even the landowner's brass rings from harness hames and Mrs. Kirk's brass from her washboards. Yet the Kirks sadly await the prodigal's return, for love and loyalty forgive much.

Lyricism and nostalgia characterize "New-Ground Corn" and "This Is the Place." Of the first, Edgar Lee Masters wrote Stuart in 1941, "I read . . . your story . . . and it is a marvel. It's beyond praise, and no more to say nothing!" Authenticity of dialogue in "One of God's Oddlings" deepens the feeling of oneness with the earth. Working close to the land, almost ritualistically the farmer chews and smokes its tobacco and drinks its liquid corn until his eyes have "a far-away eagle look in them."

Never is the hill farmer closer to his religion than when his shoes are in the dust. The moment is both elemental and spiritual, primordial and Edenic, for man is like a clod of earth into which God breathed life "as wind is breathed into the mule through his dry dusty nostrils," Stuart writes, "and he becomes a mirey beast." Biblical echoes give way to local-color epithet as both man and mule succumb to temptation of the fragrant weed, surprising the earthy young Finn: "Well—I'm a suck-egg mule. . . . I didn't believe a brute of any kind liked tobacco."

Character is delineated with sharp authenticity in "Hell's Acre," a story of a mountain feud and courtship. Stuart writes of the narrator's mother, "The weight of the pipe on the long stem sorta jimmied the pipe in Ma's mouth since she'd lost some of her front teeth." Dialect and idiom never appear merely in charming isolation in Stuart's work but combine functionally to illuminate both character and theme, as in superstition and marriage. "Don't sweep around me, Ma," Adger says. "Leave the dirt on the floor around my chear."

"Hair," the story of Jersey Harkreader's pursuit and marriage of

Lima Whitehall, is a masterpiece of comedy; the first-person narrator of Plum Grove speaks in a rhythmic Appalachian dialect as
purely rendered as that of Mark Twain's Hannibal, Missouri. "They
were kindly rich people," Jersey says, or "They think they're better'n everybody else in the whole wide world—have to watch about
getting rain in their noses." About mountain religion Jersey admits
that he saws the fiddle, plays set-back, dances, and may not have
his name "on the Lamb's Book of Life," but he will not be denied
the earthly pleasures of the mountain church: "I just up and go to
see and to be seen—that's what we all go for. It is a place to go and
about the only place we got to go." Stuart's intense identification
with his droll and obsessed narrator, and his sensuous imagery and
sustained evocation of the Plum Grove hill people and their ways,
make "Hair" a memorably different kind of love story.

   Of the other stories, "Betwixt Life and Death," which centers on
a corpse kept from burial for months while "funeralizing" parties
go on, contends with Milton Rugoff's observation that there is in
Stuart little of "the rawness of the Southern etchings of Erskine
Caldwell nor the horrifying decadence of Faulkner. Next to Caldwell, Stuart seems lyrical and classic and next to Faulkner, whole-
some and conventional." Yet with few exceptions Stuart's stories
are thematically more varied and of a more durable texture than
Caldwell's, and they are more impromptu and less obfuscating,
more gentled with humor if less Gothic, and invariably more natural and innocent than Faulkner's.

   Stuart writes out of the very intensity of life, from the inside out.
When the reader or critic looks outside in, he may mistake the part
for the whole, overlook the naturalness of Stuart's world with its
diverting variety, forgetting that he composes in the genres of
poetry and nonfiction as well as of short story and novel. The
critical questions of Stuart's sometimes ragged style and heavy pro-
duction aside, faults underlined by his reviewers for nearly half a
century, today's reader perceives that Stuart's work has survived.
Much remains in print, and daily new readers of all ages—children
and graduate students and senior citizens—come to his work.
Why? A clue to such durable appeal may be found in a letter to
Stuart, written by Edgar H. Duncan in 1943 at Vanderbilt, in
which Duncan pointed to the author's ability "to paint people as

they are (your great gift)." Perhaps this is one reason among many that Stuart's readers return again to his work.

It is in these stories that one discovers much regional substance in blend with the universal themes of love of life, resignation to death, family pride, anger and pain and exaltation, superstition and folly, passion and faith, human failings and the triumph of Nature and the life-hardened human spirit. Stuart's creative energy unfolds before the reader's eyes, fresh substance combining with a distinctive style to render the essence of literary art, assuring the reader in ways so purely natural that conscious art seems filtered out, and only the pure distillate of reality is left—that richly varied world of Stuart's W-Hollow, its stalwart mountains, trees, white-cloud skies, and real people, who have somehow been transposed to an imaginative plane of remarkable originality.

And there is a joy, sometimes a hymn but more often a lyric song of life, in most of what Jesse Stuart's pen touches; it may astonish or charm, even outrage or touch in turn, but most often it enthralls and lifts the human heart.

H. EDWARD RICHARDSON

Men of the Mountains

MEN OF THE MOUNTAINS

*Behind the sun and before the sun in misty rays of light
are the hills eternal where mortal men are laid—the
trees mark their resting places now and the briars—the
mountains are their tombs eternal. Men wrought of
mountain clay and stone and roots of mountain trees—
eat plants from the mountain earth and hear the music
of mountain wind and water—men live among the
mountains, curse the mountains, love the mountains,
plant corn among them and lift the rocks and cut the
timber—have seasons to fail and see the dry hard rocks
point to the skies—men of the mountains unafraid of
the cruel mountains, the homey mountains that give
them scanty food and take them home in the end to
sleep a while.*

"FLEM WAS ALWAYS A GOOD WORKER," says Pa, "and a good
man. I hate to hear that—poor old Flem—digging his own
grave and him just fifty-six years old. W'y he's the same
age I am and I'm not ready to leave this old world yet.
Much as we talk about being unafraid to die when we go
to getting up in years then's the time we want to live. We
watch each precious day. Poor old Flem. We got to get
over there and see if we can help him any. Do that much
for a good neighbor."

Pa puts on his little gray hat. He walks out of the house,
pulls out a package of red-horse and puts his brown fingers

in at the head of the half-opened package of sweet scrap tobacco. He brings a wad of brown cut-up in the tips of his fingers to his mouth, shoves the scrap in, shoves it back properly. Then he takes a twist of home-made from his pocket so strong that it smells in the July heat. He twists off the end and shoves that into his mouth with his thumb and index finger, tamps it in like you tamp a fence post.

"Got to take a little sweet terbacker with the home-made any more," says Pa. "My ticker ain't good as it used to be. That's what the years bring a man. That's one way I know I'm not the man I used to be. Can't take my terbacker like I ust to could take it. W'y I chawed home-made—the strongest taste-bud that we could grow and I never thought a thing about it. Look at me now. Have to buy sweet ter-backer and do a lot of mixing."

The July sun is hot—hot as a roasted potato. The wind, in dry burning sheets, moves slowly over the land and rubs the dry bellies of the poplar leaves—their green throats rattle. Pa walks slowly down the path, a dry line of dirt, a cow path where there is no grass at all.

"A awful drouth," says Pa. "Don't know what the poor people are going to do this winter for bread corn and feed for their stock. God Almighty only knows about a season anymore. We never know—I've spent my life here among these hills and the older I get the less I trust the seasons. Can't get seasons any more like we used to get. Used to just go out and plant the corn and work it a couple of times—awfullest corn crops you ever saw popped out'n the ground. Land was a lot better then—but we had a season.

"Lord, look at these brown acres—look at the corn. By-the-grace-of-God I'm ashamed for a man to go through my field. Bumble-bee corn—a bumble-bee can't suck the tassels without his starn-end rubbing the ground! Look at the hills—once the land of plenty—the land of good crops —bone-dry—kick this dust with your toe and see how hard it is for yourself. It's going to be awful hard on poor old Flem to dig his grave through such hard dirt."

The dust is flying from where Pa is kicking with the toe of his shoe. I can smell the dust. I would rather smell wilted horse-weeds—that pig-pen smell they have—any old day as to smell July dust from a Kentucky mountain road—dust that has settled on the blackberry briars and sassafras sprouts—the red-mouse-eared sassafras sprouts that are coloring in the drouth. Lean cattle on the hill—seven cows to forty acres of grassed hill side and cows lean as rails. Buzzards sailing up over wilted trees—buzzards looking down on pastures and old rail-piles. Buzzards always know when the fires run through the mountains and burn terrapins to death, the lizards, the frogs, the snakes. Their crisp bodies turned to the sun, around them the black ashes flying in the wind. Buzzards high above in the blue heavens, high in the winds, coasting with wings spread, coasting, coasting, and peering. They know when the drouth comes to the high bony hills where life is hard for man and beast.

"That hill over there," says Pa, pointing to a sag of corn that fits into a lap between two hills, "w'y old Flem cleaned that up for me when you was just a boy. Old Flem took his three boys in there—just little shavers then—and dogged if he didn't clear that land. He'd take them little boys and clear land all through these hills. That Flem was a worker. What I mean he was a worker. Great big raw-boned man, so deef he couldn't hear the wind blow. That's all I didn't like about him. Had to get right up close and holler in his ear. Then he had that eye where some man back in Carter County hit him with a rock and his eye stays open all the time. Can't get the lid down. It looks right funny to see that eye standing wide open like a snake's eye. That's what a man gets for fighting with rocks. Mountains full of rocks, and men fit with them before they ever fit with guns. Look at poor old Flem—old at fifty-six. Just my age. I get around just fine—if I just had a new ticker——"

Buzzards search the mountains—circle low down to the wilted trees. Snake marks are across our paths—long trailer-marks in the sand. Birds fly about and chirrup with a disconsolate wail.

"Poor birds are hunting water," says Pa, "poor birds. I'd rather see a man in trouble. He can help hisself more."

Pa swishes the sweat from his red forehead with his index finger and it drops in a straight line of fast-shooting white beads as he slings his hand. It hits the dry sand and sprinkles it—water to the dry earth—the bitterness of sweat to the parching lips of the earth. "Whoo-ee-ain't it hot," says Pa. "Never saw anything like this in my life. Hottest time I ever saw. Drouth. Birds dying and them buzzards up there just waiting for us all to die."

We leave the hollow road and turn to the right. We walk up this avenue of wilted weeds, of wilted trees, of brown corn-field rocks gleaming in the sun and lazy wilted corn—starving to death for water—standing in the dust down between two sweeps of hills—slanting back against the sun-scorched buff-colored clouds. We smell the burning weeds, the dying corn, the wilted sweeps of saw-briared hills and gloomy arms of scorched pine trees, the weeping fingers of the sourwoods. When we have reached the head of this little hollow, we cross the gap and go down the neck of the next hollow where Flem lives—right on the old John Kaut farm where all that big timber used to stand.

"We'll soon find out about this grave-digging," says Pa. "Son, that kindly bluffs me. When it comes to digging graves—it ain't very long. I've seen too much of it happen. These old men get the warning—they nearly always know —never hear of one missing it. But just to think of old Flem being the one called—who'd a ever thought about that? Just can't tell where the tree is going to fall, but where the tree does fall there is where the tree is going to lie——"

Flem's house is in sight—a house made from the rough oak planks and slabs from where the saw-mill used to set when it cut the giant oaks into slivers—a house there in the sun—the July Kentucky sun high in the burnt-up clouds. Windows in the house like burnt holes in a brown quilt, the color of seasoned-out lumber, brown against the wind —sweltering in the sun—the resin running from the pine knot-holes—smelly, tasty, bee-colored in the sun. Smoke coming from the rough-stone flue—smoke, thin smoke and light-blue against the wind, fat puffs of smoke with big bellies in the sun—going out with the wind—in all directions over the hot dog-tongued earth. Palings around the garden with fruit jars sunning—stone jars and glass jars and rag-rugs out on the palings to sun. Hoes with their goose-necks hung over the palings, a scythe, an oat cradle with one broken finger. Wilted corn on the mountain slopes above the house—a whole mountain of wilted corn—each stalk of corn crying for water. And the wilted arms of the corn—whispering—whispering—to the hot wind.

"Look in the garden," says Pa, "look at Flem's garden. Burnt up alive just like our garden. Look at them little tater vines. Bet you can gravel down there at them tater roots and you won't find taters bigger than a marble. Look at them cabbages. Looks for the world like wilted pusley to me. Look up that mountain—look at Flem's lean cows—and them buzzards. See them! There they are—always right around where the milk cows are trying to find grass to eat—right above the cows they snoop aroun' in the air. Why don't a buzzard wait for a buzzard to die?"

We walk in at the gate—a lean-to gate that we open and it shuts itself, weighted with a chain and plow-points—and up to the house. We smell the resin on the pine boards—scent of pine. We love the smell of pines in the spring, but the smell of pine on a hot day, the smell of pine, molted pine, wormy wood—we have to hold our noses. Around the house in the blistering heat—the smell of the wilted ragweeds—the poor wilted lady's finger and forget-me-nots drooping—the scent of pinks and iron-weeds in August.

"Hello," says Pa, "how are you, Flem." Flem does not hear. Pa goes up and he hollers in Flem's ear: "Hello, Flem. How are you!"

Flem laughs and he says: "I'm so deef can't hear nothing no more. Ain't heard the wind blow for years. The only way I can tell when the wind blows is to see the brush moving and the corn moving. It's awful to be deef. You'll never know till you get that way. When did you come over, Mick?"

"Just come," says Pa, getting up and hollering in Flem's ear. "Just come over through the hot sun and the whole air is filled with buzzards."

"Filled with buzzards," says Flem. "I'll be dogged. Sign of dead stock. Sign of deaths. Don't get me though. I got the hole dug to catch me. I'm looking for this thing."

Flem laughs. One of his eyes squints, the other eye can't, for the lid is stiff—stands open like a snake's eye—he never takes that eye off you. Flem is a big man, has a belly big as a nailkeg, doesn't have on any drawers—you can see a big white patch of his belly where his blue shirt has worked up from his overalls. When Flem laughs his belly bobs up and down—up like a hand under dough lifting it up—down like a hand over dough beating it down. His hair is gray and stiff as wires in a brush—hair that won't lie down nor sit up nor do anything. It has a little crown in it—a twisted place in the bristled stuff. He has heavy eyebrows like ferns on the edge of a rock cliff.

"Wear number ten shoes," says Flem. "I see you got a mighty little foundation, Mick." Flem laughs and his belly

works up and down. I see Flem's little pipe-stem hairy legs
with the big feet to hold them down.

Pa says, "I got little feet. I wear eights." Pa laughs and
pulls out his tobacco. He tamps it into his mouth, the sweet
with the bitter, then reaches some to Flem.

"Thank you," Flem says, "I don't chaw my terbacker.
I smoke it." Flem takes out a leaf of home-made tobacco,
crumbles it in a little red corn-cob pipe, strikes a match on
his pants leg, and wheezes as he sucks the long dry stem.
Long streams of thin smoke come from Flem's mouth—
thinner than the air and bluer.

"My ticker ain't good as it used to be," says Pa, hollering in Flem's ear, "that's why I got to take a little sweet
with the bitter any more. Can't take it like I used to take
it. Getting younger every day, too."

Flem says: "Huh—yes—ahh. Huh."

"God," says Pa, "he's the deefest man I ever tried to
talk to. He's about got me winded. You try to talk with
him a while. Let's get him to show us his grave."

Hodd is Flem's boy, twenty-two now, with two rows of
black broken teeth, freckles on his face, patches of un-
shaved beard growing here and there, a straw hat on his
head, a blue shirt on his back with two dark blue stripes
on the back where his overall suspenders have not let the
sun fade the blue out, overalls torn at the cuffs into ravel-
ling ruffles.

"Hello, Hodd," Pa says, "will you talk to your Pa a
little for us?"

"I'll do my best," says Hodd. "Pa's deef as a rock in this
hot weather and deef ain't no name for it. Just sets around
—can't do nothing—can't talk to nobody. He's got his grave
dug—guess you know about that."

"Heard about it," says Pa.

"Well, he has," says Hodd, "and he's got Ma's grave
dug with his. Right beside his. Ma's taken a cry every

day since he's done it. She says it's the sure sign when a Simpson digs a grave. He's not much longer for this world."

Flem just sits on his rocking chair and rocks. Life doesn't have any noises for him, he can't hear the jingle of the harness any more nor the sound of the hoe and ax nor the barking of fox-hounds.

"Tell Flem," says Pa, "that I want to go back there where he has got them graves dug. Tell him I want to see them." And Hodd hollers in Flem's ear.

"All right, we'll go," says Flem. "About three miles back there. But we'll go."

Flem leads the way up the path. Pa walks second. Hodd is third and Ott comes out. He says: "Where you going, Hodd?" And Hodd says: "We're going to Pa's graves out here on the hill. Come along with us."

Ott comes up the hill. He is tall, thin at the hips, with twisted legs and a hairy chest, unbuttoned shirt, a partly bald head with hair thin as timber on a hill where the fire has run over it year after year. His lips turn down at the corners like the curve of a horse-shoe. He says: "Uhuh—ahh——"

And he walks up the path, his legs working strong and fast. We move on toward the graves, the sun high on the mountain above us among the burned-copper clouds. Flem is easily winded, walks with a stick. He gets his breath like a snoring hog sleeping in the sun. Sweat drips from Pa's face. He slings it with his forefinger from his forehead, and he wipes among his scattered wire-stubbled beard with his red handkerchief.

"Ma is worried plum sick," says Ott, "the way Pa has done. He tried to get me and Hodd to come back here and help him with the graves. We wouldn't do it. Me to dig my father's grave and my mother's grave. No. I just couldn't bear it. W'y he's been coming back here and working one hour at a time for the past five weeks. He brings that crazy boy of Mort Flannigan's back here. He comes with Pa. He laid down and had Mort's boy to mark him off—right back yander on the Remines pint."

Lazy July wind seeps out of the brush. It is soft and hot. It runs fast then slow. The scent of the corn—corn sweltering in the heat on the slope to our right—corn ready to tassel—corn so small and twisted. The mountain path is slow and twisting and the wilted leaves hang in pods in the July sunlight. Sweat runs from my face, from Pa's face, from Hodd's, Ott's, and Flem's faces. Flem is in the lead, setting the walking pace. It is slow as the slow smelly wind that comes out of the brush. The buzzards are above the mountain tops, flying in circles over the pasture slope where the lean cows pick the brown grass, grass that would burn quick if Flem would throw down a lighted match-stem.

"Ma's been just crying her eyes out," says Ott, "about Pa. Corn in the ground for another year. Pa is going to die. We know he's going to die. Nothing we can do about it. He says he's going to die. Ain't worked none this summer. Ma says she hates to die and leave little Effie, the baby girl you know, just twelve now. Just us three left at home. All safe, Ma says, but Effie and she says there's so much weakedness in the world she hates to die and leave her."

It seems like we are climbing to the sun, the sun that crosses the earth, in the region of the hill man's destiny—great backbones of ridges where the crow flies, where cows wither on the bone on the dry summer grass and where buzzards circle low. Men of the mountains growing old. Pa growing old at fifty-six—mixing sweet tobacco with strong. Flem Simpson growing old and his autumn not here. His grave is dug.

"W'y," says Pa, "Flem ain't but from March to June older than I am. I am still getting around and I've worked as hard in my day as any man."

"Yes," says Hodd, "but you wasn't hit in the head with a rock like Pa. That's what got Pa. You know about that fight. He's been a peaceful man ever since. He communes with the Lord often—gets out at night and communes with the Lord."

"Lord, I'm hot," says Pa, wiping the sweat from his face.

"No hotter than I am," says Hodd. "Look at Pa, though, he's still wiggling like a young weaned calf—big in the middle and little on both ends. . . . Soon be at the top of the mountain."

The sun is high in the sky—high among the mountains, the color of a red sand-rock—floating—floating—heat below is dancing to the tune of grasshopper in the weeds. Heat on the fields of wilted corn on the mountains where the earth is baked in a big brown pone. If rain was to hit the baked earth, rain wouldn't soak down for a while—it would go up in steam. Great brown sheets of earth—wilted mountains of leaves—green clouds of leaves—clouds, wilted and drooping.

"Let the old men get their wind," says Hodd, as we top the mountain. "Won't be so bad now—it's about all going down the hill now."

Pa wipes the sweat from his face and moves faster and faster as the road on the mountain ridge goes down a knoll and up another knoll to the Remines point.

"Coming in sight of where I'm going to be laid out to rest, boys," says Flem, "just right over the pint here in these chestnut oaks. Nice quiet place out here away from the houses—back like the woods was when I was a boy."

We walk over the hill—here are the graves—two graves dug under the chestnut-oaks—twin graves—side by side. "Here they are, boys," says Flem. "Will show you this one is a fit for me. The other one is a fit for my wife. Prudy just comes to my shoulder you know. So when I laid down to measure her grave I had to make allowances. I measured from my shoulders down. But I just laid down here and had Mort's boy to measure me on the ground. He was a little scared, but he helped me here with these graves with tears in his eyes."

"God," says Pa. "Hodd, ask your Pa what made him do this. I didn't believe he had any graves out here when he told me. I thought he was just a funning me a little . . . Poor old Flem."

Pa sheds some tears. He remembers Uncle Fonse Tillman and the strange way he knew about his approaching death—now another one of Pa's comrades passing away and acting the same way about it. "A funny thing," says Pa. "I believe Flem knows what he's doing. Flem is a goner from these mountains. Gone to sleep among them forever and that before the winds of falltime blow."

"I just fit—see, boys," says Flem as he gets down in his grave and lies down, "a little wide here in the middle but it won't be when my oak-board coffin fits in here. Most people dig a hole to fit the coffin and order the coffin to fit the man. I'm making my coffin to fit me and digging the hole first." Flem's head is against the earth and he says, "How do I look down here, boys?"

He looks up at us and laughs, his belly shaking. Then he looks through the wilted leaves of the chestnut-oaks above his grave at the molten copper clouds that halfway secure the sun—hot clouds—clouds without rain. His one eye, the snake-eye, looks glassy from down in the grave. The other eye is squinted.

"Good place to be when a man is tired," says Flem, "no more worry about bread, land to tend, and pasture for the cattle. No more worry—out here where the fox-horns will blow and maybe I can hear them then. All troubles will be over, Prudy by my side, and we'll sleep here till resurrection day. A good place to sleep—right here on the mountain-top."

It touches Pa to hear Flem say this. Pa says to Ott: "Guess you'll have to run the farm when your Pa dies. Sure did pick a good place to be buried. I'd hate to dig my grave. Don't believe I could. Even if it is cool away from all the heat we been having. I just wouldn't like it."

Flem is still down in his grave. "Come on out of your grave, Pa," says Hodd. Flem can see Hodd's lips working but he can't tell what he is saying.

"Say it louder," says Flem, "like Gabriel is going to do when he blows his trumpet."

Hodd hollers as loudly as he can, down into the grave: "Come on out of your grave, Pa."

"That's more like it," says Flem, "more like the trumpet I'm going to hear on resurrection morning, when time shall be no more, and these fifty-six years ain't going to be a drop in the bucket. Help me out of my grave, boys."

Pa gets him by one hand and Hodd gets him by the other.

"I want to live where there's not any time. Then I can farm and lift rocks and cut sprouts the way I want to with a strong set of arms and a strong set of legs. We'll have seasons and crops. That's what I want and not this awful sun to burn up the crops——"

Flem comes from the grave and starts to get down in Prudy's grave to show us the length of it. "Oh, God," says Hodd, "don't get down in Ma's grave. No need of that— I don't want to think about Ma coming to this lonely place when she's always liked to go to town on Saturdays where she could see people. Ma don't like fox-horns. Has to be buried way out in these lonely woods."

"I'm ready to go," says Flem. "Can't farm any more. Don't have the legs—don't have the arms. Can't see as well. Can't talk to people. I'm in the way. Can't trade like I used to trade. Country is changing. Government telling me what to do—how to plant the mountains. Tell me I can only raise so many hogs and a lot of stuff like that. It's getting time for us old men who ain't used to that to die, Mick. God Almighty sent this drouth on such people as that. Won't let us plant—won't let us have what we want—we've always had that—even under a Republican, much as I hate that Party. I tell you, I'm tired and ready to sleep. I told the Master I was ready and I'd like to bring the old woman along with me, too. I told the Master she was ready—she'd been with me all through life and I wanted to be by the side of her in death."

Tears come in Pa's eyes. Hodd looks to the waters of the Little Sandy and keeps his eyes away from his father. Ott looks at me and I look at Ott and then at Pa. The Little Sandy River winds slowly down among the hills, down among the wilted clouds of leaves—a brown muddy river—curled like a snake crawling through the briars. Giant oaks tremble in the wind. Leaves flutter in the hot July wind.

"Great place to be buried," says Pa, "here among these mighty hills. They'll get me in the end. Oak roots will go in to old Flem. He'll go back to the mountains and only a tree some day will mark where he is buried."

Flem says: "Come down here a minute, boys. Got something I want to show you." We follow Flem down under the hill—just a little way down under the rim of the hill to a rock cliff—where lichen is bluish-gray and dying—the sourwoods lean over and twist their slender bodies groping for the light.

"Come in here," says Flem. "Look here, see these barrels of salt—seven of them—four for me and three for the old woman. The children can take care of themselves. I'm going to have four barrels of salt dumped in on my oak-board box—and three dumped in on the old woman's. We're going to keep like a jar of apples till the judgment. Going to keep right here on this mountain till resurrection day, looking fresh as two lilies. We're not going to be a

couple of skeletons coming out of the grave. We're going
to come out of there—the whole of us just like we went in.
Salt around us and oakboards from our hills—buried on
our mountain-top where only the fox-horns blow and the
wind and the hound-dogs bark—w'y we'll keep forever."

"We got to get home and feed," says Pa, "got to be going. Come over, Hodd, you and Ott—come over when you
can. Come over, Flem," says Pa, hollering in his ear. "Come
over and see me before you change worlds. After you
get out of here you won't be at a place where we can
neighbor like we used to neighbor."

"I want to get around to your place and Hankas's place
before September and see all you boys once more," says
Flem, "then I'm ready for my rest. No drouths then, no
crop failures, and people telling me what to raise and how
to raise it. I'll still be a Democrat, though. You can't change
a mountain Democrat or a mountain Republican."

"That's right," says Pa, "you know me. I'll be a Republican in Heaven or in Hell. But I like you Flem because
you are what you are and a good neighbor. I hope we get
to neighbor again in other mountains."

We walk up the hill—we take the near cut across the
spur home. The path is dry and white as a crooked dog-
bone. Pa walks in front. Pa's shirt is wet with sweat as a
dish-rag—sweat has come through the crown of his hat in
places. We see the sun sinking—we look back at the vast
hills, timber-covered, the great green clouds of wilted
leaves that dry-rustle in the wind, and the houses down in
the valley. "A good neighbor," says Pa, "a good neighbor
if I ever had one on this earth."

THE PEOPLE CHOOSE

I saw a streak of dust rise like white soup-beans toward the sky. The streak of dust was comin' toward me. It followed the Tiger River road. "Who could that be," I thought, "comin' that fast down that crooked road?"

I wasn't long findin' out. I saw two black horses, slim as racer black-snakes, loapin' in front of the storm clouds of dust. I heard them gettin' their breath long before they reached me. I saw a little driver sittin' on the front seat of the two-horse surrey. I heard a voice cry out from the back seat: "Pewee, stop the horses." Then I heard a big laugh like low thunder from the back seat of the surrey.

Pewee pulled up beside of me and stopped. The horses' sides were working in and out like a bee smoker. Their tongues were out where the bridle-bits go in their mouths. Flakes of white foam dropped from their mouths to the dusty road. Their sleek black skins were covered with patches of foamy sweat that looked like patches of snow the sun didn't melt on the dark winter hills.

"Dog my hide if it ain't old Dusty Boone," says a big husky voice from the back seat. "Where you goin', Dusty?"

"I'm out to skeer me up a few votes," I says. "You ain't seen any up the river, have you?"

"You don't mean to tell me you're out tryin' to beat me," says Jason Mennix. "If that's what you're doin' you'd as well go home and smoke your pipe. I've done skeered all the votes out'n the brush. They're goin' to vote for old Jason. They call me 'Suits the People Jason Mennix.'" Jason bent over as far as his stummach would let him. He laughed and laughed and hit his knees with his big fat hands. He puffs big clouds of smoke from his long black cigar that he held between two rows of gold-covered teeth.

"Jason, I'm out to beat you," I says. "I'll tell you what I'll do. If you beat me, I'll let you roll me off'n Town Hill in a barrel. If I beat you, you let me roll you off'n Town Hill in a barrel. We'll invite the people out to watch one of us roll."

"I hate to roll you off'n that high hill in a barrel," says Jason, "but I guess I'll haf to do it.

"You hear the bargin, Pewee," says Jason. "Now remember it to me when I get into office."

"Yes-sir, Mr. Mennix," says Pewee holdin' to the leather check-lines and lookin' straight ahead at the road. "I'll remind you of it, Mr. Mennix."

"I've got the Boone Mountain precinct in the bag," says Jason. "I've got all that Boone tribe. You know when I get them I've got a big vote. I've got all the Reffitt vote over on Reffitt Mountain. I'd get 'em all but they think the Boones are fur me. They won't vote for a man the Boones vote fur."

"It looks like you have the election in the bag," I says, "when you get the Boones. They are my kinfolks."

"You ain't akin to the Boones, are you, Dusty?" says Jason. "It's too fur back fur the blood to count."

"I'm akin to 'em today," I says. "You never got back on the ridges and in the heads of the hollows with that rig. You are too big to walk over the cow paths and shake their hands and ast them how their crops are gettin' along. I'm goin' back and visit among my people today."

Jason bends over and laughs and laughs. He throws his cigar stub down on the dusty road. He takes another cigar

from his coat's front pocket. He takes a match from his big
black hatband, strikes it on his blue-serge pant leg and lights
another cigar. He puffs out a big blue cloud of smoke. "Go
amongst all of 'em, Dusty," he says. "Remember I was in
the American-Spanish War. See my medals pinned here on
my coat! People like medals pinned on a brave man!"

"My scars will mean more than your medals," I says, "if
I take my shirt off and show my scars. There's not a place
on my body big enough to lay a pin down but what there
is a scar. I ain't been in just one war. I ain't never been out
of a war, Jason. I've been fightin' ever since I could remember! Look what the Boone tribe has been through with
among these hills! Fightin' the Reffitts ever since I could
remember!"

"Sorry you come out agin me," says Jason. "I'll haf to be
movin' along. Pewee, tack up one of my pictures on that
locust tree over there. It's a good place to catch the eyes
of the people when they make this bend in the road."

"All right, Mr. Mennix," says Pewee. "Yes-sir, Mr.
Mennix."

Jason reaches him the picture, the hammer, and tacks.

"You ain't got a picture tacked up anyplace," says Jason.
"What's the matter? Don't you know people want to see
your mug along the turnpike? You might get a lot of wimmen votes. If it wasn't fur my picture you would." Jason
laughs and blows smoke to the hot July wind. Pewee tacks
up Jason's picture on the locust tree. He walks back to the
surrey, steps on the stirrup and unwraps the lines from the
whip-holster.

"You'd better take care of your team," I says. "If you
don't quit runnin' 'em so hard this hot weather you'll give
'em the thumps."

"Won't matter," says Jason. "I've got to canvass the
county with this team. When I go back into office, I'll buy
me a better team and a rubber-tired surrey. Here, Dusty,

take one of my pictures as a partin' gift before I roll you over Town Hill in a barrel." Jason laughed and laughed— I heard him long after the surrey had disappeared behind the clouds of rollin' dust.

"I'll beat him," I says. "I'll beat 'Suits the People' Jason Mennix. He's had the office six years. I'll have it the next six years, durned my hide if I don't. He's never been back amongst the Boones. He's just rid along the turnpikes and stopped at the houses. I'll go back among them."

I looked at Jason's picture. A big man with three chins and a big cigar in his mouth. Medals pinned all over the front of his coat. A half-dozen cigars and a fountain pen in the front pocket by his coat lapel. A row of matches behind the band of his big black hat. Down below the picture it said in big black letters: "Vote for 'Suits the People' Jason Mennix. I am for good roads, churches, schools and the farmers. I am a veteran of the American-Spanish War. If elected, I will faithfully fulfill the duties of my office, Sub- ject to your approval, August 8th."

"He's got a good speel here," I thought. "I'll haf to go over to Uncle Tobias Boone's. I'll haf to see Cousin Subrinea Boone. I know that she's one of the Boones that loves a Reffitt—too bad but she loves Roosevelt Reffitt."

I rode Nell up to the Spruce Pine Gap. I turned to my left. I followed the little path under the dark fir trees that led me to the home of Uncle Tobias Boone's. I was in the land of the Boones—a land of log-shacks, terbacker patches, and cornfields. I saw Uncle Tobias hoein' taters on the bluff back of the barn.

"Howdy, Uncle Tobias," I says, "Do you need an extra hand to help you with your taters?"

"Shore do, Dusty," says Uncle Tobias, looking up at the sun and stroking his long red beard with one hand, holding to his hoe handle with the other. "I need another Boone

down here. Fetch that hoe from the fur-end of the tater
patch and come along."

I got the hoe and walked down the bluff. I started diggin'
in a row right above Uncle Tobias. I hadn't been in the
tater patch a minute until Uncle Tobias says: "How's the
election goin', Dusty? Gettin' purty warm, ain't she?"

"It all depends on you, Uncle Tobias," I says. "If the
Boones stand by me, I'll have a chance."

"I planned to vote fer Jason Mennix," says Uncle Tobias,
"if you didn't get around to see your kinfolks. We're akin,
Dusty. The same blood flows in your veins flows in my
veins. It's a way back yander where we branched off and I
could explain it to you if I had time. I've got to get my
taters out'n the weeds!"

"I'll help you with the taters," I says. "I know we are
akin. The reason I ain't got to see you before now, I've had
to canvass the whole county. I've come here last for I
know how you stand. I know blood is thicker than water.
What ever you say, Uncle Tobias, the Boones will do. If
you fight for me, all of the Boones will fight for me. I just
want to show you the picture Jason gave me over on the
Tiger River Turnpike a few minutes ago." I took the picture from under my coat.

"Look, Uncle Tobias," I says. "See the medals on his
coat! Says he's a brave man in the American-Spanish War.
I'll show you what a brave man really is. Wait until I strip
my coat and shirt off." I took them right off in the tater
patch.

"Look at the scars on me," I says. "How do you think I
got these?"

"I don't know," says Uncle Tobias—"fightin', I 'spect,
like the other Boones."

"You're right," I says. "I got them fightin' Reffitts."

"Lord hep me," says Uncle Tobias, "I'll let the weeds

take the taters, I'll ride a mule among the Boones day and night until the election. I'll see you get every Boone of the name. Put your shirt and coat back on and go to work."

"Jason told me he'd carry the Reffitt vote," I says. "Said he'd carry the Boones' vote too. I ast him how he expected to take my blood and kin vote. I thought if you all turned agin me, I wouldn't have a chance."

"We ain't turnin' agin you, son," says Uncle Tobias as he sticks his hoe in the ground. "I'm saddlin' my mule and ridin' and ridin' right now until I see every Boone of the name old enough to vote and a lot of 'em not old enough to vote. We'll show Jason who'll be the next Prosecutin' Attorney. He's had it six years nohow. Dad-durned if I don't beat that Jason! Goin' over there and cavortin' around with that bunch of Reffitts! Then he comes over here and talks wild honey to me. His words were sweeter than wild honey. You've got to be on one side or t'other. I'm standin' by a Boone first, last and always when he thinks enough of his kinfolks to visit them."

"I'm trustin' you, Uncle Tobias," I says. "I'm dependin' on you. I'll see Cousin Subrinea. Then I'll be on my way."

"I'll go to the barn-lot and get my mule and I'll be on my way," says Uncle Tobias. He hopped over the tater ridges toward the barn-lot like a sparrow-bird. I put my shirt on and carried my coat under my arm. I took Jason's picture with me. I clim into the saddle, waves good-by to Uncle Tobias as he clim on his mule and rode away—up a rocky path under the dark spruce pines.

The mule galloped away and his red beard was bent back by the wind against his body. I rode toward the log-house under the pines.

"Howdy, Subrinea," I says—"Looks like you're puttin' out a pretty good-sized washin' there."

"Howdy, Cousin Dusty," says Cousin Subrinea.

Subrinea stood straight behind the wash-tub she had

placed on a stool under a spruce pine. I thought she was
the purtiest woman I'd ever seen. She was tall and fair. Her
hair was golden as the moonbeams when a harvest moon
shines over a ripe wheat-field. Her sleeves were rolled halfway up her lily-white arms and the soapsuds clung to her
long slim fingers. Her teeth were two rows of agate-white
marbles.

"You're the purtiest woman that ever wore the name of
Boone, Subrinea," I says, "if you don't mind my tellin'
you."

"Any woman loves to hear that," says Subrinea. Her
lips curved in a smile and her teeth beamed in the sunlight
that filtered through the dark fingers on the spruce pine.

"If you weren't my sixth cousin," I says, "and I wasn't
a married man, I could love you, Subrinea. And you love
Roosevelt Reffitt! You love him, don't you, Subrinea?"

"Shhhhh," says Subrinea. She flings the suds from her
hands. She walks over to the fence. "I don't want Grandma
to hear you. You know how they feel about the Reffitts.
I'll tell you, Dusty, this fight has gone on long enough. It's
dangerous fur a Boone to go beyond that Gap where you
turned away from the turnpike. That's where the Boone
territory ends and the Reffitt territory begins. We've been
fightin' 'em for seventy-five years. They've killed us and
we've killed them. I guess we'll keep on killin' one another
if something doesn't happen to bring us together. The last
time the Reffitts and the Boones met, two Reffitts were
killed, and two Boones. Uncle Charlie and Fonse were
killed. Grandpa will never git over it."

"But you love a Reffitt more than words can tell," I
says. "I know you love a man when you hide out to see
him."

"Yes," says Subrinea. "There's no use of this killin' goin'
on forever and forever. A Reffitt is afraid to poke his head
over on Boone territory. He's even afraid to squirrel-hunt

over here. He can't own land on this side of the turnpike. He can't fish on our side of the river. There's been gun battles across the river when we fished down there."

"Subrinea," I says, "I don't blame a Reffitt for lovin' a girl purty as you are. I don't blame you for lovin' a Reffitt handsome as Roosevelt Reffitt. If you'll git the wimmen vote out among the Boone wimmen for me, and I am elected Prosecutin' Attorney, I'll get the Reffitts and the Boones together. You'll never regret all you've done for me. You won't haf to meet Roosevelt Reffitt where neither Boone not Reffitt eyes must see you. I'll fix everything. These murder trials never come to court, did they, while Jason Mennix was Prosecutin' Attorney?"

"No they didn't," says Subrinea—"but you know, Dusty, they can't come to court. They must never come to court. It would take thirty years to try all the trials betwixt our families. Our killings are even now on both sides. We just don't want any more. And I'll tell you, Cousin Dusty, it would take all of Kentucky's National Guards stationed at the courthouse the thirty years it took to try the cases. Long as there is a Reffitt left and a Boone left, they'll fight at the trial. If you can do anything about it, I'll wear my shoes out over these hills to git the wimmen out to vote for you."

"Get 'em out, Subrinea," I says, "but don't let Uncle Tobias know what I am doin'. You love Roosevelt Reffitt and I'll see that you get him. I'll see that this killin' stops."

"It's an awful promise for you to make, Cousin Dusty," says Subrinea, "but I'm goin' to work for you soon as I finish my washin! I'll go from house to house."

"I'll be ridin' on, Subrinea," I says. "Just a few more days, you know, and I've got a lot of work to do. Good-by, Cousin Subrinea."

"Good-by, Cousin Dusty," she says. "You can depend on my gettin' the wimmen to the polls."

I reined Nell away from the palin' fence. I left the purtiest girl I'd ever seen standin' like an angel under the
tall spruce pine with her sleeves rolled up, her golden hair
frizzled by the wind. I rode out the path and down over
the big mountain to the Spruce Pine Gap. "How can I
win the Reffitt vote?" I thought, as Nell stepped over the
big rocks layin' along the mountain path. I rocked from one
side of my saddle to the other.

"The Reffitts are great moonshiners," I thought. "Last
year was a dry season. The corn crop was light on the
mountain slopes. The Reffitts need corn to feed their moonshine stills. I'll see Uncle Roosevelt Reffitt, the head of the
Reffitt family. I'll send him a carload of cracked-corn to
feed his moonshine stills if he'll line up the votes just
right."

I reined Nell to my right after I'd gone one mile from
Spruce Pine Gap down the turnpike. I went up a rough
mountain path under tough-butted white-oaks, tall chestnut oaks, and black oaks. "Funny," I thought—"even the
timber changes when a body rides across that valley. Over
here are the Reffitts under the oaks—over there are the
Boones under the spruce pines. They are about as much
alike as their timber is alike." And then I thought: "What
if Uncle Tobias ever finds out I run into a barb-wire fence
huntin' one night and got my scars where barb-wire cut
me?" Another thought come to me as I rode along up the
narrow path—over the big rocks, under the shade of the
tall oaks.

I reached the top of the mountain, rode along and
watched the squirrels jumpin' from oak to oak over my
head. Soon I saw the log-shack under the oaks where
Roosevelt Reffitt lived. I rode down before the house. I
hollered, "Hello! Anybody at home!"

"Yes, young man," says Roosevelt Reffitt. He walked
in a dog-trot from the house with a Bible in his hand.

"What might your name be and what do you want?" He stroked his long white beard with his hand.

"I want a drink of cold water," I says. "I've been ridin' hard and I'm dry as a bone!"

"Get down off'n that nag," he says, "and go over to the well under that oak yander and hep yourself. There's a well-bucket there and gourd hangin' on the well-gum. What might your name be?"

"Dusty Boone," I says.

"Boone," he says—"you ain't welcome to drink of water here. You're on the wrong mountain! The quicker you can get off, the better it will be fer you, young man."

"I'm not akin to the Boones on yan side of the Mountain," I says. "I'm another Boone. I'm runnin' for Prosecutin' Attorney. I met Jason Mennix down yander on the turnpike and he told me he'd get every Boone vote of the name. He's got all the Boones lined up for him. If he gets the Boones I ought to get the Reffitts. Here's a picture, Uncle Roosevelt, I want you to see, then I want to show you something."

I got off the mule. I walked over to the dog-trot. Uncle Roosevelt took the picture of Jason Mennix's. "Here's the fellar," I says, "that told me he had the election in the bag. He said he had all the Boone vote. He's not a common man like I am. Look at the big cigars in his coat pocket! Look at the medals pinned on his coat! Read the words where he calls hisself 'Suits the People' Jason Mennix."

"Uhhuh," says Uncle Roosevelt Reffitt—"a betrayer. He may suit the Boones but he don't suit us Reffitts. Anybody that suits them can't suit us. There's as many Reffitts, young man, as there are Boones. If the vote ain't here we'll get it nohow, I'll call the Reffitts together and let them know what's goin' on. I'll get the Gullets, Rayburns, and Ratcliffs too. They've married into the Reffitts in so many places. We'll show the Boones."

"You see them medals, Uncle Roosevelt," I says—
"Jason said he got them for bravery in the American-Spanish War. Let me show you something. I ain't never been
out'n a war since I was a little shaver. Wait until I haul off
my coat and shirt. I'll show you." I pulled my shirt and
coat off. "See these scars!"

"Uhuh," says Uncle Roosevelt Reffitt, strokin' his long
white beard with one hand and holdin' the Bible with the
other. He walks up close and looks at the long white scars
across my body. "How did you get 'em, young man?"

"Fightin' Boones," I says. "They knifed me there but I
used a club. A club was all that saved me."

"Young man, put up your nag in my barn," he says, "and
stay the night with us. You'll find a little feed out there.
You air welcome to all the feed we got."

"Had a bad corn-crop last year?"

"Yes," says Uncle Roosevelt. "Everything purt nigh
burnt up on this mountain last year. This year has been a
golly-whopper on poor people."

I took Nell to the barn, let her drink from the trough,
put oats in her manger and corn in her box. I took the saddle off and hung it up by a stirrup to a spike nail on the
barn-post. I walked back toward the house.

"I ain't got but one boy at home," says Uncle Roosevelt.
"He bears my name. He's my baby boy and he tries to
marry a Boone gal. He's plum wild about her. I ain't had a
youngin to ever look at a Boone but him. He's wild about
old Tobias Boone's granddaughter. I think her name's
Subrinea."

"Too bad," I says. "Maybe I can help you a little. Let
me talk to him tonight."

"It's a funny thing," he says, "out'n seventeen youngins
my last cne—and the one that bears his Pap's name wants to
marry a Boone. Went hogwild about her at a pie-supper.
That was the night he lost two brothers. Her Uncles kilt

'em. I can't understand it fer the life o' me. The only good Boones I know air dead Boones—sleepin' on that mountain over yander under the spruce pines. Roosevelt's comin' now. He's comin' dog-tired from th' terbacker patch."

"Roosevelt," says Uncle Roosevelt Reffitt, "this is a Boone—the first one that will ever sleep in this house. I want you to meet 'im. He ain't no kin to the Boones on yan side of the mountain."

"Glad to meet you," he says reachin' me his hard brown hand. His eagle eyes looked straight at me. His black wavy hair was mangled by the wind on the mountain. "It's funny to see a Boone in this house. I guess you're the first one in seventy-five years."

"Let me have that Jason Mennix's picture again," says Uncle Roosevelt. I handed him the picture. He held it before him. "A Boone betrayer," he says. He spit a bright sluice of amber in one eye. He waddled his cud behind his jaw. He spit a bright sluice of amber into the other eye. He tore the picture in two, threw the pieces on the dog-trot floor and stomped them. "Boone betrayer—that's old 'Suits the People' Jason Mennix. That pot-bellied Hellion! He'll never get a Reffitt vote if I can hep it. I'll show 'im who the people's choice is. You fellars dabble in the pan and git ready to eat. It's on the table now."

I never set down to better grub. The table was filled.

"My Spouse Manda, Dusty Boone," says Uncle Roosevelt Reffitt. "Mother of seventeen and gettin' younger every day."

"I'm glad to know you," I says.

"Glad to know you," she says, "but I don't like your name."

"Forget about the Boones, Ma," says young Roosevelt.

"You would say that," she says. "Young man, don't ever bring one in under the Reffitt roof." Her black eyes danced when she said these words.

"I can see her," says young Roosevelt Reffitt. "I can see her golden hair and her blue eyes. I can remember how tall she was. I can remember the dress she wore. I couldn't believe she was a woman. She looked like an angel to me. I wanted to see her again—and again."

"If I thought you meant that, young man," says Uncle Roosevelt, "I'd take a five-year-old club to you. You ain't too big fer me to whip. You might be six feet and four inches tall—but I can limb you yet. Git to eatin' the grub before you——"

"Moonshine, milk 'r water to drink, Mr. Boone?" says Mrs. Reffitt.

"Moonshine if you please, Mam," I says. "I'm a man of mountain ways and I can't git high-kaflutin' and go back on what I was raised on like Jason Mennix. He used sicha big words today I couldn't understand what he was talkin' about."

Then I reached for my glass. It looked clear as water but there were beads in it clear as crystals. I put it to my lips. I couldn't take it away until I drained it dry. "Lord, this is the best I have ever tasted," I says. "Another glass, Mam, if you please."

"Go a little light, son," says Uncle Roosevelt—"it will lift your heels on an empty stummick. I've got a little heady in my time but never once has it lifted my heels. I never let it defile the temple of clay!"

I don't know how much grub I put away. It was before me. I know I helped myself. I remember leavin' the table. I remember takin' Uncle Roosevelt Reffitt by the arm. I remember sayin', "We are brothers, ain't we, Uncle Roosevelt?"

"Yes, we are brothers," he says. "We Reffitts will stand by you. We will give you every vote there is in our family and then some."

"And you need corn," I says—"you need cracked-corn.

You need what we call 'chop.' You need a carload of it and I will send it to the foot of the mountain. I will put it in that rock cliff for you. You will have chop to make good corn licker. You have had a bad season and you'll have corn for your stills. It is because of that good drink I had for my supper."

"And young man, you need not fear," he says. "You will git your votes. You must go upstairs to bed now. You don't mind sleepin' with young Roosevelt, do you?"

"Of course not," I says—"I want to talk to him. I want to have a talk with him. I'll tell him about the Boones. I'll tell him about the girl he thinks he loves. The boy is tired out but I'll wake him and I'll tell him."

Uncle Roosevelt took me to the door. He lit the lamp and showed me to the bed. He left the lamp on the dresser —I undressed, blew out the lamp and crawled in beside of young Roosevelt Reffitt. The moonlight fell across the bed.

"Young Roosevelt, wake up," I says—"don't be a sleepy head. I've got a message for you——"

"Huh," he says.

"Wake up," I says, "I've got a message of love from Subrinea for you."

"Oh, what is it," he asks— "When did you see her?"

"Today."

"What did she say?"

"That she loved you. Said all this trouble betwixt your families was all foolishness. Said she loved you and always would. That is why I am here. If you'll git all the young vote out and help put me over—I'll help you get her. Maybe we can stop all this fightin' between your people and her people. Her grandpa—Uncle Tobias—hates your Pap as much as your Pap hates him."

"That's a shame. We ought to let bygones be bygones. We ought to lay our rifles down and put our knives away.

Jist because they live under the spruce pines on yan mountain and we live under the oaks on this mountain—ain't no
sign we should go on and hate each other eternally."

"That's the way I feel. Honest, I think Subrinea is the
purtiest woman I ever saw. She was washin' clothes under a
spruce pine. She looked like an angel to me. I could love
her."

"Don't talk like that. If I knowed you loved her you'd
never get out'n this bed. I'd slit your throat from ear to
ear."

"I'm her cousin. I couldn't marry her. Don't tell your Pa
I'm her cousin. She is workin' in the election for me. She
said for you to. She sent me to you. I am a married man. I
don't want to leave my wife nohow. I want to be your
next Prosecutin' Attorney. If I am elected, I'll surprise you.
I'll get all of you people back together, that is if you'll
help me."

"I'll work my toenails off for you."

"Thank you, young Roosevelt Reffitt."

We went to sleep. I heard young Roosevelt say
"Subrinea" throughout the night. He talked in his sleep.
"I love you," he said. He flung his arms out and tried to
grab me. He would hug his pillow. I could see him in the
moonlight that fell across my bed.

"This election is mine," I thought. "I'll run neck and
neck all over the county with Jason. I'll carry the Reffitts
and the Boones—something no man has done for seventy-
five years. I'll beat Jason two to one when all the votes
are counted."

We got up at five o'clock. Breakfast was waitin' for us.
I et my breakfast with young Roosevelt. He had a big grin
on his face. He would look at me and he would eat. When
breakfast was over Uncle Roosevelt Reffitt stroked his long
white beard and says: "I've fed your horse. I don't want to
run you off but I'm takin' young Roosevelt and we're goin'

on mules amongst all of our people. You won't need to go with us. You go amongst others. We'll take care of this mountain. We'll soon be startin'."

"I'm ready, Pap," says young Roosevelt, "I want to help Dusty. He's a good man. I listened to him last night. He told me a lot I didn't know."

"I thought he could," says Uncle Roosevelt—"I thought he could give you a little light on the boogers on t'other side of the mountain."

"He give me a lot," says young Roosevelt. "I'm a new man this mornin'. I feel like one of the flock that has strayed away and just come home."

I thanked Manda Reffitt for the good grub. I ask her for a vial of drink to take along. She fixed it for me. I put it in my pocket, went to the barn and saddled Nell. I climbed in the saddle and waved good-by. I saw Uncle Roosevelt and young Roosevelt ridin' their mules out the ridge road—both waved good-by to me. "No need for me to do anymore but send the carload of chop to Roosevelt Reffitt," I thought—"just lay low and wait a few days." I rode over the mountain and down the river turnpike to town.

On August 4th the carload of chop was set off on the switch. I started four trucks haulin' it to the foot of Reffitt Mountain. "Ast me no questions, fellars," I says, "you just deliver the chop and stack it under the rockcliff on the right-hand side of the road that goes over the mountain. You'll have a little totin' to do. Just get the chop safe from the rain."

August 8th, I saddled Nell and rode to Spruce Pine Gap. I rode up a little drain where the bright water dashed over the rocks. I hitched Nell to a saplin' where people couldn't see her when they passed the road. I had my precinct workers all lined up. I was ready for the election—the biggest Primary election ever held in these parts. I wanted to watch the wagons loaded with voters goin' down the turnpike. I wanted to watch them comin' off'n the mountain.

I laid in the shade and smoked my pipe. I saw wagons loaded with Reffitts goin' down the road. I saw wagons loaded with Boones goin' down the road. I never heard the people speak to each other or as much as wave a hand. They looked at each other hard. They were goin' to the polls in great multitudes. Sometimes I saw boys among the Reffitts that didn't look sixteen years old. They were all goin' to vote. It was fun to lay in the shade and think about old Jason. I wondered where he was goin' and if he was smokin' his big black cigars. I wondered if young Roosevelt saw Subrinea at the polls. I wondered if he thought she was as purty as I thought she was. I wondered what Old Roosevelt Reffitt would do when he saw Jason. I wondered if Uncle Tobias Boone and Uncle Roosevelt Reffitt got into a fight on the election grounds if they would pull each other's beards. I just laid in the shade and had a lot of wild thoughts.

At five o'clock I clim into the saddle. Nell was a-prancin' and rearin' to go. I let her have full rein toward town. By the time I got there the votes would all be in from the precincts and we'd start countin' them. The Reffitts and the Boones would be there. They'd be there to see if their man winned. I was their man. Nell took me home in a hurry. There weren't any dead this time to count. The vote count started.

It was the Primary in our party and we counted the vote fast. Just a gun pulled now and then but the Sheriff Holliday took the guns. We were runnin' neck to neck. Jason stood over in the corner. He laughed and puffed a big cigar. "Just wait until the big vote come in," he says. Then he laughed a big horselaugh and looked at me. I smoked my pipe and waited. I saw Subrinea among the Boones. The Boones were on one side of the courthouse and the

Reffitts on the other. I saw young Roosevelt Reffitt among the Reffitts. He looked at Subrinea and she looked at him. She couldn't go to him and he couldn't go to her.

"Ready for Boone Mountain Precinct," says the Sheriff. "Count 'em, boys. Let's git through with this election sometime tonight."

"It's one way," says the tally-men. "Ain't but one man gettin' any votes here."

Jason puffed his cigar and laughed and laughed. He handed out boxes of cigars to the men. He thought the vote was goin' his way. He thought he had it in the bag. I saw Subrinea laugh like an angel out among the crowd of Boones.

"Ready for the Reffitt Mountain Precinct," says Sheriff Holliday—"the last precinct. This one will decide who your Prosecutin' Attorney will be."

The men started to tally the precinct when the Sheriff brought the box out and unlocked it. The tally-men counted the vote. They looked at the Boones on one side the courthouse and the Reffitts on the other side. Their eyes got big as they counted the vote. There weren't much talkin' amongst the people. They squirmed and twisted in their seats and waited. Jason smoked his big cigars and laughed. His gold teeth shined brighter than gold dollars under the big lamp in the courthouse.

"The count is over," says Sheriff Holliday. "Gentlemen, Dusty Boone is your next Prosecutin' Attorney. He winned by a big vote—Jason Mennix 1755 votes. Dusty Boone 3456 votes."

A big cheer went up from the Boones. A big cheer went up from the Reffitts. They looked at each other. Uncle Roosevelt Reffitt stroked his long white beard. Uncle Tobias Boone stroked his long red beard. Subrinea Boone walked among the Boones to the middle aisle in the courthouse. Young Roosevelt Reffitt walked amid the Reffitts to the middle aisle and stood beside of Subrinea. The Boones started talkin' among themselves—the Reffitts started talkin' among themselves.

"Just a minute, Gentlemen and Ladies," I says. "I've got something I want you men to witness. I made an agreement with Jason Mennix if he winned this race he could roll me from the top of Town Hill in a barrel. If I winned this race, I got to roll him off'n Town Hill in a barrel. Uncle Tobias Boone and Uncle Roosevelt Reffitt will roll Jason Mennix in a few minutes from the top of Town Hill in the barrel." The crowd roared. Uncle Tobias looked at Uncle Roosevelt Reffitt. Uncle Roosevelt Reffitt looked at Uncle Tobias.

"Gentlemen and Ladies," I says, "I have something else to witness. I hope you will excuse me for it but this is the greatest minute of my life. For nearly one century the Boones and the Reffitts have shot at each other across the river and the mountain valley. Tonight, these people have ceased to fight. I, as Prosecutin' Attorney, dismiss all old indictments. They stop with the same number dead on both sides. There has been a draw. Tonight, they shake hands and renew friendship. The young couple you see standin' in the courthouse aisle will be the first union of the Reffitts and the Boones, I must be on my way with them."

FOR THE LOVE OF BRASS

THORNY KIRK WALKS OUT TO THE BARN. He has a bucket of slop for the red brood-sow in his right hand. In his left arm he carries twenty ears of white corn for the horses. Thorny jerks the gate open with his elbow, kicks it back with his foot, walks into the barn-lot, sets the slop down. He puts the corn in the feed boxes to the horses. He takes up the bucket of slop and starts to the pen.

"Howdy-do," says a man coming from behind the pigpen. He is a little man with scanty blue stubble beard on his dark face—face the color of a stunted corn-blade in July.

"Good morning," says Thorny. "Did you sleep behind my pigpen last night?" Thorny's voice is gruff as a winter wind in the oak-tops.

"Yes," says the little bird-necked man. "I slept over there. Heard you had a big farm here and needed a man. I come over here last night and looked the farm over. Thought I might like to work for you."

"Well, old billy-hell—you work for me on this farm!" says Thorny as he puts the bucket of slop down. "I'll be dad-durned. If that's what you come for, see that road out there? Had your breakfast?"

"Ain't had a bite," says the man, shaking in the chill of a May morning. "But I didn't come for my breakfast. I come to get work."

46

"What is your name?" says Thorny.

"My name is Bud," says the man, his teeth chattering, his thin coatless arms limp down his side, his hands in his pocket.

"Just Bud?" says Thorny.

"Yes," says the man, "just Bud. Just call me Bud. That's all." Bud smiles and shows his two rows of broken discolored teeth.

"I can do an awful lot of work," Bud says. "Can do much as anybody I ever worked with. I'll do devilish nigh as much work as you will."

"I'll be dad-durned my pictures!" Thorny Kirk laughs and laughs. "You do as much work as I will." And he takes one hand, lifts the heavy can of slop to the railing, catches the rim of the bucket with the other hand, and pours the slop in the slide to the trough. "I'd like to see any bird-necked runt of a man," says Thorny, "do more work than I can do, my man; that has yet to come, for any big well-fed man that can work with old Thorny. I put 'em all in the shade. I can't keep a hired man. I don't ask 'em to do as much as I do, either. Hell, I'm a worker. That's how I got this big farm here on the river. Made it with these hands and arms."

"I don't have a home," says Bud. "Oh I got one, but I don't like it. It's just a part-time home. I go and come from it all the time. I might be able to stay with you awhile, then I'll go home and stay there awhile, then I'll come back. But I'd like to stay on this farm with you long as I can. Stay here till I haf to go home again."

"You got a wife," says Thorny, "and children?"

"No, I've not got a wife nor children," Bud says.

"I got a wife, but no children," says Thorny. "I'll tell you what I'll do. You go out to the house and get your breakfast and come down to the field. Right down here on the hill. And if you hoe one half of a row of corn to my one row you have a job. Come on and we'll go to the house and have Lydia to fix your breakfast."

Thorny starts toward the house. Bud does not start. "What's the matter?" says Thorny, as he turns and sees Bud standing there. "Don't you like the bargain I offered you? Can't you stand that much?"

"Not that," says Bud, "I just don't like to go in a house."

"Why," says Thorny, "what is the matter with my house?"

"Nothing," says Bud. "I just don't like to go in a house. Bring my breakfast out here to me if you will. I forgot to tell you I don't eat in houses. I eat out in the open, away from houses and fences."

Bud stands shivering in the early May morning wind. It comes from the dewy corn in the fields. It comes from the dewy dwarf-willows along the river. It is a cool wind, laden with mists, and the sun is coming up now, a patch of sun strikes the roof of the barn and is clearing up the mists. Thorny is in the house now. Bud does not hear what he says to Lydia. "Fix up a breakfast for a man. Looks a little like a tramp to me. Says he can do more work than I can, and when he said that it kindly riled me. W'y, I'll hire a tramp and bring him in here if he'll do more work than old Thorny Kirk. Fix him a good breakfast with plenty of hot biscuits and good coffee."

"Reckon, Thorny, that the man's all right," says Lydia. "Reckon he ain't some kind of a spy. Reckon he won't hurt one of us."

"Fix the breakfast," says Thorny, "something about him, I like. I'm willing to risk him. No man on this river or any other river that I have ever worked with has ever took a row of corn and raked the weeds down on me." Thorny takes the pot of coffee, the hot buttered biscuits, and fried apples and goes out to the pigpen. As he leaves the kitchen Lydia says, "Be careful, Thorny, about that man."

"Here's your breakfast, Bud," says Thorny. "While you eat, I'll turn the horses in the lot. We'll hoe corn today. I'll not do any plowing. I want to hoe corn with you." And Thorny stands awhile to watch Bud eat. He will not eat in front of Thorny.

Thorny goes to the barn and lets Tom and Kate out of their stalls. He drives them to the gate, opens the gate, turns them loose in the pasture. He sucks his pipestem and blows out wisps of blue smoke to the morning wind. He walks up toward the pigpen. Bud walks from behind the pigpen. He is wiping his mouth and carrying back the empty dishes and an empty coffeepot.

"Was a good breakfast," says Bud, "such good coffee. A lot better than I find at home. Good biscuits too. Good fried apples. Your wife is a wonderful cook. Have you got any good homemade chewing?"

"Got some cured-out burley out there at the barn-shed," says Thorny.

They walk toward the barn-shed. Thorny reaches across the manger and pulls off a hand of tobacco. "Here," he says, "put that in your pocket." Bud strips off a handful of the dry-leaf, crams it into his lean jaw. He takes his lean bird-claw fingers and puts the rest of the dry-leaf in his pants' pocket, blue-serge pants with patches on the seat and frizzled cuffs.

They walk past the smokehouse and Thorny picks up two hoes hanging on the palings. "Get me a bigger hoe than that," says Bud. "That hoe's too little. Won't cut a wide enough swath of weeds." Thorny looks at Bud, puts the hoe back and gets a big one-eyed sprouting hoe.

"This'll hold a big man like you," says Thorny. "Pap made this out'n a old saw-mill saw—pure steel and fourteen inches wide. But I'm taking the other one in case you can't stand this one." Thorny picks up three hoes.

"We're getting a late start," says Thorny. "I'm always

in this field at the break of day. Like to work while it is cool."

"It don't matter to me," says Bud, "any old time suits me."

And they walk down the field. Corn is still covered with dew. A white fog leaves the corn in the rays of the sun.

"I'll take this bottom row," says Thorny. "You see I need help, don't you? Look how foul this corn has got on me."

"Looks like it ought to be snaked," says Bud, "I don't believe you are the worker you think you are or you would have had this corn out."

"What do you mean by snaking corn?" asks Thorny.

"W'y, Pap used to tell us," says Bud, "when we's little boys back in the Kentucky mountains that when weeds got knee high in a corn patch, we ought to go through with a stick and shake the weeds and run the vipers, copperheads, rattlesnakes, and blacksnakes out. He said only lazy men had to snake their corn." And Bud laughs. Thorny gets in the bottom row. He bends over with his goose-neck hoe and he tap-taps, the grass falls and he rakes the loose dirt from the plowed furrow across the balk and levels the corn-row. Bud takes big long rake-like swaths and he cuts the grass, levels the balks and draws loose dirt to the corn. He does it with ease.

"This is a good hoe," says Bud. "Never used one that suited me any better." And he plays behind Thorny with ease. Thorny looks up at Bud standing half the time above him and him peck-pecking away, moving slowly with a row of corn through the crab-grass and devil-shoestrings vines. "Let me have that bottom row," says Bud. "You can't hoe corn. Who told you that you could hoe corn?"

A frown comes over Thorny's face. "But you can't keep that up for long in this hot sun and you with that big hoe," he says.

"I'll keep it up all right," says Bud. "If not, I'll do it just like you want it done." And Bud smiles and shows his broken discolored teeth.

"You are doing a good job," says Thorny, "better than I am doing. Not a weed left in the row. Looks like some machine has done it, it's done so smooth."

And Thorny gets down in his row—takes up his hoe again. Peck. Peck. Peck. Peck. Click. Click. "It's all in the sleight," says Bud, "the movement of the hands and the body. No man can tell you just how." The sweat streams from Thorny's face. His bull-neck is beet red. His great hairy arms are running streams of sweat down from his armpits. His shirt is wet with sweat as if he'd jumped in a river of water.

"The rows are long around this hill," says Thorny, "we'll just about make one round before dinner." And Thorny digs down into the crab-grassed earth. "It's awfully pretty corn," says Thorny.

"Awfully pretty," says Bud, "but it needs the weeds out'n it. If I stay here the weeds will come out'n it, too." Bud is not sweating.

"Why do you stay so cool?" says Thorny, looking up at Bud and wiping the sweat from his eyes.

"I'm not working," says Bud. "I sweat when I work just like you do. Give me the bottom row and I'll show you how to hoe corn. Turn me loose in these weeds."

"Here, take my row," says Thorny. "It breaks me in two to let a man like you take the lower row on me. First time in my life this has happened." And Bud steps down in Thorny's row.

The May sun is beaming down now. The wind has laid. The heat glimmers over the field of corn. It dances like the heat above a burning brush-heap in the early spring. Bud takes the big hoe and with all the ease in the world, it seems like, he leaves Thorny standing in his row. "Dog

my cats," says Thorny to a hill of corn he is raking dirt
around, "if I don't believe I'm dreaming. This can't be so.
Yesterday I was the champion corn-hoer in this county.
Today I'm just a slow hand, the kind that used to aggra-
vate me. And I'd want to tell them to hurry up. A little
bird-necked man with arms no bigger than wagon wheel
spokes, a man I don't know nothing about who slept behind
my pigpen in the dew like a cow-brute, stepped right
down and beat me. It must be a dream."

Thorny wipes the sweat from his eyes. He works fast
as he can. It is a long way around the mountain bluff above
the river. The corn is weedy. The crab-grass, the sourwood
sprouts, the cockleburrs, the horseweeds and the smart
weeds are just about to take the corn. "I could go a lot
faster," says Bud to a stalk of corn, "if I didn't have to stop
and hunt for you in all these weeds. A lot of lazy men in
this world. A lot of men lazier than old Bud." And the
weeds and the sprouts fly. Bud is out of sight now from
Thorny. He has left him far behind. "I can see daylight,"
says Bud. "Here's the other end of the field. I can get two
more rows before noon. If Thorny can just get two rows,
then we'll be doing fine."

The sweat is breaking on Bud's face now. Sweat flows
from his face the color of white soup-beans. Weeds fall
before his big hoe. "Old hoe, you are a good'n," he says.
"How do you like old Bud? Stay with me, old hoe, and
I'll stay with you." And Bud is moving back to meet
Thorny coming with his row. When Bud turns the bend
of the hill he sees Thorny coming with his row. "Yahho,"
says Bud, and he waves his hand to Thorny. Then he bends
down. "Stay with Bud, old pet," says Bud. "Stay with
Bud, my darling hoe."

And Bud digs around the stumps. He does not leave a
sprig of crab-grass. He does not leave a weed in any row.
He moves almost as fast as the lazy heat-struck wind of

May. He is meeting Thorny a third of the way back. He hoes up to Thorny, meets him. They step up in the row above. Bud goes in his direction and Thorny keeps plodding his direction. "Bud, am I dreaming," says Thorny, "is this a dream? Am I in my right mind?"

"Is he, old hoe?" says Bud and Bud smiles. "My hoe says you are," says Bud. "Good old hoe." He bends over and digs that much harder. His little bird-neck is wet with sweat and his little arms no bigger than wagon-wheel spokes move like greased pistons. The big hoe falls on the loamy earth. It cuts the weeds and pulls them out by the roots. Bud's row of corn looks prettier than where Thorny has hoed. He moves on back from where he started from. Bud looks at the sun. He says: "Nine-thirty. Time for another row and to help Thorny out on his second row. We can do it, can't we, little hoe?"

Bud stops and looks at the sun again. He puts a dry wisp of crumbled tobacco leaves in his mouth with his little shriveled bird-claw hand. Then he starts digging in the loamy earth. The weeds start falling and the dirt starts rolling. He meets Thorny coming back on row number two.

"I'm about petered out," says Thorny. "You'll be petered out, if you take that row and keep it ahead of me when I get started to the other end of the field with my fourth row; won't he, little hoe? The hoe says 'yes.' "

Bud digs into the earth. He soon steps out with row number three. He steps up in row number four. He cuts the sprouts and weeds, he rakes the dirt. He moves.

"God, I need water," says Thorny. "Maybe I can make it to the other end without a drink." Thorny digs into the earth. "I'll beat 'im out," says Thorny, "or I'll strain every muscle. First man that ever beat me with a row of corn. Dad-durned my pictures if he hoes two rows of corn to my one. I can't stand that. It's bad enough for him to beat old Thorny Kirk, once champion corn hoer of these mountains."

"Lord, but you are hot, Thorny," says Bud.

"Hotter than a roasted tater," says Thorny. "I'm about a goner. Let's get to the house. All the water went out'n my biler into sweat and steam. Got to refill my biler."

"It's just barely eleven," says Bud.

"You ain't got no watch," says Thorny.

"Yes, but I can tell by the sun," says Bud. "When my shadder gets so I can step on it, it's twelve o'clock. It's not quite eleven. Look at your watch and see."

Thorny takes his watch from his sweaty overall bib-pocket. "My old turnip says it's ten minutes till eleven," he says. "But my old belly says it's time for beans."

"Just as you say," says Bud. "It suits me."

They throw down their hoes at the end of the corn-rows. They walk up the hill, two men—one a bean-pole, the other a mountain of a man. They look like they have swum the river with their clothes on. They walk up the hill to the house. Lydia walks out on the porch by the black-locust tree. "Oh, Thorny, is anything ailing you?" she says.

"Nothing, Lydia," says Thorny, "just don't talk too much to me. Is dinner ready?"

"Just a matter of minutes, Thorny," she says. She runs back in the kitchen.

"Bring my dinner out to the barn," says Bud.

"You just got to eat in the kitchen," says Thorny. "A man that can work like you, Bud. You can't live in my barn like a cow-brute or a horse." But Bud walks toward the barn. Thorny watches him pass the smokehouse, go by the woodyard, the pigpen, and into the barn lot.

"Lydia, that man out-hoed me this morning," says Thorny. "He's nearly killed me. He hoed two rows of corn to my one. The best man with a hoe I ever saw in my life. Talks to his hoe like I talk to my horses. And he's got the sleight of hand. Says that it was handed to him by a Higher Power. Beats anything I ever saw. Believe to my soul and God I got over-het down there this morning in that hot corn. Head's a-swimming."

"Did he go to the barn?" says Lydia.

"Yes," says Thorny, "struck out for the barn hard as he could go. Couldn't get him in the house."

"He might be a great corn-hoer," says Lydia, "but I believe he's a little off. Did he tell you his last name and where he's from?"

"No, he never told me anything. Just told me he's from a big family and he had to work pretty hard. Never laughs very much. Just digs down and works."

Thorny lights his pipe. He sits by the table and blows smoke across the heat-glimmering kitchen. Lydia fixes a lunch for Bud. "I'll take him his dinner before I eat," says Thorny. "When a man can do twice as much as I can do, he's got his beans a-coming to him first."

Thorny walks out toward the barn—out the path with the basket past the smokehouse, the woodyard, the pigpen. He walks into the barnlot. He hears two people talking in the barn. He slips up and listens. "Now, Sheriff, old Bud ain't done nothing. What are you after me again for? I didn't steal that brass. Old Bud is a good man, trying to be a good citizen this time. Ain't done a thing and I don't want to go back to the pen. No sir, old Bud ain't going back to no pen neither. What do you always want to pick on me for when I get out and work and make my living?"

"Now," says the other voice, "Bud Logan, I'm after you this time. Seven years. You'll have to serve it out too. Seven years and one day. I got you, Bud. I watched you down there in the cornfield this morning. You down there a-showing off and trying to kill old Thorny Kirk. You know that big bull-brute of a man can't hoe no corn. He ain't fast enough. He's too clumsy to hoe corn with you,

Bud; he don't have no sleight of hand from God Almighty. I'm going to take you back home, back to the state pen."

Thorny runs around the corner of the barn with the basket of hot grub. He says as he turns the corner: "Sheriff, you might be after Bud, but you quit talking about Thorny Kirk. I can hoe corn, too." But Thorny Kirk does not see anyone but Bud sitting on the manger. "Where's that sheriff?" says Thorny.

"I never saw any sheriff," says Bud. "Is there a sheriff here?" Bud looks wild out of his eyes. He looks up at the hayloft and he jumps down and looks under the mangers. "I don't see no sheriff," he says.

"Well, I heard two men talking," says Thorny, "or, I heard spirits in the air. Maybe I'm not right after getting so hot this morning. But it 'peared to me I heard two voices in this barn. You was talking to the sheriff. And the sheriff was talking to you. And the sheriff started talking about me."

"You never heard me," says Bud.

"Where is that sheriff? He called you Bud Logan. Dad-durned my hide if I didn't hear it or I ain't all here. I brought you your dinner."

Bud takes the basket. He does not look at the food until Thorny turns and walks out. "Like a wild timid brute," says Thorny to himself. "Durned it's got me all puzzled. I can't figure this thing out. I'll not work this afternoon. I'm about petered out, nohow." And he walks to the house. Before Thorny is done eating he looks out at the kitchen window. Bud is sitting on the wood-block.

"He's waiting on me," says Thorny. "Just tell him, Lydia, I'm sick this afternoon. Tell him I got overhet this morning in the field and that he can just go down there and work by himself."

Lydia goes to the door, her red hair flying in the May wind. "Bud, Thorny says for you to go ahead and work

this afternoon by yourself. He come nigh as a pea kicking
the bucket here a few minutes ago. He gorged on water.
You just go on by yourself and do what you can." Bud
does not speak. He goes to the corner of the house, takes
the path down to the mountain bluff above the river.

Wind is smothery to breathe. It is a hot glimmering
wind. But the wind can't stop Bud. The weeds fly and
the dirt rolls. "We can hoe six rows through here ourselves, can't we, little hoe?" says Bud. "Glad you said yes,
little hoe. Old Bud wants water, little hoe. Old Bud does.
Go to the river and drink. Glad you said go to the river
and drink, little hoe. Old Bud will go down to the river
and drink. Old Bud won't gorge on water like Mr. Kirk
done. Old Bud will drink water like a muskrat. Old Bud
knows how to drink water."

Bud leaves his row of corn long enough to go beside the
river, to lie down flat on his stomach, brace his hands on
the earth and drink water from the river. Bud pulls himself
up with his hands, leaps to his feet, wipes his mouth with
his hand, crumbles the dry tobacco leaves in his hand, puts
them in his mouth. He takes back up the hill like a squirrel.
"Fresh as I was this morning when I started," says Bud
to a stalk of corn. "Leave it to old Bud; he'll get you out'n
the weeds. Old Bud can kill 'em all, little hoe, if you'll
just stay with old Bud."

Bud looks over the field. When a blade of corn rustles
behind Bud, he turns and jumps. But the weeds fall and
the loose dirt goes to the corn. The corn does not speak
to Bud. It waits to have the weeds cut from its spindling
stalks.

"Lydia, I'll slip down there and watch that man work
awhile," Thorny says. "Maybe I can catch his sleight of
hand. I'll tell you the truth, Lydia, something funny about
this whole thing. I don't guess I'm losing my strength and

my mind, am I? Have I been talking funny the last few days?"

"No," says Lydia, "you are talking funny now to say that."

"Well," says Thorny, "when I went out to the barn awhile ago I sure to God thought I heard the sheriff talking to Bud. Told him he was going to take him away. I thought I heard Bud talking to the sheriff and telling him Bud Logan was a good man and a lot of stuff like that."

Thorny gets up and walks out of the room. Lydia watches him as he turns over the bluff toward the corn-bluff by the river. Thorny walks through the glimmering heat. He wades out among the wilted weeds at the edge of the field. He lies down on his belly and waits to see Bud come toward the east end of the field. "Lord," says Thorny, "how many rows has Bud hoed on the bluff already? One, two, three, four, five, six, since noon. Much as we both done this morning. And it ain't four yet. It's all a dream and I'll wake up in the morning laughing about it all."

But it is not a dream. Here comes Bud with the big hoe. It is worn bright as a silver dollar now. It shines when Bud lifts it up in the air and brings it down again. Thorny lies in the weeds and watches Bud. Bud is coming fast on row number seven. "I'll get you out, little corn," says Bud. "Bud wouldn't have corn this weedy. Stay with me, little hoe."

Thorny lies in the weeds. Tears stream down from his eyes.

"Old Thorny just in Bud's way," says Bud to himself. "Can do more than both of us in the field, while I'm by myself. Stay with me, little hoe. This is row number seven. Want to get ten rows by five o'clock. Want to help Mr. Kirk get his corn all out'n the weeds. Might be called back home pretty soon and all this corn in the weeds. Want to get them out for Mr. Kirk. Old Bud can do it, too."

"I'm not hoeing corn with a man like that," says Thorny, "my reputation is ruint. Don't want people to know it. I'm going to tell Lydia I ain't the champion corn-hoer of the hills anymore. I'm going to tell her my mind is all right. Bud talks to himself. Guess he was talking to hisself in the barn and didn't know it."

Thorny slips up through the wilted weeds to the house.

"Row number ten, little hoe," says Bud. "Stay with me, little hoe. This will be all today. Old Bud needs a little sleep but Bud will be with you tomorrow morning if the sun shines and the ground is dry."

At five o'clock when Thorny goes to put the horses in their stalls, he walks in the empty stall to the left of where his horses are to stand. He finds Bud in his stall. Bud's eyes watch every move Thorny makes. "Do you want all that hay?" says Bud.

"Yes, but I got more," says Thorny. "What do you want with it?"

"Want to sleep on it," says Bud. "I want this stall right over here from big Tom."

"Why don't you go to the house and sleep in a feather bed?" says Thorny.

"Feather beds ain't for old Bud," says Bud. "Feather beds are for other people. Give me a fork of straw and this manger and that's all I want."

Thorny throws a pitchfork of hay over into Bud's manger. Thorny leaves the barn. He goes back to the house.

When Thorny comes back to feed the horses corn, he brings Bud's supper. He brings Bud two quilts to use over the hay. He feeds Bud in his manger like he feeds the horses.

Thorny goes to the barn after he eats supper to see how Bud is getting along. He walks out past the smokehouse, the woodyard and the pigpen. He hears two men talking in the barn: "Now, Sheriff, what have you got again' old Bud? Ain't I always paid my debts? Ain't I always been a honest man? You can't take old Bud back home. He won't go! He likes this farm. He likes to hoe. Bud likes Thorny Kirk. Thorny is a good man. But he's a little slow about his work. Let the weeds take his corn, Sheriff. Old Bud just got here in time to save the corn. You can't take me back now, Sheriff. Let old Bud stay on this farm. This is Bud's new home."

"I'm going to take you, Bud. You got that brass. Bud, you served your sentence. It was your third time. Now you'll have to go home. You'll have to serve more time this sentence. I hate to take you, Bud, but I'll have to."

"You can't have me, Sheriff. I didn't get the brass this time. I just didn't do it. I'm going to stay here with Thorny. Poor old Thorny thinks he can hoe corn. Old Bud can hoe his corn out if he'll let Bud stay here. But I don't like to be hemmed in. Bud is afraid of walls. Bud likes the open air in the cornfields. Bud ain't no bad man, Sheriff. You know he never harmed no woman nor shot no man. Why do you just pick on old Bud? Let me stay, Sheriff. I promise you, I'll do my best not to steal any more brass."

Thorny listens to Bud and the sheriff talking. He cups his hand over his ear to catch every word. "W'y, there's two different voices there," says Thorny. "I know Bud's voice. It's another voice too. That sheriff, w'y he's back after Bud. I like Bud and I aim to help him. I'll take care of that sheriff myself." And Thorny runs into the barn. Just Bud by himself. He is sitting on the manger chewing his tobacco and patting Tom's nose. Tom is chewing hay.

"I thought I heard two men talking in here," says Thorny.

"Nobody in here," says Bud. "Not a soul."

"Thought I heard a sheriff talking," says Thorny.

"Lord, the sheriff!" says Bud and he looks wild under the manger and up in the hayloft.

"Don't guess I did," says Thorny. Thorny goes back to the house.

The next day Bud goes to the field just at daylight. "Mr. Kirk, you stay here and get the weeds out'n your garden and get your ginwork done up," Bud says. "Just let old Bud take care of the corn." Thorny turns and the tears stream from his eyes. He wipes them with his big rough hands.

"All right, Bud," he says. Bud goes to the field. At twelve he is back at the barn. Thorny takes his meal out to him.

"Will be done by four this evening," says Bud. "Will have all the weeds out, Mr. Kirk. My little hoe has whipped the weeds. We got that field just a-shining, so pretty and clean. Won't have to snake your corn."

Bud goes back to the field as soon as he eats. No one sees him go. But when a wind rustles the corn, Bud stops and looks and listens. When a wind shakes a briar Bud stops and listens. He is afraid of the wind. His eyes watch everything. By four o'clock, Bud goes around the bluff on the last row of corn. "I told you, little hoe. And you told old Bud what we'd do. Got the corn done, didn't we?" Bud puts the big hoe across his shoulder and goes past the house to the barn. He does not stop at the house. He takes his hoe to his manger. Lydia sees him pass the house. She goes to the window and looks at him.

It is Saturday and Bud has been with Thorny all week. Thorny pulls out six one-dollar bills. "Here, Bud, is your pay for the week. You have earned it. You have a home with me and work as long as you care to stay. I believe you need some clothes." Bud takes the money. He goes across the river to Carlton. He comes back with some new overalls and shirts and a pair of shoes.

May has come and May has gone. The corn is clean now.

Bud lives in the barn. June comes with growing rains and warm fertile earth shoots the corn skyward. "That's the way I like to see corn grow. I like to see it shoot out'n the earth," says Bud as he peeps over at the bluff of corn that he hoed in May. Bud goes over the farm to see about the wheat, the corn, the cane, and the tobacco.

July comes and Bud hoes the late potatoes. He rides the mowing machine and cuts the hay. He hoes the melons. "I look after this farm for the old man Kirk. Just like it was my own. Poor old Thorny, a good man but mighty slow." And July passes. August is here. The swallows gather over the housetops.

"W'y, even the brass rings are gone off my harness hames," says Thorny.

"The brass is gone out'n my wash-boards," says Lydia. "It's funny. All the brass around this place is gone."

Lydia goes to the barn and tries to get Bud to come to the house. It is September and Bud has never been in the house. "Bud, come to the house and be our son. You've not got anything in here but that old hoe and a fork to hang your clothes on, two quilts and hay to sleep on." But Bud would not go. He rubs Tom's nose all the time Lydia talks to him. And Lydia leaves the barn. She says to Thorny, "Can't do a thing with him."

"Leave him alone," says Thorny. "Bud is satisfied here in the barn with the horses. You can't make a house-cat out'n Bud."

The corn begins to ripen in the fields. "I'll get to help Mr. Kirk gather the crop now," says Bud. "Good crop of everything. Fall time here. Old Bud likes the time when the leaves turn."

Thorny picks up the newspaper. It is the *Claymore County Weekly*. He puts on his glasses and he reads. The headlines are: "BRASS STOLEN FROM ENGINE." And it goes on to say that the thief was a small man. He

was shot at. It was supposed that he was killed as he swam
the river. The engine was one of the Old Line Special's
engines. The paper stated that the little man ran like a fox
to the river and the sheriff was after him and a posse of
men. Said several took pot shots at him but he ducked in
the tall horseweeds on the river bank and carried a big
brass rail and threw it in the river.

"W'y, if Bud ever swum the Ohio River, I don't know
it," says Thorny. "He ain't been shot. I can tell that. Spry
as he ever was. If that paper told the truth about the shooting it wasn't Bud."

Rap-rap on the door. Thorny comes to the door. A
posse of officers are standing on his porch. A big man with
broad shoulders and a Winchester across his shoulders
says, "Is this man staying with you?" He shows Bud's picture. It says below, "Wanted for robbery."

"Yes," says Thorny, "he's with me. Bud is in my barn.
But when you start shooting at him, men, there'll be more
shooting. He's the best worker I've ever had on this farm.
He's like a son to me."

"This is Bud's fourth trip for stealing brass," says the big
man with the Winchester. "He's never done another thing.
Just stole brass. He's bad after brass. You men surround
the barn and don't shoot." And they surround the barn.
The sheriff and Thorny go in the barn. Bud is sitting on
the manger rubbing old Tom's nose.

"Don't take me, Sheriff," he says. "I ain't done nothing.
Old Bud just stole a little brass. I want to help Mr. Kirk
get his crop gathered. I like it here. I don't like my old
home. I like this one better. No fence nor walls."

"Got to take you, Bud. It is our duty. I hate to, Bud."

Bud steps off the manger. He does not try to run. He
gives up.

"Sheriff, you got me at last," he says.

Thorny turns his head. The tears fall. They stream down

from his eyes. "No use of that, Mr. Kirk," says Bud, "I'll be back to see you sometime or you'll hear from me. I'll be back to help you with the work. Just ten years this time. Old Bud won't bother any more brass. If he does it'll be twenty-one years."

They lead Bud away. He leaves the buff-colored corn. He leaves his stall beside the horses. "It was a good home, Sheriff," says Bud. "Best I've ever had. You've been mean to me, Sheriff. You ought to let me a-stayed. That big brass rod is down there in the river. I can show you. I can get it for you."

Through the years of waiting Thorny often speaks of Bud. "W'y, Bud was the best worker that's ever been on this farm," he says. "If Bud could just have helped gather the big ears of corn he raised. I'm looking for old Bud back one of these days."

Bud did not come back. Eight years pass and Thorny gets a package from the post office. He opens the package. "Mr. Kirk, I'll not be back. Here are my clothes. I don't like my old home nigh as well as I liked my home with you. I won't need this home much longer. I am forty-two years old next month. I have spent twenty-one years of my forty-two here. It's been all for stealing brass. Take care of Tom and Kate and keep the farm goin!"

The month of August comes. Another message comes from the state pen. "We were requested to inform you that Bud Logan is dead," it read. "He requested that we send you this message. He was buried here by the state. He died on August the sixth at two P.M." Thorny reads the letter. Tears stream from his eyes.

"Bud ought to have had a better life," says Thorny. "Poor Bud, I loved him like a son. I can't help it if he did steal brass. I wish Bud was buried on this farm. No one can put even a bunch of corn blades on his grave." Thorny keeps Bud's big hoe hanging today in his manger in the barn.

NEW-GROUND CORN

"THIS IS PURTY CORN," Pa says. "Shan, this is the way I like to see corn grow. Look at the stalks of this corn won't you! Big nearly as our hoe handles! It is the deepest green I've ever seen in a patch of corn. Looks like a green wave in the sun. And the blades lap in the rows and rustle when they touch each other. I don't believe we'll get to plow this corn again. Just haf to come in here with our hoes and chop it out!"

Pa bends over and pecks with his sprouting hoe. He cuts the soft tender sprouts from the stumps. He rakes the loose loamy new-ground silt from the balk around the tall sturdy stalks of corn. The corn is so heavy the guard roots cannot hold them stalks in place. The wind leans the heavy stalks of corn.

"It's gettin' hot and smothery to work in this corn now," I says. "We'll not be able to plow it again. We might come in here with our hoes and chop the weeds out. If we don't it will be mighty foul by corn-cuttin' time."

"Yes," says Pa, "these black locust sprouts will rake a body's legs and cut his hands all to pieces. He'll haf to get in here and cut corn when the dew has softened the ripe fodder blades. The dew will be on the sprout-leaves too. The dew will be on the crab-grass. A body will get wet to his waist. I can't help how hot it is—we'll haf to cut it out again with our hoes!"

"Funny," I says, "about this big rock-pile here in the middle of this new ground piece of corn. Funny about the two little rocks down there in that corn balk with the bull-grass growing between them. I can't understand why you didn't plow that little place. It makes an ugly spot in the cornfield! Funny about this good land in the middle of a new-ground. It is like a garden-spot."

Pa stops the click-click of his hoe. He takes a red bandana from his hip overall pocket. He spreads the big red bandana over his red face. He wipes the white drops of sweat that trickle down his graying beard. He pulls off his black hat. He wipes the sweat from his thinning black hair. He puts his hat back on his head, and his red bandana in his hip pocket. Pa looks at the sun above the corn. He holds his hand up and feels the slow lazy wind above the corn.

"We can get too hot in this smothery corn," says Pa. "We'd better sit down and wind a minute. A fellow don't know how hot he can get down among this corn until he reaches up and feels the wind above him. It feels like ice atter a body digs through one of these long corn rows with his head down lookin' at this rich ground. Ah, Shan, I remember the day when I could stand anything! I can look at this ground and I can remember. You do not know —you do not remember. You were not in this world then. That was when Bill McKinley was President of the United States!"

Pa sits down on a stump in the corn-row. He takes his hat off and fans his face and head with one hand. He looks at the clumps of bull-grass in the corn-row. He looks at the giant rock-pile in the middle of the new-ground cornfield. He watches the corn blades slapping each other across the balks. He hears the rustling of the corn-blades in the wind. Pa's face is red as a beet. It is tanned by the wind and the sun. Pa's face is hard as a brown sand-rock. His

flesh is hard and his muscles are tough as hickory withes
that you tie fodder bundles with in the fall time.

"Son," says Pa, "I ain't told you a lot in my day. I've
give you good advice though. You'll haf to say I have. I
can remember, Shan. I can remember lots of things. I can
remember things I don't want to remember! They won't
go away. They stay in my head. They come back to me
in dreams. They come back to me when I see this new-
ground corn. They come back to me when I see this rock-
pile. You remember this place as our hunting ground don't
you? You remember when we used to bring Black Boy into
this hollow on rainy nights—how we used to get the minks,
possums, polecats and coons. Remember how Black Boy
would tree a coon and how we'd build a fire up under the
tree to keep the coon from coming down—how we'd sleep
there all night and shoot the coon out'n the tree the next
morning?"

"Yes I remember," I says. "I remember how you'd send
me to the house to get more shells. I'd be afraid of this long
dark hollow. I'd pray to myself a hant wouldn't jump
out'n the place where the old Hylton house used to be
and get me—yes, I remember—that too, is like a dream——"

"You didn't know then that there used to be a house
here," says Pa—"well there was. About the time Bill Mc-
Kinley was killed this house burnt down. I can remember
where the apple trees used to stand in the yard—where the
rose bushes stood by the palings. This stump I'm sittin'
on—this stump——"

"What about it Pa?" I ask—"what about the stump?"

Pa pulls his bandana from his hip pocket and he wipes
more sweat. He lets his hoe handle lean against the stump.
He fans with his hat in one hand. He wipes sweat with a
red bandana in his other hand. The corn is above his head.
The wind is above the corn and it is nosing slowly through
the corn. The sky that holds the sun is above the wind and

the glimmer of heat is over the land. The corn is wilted and it is begging for a drink of water from the water-over-gravel color of sky. There is not any water to beg from the waterless sky but it is thirsty and it begs for water and the rain crow croaks for water at the corn-field's edge.

"I remember when this stump was a tree," says Pa. "God in Heaven only knows why it ain't rotted sooner. It's a black-locust stump and black-locust is slow to rot. You know that, Shan, by the black-locust fence posts we have put in the ground. When this stump was a shade tree in this yard, I used to be under it every Sunday before McKinley was killed. Yes, I was here. Time goes by so— I can count back the years—I can remember by Bill Mc-Kinley. I used to come here all the time. I'd ride my sorrel mare around that ridge. I'd have two pistols on my hips. I'd shoot all the way around that ridge just to be shooting. God knows why I'd do it. I'd just shoot to hear the crack of my pistol. Son, I could take a row of corn and hoe it through the new-ground in them days!

"I could tell you for days," says Pa, "all that used to happen here. Son, you think this has allus been a wilderness. Well it ain't allus been a wilderness. I used to take Lucretia Hornbuckle from this house—she rode a sorrel pony—I rode my sorrel mare. We'd go side by side up that pint where you can still see that dip in the ground. Only that is left now. That used to be the main road to the church. I'd go to church with Lucretia and of all the times—you never heard sicha shoutin' and house warmin' as we'd have in that house. That was called the Six Hickories Church House. Six big hickory trees stood in front of the house. I saw the cattle snake them away to the saw-mill years later. I stood there by the church the day the mighty cattle got down on their knees—straining to pull sicha mighty trees! While Old Brother Litteral was praying for the Lord to come down through the loft, we's on the outside seeing

whose pistol would crack the loudest. We'd hold them in
the air and shoot at the moon, Son, I hate to tell you this—
but you're a grown man and I'm a old man and it comes
back to me and I've got to tell it to somebody. It comes
back like a dream comes to a man—when I see this rock-pile
—when I see that patch of bull-grass and the two rocks at
each end of it. I think that I can tell you now. You wanted
to know why the corn was so tall here. There was a good
garden here then. It is still rich where the old house used
to be."

"Where did all the people come from to the Six Hickories Church?" I ask. "I didn't think there were many
houses here then. You can go for miles now and can't find
a house. It is a wilderness now."

"Shan," says Pa, "you can find old roads, can't you?
You can find them on every ridge. You can find them running down the pints and across the hollows. You can see
these great sinks in the land. They used to lead to houses.
This land was covered with houses. Son, that's when people
had to dig a livin' out'n the ground or they starved—not
like it is now-a-days. We used to have old iron-furnaces
in this county. People moved here to cut charcoal cord
wood. The old men told me they used to see these hills
ricked with cords of charcoal wood fir the furnaces. They
saw as many as twenty yoke of oxen pulling cord wood
and pig-iron—all hitched to one big wagon. Now you
know about these roads—ah, the strength that has been
spent on them! When the ore was dug from the hills, and
the trees all cut into cord wood—the people didn't have no
place to go. They just lived on in their little shacks. They
piled the brush where they had cut the cord wood. They
burnt it—plowed the land and dug a living from the land
as we are doing still today, Shan."

"About Lucretia, Pa," I says—"I never——"

"Like a dream, Son," says Pa—"I never talk about her.

She is gone. She went the way the timber went; the church house went; the iron ore went; she went the way our horses went and the houses went; the big yokes of oxens went; the merry crowds in the days of Bill McKinley went—Lucretia is gone. She went young. Now who knows all of this? No one knows about it but a few of us that time is withering on the stem. I've seen the wild game go. I've seen the timber go. I've seen the oxen go. I've seen the horses go. I've seen the surreys go. It seems like I am lost. And, I've seen the people go. The boys and the girls I used to know are under the dust and scattered somewhere among the four winds of the earth—beyond these dark hills. They never come back any more than the otter, mink and coons come back!"

"But about Lucretia, Pa," I says—"you never told me about her."

"She was a woman for a good time," says Pa—"and I couldn't help lovin' her. I knowed it wasn't best. Son, she wasn't a woman for a living—it was always a good time. I can see her ride today. I can see her pony goin' over the fences leadin' my sorrel mare—I remember how I used to follow. I can hear her laugh—that laugh has not died on this wind. That laugh still re-echoes on this hill. When I used to coon hunt here when you was a little boy—it seemed like I could hear laughing—I could hear it sound against these hills. I could hear her voice. I can't forget. I was warned but I was mad with life and fun. She wasn't a woman for a wife, Son—She wasn't a woman for a living but I just can't forget."

"Somewhere back in a tin-type album," I says, "I saw a tin-type turning yellow with age—a young man standing with his hands on the back of a chair and a young woman with flowing hair—sitting in the chair with her hands across her lap—and the dress—the full-bosom and the big sleeves—I remember and the combs in her hair. And the

man with a black mustache, and the high collar and the
black bow-tie—I remember——"

"Right where we are sittin', Son," says Pa. "That picture was taken under this tree. That picture was taken
where you see this big new-ground corn—where the corn
is tall and stalwart—where it grows from this dark loamy
earth—I remember the day the man walked down that hill.
He carried his camera with him and it was on a three-
legged contraption. It was on Sunday when he came. And
you see where that tall timber stands over there on that
slope—that was in corn then. I'll tell you times change a
lot. It took him two hours to take our pictures. 'Look at
the birdie and smile', he says. He had a cloth spread over
his head. He had us get fixed this way and that. 'Don't
move now,' he says and then he pulls a little rope. Honest
it's funny to think about him. He was a little bird-like man
with a long beard. He had tiny hands and bird-claw fingers.
I paid three dollars for six pictures. I made fifty cents a day
working for Bill Fultz. I plowed corn for him. I tell you
there wasn't much money then. Pictures cost me six days
work—harder work son, than hoein' in this new-ground
corn."

The wind that blows through the corn and over the
corn moves the thinning locks of graying black hair on
Pa's head. The sweat trickles down his arm where he holds
the hoe handle. It drips to the dry loamy ground and makes
a little damp puddle. The wind smells of corn and pusley
and careless and saw-briars. The wind smells of shoemakes
and sourwoods sprouts. It smells of pumpkin vines that
run across the corn balks with big yellow blossoms and tiny
green pumpkins setting on the vines. The wind smells of
the bean vines that climb the corn stalks where Mom has
planted her a patch of fall beans. And the wind smells of
morning glories. It is a strange wind to smell but it is a

good wind to smell and it makes one lazy. It makes one's nostrils open wide and it makes one inhale deeply and exhale slowly. The work and the wind give one an appetite so that he can't get enough to eat when he puts his feet under the table. He just eats and eats after he feels full and then he wishes he could eat more.

"Son, you remember," says Pa, "that I have warned you —ain't I?"

"Only about one woman," I says. "You told me not to go there. You heard I was going to see Daisy Hornbuckle twice a week."

"Yes," says Pa—"Lucretia was her Aunt, Son. That is why I warned you. That set of wimmen didn't make good wives. I don't know about 'em now. I heard she was as much like Lucretia as two peas in a pod. That is why I warned you. I have the years behind me. You have the years before you. I remember this spot. I wouldn't talk about it so but we are working here today. I never dreamed I'd be hoeing corn here with a grown-up son. I never dreamed things would be changed in forty years and the old life would be replaced by things that are new. I never thought the church at Six Hickories would go and all the houses on this tract of land would go as time went on and on like wind over the corn. But things change and change. They just keep changing and you find that if you loved the things of yesterday you are lost today. I just often hear the pounding of the horses' hoofs on this ridge road. I can't hep it if the road is old and choked by briars. It's still a road to me. I can't hep it if the little trails that led from the main ridge road down these pints to the houses in the hollows and on the flats are just dips on the land today —I've run my horse over all of them and emptied my pistol over about every foot of these roads. Today, no one remembers. I remember—and I remember most of all, Lucretia!"

"Mom never dreams of all of this," I think, "when she comes to hoe her fall beans in the corn. She'll never dream of all of this when she comes and picks her apron full of beans—Mom with a slat bonnet on her head and drops of sweat standing like white blisters over her face and on her nose—Mom with her pipe in her mouth and blowing long streams of blue smoke to the wind. Mom will not know about this locust stump and where Pa and Lucretia had their pictures made. Mom will never know when she steps over the big yellow pumpkins ripe in the corn-balks after the frost has hit the corn and the blades have ripened into buff-colored fodder;—no, Mom will never know. Mom has seen the tin-type in the album. Mom has seen the young man with the high white collar, the black bow-tie and the black mustache—the heavy head of hair parted on the side. But Mom doesn't know the rock-pile in this cornfield is a chimney that stood at a house where Pa used to come three times a week before McKinley was assassinated. She doesn't know about the two rocks and the clot of bull-grass growing between them. Mom would wonder then and she would ask questions. Something would come back to her that she would not like; though, the years have pressed upon her and her youth is done. Yet, there is something she hasn't known and she would like to know."

I do not ask Pa about the stones and the clot of bull-grass. He sits and stares as the sunlight falls upon us—as it twists and shifts through the green leaves on the oak at the edge of the field. Shadows are shifting now. Shadows are shifting over the green stalwart corn that will make us bread and feed our hogs, mules, and cattle for the winter. It grows from the dust of Pa's dreams. It grows from the earth he knew and played over when Bill McKinley was President of the United States—a time that I have lived because his coming measured time for Pa. Time then covered the earth like a yellowing wind and kissed the blades of corn where the bird-like man with the long beard carried the three-legged contraption down the road—where now is only a dip of land and where the tall trees grow on both sides to mark out the time and foot-prints of man—to cover it over with time and wind and leaves and the roots of trees. It is strange and something far back of the days of McKinley calls me—something back to the days of Grover Cleveland when Pa first rode this ridge road and emptied his pistol at the big snakes that sunned on the rocks. Something time has done to these hills that makes me weep. Time has not only covered the foot paths and the ridge roads where the cattle pulled the pig-iron and the charcoal cord wood but time has covered a civilization —time has left it and it will never be unearthed for only their foot-prints were left, the traces of the hoes and the axes—and these are gone.

"And that hump of earth covered by bull-grass," I think, —"that hump of earth—that spot that Pa has left. If I had plowed this land—but Pa wouldn't let me plow it. He let me plow the rest of the land but he took the plow handles here. Pa skipped that little spot of land as if it were something sacred—and the two stones—and the tall corn that overshadows it—the talking of the corn blades that seem to whisper something ghost-like and strange about the love and the joy and the dreams of a civilization gone with the floating winds of time—I would like to know about it——"

"Son," says Pa—"this ain't gettin' the corn hoed, is it? Remember, we'll never be able to go over this corn again only with our hoes. It will be over the mule's back. It will be too tall to plow. The single tree will knock it down when the mule has to go around the stumps in the balks. Ah, just one more time with our hoes—and the pumpkin vines will cover the black loam here! Mule steps on one he'll squeeze the life out'n it——"

"Yes, Pa," I says——

"And, Son, you know the ways of man?" Pa asks.

"A few," I says—"I didn't know that a house had once stood here until you told me today. I didn't know that rock pile was the bones of a chimney and the foundations of a house and that locust stump was a shade tree where you made that tin-type picture that is in the family album—I didn't know but that picture connects something back for me with the days of Bill McKinley—the dream I have of them. There are so many things I do not know——"

"No," I says—"lots of things I don't know. I don't know why you have left that hump of earth with the two stones down there. I do not care to know. I know you have left them for a reason. I do not know that reason. I know you wanted to plow this hill and you plowed the mule slowly here. The mule acted as if he were dreaming and you followed between the handles of the cutter plow as if you were in a deep study as if something were calling you back —and now I can understand——"

"Son," says Pa, "that is sacred earth to me. I put rocks there. I've kept them there throughout these years; though the fire has run over that spot time again and again—the bull-grass has always marked it. Timber has been cut nigh it and coons caught from the tall trees over it—cattle have pawed hard down upon it when they strained behind their yokes—the mighty poplars and black oaks have crossed it —and now the corn grows around it—but that is sacred earth to me. The dust is the dust of you and me. That is the dust of my people. It is there under that bull-grass between the two rocks. You do not haf to talk about it. Let it pass over now as the wind blows over—remember I'm not as young as I used to be. I am not sorry about it. It just makes me remember. It is a dream. It is a love that has always lingered and I ain't a man to talk about love. I don't think you ever heard me sit around and talk about love. I always got sick of hearing a lot about love. But

something about Lucretia that always lingers—and if she
hadn't gone—if she hadn't gone—my life would have been
different—and she wasn't a woman for a living. Son, that
is why I warn you——"

"If Mom ever wonders about this spot of earth," I think
—"she is bound to see it. I wonder if she sits on one of the
stones and smokes her pipe when she comes to hoe her
beans in the tall corn rows. I wonder if she ever thinks to
cut the bull-grass—if she wonders why it stands in a row
of corn. I wonder if she knew about it if she would lay
a wisp of corn flowers and pumpkin blossoms there. I
believe Mom would. But that is Pa's dream; something he
has held all of these years; something buried by dirt and
time and wind and leaves. I wonder if Mom would think of
other hidden dreams as she picked the beans and looked at
the big yellow pumpkins laying in the corn balks. And the
dead bull-grass when the frosts come and the hump of earth
barren to the winds—weighted by snows and soaked by
rains and covered by the yellowish flowing of wind and
time!"

"The shadders are creepin' upon us, Shan," says Pa—
"We'd better get up and get to work. We'll never fill a
corn crib for this winter settin' on stumps. I believe in the
old way—one dream I've never lost—that is, Son, makin'
your livin' by the sweat of your brow. I believe in diggin'
it from the earth and not asking a red cent from any man.
That is what I learned when I was a boy and I am too old
to forget it now—that seems to be old too now-a-days! It's
the only sure way I know. Look at the pumpkins to roll in
the fodder shocks here this fall. Look at the beans there
will be to pick. Look at the corn to cut and the big white
ears of corn that will hang down two on a stalk like sticks
of stove wood—all these to shuck and we'll come with the
mules and the sled and haul big white piles of corn away
from each fodder shock and big yellow heaps of pumpkins.

Lord, atter we get all we want we'll have plenty for the cows and the fatten-hogs! And I love the smell of ripe corn and big fat pumpkins! I like to smell them when the frost hits the land! Everything is so purty then!"

Pa gets up slowly from the stump. He puts his hat back on his head. He pulls a wisp of home-made tobacco from his hip pocket. He twists a chew into his mouth of the bright burley leaf—he puts his bandana into his hip pocket. He takes his hoe and starts to peck-peck the earth—to cut the sprouts and rake the rich loose loamy silt around the guard roots of the rank growing corn. The sprouts fall behind his hoe and they wilt in the lengthening shadows of the sinking sun. They fall with the underside of their soapy leaves upturned—milk-white in the shadows of approaching evening. I follow Pa with my row of corn, my hoe white-gleaming when I raise it from the earth. We move toward the far end of the field. The rain-crow is still croaking for rain but the cool of the evening has made the corn look fresh again. The wilt has gone from the stalks and the dew has dampened the corn. They do not look to the bright heavens and pray for rain as they prayed under the blistering heat of a fire-ball sun. The dew has quenched the thirsting blades and the lengthening shadows of approaching night have cooled their parching tongues.

"We'll make a couple of rounds," says Pa, "before we turn in to do up the work. This is a good time to work. It is cool now and a body can do twice as much work as he can in the heat of the sun. I like to work this time of day. I feel as fresh as the corn."

I do not speak to Pa. I dig behind him. I keep my row of corn up with him and the weeds from my row, above his row, fall at Pa's heels. I work hard to get my row to the end of the field.

"Where is Lucretia?" I ask Pa.

"Under the earth at Plum Grove," says Pa—"where a lot

of my generation has gone—but she went too young—she died three months after I set the bull-grass down there between the two rocks! Just three months later!"

Silence. Shadows keep lengthening. Evening is coming on. Night will soon be here and the stars will come to the water-over-gravel colored sky. Night will come and the stars and the moon will look down on the tall new-ground corn. The stars will explode in the sky above the corn, beans, and pumpkins. Night will come and cover all. Night will come quickly as a dream—creep stealthily as a shadow —quietly as the footsteps of a fox.

"Two rounds," says Pa, "to yan end of the field and back. We can say then that we have done a good day's work. We can look at the clean corn below us and go home and be satisfied. I've always liked to see my work when the day is done. It puts something in me to see a clean cornfield."

We hoe the row to the end of the field.

"I'm quittin' Pa," I says. "I'm quittin' for today."

"Why, Son?" Pa asks. "Can't you stay with you old Pa?" You ain't all pooped out, are you?"

"No," I says, "I can take it. I could work all night if the moon and stars put enough light on the earth until I could see to dig the crab-grass and cut the sprouts. I could work tonight and all day tomorrow—but I've made a promise."

"What kind of a promise?" Pa asks.

"To a girl," I says.

"Who?" asks Pa.

"Daisy Hornbuckle," I says.

"I've warned you," says Pa.

"I know," I says. "Just seems like I can't take warning. I've been warned by people of no blood kin to me. I just can't break away from her."

"I've never seen the girl," says Pa—"but I'll bet she has brown eyes."

"Yes," I says——

"And purty white teeth and every one sound as a silver dollar," says Pa.

"Yes," I says—"not a cavity in a tooth she says. And I believe her. I believe everything she says."

"And wavy black hair?" Pa asks.

"Yes," I says—"like love vines on a fence——"

"And she is big and robust?" Pa asks——

"Yes," I says——

"And she laughs, laughs—laughs like the wind?" Pa asks.

"Yes," I says—"how do you know all of this?"

"It runs in the blood, Son—" says Pa—"Her father—I remember him. Just looks like Lucretia and they looked like their mother. I'd know a Hornbuckle when I met one."

"Son," says Pa, "you will haf to live and learn. Don't come to me and say I didn't warn you. Your life is your own. No one owns your life and your life is all you really own or ever own. So it belongs to you."

I stand my hoe against a stump at the end of the field. I walk down across the clean corn rows. Pa stands and watches me as I leave the new-ground corn field. He leans on his hoe handle and he looks at the heap of rocks and the hump of bull-grass, just below it. I look back to see him look at them and then he takes his eyes away to watch me go down the hollow.

"You are certainly my son," I hear him say to himself.

ONE OF GOD'S ODDLINGS

"GET YOUR HOE," says Pa, "and let's get to the knoll-piece first. Weeds takin that terbacker. Bottom leaves are fired already." I get a goose-neck hoe hangin on the garden fence. I pick up the dry seasoned handle and lift the hoe up betwixt me and the sun.

"See that hoe," says Pa, "how rusted it is. It ain't been in use now for three days. The damn rain and the terbacker runnin away with the weeds. That hoe ain't strong enough for a man like you. Hang it back on the fence and go look under the crib and bring me that old one-eyed sproutin hoe. It's the darb for cuttin sprouts and killin copperheads. Break a handle out—cut down a hickory saplin and stick another handle in."

I go to the crib and get the sproutin hoe under the crib. The hens have been wallowin under the crib in the dry dust and sprinkles of sand have grained the dry-seasoned sproutin hoe handle. I put it across my shoulder and we walk down past the house. We walk down the path by the spring toward the knoll-piece of tobacco.

Finn is behind us with the mule. He is ridin the mule. I can hear the trace chains rattlin. I can hear the patter-patter of the mule's feet on the hard dry earth. I can hear the wind ooze through the green wilted leaves beside the path. "Boy's comin with the mule, ain't he?" says Pa.

"Yes," I say.

"Didn't know about that boy," says Pa. "He's liable not to come as he is to come on a day hotter than hell."

80

The sun is hot. It is like a brushpile in the sky—a brushpile right above our heads. It is so hot one keeps lookin for
the ashes to drop from the air. The sun dances on the dead
logs where the lizards play. The lizards pretend they are
half asleep to catch a fly. They are out to get their bellies
filled with green flies.

"I like a damn lizard," says Pa. "it's a lot of help to us.
These fires burn up so many of them every year. W'y the
blasted things can catch more flies than a man can shake a
green bush at. I wouldn't kill a lizard a-tall."

I see Finn. He sits on the mule's back. He takes a sling
from his pocket, loads it with a rock. Whiz. "Lord, I made
the fur fly." Whiz. "I got him. He won't need no more
flies for his bark-colored belly." The lizard tumbles from
the log. Its gray belly upturns to the hot sun.

"Boy, I dread 'er this evening. Nothin a body can do but
stand 'er though. Weeds will die quick as snowballs melt
in hell on a day like this. It's the right time to murder
weeds," I say to Pa. We walk up the hill and Pa takes his
red bandanna and wipes the sweat from his neck the sun
has made redder than a turkey's snout. After Pa has wiped
his neck he twists the sweat from his red bandanna. It
runs like water and the stream is silver-colored in the sun.
I see a lizard on a stump. It catches a green fly. Finn is
comin up the hill on the mule's back and his big feet are
restin on the trace chains—and his hands clutch the hames.
Finn motions back and forward as the mule moves.

"Look at that mule how he's sweatin," says Pa, "funny
to ride a mule to the field, a big boy like Finn, when the
mule has to pull a plow through roots and stumps all evenin
hot as it is here.

"You take the bottom row," says Pa, "you're young and
on your first legs. I'll take the row above you and rake
the weeds down on you and the dust in your eyes."

"A go," I says to Pa, "and when you rake the weeds

down on me I'll dance in a hog trough at your second weddin." Pa laughs. Finn has hitched the mule to the plow. "Get up there, Barnie. Damn that stump to hell. Hitched a-ready. A hitch here and a hitch there—can't you dodge a stump once in a while, you stubborn devil you—Come on—Get along—" Barnie plods along like a snail on a dry rotted log on a hot day.

"It'll take him a long time to get this piece plowed the way that mule moves and hot as the sun is—" says Pa.

"We'll about get it hoed, won't we," I say, "by the time he gets it plowed?"

"Yes," says Pa, "goin like a snail you know we will——"

Click. Click. Click. Our hoes ring against the stubborn roots and the hot rocks. The dust flies up in little clouds. The wind blows the dust into our eyes. The sun beams down upon our backs. Click. Click. Click. Shadows go slowly over the field—trailin shadows—shadows in circles —a light-blue somethin—thin as the air movin in circles on the ground.

"See that buzzard," says Finn—"huntin for some pickin. Won't get it just now. Might this winter if they ain't nothin raised. Might get to pick a few cow ribs and calf ribs."

"Wonder what that buzzard smells," says Pa, "they tell me they smell like a hound dog, would have to smell or they couldn't find anything." Crows fly over and the sun moves around the deadened new-ground trees with wide rings of bark peeled from their bodies. Long shadows from the trees and little slow-moving shadows from the buzzards.

"Somethin's dead around here," says Finn, "or a body wouldn't see so many buzzards." Now Finn starts to plow again. Pa starts the hoe. I have stopped lookin at the sky and the cloud shadows and buzzards that trail the dry hard dusty dirt.

"Finn, ain't it about time we have a little snort?" says Pa.

"Just as you say, Pa," says Finn. "When you say the word you know I'm right on your hip."

So, Finn walks slosh-slush barefooted across the dry clods of dirt. Little dust pods pop up when he lifts his feet up—across the plowed rows—down under the flat to a big black stump where the water oozes from the ground, right above where the mules drink. I see Finn get it. It is a jug, a white jug with a brown neck and a corncob stopper. Finn puts the strap across his shoulder and comes up to Pa.

"A little eye-opener on a hot day like this when a body's got dust in his eyes and a little drowsy," says Pa.

Pa puts the jug to his lips and the white body gleams in the sun. "Gurgle—gurgle—gurgle—" Pa drinks.

"Give me a snort, Pa," says Finn. Finn drinks with Pa.

"Have a drink, Shan."

"Don't like it, Finn."

"Can't take it," says Pa. "He's one of God's oddlings. Some funny about old Shan. He thinks a lot about books and writin things down."

Pa drinks again and then he hands the jug back to Finn. "Another snort, son, and then take it back to the water where it will keep cool."

"All right, Pa." Finn drinks from the jug. He puts the corncob stopper back, walks across the field with little clouds of dust trailin him.

The tobacco is pretty in long rows where we have cut the weeds from the plants and heaped loose loamy earth around the green-sticky stems. Below us like thin dry hay cut green and cured green—the weeds are cured and strewn on the ground. The tobacco plants drink in the sun and wave wilted fingers to the slow lazy summer breeze. This wind is lazy. It is not lazy as Finn. But Finn will take new courage now.

Pa says: "That's a boy atter my own heart. He likes the things I like. We like to do things together like takin a little snort unbeknowns to your Ma. She says it's bad on a body's heart that stuff that Toodle Powell makes. But it ain't. It would a killed me long ago if your Ma had a-been right."

Pa is workin harder now. The sweat streams. I work hard to keep my row ahead of Pa so he can't rake his weeds down on my row and make work harder for me. Here is a stump in my row. I say, "Go easy here, Pa, I got a stump and a lot of high weeds and crab grass around it."

"That's all in the game, son," says Pa. "You either hump to it or I'll smear your baulk with weeds and weeds a-God's plenty."

Finn moves faster than a snail above us now. The mule goes around the hill slow gaited and pulls the plow slowly but surely up against the black oak stumps and the rocks. Click. Click. Click. Looks like these hoes would strike fire hot as the hoes are and hot as the ground is.

"Men ain't the men they used to be," says Pa, lookin up at the buzzard, "but that's just what the Bible says—Men will grow weaker and wiser and pon my word that's the gospel facts. I ain't the man old Dad was. He could hold more whiskey than me, cut more timber, clear more land —better with his fists than I am or ever hope to be. He was a man. Here I am not nigh as big as one of my boys and I can whop 'em on less ground than they can stand on. I can do more work. I can beat you boys at anything but cipherin and schoolin. See you boys are a little wiser than me, but I got everythin else on you."

"Yes, Pa—You're feelin that jug now."

"Grandpa cleared the land. He built the houses. He helped fight a war for the nation and several at home. But look today! The fields grow up in sprouts again that he cleared and the houses that he built have rotted down some of them and them left standin is soon goin to fall. The lizards play on them. These sprouts whip the men that fight them. What's the use in all this work——"

"That's why I said you was one of God's oddlings, son. You won't even drink the licker like your Pap drinks and your Grandpa drunk. You won't smoke the weed that we are plowin. You ain't like your people. You are goin to get weaker and wiser if you ain't careful."

"It takes a strong will and a weak mind," says Finn as he stops the mule above us, "to stand this. W'y a mule, little sense as he's got, he wouldn't come out here and work like us if we didn't make him."

"That shows he ain't got the sense," says Pa.

"Have it your way," says Finn, "but you can work it either way."

"Ready for another round," I say to Pa, "let's get up to that black oak snag by sundown. We'll be makin a showin then."

"We'll go two rounds above that snag," says Pa—"We'll be way up there by quittin time." Click. Click. Click. Click. Click. The hoes whetted bright gleam in the sun, when we lift them up to hit the weeds. Finn lifts the plow up. He kicks the trash from behind the cutter. He sets it back on the other side of the stump.

Finn says: "Get up there, Barnie. Whoa back, Barnie." And the mule creeps out along the furrow.

"Terbacker is damn hard stuff to raise and make money out'n," says Pa, "all I ever try to make out'n it is tax money. You know it's a little money crop. Raise enough corn to do us and other truck and sell the terbacker. Sow beds for plants when the March snow is on the hill. Strip it at damp spells in the winter time. Terbacker is a all-year crop. Never get through with it. Then sometimes don't get enough out'n it to pay the taxes."

"We didn't make anything off'n this when we had it in last year, did we?"

"Atter we paid to truck it down to Maymore and paid a man to handle it for us—we owed the house thirty-five cents, not countin all our work for the summer. A fellar wrote me a letter for that thirty-five cents. I had Finn to write him a letter and tell him if I ever got the thirty-five cents I'd pay him here on earth. If we went to Heaven both of us and raised terbacker and had better luck with our prices I'd pay him in Heaven and if we both went to Hell the debt would be canceled, for we wouldn't need thirty-five cents there. We'd both be shovelin coal. He never did answer the letter. Guess he thought I was a goodin."

I look at the rows of tobacco—pretty in the sun and wind—pretty in the hot sunlight—pretty in the lazy wind. And I think. "We give our blood to you. We give our life. We do not get back what we give. The land does not get anything back. We cannot give the land anything until we can get something to give the land from the pretty plan of tobacco. Yes, I love to write about you. I love to throw the dirt up around you with a hoe. I love to cut the weeds from around you and give you a chance to grow. I love the smell of you in the wind. I love to hang you when you are the color of black oak leaves in September. I love to hang you to poles in the barns. I give my sweat and blood to you because I love to give them to you or I would not do it. Who gets my love for you?"

Click. Click. Click. Click. Click. Click. See our hoes gleamin in the sun. The sun is gettin low. The sun is goin down over the Seaton Ridge. There are chestnut tree snags pictured against the sun. If I did not know about the sun and the sun had been above hours ago—right up above the buzzards in the lazy sky—I would say the snags are growin in the sun. But the sun is a brushpile on fire and it is tryin to burn us up and the tobacco up. It has made the sweat roll off the sleek mule's back and run down to the few long hairs on his belly and drip off white beads to the ground on the dry clods of earth. Click. Click. Click. Click. Click.

"Someday," says Pa, "when you get out in the world—when them books takes you out, you'll smoke big cigars maybe made out'n this terbacker. You remember, will you, what you pay for—you remember. God's oddlings. My Pap used terbacker and my Ma used it. I use it. Finn uses it. Your Ma uses it. You don't. Odd, ain't it."

"This round puts us above the snag," I say to Pa.

"I told you we'd get there before sundown. We're comin back atter supper and go a couple rounds more."

"You're dog-tired now, Pa, and you'll need rest."

"No rest for the wicked when the terbacker's in the weeds."

"You can't stand work like this."

"What I can't stand old Finn and his Pa's got it right down there in the jug. Hell, I go long as I can go and the spirits carry me on further."

Pa's overalls is wet as if he'd waded Little Sandy. There is dirty streaks on Pa's face of dust and grime like little maretails rubbed on clear-as-mountain-water sky. The skin on Pa's hands is rough as black oak bark. His neck is redder than a turkey's snout. Finn's face is the color of a wet clod. I feel sorrier for the mule than I do for my brother Finn. The mule has had to take it on the shoulder all day, the collar that the trace chains pull against. He has not been able to tell Finn when he wanted water and what was hurtin him. He just went up against the plow and smelled the dust. Finn followed him through the dust. Old tall Finn, young and strong, his body awkward wrigglin between the handles of the plow, his eyes set to the far end of the field. No wonder he takes it slow. He could not take it faster. Finn knows what the mule can stand and what he can't stand. Oaths, the Lord's name in vain, have gone from Finn's mouth all day under the hot sun. Wonder if the Lord heard Finn! Maybe, if he did the Lord won't condemn, for there's two ways of lookin at it. Finn does want the Lord to damn the stumps and the rocks when they made the plow handles kick him in the short ribs hard enough to crack a walnut.

"I hope they ain't no rough ground and rooty ground to plow in Heaven. If there is," says Pa, "a lot of us if we get there's goin to get into it with the Lord—A body's got to cuss when a plow handle jabs his ribs or punches him in the belly.

"Ain't no wonder so many men get their religion all over again atter they get through plowin the new ground."

"It's about time for beans, don't you think?"

"I told you I'd put you in the shade, son. You're goin to get weaker and wiser foolin with books. You can't take it like you use to take it. You, big as a skinned ox. Me, a old dried-up man. I can take it. But not like Pap."

The sun is behind the ridge. The place where the sun went down is redder than a sassafras leaf in October. It is red on the water-colored sky as brush pile just burned to the earth and the wind refreshin the embers. Finn comes around the hill plowin the earth where there is no sun now —where the earth is but a solid shadow.

"Gettin cool now," says Finn, "just the right time to plow land like this and this time o' the year. It's been so hot a body could hardly plow. But we've clumb up on it right sharply this evenin." Pa's eyes and Finn's eyes have a far-away eagle look in them.

Pa says: "Books has hurt your eyes. You are a oddlin. Books. Books." And Pa kicks a dry clod. Books are second-life. Books are dry as a clod. Man is made of a dry clod or a wet clod. Life was breathed into man and he become a livin soul as wind is breathed into the mule through his dry dusty nostrils and he becomes a mirey beast—sweaty, grimy

—with white pretty beads of sweat drippin from his belly
onto the dry-as-dust clod that is man.

"I never smoked or chawed terbacker till I was twenty-
one years old.

"I was attendin a funeral—old Wilkes Thompson was
buried that day—plow kicked him in the touchy parts and
they brought him to the house on a sled. He was dead in
two hours. Well, I helped dig his grave. I helped make a
coffin for old Wilkes and I hauled him in it. Well, Red
Callihan was there and he pulled out a twist and offered
me a chaw. I told him I didn't chew terbacker nor smoke
it. He called me a oddlin and I says to him, 'Red, give me
that damn plug o' terbacker and I'll show you who's a
oddlin around here.' I took a chaw and I been a terbacker
worm ever since."

"Ma smoked when you married her," I says.

"Yes," says Pa, "she has smoked ever since she was a little
tot—smoked ever since she used to light her grandma's pipe
and she drawed the stem to see if it was lit and she got a
taste o' the smoke and you know how it is. She's been
smokin ever since. Pap never did remember the first chaw
he ever chewed."

"Time to unhook the traces and take the mule to water,"
says Finn—"hear that whippoorwill! Boy, ain't we walked
things here this evenin! Look how we've walked upon this
hill."

"Yes," says Pa, "we've walked this work today. Look
behind us. Look at the dead weeds. I like to look up the hill
at the livin weeds. I want to lay 'em low. Tomorrow we'll
do it. We'll walk out'n this knoll-piece tomorrow. Get the
jug, Finn, and let's take a snort. My legs ain't what they
used to be or I'd run down there and get that jug."

"I'll get it, Pa." Finn crosses the field with a fresh stride.
Finn is not tired as Pa. He gets a jug from the spring. Here
he comes back up the hill. His stride is slower up the hill

than it was down. "If a body planted taters on this hill all
he'd have to do is dig the bottom row and the rest would
all run out."

"Lord, that looks good to me. Unstopper it, Finn. Get
that cob out. Give me a snort. I'm thirsty as a dry goose."

"All right, Pa."

"Juggle—juggle—gurgle—gurgle—juggle—juggle——"

"Pa, you're dry as a chip. You're a dry clod of dirt soakin
it all up, ain't you——"

"Plenty left."

Finn drinks and drinks. Finn is a pile of sand if Pa is a pile
of sand and I can almost see it runnin out in the dry pile
of sand and the sand turnin to the color of a shadow.

"Lord, that's good."

"Son, if me and you get to Heaven and they have a lot
of new ground to plow there, what are we goin to do for
spirits?"

"Do without," says Finn. "Don't think they'll be any
terbacker raised there if old Brother Toady Leadingham is
right. He said before a man got to Heaven he had to change
the color of his spit."

"Cuts me and your Ma and you out."

"If anybody gets to Heaven," I says, "it'll be poor old
Ma—Brother Leadingham's just got smoke in his eyes. It
makes me mad to hear a preacher say a lot o' stuff like that
and get off'n the Gospel when they's so much of it to
preach."

"Time to go, boys—whippoorwills singin everywhere
now. Hear em. It's time to get in and get a bite of supper."
Pa puts his hoe by a hickory stump. I put my hoe beside of
Pa's hoe.

"Stand that hoe up so it won't rust. Ain't you learned
that yet?"

So I stand my hoe up. Pa starts down the hill. "I'm leadin
old Barnie in—he's worked so hard. He's worked harder 'n

any of us. And he never gets no benefit of this terbacker. Just think o' it."

"Think o' it," says Pa. "That's all you know about it. You know when Mart Henson stuck over there on the Runyan Hill that time and started to put hay under his mules and set fire to it and his old woman stopped him. I went over there. Well, I said to Mart, 'Mart, I got one mule that I can hitch to that wagon and he'll fetch it out of there.' And Mart said to me, 'I'll bet you two tens and a five spot against your mule he can't!' 'That's a called bet,' I said to Mart. Well, I come back over to the house. I geared old Barnie up and took him over there. The first pop out'n the box and Barnie snapped that wooden singletree in two just like it was a holler milkweed. And I said to Mart then, 'Loan me one of your iron singletrees.' And Mart loaned it to me. He laughed and said, 'I guess that mule of yours will bend that double.' And I says, 'If the wagon don't move, he will.' And Mart laughed. Well, the first time old Barnie yanked on it he didn't shake it and the singletree didn't bend neither. And old Mart just haw-hawed and laughed and said, 'He's my mule.' So I remembered old Barnie and me is right good friends. When I used to buy sweet scrap Red Hoss terbacker to mix with my homemade I used to give old Barnie a little nibble now and then and he followed me all over the pasture for a nibble o' terbacker. Then I got to mixin his terbacker just like I did mine. What I chawed I give the same mixture to that Barnie mule. I knowed if I had a little Red Hoss scrap mixed with a little homemade and hold it out'n front of that mule, that he come out'n there or break a hamestring. So I says to Mart, 'Mart, give me a chaw o' Red Hoss.' He reached me the terbacker poke. I gets in front of the mule with that terbacker poke and of all pullin that I ever seed in my born days it was right there. I thought he'd strip the gears off'n his back. But he didn't. That wagon begin to

move and right out'n there she come up out of that chug
hole. And I give old Barnie the whole poke of Mart's terbacker. Lord, he got raw—pretended it was over the poke
o' terbacker, but it was over the two tens and the five spot.
I took my mule and the money and went home. That
helped pay the last land note on our place.

"That mule just loves terbacker. He'd break a man up
keepin him up in terbacker. I don't give him but a chaw
every mornin. Ain't you seen him out followin me around
the pasture?"

"Yes," I says——

"Well he was wantin terbacker."

"Well—I'm a suck-egg mule," says Finn, "I didn't believe a brute of any kind liked terbacker."

"W'y anybody when they get the taste of it will like it.
Look at your Ma when she's a little tot she got the taste o'
the smoke and she hid her pipe out a long time and smoked
—even after she married me. I knowed it all the time. I
caught her at it one day and I says to her, 'W'y Sall, bring
your pipe on to the house. It's perfectly natural for you to
like terbacker.' Finn there was slippin out in the brush at
five and smokin. I knowed it. I never said a word. It's in
the blood. Brutes like it when they get the taste. And you
know the taste o' the devil is allus better 'n his broth. So
when you get a taste o' the terbacker it's better'n the
smoke."

Now we are down to the waterin hole. Barnie drinks and
drinks. Finn gets on his belly and puts his head down to
the waterin hole and drinks beside the mule.

"Tinnn-tinnn—tinnn—tinn——"

"That's Ma hittin the plow pint with the hammer and
a-callin us to supper. We'd better hurry along," I says.

"Now someday," says Pa, "I don't care if you are a
oddlin. God's got a lot o' oddlins, you know. Well, you'll
go back to the weed. The weed that grows over there on

that hill under that thin moonlight. The weed we've
sweated in today. You'll go back to that. It's in your blood.
Men come back to the waters o' the mountains, don't they,
atter they've spent their boyhood days where they can
drink them and hear them squall around like a panter at
night. Well, you'll come back to the weed. Remember
what I tell you if it don't come true. The Devil nor books
nor nothin else can stop you from it. Not even Heaven.
They'll be a pile o' 'em that don't go there if they have to
change the color o' their spit."

Pa walks slowly up the path. Finn leads Barnie—Finn,
the big tall barefooted thing. But old Finn can take it. He
knows how to take it and keep goin. He's good when the
day ended as when the day started. He does a day's work
too. "I think I got that big green scorpion down there.
The rock busted, but I turned him over."

Behind me, I see the moon come over the field. "The
moon always shines pretty in Kentucky," Janey says.

I see the tobacco plants under the light of the moon.
They are pretty under the light of the moon. The hill is
clean of weeds. The dead oak trees are bigger than hoe
handles against the sky. The stars are goose-eyes in the
color of a dirty-drake's-back sky. The lizards must be
asleep on the hoe-handle trees. Here is the well box and the
big sassafras tree by the well box in our kitchen yard.

"I want a gourd of that water," says Finn.

"Biggest sassafras I ever saw in my life," says Pa. "I
would a cut it when I built this house, but it's pintly bad
luck to burn it and I didn't want it a-layin around the place
here in the way."

HELL'S ACRE

"WHAT ARE YOU SITTIN HERE FOR, Adger?" Ma asks. "Can't you hear the guns a-boomin at the fur-end of the pasture field? Why aint you a-helpin out?"

Ma stopped sweeping the floor and looked at me. She looked at me with her gray hawk-eyes. The weight of the pipe on the long stem sorta jimmied the pipe in Ma's mouth since she's lost some of her front teeth. Ma stood in front of me solid as an oak tree. She looked mean out'n her eyes when she spoke to me.

"You know why I aint out there," I says. "You know I was jest a boy when I first picked up a musket and went out there to fight the Sturgins. I didn't know how to fight. That was in 1929. I've had enough of that damn war over a line fence. We've been fightin all this time and we aint got a thing settled."

I laid my pipe down on the bottom of a hickory split-bottomed chair. I pulled up my overall leg above my knee.

"Here is part of what I got," I says. "This aint nigh all. I was shot through the hip. I was shot in the shoulder blade and the bone was nicked. You can see the fat part on my right ear is shot off. Ma, I've had enough of this war. I've been thinkin about some sort of peace."

Ma took her pipe out'n her mouth. It was too hard to hold in her mouth while she talked. She looked down on my leg at the tiny scars that glistened like white-soup beans from my ankle up above my knee. It looked like there's two hundred tiny scars on my leg.

"I was shot down with a autermatic," I says. "Kam Sturgin pumped six loads of buckshot at me. If he'd a-been ten yards closter to me I'd a-been a gone-goslin. I'll never forget how I felt when I's shot. Jest seems like the props went from under me all of a-sudden."

"You was shot in the leg in 1930," says Ma.

"And I was shot through the hip in 1933," I says. "My shoulder blade was nicked in 1935. My ear was shot off in 1936. I've been sprinkled with shot so many times I don't mind it any more than I do a light shower of April rain."

Ma put her pipe back in her mouth. She took a draw on her long pipestem. The fire was out in Ma's pipe. She reached in her apron pocket and got a match. She struck it on the jamm-rock above the fireplace. Ma lit her pipe again.

"Don't sweep around me, Ma," I says. "Leave the dirt on the floor around my chear."

"You talk crazy, Adger," says Ma.

"That aint crazy," I says. "If you don't sweep around me it is a sign I'll get married."

Ma laughed and laughed. She thought I was crazy. I was glad to see Ma laugh. She laughed more than she had laughed the past nine years. I'll tell you since we've been at war over the line fence there aint been much laughin at our house.

"You air old enough to get married," says Ma. "If you live until next August you'll be twenty-two."

Ma swept around me. She left a circle of dirt around my chear. I sat before the fire and baked my scarred leg. Heat felt so good to it. Seemed like it lost a lot of feelin in it since Doc Holbrooks spent two days pickin the buckshot out. Some are left in my leg. I can feel them under the skin. They feel like hard dry grapes. I put my overall leg down atter my leg was baked until it was red by the wood fire.

"You aint very stiff in that leg, air you?" Ma ast. "None of the jint water run out'n your knee, did it?"

"Nope," I says. "The buckshot didn't go in deep enough."

"Listen to the guns this mornin," says Ma.

"I've been settin here listenin," I says. "That aint nothin. We hear 'em all the time. Pears like the fightin is the hardest in February and March when the ground is froze and we can't plow. I'd better get my gun and get out there."

"Be careful, Adger," says Ma. "Your body is a wreck now. Don't get shot any more. You'll not be able to stand many more bullets in your body."

"My body's good fer a lot of bullets yet," I says. I picked up Hulda. Hulda is my long-range single barrel. She's thirty-six inches in the barrel, a ten-gauge, and full choked. Use super shells loaded with two extra grams of powder and chilled buckshots. Sometimes I ring the shell so it'll shoot like a rifle when I'm shootin at a Sturgin at long range. I put Hulda across my shoulder, I sorty dragged my stiff leg and walked out'n the house. Ma came to the door with her broom in her hand to watch me go.

"Do be careful, son," says Ma.

"I've been there too many times," I says. "I'll watch what I'm doin."

I walked out past the barn. Then I went around the path through the wood's pasture to the fur-field. The wind blowed lonesome-like in the bare oak-tops above my head. The winds made a lonesomer sound in the pine-tops. The closter I got to the fur-field the louder the guns got. I clim to the top of the yaller clay bank. I looked over at the cedar tree. That was where Pa give his men orders. I whistled our signal—two longs and a short whistle. Pa answered me with two short whistles. That was the signal that all was well. I crawled on my belly over the frozen ground down to the hole where Pa was under the cedar tree.

"They air takin pot shots at us from that beech grove down yander," Pa whispered. "The damn dirty cowards air in the timber on us. We're jest shootin enough this mornin to keep 'em back. We can't hit 'em in all that timber. We've skint a lot of trees around 'em though."

Pa was layin down in the hole chewin his home-twisted burley terbacker. He had two big sand rocks above him and his musket was pinted between the two sand rocks. Pa had a pot of coffee on a little fire down in the hole. Smoke went out'n the hole and up among the limbs on the cedar tree.

"The Sturgins can see your smoke here," I says. "They'll get you, Pa."

"They know who's in this hole," says Pa. "This is the place they can't get. I'm upon this little rise here. I can look every way and give my men orders. I think I put another bullet in old Kam Sturgin this mornin. If I did, this makes eight times I've shot 'im. He's a hard booger to kill."

"Spat—"

The cedar bark flew over us. Pa opened fire with his musket toward the beech timber. Pa shot until his musket was hot. He shot from between the sand-rocks. Our men opened fire plum across the end of our pasture field. They knowed the Sturgins were tryin to get Pa.

"The Sturgins can't take my land," says Pa. "Our war started in 1918. We fit 'em with the courts until 1928. I've sunk fifteen hundred dollars with lawyers' fees and court costs. Then the Supreme Court give the Sturgins that acre of ground. They've lost nearly all their land payin lawyers' fees to get it and they aint got it yet. I jest decided powder and lead was cheaper than lawyers' fees and court costs. That's the reason we've been fightin another ten years fer that acre of land."

Pa put Hulda between the sand-rocks. Pa started feedin 'em the ringed shells from Hulda's muzzle, and we heard 'em screamin and hollerin. They thought we'd turned a cannon loose on 'em that shot buckshot.

"We'll win this fight with this kind of a gun," says Pa.

"Did the Hillmans ever fight their kinfolks?" I ast Pa.

"Never in my lifetime, Son," says Pa as he opened fire with Hulda at the beech grove. Pa jest talked like nothin had happened and kept shootin. "Never in my lifetime, Son. We respect our own people. We've had little fist fights among ourselves but they don't amount to nothin. We've never used a gun or a knife. We've never even used a rock or a club when we had our little skirmishes with our own folks."

"Gee," I says, "that's fine!"

I jumped out of the hole and started over the bank. I think every Sturgin's gun barked at the same time when I hit the open field bent over half-double, runnin. The bullets hit all around me. They wheezed over my head. One went through the elbow of my coat-sleeve.

"Take kiver," Pa hollered. "What's the matter? Have you gone batty? You'll git shot again."

"I aim to end this damn war," I says.

I leaped over the yellow clay bank safe from the flyin bullets. I can't tell you how I felt. I took down the hollow to Kam Sturgin's farm. I took down the hollow behind the winter-fern-kivered bluff. I was safe from their battle lines. I was soon behind the Sturgin lines. I could still hear the guns boomin over toward our house. I walked down the hollow with a pipe of terbacker until I come to Kam Sturgin's big log house. I'd allus wanted Effie Sturgin. I would get her.

The hound dogs run out to the gate and started barkin through the palins at me. The palins were tall and the tops sharpened so a body couldn't climb over the fence. Kam was fixed fer us so we couldn't attack his house. I was goin to make an attack a different way.

"Howdy-do!" I hollered. "Is there anybody at home?" I could peep through the palin cracks. I could see eyes peepin from the winder glasses at me. No one dared to come outside the door.

"Kam Sturgin and his men have been whopped," I hollered. I thought that would bring somebody out'n the house. It did bring somebody out'n the house. It brought Effie Sturgin out'n the woodshed. She walked out with her sleeves rolled to her elbows. She looked like an angel to me.

"You might say Pa is whopped," says Effie, "but I don't believe it. He will never be whopped by the infernal Hillmans and their click. They might kill 'im but they won't whop 'im. Is that you, Adger Hillman?"

"Yes, mam, this is Adger Hillman," I says. "This is all that aint been shot away by Sturgin bullets."

"What are you doin here?" she ast.

"I've throwed my gun down and quit fightin," I says. "I'm tired of fightin."

"Have the others quit fightin?" she ast.

"Hell, no, Honey," I says. "Can't you hear the guns crackin? I'll tell you what is wrong with the Sturgins. They can't shoot."

"They can shoot," says Effie. "They are good marksmen."

"They couldn't hit me," I says. "I was runnin fast as a rabbit."

Effie looked at me and I looked at her through the palin fence.

"I've got to get back to washin clothes," says Effie.

"Let me hep you," I says.

"I can't let you come in here," she says.

"Yes you can," I says.

"Ma would take the top of the house off if she's to see you come in at this gate!"

"Aint there another way around?" I ast.

Effie stood and looked at me. She shivered in the February wind. She stood a minute before she answered me.

"I don't believe you are up to a trick, Adger," she says. "You know we aint on good terms with your people."

"I'll cross my heart," I says, "that I aint up to a trick."

"Jest don't let Ma see you slip behind the woodshed," says Effie. "There's a trap door there. I'll open it. Come in from the backside."

Effie walked back in the shed as if nothin had ever happened. I slipped along beside the palins. I slipped up behind the woodshed. Effie opened the door from the inside. I walked in the woodshed. The palin fence tied onto each side of the woodshed and that made it part of the fence.

"Thank you, Effie," I says as I walked into the shed. "I've come to see you. I have something to tell you."

"What?" Effie ast.

"We can stop this war among our people," I says.

"How can we do it?"

"Get married," I says, "if you love me enough."

"You've ast me too suddenly," says Effie.

"Honey, we can," I says. "You know we can. All that's ever kept us apart has been our people. Your people hast nearly got me four different times. You see me limpin, don't you?"

"Yes," says Effie, "what is the matter?"

"Your Pa filled my leg full of buckshot."

"Pa did?"

"Yes, your Pa did," I says. "Kam Sturgin shot me."

"I can't hep it if he did shoot you," says Effie. "You was out to get Pa."

"You can hep it," I says. "You can kiss me for every buckshot that went in my leg."

Effie didn't answer me.

"You know kinfolks don't fight each other here," I says. "We won't fight our kinfolks. Do you fight yourn?"

"You know we don't," says Effie. "You know that kinfolks don't fight each other here."

"Then we can stop this war."

"Yes."

Effie put her arms around my neck. I helt her close. I kissed her and she kissed me. We jest let the washin tub of clothes stand. We loved and loved in the woodshed. I'll tell you she's the purtiest woman I'd ever seen. Her tiny white wrists was just about the size of my middle-finger and my index finger put together. Her eyes were green like a cat's eyes. Her lips were clean and purty and red with bloom as the petals on a spring pink. Her teeth were white as grains of corn when the shuck has just been stripped off. She was nearly as tall as I was.

"I can't love you all afternoon," she says. "I've got to get my washin out on the line."

"I never washed clothes in my life," I says, "but I'll hep you. I'd rather wash clothes than carry a gun and fight all the time."

I couldn't wash clothes very well. I washed them the best I could. I'd work awhile then I'd hold Effie in my arms. I washed clothes and loved Effie all afternoon in the Sturgins' woodshed. It was the best way to end a war I'd ever seen. I jest wondered why I hadn't thought of it before. I'll tell you it was a pleasant way to end a war. Effie wondered why she hadn't thought of it before. I never even thought about my brothers, cousins, uncles, brothers-in-law over there layin in the broom-sage on the frozen ground on their bellies and poundin away over an acre of land. I didn't even think about Pa in the hole under the cedar tree drinkin coffee and chewin terbacker fer his nerves. They could all fight and be damned. If it did or it didn't stop the war—I was marryin Effie Sturgin and takin her out'n the mess and

gettin out'n it myself. You don't know what one of these
damned long fights is until you've been in one. I was gettin
out and stayin out.

"You'll haf to go, Adger," says Effie. "It will soon be
dark and our men that are alive will be slippin back through
the woods to their homes to do up their work. A lot of
them will never slip back. Pa has been shot seven times.
He's still alive and fightin. Uncle Charlie was shot in the
leg. He's got white swellin in his leg now and he hast to
drag it along. Cousin Eif, Charlie, Bill and Van sleep on
the hill—brother Cy and Mort sleep beside of them. Uncle
Dave, Uncle Martin, Brother-in-law Did kilt—nearly all
the men hast been shot sometime or the other—or they've
been skint with bullets."

"We aint been shot up that bad," I says—"I've lost one
brother, four cousins, one uncle and a brother-in-law.
They are buried on the hill jest across from the hill where
your people are buried."

"What kind of a place is it where they are fightin?"
Effie ast me.

"You've got your pasture fence set behind the line fence
five acres deep and ten acres long," I says. "We've got our
fence set back the same way. We're losin fifty acres of our
best land. You're losin fifty acres of your best land. Our
bull was shot through the brisket with a stray ball behind
our lines. We've had two calves and a cow shot. We're jest
fightin on it to get one worthless acre. Look at the money
spent in the courts and look at the men kilt and plugged.
Men that will never fight again and the men that will never
be able to work again. Look how our neighbors air gettin
ahead of us over behind the ridges. They are raisin terbacker and corn while we are raisin hell. When we marry,
Effie, it will be ended. We'll all be kinfolks then."

"Give me time to think," says Effie. "You know I love
you, Adger. I've allus loved you. I've been afraid to go

with you. I hate your last name. I'll allus hate the name of
Hillman. It's a mean name. It's the name the Devil wants
it to be. You must come and see me. Come when you can.
Give one long whistle. I'll leave the door unfastened to the
woodshed. Don't let anybody see you. You must go now."

"I'll see you," I says.

I pulled Effie close to me. I kissed her purty face over
and over. I was fightin a different kind of war now. I loved
this kind of war.

"Good-by, Honey," I says. I grabbed my cap and I went
out at the trap door. I hit the road runnin with my cap in
my hand. I took up the crick the way I'd come. I heard
people talkin around the bend in the road. I jumped over
the bank and hid behind a rock. I hadn't more than got
behind the rock until I saw about a hundred men comin
down the road with their guns on their shoulders. The men
in front were walkin fast and a-cussin the Hillmans.

"I'd soon shoot a Hillman as a rabbit," said a tall bearded
Sturgin.

"They air a bunch of polecats," says a small man walking
beside of the tall bearded man, "and we got to get 'em
thinned out when the green gets back in the trees and we
can snipe 'em from the cliffs."

Then I heard a man groanin and hollerin. Four men were
carryin him. Two men walked behind and carried a leg
a-piece. Two walked in front and carried an arm a-piece.
They had their muskets strapped around their shoulders.
The man's head was bent over with his face turned toward
the sky. He would groan when the men shook him. His
long red beard stuck out from his chin like the handle of a
cane. The wind moved his beard as the men walked. His
clothes around his waist were red with blood.

"Oh, my side," he would groan.

"Don't go on so, Kam," says one of the men a-hold of his
leg. "We can't let the Hillmans know you've been plugged

again. It gives them a fresh start. They'll be right over on
our side of the fence tearin up the dirt. Old Tarvin Hillman
will have his hole dug over on our side the fence blastin us
with buckshots."

"Oh, if you'd been plugged through and through like I
have," Kam moaned, "you'd groan too. You know I'm
tough. I can take it. This is eight bullet holes I have in me.
I'm plugged through and through and that silk handkerchief feels funny in my stummick."

"It's in place though, Kam," says a short stocky Sturgin
carryin one of Kam's arms. "I know it is fer I pulled it
through the bullet hole and tied a knot in each end so it
couldn't slip out. Take it easy. We'll soon have you home.
We can give you some hooch and you'll feel better. It's
three-ply hooch and it will put the spirit in you."

"Hooch, hell," Kam mutters—"I'm hurt. Old Tarvin
Hillman plugged me with a rifle. I know he plugged me.
I saw a cloud of smoke under his cedar tree the second I's
plugged."

I was glad when that crowd of Sturgins got past me. I
changed my path. I went over Sturgin land to the acre of
land we'd been fightin over. It got a little dark before I
got there and I got afraid. I thought I might meet the
spirits of the dead men that had been kilt by Hillman bullets. I'll tell you the trees over in Sturgins' pasture field
clear back to the second fence was riddled by our bullets.
The bark was all skint off'n the trees. It was a ugly dark
field. You could feel empty cartridges all over the ground
with your feet. You could find holes dug out everyplace.
Our side of the line fence wasn't shot up half as bad as the
Sturgin side. We must a-had better guns. In all our war
with the Sturgins Pa had jest lost one finger and had been
plugged in the thigh once when he crawled out'n a hole.
I had sad thoughts though as I dragged my numb leg across
the pasture-field of brown broom-sage in the moonlight.

It was before daylight when Pa took his men and went
to the field to shoot at Sturgins across the line-fence. I
stayed behind to hep Ma feed the hogs, milk the cows,
carry in water. I made up my mind not to go to the pasture
field anymore and shoot across the line fence at the
Sturgins. When I thought about the Sturgins I couldn't
hate that name. It was a good name to me anymore since
I'd seen Effie Sturgin. I could see her cat-colored eyes looking at my beardy face. I could see her purty hair and her
purty white teeth. I could feel her soft hair in my hand
and her tall body clost to me when I loved her. Hell, I
didn't want to fight anymore. I'd had enough fightin. I
didn't ever want to fight again. I wanted to get out'n it.
I wasn't a-goin to get kilt over an acre of old poor worthless land when there was a girl in the world as purty as
Effie Sturgin.

As I set on a milk stool and milked Old Roan, I could
see Effie Sturgin in a little house. It was fur away from our
pasture field. It was out'n the range of the bullets. It was
over in Hog Hollow. I could see her washin her clothes and
my clothes under the shade of a big oak tree in our yard.
I could see hollyhocks bloomin by the door of our shack.
I could see geese, pigs and chickens about our door. I could
see some little Hillmans running around loose in the yard
—free as the wind that blows. That was what I could see
when I looked over our barn lot and zigzaged two streams
of milk into the three-gallon zinc bucket.

"What's the matter with you, Adger," Ma ast, "that
you aint goin out there anymore and heppin your Pa
fight the blasted Sturgins?"

"I'm on furlough," I says, "and it's goin to be a long
furlough too. It's goin to be forever. I'm through."

"What's the matter?" Ma ast. "Hast the color of your
blood turned from Hillman red to Sturgin yaller?"

"Nope," I says, "my blood is still Hillman red but my heart has changed."

"Who's the gal?" Ma ast me.

"Effie Sturgin," I says.

"My Lord," says Ma—"a Sturgin——"

"Yep," I says—"a Sturgin."

"She can't come under my roof atter I've lost a boy by the Sturgin guns."

"They've lost more than we have," I says. "They are crippled up. If you'd see their men hobblin along the road then you'd know. Looks like they've all got the jake-leg. Old Kam Sturgin has been plugged eight times. He's still alive and fightin. Look at me Ma! I'm a cripple fer life if some feelin don't get back to my leg."

"A Sturgin gal in the Hillman family," says Ma as she reloaded her pipe and lit it with a match. "You aint standin by us, Adger."

"I'll end this war," I says, "and it's right now time it was ended. The trees hast started gettin green. You know what that means. It means bush-whackin."

I couldn't hep it. I jest set the milk bucket down in the barnlot. I jumped over the fence. I never said another word to Ma. I left her talkin to herself in the barnlot. I'd been goin to see Effie a month now. I'd been slippin around the battle lines. I'd been slippin like a fox when he goes to get chickens. I had to come back in the dark. I had to dodge the Sturgins all the way. They'd be comin home carryin their dead 'r heppin their wounded. I could allus smell their terbacker smoke and hear 'em cussin Hillmans before they got nigh me. Now I was makin my last trip.

I whistled fer Effie behind the palins. She come to me. Effie looked like a queen when she come through the trap door of the woodshed. We didn't do any talkin. We jest helt hands and run like two turkeys up the road. We walked five miles to town and got our license. We walked

six miles back to Brother Tobbie Bostick's and jumped
the broom.

"I'm glad to see this," says Brother Tobbie, "fer I believe it will end that fightin over there. I've heard guns
over there jest like a field of men huntin rabbits. I've
preached the funerals on both sides. I've prayed a lot over
that trouble. I hope this will end it."

"We haf to be goin," I says to Effie. "We got work to
do."

We left Brother Tobbie prayin over our family troubles.
We took up the sand-rock path, and over the cow-path
hill to the hollow. We could hear a gun now and then. We
walked up the hollow to where the little crick branched
off the main hollow. We slipped up this crick toward the
beech grove. We slipped up behind the Sturgin lines.

"You'd better holler, Honey," I says, "to one of your
men. We might get shot."

"Oh, Pa," Effie hollered. "This is Effie. Please don't
shoot."

"Take kiver, youngin," said a coarse voice. "What air
you doin here nohow? This aint no place fer wimmen
folks!"

Jest somehow the guns stopped barkin on our side of
the fence. Guess our men heard a woman's voice and bad
as they are to shoot they'd never shoot at a woman. We
didn't take kiver. We walked up in the beech grove.

"Papa," says Effie.

Effie walked toward Kam Sturgin. He was propped up
behind a big beech tree smokin his pipe and givin orders
to his men. He had bandages and plasters all over 'im.

"What brings you here?" Kam ast, "and who might
that young man be?"

"My husband," says Effie—"Adger Hillman!"

"My God," says Kam—"you married a Hillman!"

"Yes," says Effie—"I married a Hillman. We want you to stop shootin right now. We want this war ended."

"Atter I've lost this much blood," says Kam, "I'll lose the rest of my blood or win this fight and my acre of ground."

"How about dividin that acre of ground, Pappie Kam?" I ast.

"Don't Pappie me," he says. "I'll plug you on the spot."

"No you won't," says Effie.

"I'll Pappie you too," I says.

"Stop your men from fightin," says Effie.

"We'll stop the Hillmans," I says. "We don't fight our kinfolks. Aint that a rule among you?"

"Come to think about it, that's the rule among our people," says Kam. "I jest hate to be licked."

"We aint licked," says Effie.

We turned and walked down the hollow. We heard two short whistles. We didn't hear anymore guns.

"That's our signal fer retreat," says Effie.

"Let's hurry and get to the other side," I says.

We run down the beech grove hollow. We kept under cover by the fern-kivered bluff. The trees had started to put out their new spring coats of leaves. March was nearly over. April would soon be here. We hurried to the top of the yaller-clay bank.

I gave Pa two short whistles. Pa answered me with two longs. We jest walked over into Pa's headquarters. He was makin coffee.

"This is my wife, Pa," I says.

"Son, wasn't you afraid to bring her out into the open? Don't you know what is goin on here?"

He had his musket pinted between the sand-rocks. Pa didn't pay us no minds.

"We aint afraid," says Effie. "There won't be anymore shooting from the other side. It's all over."

"I thought something funny," says Pa—"We heard a woman's voice down there awhile ago. I signalled my men not to shoot that way. Then the guns stopped. Who might your wife be, Adger?"

Pa turned and looked at me. He twirled the corners of his mustache with his big fingers.

"Effie Sturgin," I says.

"A right purty gal," says Pa, "but I don't like that name, Sturgin. Child, you've changed it fer a better one. And this is the reason, Adger, you've been layin down on the job since last February—right when we've been doin the hardest fightin. We lost three of our best men last month. I know Sturgins lost five men last month."

"Pa, you'd better give a signal fer the men to come in," I says. "The Sturgin men have gone home. You know we don't fight our kinfolks."

"You air right, Adger," says Pa, "but what air we goin to do about that acre of ground?"

"Divide it."

Pa give three long whistles again. Not a man stuck his head up out'n the broom-sage.

"They will come," says Pa.

Pa give 'em seven long whistles. Effie didn't know what it meant. It was our victory signal. Men popped up all over the field. They started talkin. A lot of our men limped as they walked toward the cedar tree. They looked beardy and tired. Effie was afraid when she saw their muskets.

Effie put her arms around me. We loved and loved above the coffeepot. We could see the long line of men trailin around the path fer home. I could feel the life comin back to my own leg now.

THE BASKET DINNER

"DAD-DURNED MY CATS, Ma," says Bill Dingus, "if I ever seed sicha hands on a man in my life. They air nearly big as coal scoops. His fingers air long as pitch fork prongs. W'y hit's hard for him to hold a knife or spoon at the table with them big hands. Then you air goin' to let little sister Rilda marry 'im."

"Hit ain't in my power to help hit son," says Murt Dingus. She takes a stick of stove wood from the box beside the kitchen stove, opens the hot stove door and dips her pipe in the embers in the fire box. She wheezes on her long-stem clay pipe. A cloud of blue smoke rolls from her wrinkled lips.

"Jist a minute, Ma," says Bill, and he pulls on the end of a homemade twist-bud cigar that he rolled from the ripe hands of tobacco left in the barn shed for summer use. He puts the end of the cigar on the red embers in his mother's pipe. The smoke rolls from Bill's bearded lips. There is another big homemade cigar in his faded blue shirt pocket. Murt closes the stove door with the stick of stove wood and throws the stick of wood back in the stove wood box.

"When a girl loves," says Murt, "hit ain't nary bit o' use to try and break hit up. Little Rilda won't never be happy nohow. Besides she's eighteen years old and her own boss. She's sparked Sweet William goin' on four years now. Hit's time to marry. Somethin' might happen. A body jist can't pry into love. I was told not to marry your Pa.

I was told by the old men that the Bridgewaters would git him sooner or later. Your Pa was a bad man to fight. A bad man to fight never lasts long here among the hills. A man jist a little better comes along and gits the drop. You know where your Pa is now!"

"Yes," says Bill, "I know where Pa is. Sleepin' back yander on the pint. If we's to ever git in a fight with the Bridgewaters and Sweet William was married to Little Rilda he wouldn't be no 'count to help Eif, George, Harry and me. He's too big to fight. Too big to stand up on a steep hillside and plow. Not even a bed on this place that would hold Sweet William up. He's jist goin' to be in everybody's way when sister Rilda marries him."

"He might turn out to be a good provider for Little Rilda and a good man," says Murt Dingus, leaning back in her hickory-bark split-bottom chair and blowing a swirl of blue smoke to the top of the log kitchen where she has long strings of drying red-pepper pods tied to the rafters and hanging down over the stove to dry. Long strings of leather-britches beans drying too above the stove for winter use. "Hit's hard for a woman to be left without a man and bring up a family like I have here among these lonesome hills."

Bill Dingus looks out at the kitchen window. He sees on top the clapboard roof of the log smokehouse, the apples his mother and sister Rilda have peeled and sliced to dry. There is a quilt frame stretched down along the board-drip to catch the dried-apple slices if they try to slide off. The yellowjackets fly around the dried apples like honeybees around apple blossoms. The hornets come and catch the flies that try to pilfer among them. He puffs his cigar and looks steadily at the work of his wrinkled-faced mother whose clear blue eyes are surrounded by shriveling skin same as a shriveled piece of dried apple.

"Yes, Ma," says Bill, "you've been a good provider.

You've stuck with us through thick and thin. If you say so we'll not bother Sweet William. But tonight, Eif, George, Harry and me intended to tell him to stay away from here. If he'd a-tried to a-come back, he'd be sleepin' in the same place Pa is sleepin'. That's the same place the Hawthornes bury their dead ain't it?"

"Yes," says Murt, "but no more killin'. I've seen too much of hit. Sweet William will be here in th' mornin' to go with us to th' basket dinner at th' Gap Church. See all them pies over there on th' table that Little Rilda's baked! We're goin' to have th' best basket dinner there on th' ground tomorrow. I want you boys to quit lookin' at Sweet William's big hands. You ain't got sicha small hands yourselves. Want you to wear your silk shirts and blue serge suits and git dolled and spruced-up for once this summer."

"Will sure do hit Ma," says Bill, "if you say so. See if we can't catch us some girls. Be a lot of good-lookin' girls there. Allus is at the basket dinner at the Gap Church!" Bill's cigar is getting short now. He blows a wisp of smoke from his blue-bearded lips. His narrow long-slit upturned blue eyes look through the dingy window panes at his three brothers coming up the hill path with the mules to the barn. George is riding the mule in front, Eif is riding a mule behind and Harry is walking between the mules. They are tall bearded men with sun-tanned faces who work bareheaded and shirtless in the tobacco fields.

"What did Ma say," says George, "about us puttin' the skids under that big capon comin' to see Little Rilda?"

"She says," says Bill, "to leave 'im alone. She says for us not to mess with a love affair. Somethin' worse might come of hit. When Ma says that hit means we air goin't to leave them alone. Sweet William will be here in the mornin' to take Little Rilda with us to the basket dinner. Rilda and Ma's got the awfulest lot of cookin' done already. Goin' to have the best basket dinner on th' hill so

Ma says. Rilda's ironin' our silk shirts now. Boy air we goin' to show 'im somethin' there tomorrow."

"Hit jist always looked bad to have to haul that big clumsy capon around with our family," says George. "My Lord, when he's in the wagon, hit makes a load fer the mules. But if Ma says so we'll take him. I jist hate like hell to see Little Rilda marry 'im, that's all. Pears like a pretty little woman allus gits a big ugly over-grown clumsy brute of a man! Funny how pretty women fall for ugly men! Guess I must be a good-lookin' man!"

George sits on the front seat and drives the mules. The red tassels on the mules' bridles are flying to the bright July wind. Every buckle on the harness is shined until it glistens in the sun. Murt Dingus sits between Eif and George on a plank seat fixed across the jolt-wagon bed. Harry sits on a quilt spread on the bottom of the wagon bed and holds the big basket of grub to keep it from turning over as the wagon hits the big ruts in the streak of yellow roads over the Kentucky hills. The crows fly above them and caw . . . pairs of winging crows going over to their nests. There is a smell of penny-royal penetrates the bright Sabbath-morning wind. The dry wind stirs the soap-slick poplar leaves above them and dryly shakes the oak leaves on the boughs of the tough-butted white oaks that grow alongside the yellow streak of rutty road in the poor clay gravelly earth.

Sweet William and Little Rilda sit on a quilt on the back end of the wagon. Sweet William has his arm around Little Rilda. She is almost hidden in the loop of his big-as-a-pillow arm. He is too big to sit on a board across the wagon bed. He has tried it before. He smashes them and drops to the bottom of the wagon bed. He wears a black bow tie that looks like two sourvine leaves tied on the side of a big walnut tree. He wears a white shirt and a double-breasted blue serge coat. He pays no attention to the crows

and the basket of grub. He keeps his eyes looking down at
Little Rilda Dingus. She looks like a little playhouse doll in
the coil of his arm. Her black curly hair, her black crow-
beady eyes, and her brown cornshuck complexion and her
white grain-of-corn fresh-October-husked teeth, her little
hummingbird claw hands and mouse-claw-pink fingernails!
She sits contented with his big arm around her while the
big wagon, filled with her four big brothers dressed fit to
kill in their silk shirts and blue serge suits, rolls along over
the Kentucky hills bound for the Gap Church.

"Now," says Murt, "if the Bridgewaters air there, jist
don't pay no mind to them. Jist pass and repass with them
and let that be all. After all the Bridgewater boys air your
own flesh-and-blood second cousins. They promised the
Dinguses never to knife in a fight. In all th' fights your Pa
ever had with 'em a knife was never used. They killed
Pa with a sled standard. Brained 'im right over the head
with hit. The sight of a Bridgewater makes my blood bile.
But boys, today, let's be peaceful. Hit's the day of the
Lord and let's don't break hit!"

"All right, Ma," says Harry. "We won't start nothin'.
We aim to be peaceful. If they start hit we aim to take our
part though. You can bet on that." Sweet William Hawthorne does not hear. Little Rilda Dingus does not hear.
They are loved up like two spring black snakes in the
back of the wagon bed. They look into each other's eyes
with that come-and-get-me-honey look of spring in their
eyes! The wagon rolls around the ridge road, across the
coal-mine wagon ruts, over the sandstones, up the little yellow clay bank, over three sand heaps and down to the Gap
Church in a grove. George drives the mules under an oak
and says: "Whoa boys! Whoa—hooo, boys!" He rough-
locks the wheels to a dead stop. "Roll out, everybody,"
he says, "and I'll unhitch the mules and feed 'em corn
here in the boxes under the shade."

Eif jumps out and helps his mother out of the wagon.
She steps on the rough-lock of the jolt wagon. He lifts her
on down to the ground. She wears a big hat, a tight fitting
silk waist with a big pin at the collar and a long sweeping-
the-ground skirt. "All right, Ma," says Eif as he sets her
carefully on the ground. "I ain't too old to have made
hit all right," says Murt. Bill and George handspring over
the sides of the wagon bed onto the ground. Then they lift
the big basket of grub from the wagon bed onto the
ground.

"Hit's time," says George, "Sweet William fer you and
sister Rilda to know you's on the Church grounds!"

"Oh," says Sweet William, "we air here Rilda, Honey.
Let's git out'n the wagon!"

Sweet William stands up in the wagon bed and stretches
his arms like a crow lifting its wings when he starts to fly.
His head is up among the white-oak limbs. Little Rilda, the
little tiny doll-girl stands up beside him and her curly head
comes no higher than his belt buckle.

"What air they bringin' that big clumsy rooster over
here fer," says Boliver Bridgewater. "Bringin' 'im over
here if trouble brews! He won't amount to a hill o' beans!
One lick and he'll hit the ground from one of my old fence-
post mauls!" Boliver looks mean out of his narrow bean-slit
black eyes! He is standing down among the group of
Bridgewaters who are putting their basket on the ground.
There are nine Bridgewater men! They stand and eye
Sweet William and their second cousins, the Dingus brothers. "I never liked a Dingus in all my born days," says
Boliver. "Wished they'd never made that agreement back
yander between old Bill Dingus and Pap not to have fit
with knives. I'd like to fight 'em with knives. I'd cut 'em
up into sausage meat for the ants damn 'em to hell nohow.
Hit makes my blood bile to look at a Dingus."

"We don't want no trouble," says Flora Bridgewater.

"Your Ma has come here to worship on the Lord's day. This ain't no day for fightin'. Now you boys all git around the basket dinner here and eat and listen to some good preachin' this evenin'. Fill your bellies now on good grub and fill your hearts this evenin' on the Word of the Scriptures."

"Well, Ma," says Trevis Bridgewater, "Boliver is right. Look what happened to Pap that time atter old Bill Dingus hit 'im with that rock. Went around like a addled goose and drapped dead six months later. A death by degrees! Pap never did come to hisself!"

"Yes," says Flora, "look what your Pap done to Bill Dingus. Got 'im didn't he? Brained 'im with a sled standard. Hit was man for man and let's quit at that. I'm too old to see any more trouble. So is Murt over there. We don't speak to one another but you boys behave. They didn't bring Sweet William Hawthorne over there to fight. He can't fight nohow. A man that big is jist in the way. He's in love with that little sweet doll-baby of Murt's. Watch 'im over there lookin' in her eyes!"

"Some love," says Lum Bridgewater. "Watch 'em castin' sheep eyes at one another." He laughs and all the Bridgewaters laugh. Flora starts spreading their dinner on the ground!

Sweet William looks over toward the Bridgewaters. He hears them laughing and heard them speak his name. They are looking at him and bending over and laughing. "Honey, air they makin' fun o' me," says Sweet William to Little Rilda. "If they air I'll go right among 'em!"

"No, Honey," says Little Rilda, "they ain't makin' fun o' you and don't you start among 'em. You might not git back to me. And I want you more than anythin' in this wide world! You jist don't pay 'em no minds. Silence is the best contempt!"

"Say, Ma," says Bill Dingus, and he whispers in her

ear, "they've started makin' fun o' Sweet William. I hear
'em over there. Nine of 'em and four o' us. Two men
a-piece for us boys to fight if hit starts and one for Sweet
William!"

"SSSSS HHHHH," whispers Murt, "no fightin' here
today. Let's git our dinner spread out on the ground and
eat. Fill yourselves on good grub now and this evenin'
we'll fill our hearts on the Word of the Scriptures. Goin'
to be some good preachin' in th' house this evenin'."

Around the churchhouse is a graveyard. There are a
few white tombstones. Among them are cornfield stones
set up for tombstones with names and dates of births and
deaths. Many of the letters are carved backwards. One of
the names is Bill Dingus. It is one of the brown cornfield
stones. Another name is Silas Bridgewater. There is just
a big tough-butted white-oak tree between the graves. The
churchhouse stands under a clump of trees. It is old and
the peckerwoods fly in and out of the holes they have
bored in the gable-end white-pine logs. They fly over the
gravestones in the bright July wind. The churchhouse is
old and crippled. It has seen a lot of the Dinguses and the
Bridgewaters hauled here. It has seen them come inside
the house and sit on the half-log split benches, the Dinguses
on one side, the Bridgewaters on the other. It has seen them
sit and listen to a sermon together and yet never speak to
each other after church. It has seen the Dinguses get up
as a group and go out of the churchhouse one night first
and the Bridgewaters get up and go out the next night first.
Never a Dingus spoke to a Bridgewater or a Bridgewater
to a Dingus! For one hundred years this has gone on. The
graveyard is filled with Dingus graves and Bridgewater
graves. Yet, a row of tough-butted white-oak trees separ-
ates them in death. No Dingus is buried on the Bridgewater
side and no Bridgewater is buried on the Dingus side. Once
a Dingus married a Bridgewater. They were buried side

by side. Trouble started again and the Dinguses dug their kinsman up and took him over on his own side of the lot and left him among the dead who bore his name!

Not many names at this basket dinner. Each family brings its own dinner. Down over the hill are the Mac-Guires. They have their dinner spread on the ground now and are eating. The Blairs are on the far corner of the churchyard. They have their dinner spread out and are eating now. The Crumps are near the Bridgewaters. They have their dinner spread out and are eating. The Scotts are up near the churchhouse door. They have their dinner spread out and are eating. The Tizzels are to the left of the Scotts, facing the churchhouse and they are eating now. The churchhouse looks at these families. The Dingus family is eating now. It is the smallest family. Just across from them is the Bridgewater family. It is the second smallest family there. There is a little patch of sassafras sprouts, thick as the hair on a dog's back behind the Dingus family. The sprouts are higher than Sweet William Hawthorne's head. The churchhouse sees them all eating now.

"Look at the grub on this ground, won't you," says Bill Dingus. "Ma, jist to tell the truth I believe you have fixed the finest dinner here. Lord look at this turkey. Great big brown drumstick don't go half bad! Dumplings, pickles, cake, pie, ham, fried chicken, apple preserves, plum preserves, apricots, apples, cornbread, biscuits, light-bread, jelly, Irish taters, sweet taters, squirrel, soup beans, green beans, leather-britches beans, blackberry cobbler, raspberries, dewberries, strawberries, wild-plum jelly, wild-grape jelly . . . ah, Ma . . . you're the best cook in the world. None to beat you!"

"Who said so," says Boliver Bridgewater across from the other table. "That's what you think!"

"I said so," says Sweet William, pulling the fried brown crisp meat from a young fried-chicken's leg.

"You big son o' Satan," says Boliver Bridgewater, "when I want a dog to bark I allus pulls on his chain! What air you doin' with the damn Dinguses nohow!"

"Quiet children," says Murt. "Let's have no talkin' across the tables now!"

"Quiet boys," says Flora Bridgewater. "We don't want no trouble now."

The people at the other tables listen. They stop eating and listen. There are four hundred people or more on the ground.

"Hit ain't none of your business what I'm doin' with the Dinguses," says Sweet William Hawthorne. "If you could see a little better out'n them ferret eyes of yourn you could see what I'm doin' with all o' the Dinguses!"

"I told you, Ma," says Harry Dingus, "he'd bring us bad luck sometime or another. Hit's goin' to be a fight sure as God made little green apples!"

"The only reason you air talkin' like that," says Bill Dingus, "is because you got us out-numbered two to one. You know hit. I'd like to take a corn-cuttin' knife and go among you. I'd like to mow you like cornstalks."

"The only reason Bill Dingus you talk like that is because you know you ain't allowed to use knives. Damn your soul to hell nohow! You, the likeness and the name of the man who put Pap over there under that oak!"

"You ain't said nothin' about Pa over there," says George Dingus, "under a oak, have you? No you air very careful not to mention that, damn you to hell nohow!"

Brother Ward Scott stands up and says: "Boys let there be peace. This is the Day of the Lord. Let's stop talkin' about the Brothers done departed! Let's make this a day of Glory!"

"Wow!"

"Look Ma," says George Dingus, "look on Sweet Will-iam's pretty coat! Boliver Bridgewater hit 'im with a biled egg! Look at the yaller on his coat! Do we have to take that Ma?"

"I ain't goin' to take hit," says Sweet William Hawthorne. "I ain't goin' to take hit!" He jumps up, the yellow fluid streaming down the front of his clean coat. He runs the other way. He runs to the patch of sassafras sprouts.

"The dirty coward," says Bill Dingus, "a-runnin' from a Bridgewater! Can't run me to no sprouts! Damn their dirty hearts nohow! What do you say Ma? Must we take 'em? Can't defile Pa's name. Pa over there in his grave!"

"You have to take hit," says Boliver Bridgewater, "the whole dirty low-down pack has to take hit!"

"Go atter 'em boys," says Murt Dingus. "One for two men! Git 'em boys! And you come over here, old Flora Bridgewater, I'll give hit to you!"

The boys meet between the two dinners-on-the-ground. Plates are flying! Fists are flying. Men and women are running and screaming! Men are hitting the earth. Men are getting up and falling again. Blood is spurting from the noses. The other families are standing up now. Brother Scott is crying: "Peace, Brothers, peace! Peace, Brothers, peace. Let there be peace!"

"Git that big thing in the bushes," says Boliver Bridgewater. "You take keer of that big capon, brother Tim!" Tim Bridgewater runs into the sassafras sprouts to get Sweet William. Little Rilda stands and screams! "He's comin' atter you Sweet William! Watch 'im Sweet William."

He runs into the bushes but then he doesn't come out again.

"Tear off the damn Dingus silk shirts," says Boliver Bridgewater, "strip off all their fine terbacker clothes for to make skeery-crows out'n for the pea patch! Tom you run up there and see what's happened to brother Tim!" Tom Bridgewater runs into the sassafras bushes. The tops of

the bushes shake, there is a scream and he doesn't come
out again!

The mules sniff the scent of blood and snort and heave
at the halters! The Dingus brothers don't have coats on
now. The Bridgewaters are ripping off their silk shirts!

"See what the hell's happened to Brother Tom, Lum,"
says Boliver Bridgewater, giving orders for his brothers.
"He ain't come out'n the bushes yet!" Lum Bridgewater
runs to the patch of sprouts and dives headlong into them
and is hidden from the crowd.

There is a scream. The tops of the sprouts shake. He
doesn't come out again!

"He must a-got Brother Lum," says Boliver. "Must be
a knifin'. Don't know the Law of this family! Damn that
big capon to hell nohow, he won't git old Boliver." Boliver
Bridgewater picks up a stick and runs for the sprouts.

"Watch 'im if you are alive Sweet William . . ." says
Little Rilda, "he's a-comin' with a club atter you Honey!"
And above the sprouts two big hands are seen to rise up
and fall again . . . then there is a shrill scream and Boliver
Bridgewater doesn't return. "Got Brother Boliver," says
Young Silas. "I got Pap's name. I'll fight 'im till I die. He
won't git me." He grabs a rock and runs for the sassafras
sprouts. "Watch 'im Honey," says Little Rilda, "if you
are still alive. He's got a rock comin' atter you Honey."

Two big hands are above the sprouts in a different loca-
tion this time. Silas Bridgewater runs in. There is a loud
shrill scream when the big hands fall. He does not come
out again. "Man fer man now," says a voice from the
sprouts. "Stay with 'em Dingus Brothers."

The Dingus boys don't have a shirt on their backs. Their
noses are broken, eyes are closed, people are screaming.
The Bridgewater boys are trying to tear their pants off.
Got George Dingus' pants torn off. The women are run-

ning from the hill screaming. The men are staying out of the family fight.

"Let hit be fair," says Brother Scott, "if they have to fight hit out. Let hit be over and done with. . . . stay out Brethren! Stay out! Hit's the Dingus Brothers and the Bridgewaters! The Bridgewaters started the fight. I saw hit and heard hit from the start! Now the tide has turned! Hit's man for man!"

"Hit's that pretty little doll-baby over there tellin'," says Flora Bridgewater. "That pretty little Rilda. I'll glomb them wax eyes from her pullet head." She runs over the broken plates on the ground. "Watch her Ma," says Bill Dingus. "She's goin' after Rilda!"

"She won't git to 'er," says Murt, as she comes over Flora's head with a big platter of turkey. The dish flies into a hundred pieces and Flora hits the ground a-moaning! The turkey meat and gravy are strewn on the ground. There's not a dish left now. Murt runs in to help the boys. "Stay out'n this Ma," says Bill as Lonnie Bridgewater floors him with a short stick over the head. He starts to hit George and Murt catches his lick in time. Sweet William runs out of the sprouts. He waddles like a big turkey gobbler! "Stick, boys, till I come," he says. He runs down and Lonnie has wrenched the club from Murt's hand. She cries: "Oh my Lord . . . hit's another sled standard." Sweet William just in time, slings one of his big open hands like a fence-post maul and hits Lonnie on the side of the head. He falls like a rifle-shot fattening-hog.

Then he grabs Mort Bridgewater by the neck as he knocks Harry Dingus cold as a cucumber. He gives him one big choke and throws him down, wilted like a new-mown weed in the July sun. One lick to Pert Bridgewater and he curls up like a dog . . . Deb Bridgewater takes to the bushes screaming!

"Let's git the mules in the wagon," says Sweet William,

"and git back home. Come on Honey. Help unhitch the mules and be puttin' 'em in the wagon. Help Eif there." Eif just has on his underwear. He can barely walk. He is so weak, bloody and bruised. He unhitches the mules, they snort and caper. Sweet William picks up Bill Dingus and carries him like he would ten pounds of sugar and throws him in the wagon bed. Murt is climbing into the wagon bed without help. She lights her pipe. Sweet William goes back and gets George Dingus and carries him to the wagon bed and throws him in beside of Bill. Harry Dingus climbs into the wagon bed and lies down. He says: "I'm hurt on the insides." Murt spreads her shawl over Harry in the wagon bed.

Dingus boys got all their clothes torn off. Tombstones in the graveyard are turned over where they fought. The ground is littered with broken dishes and blood. The weeds are tramped down flat on the earth!

Murt smokes her pipe and drives the mules away. The Bridgewaters are lying all over the earth. The other families rush out to them now that the fight is over. She says: "What I hate about hit all the boys' clothes air gone. Will take all this terbacker crop to git 'em new clothes and terbacker for our own use. All my dishes broke to little pieces. But we winned that fight. We cleaned 'em with Sweet William!"

"They won't git out'n them sprouts," says Sweet William, "until they air carried out. I seed to that. When I rech over and got a neck I pinched hit, Honey, like you would a gapy chicken's neck! Them Bridgewaters that I fit with won't come to fer some time! They'll sleep a long time! That's th' way I fight, Ma Dingus. That's the way Pa and all his people allus fit. Run to the sprouts air the dark woods and bushwhacked their men! I pinch their necks with my big hands!"

"What happened?" says Bill Dingus. "Who winned the fight?"

"Who winned hell," says Eif. "Sweet William winned the fight hisself. He's got a new way o' fightin'. Runs to the bushes and fights. He's our new-found Brother. He ain't goin' no further than our house tonight. He aims to stay right there!" Murt smokes her pipe and drives the mules over the rough rutty road back home. The sun is high in the sky. The wilted pennyroyal is smelly. The hawks fly high above the wilted hills and circle in the bright-blue air.

George and Harry are lying on the bottom of the wagon bed groaning. There is a shawl spread over George. His clothes are torn in shreds, too fine to build a scarecrow with.

Sweet William has Little Rilda in the loop of his big fence-post arm. She never got a scratch. Neither did Sweet William Hawthorne.

Sweet William says: "Ma Dingus, I'd drive the mules but I'm busy. None o' your boys able to drive them. I think your boys got good pluck. I used to think they's a bunch o' soft hands and didn't know whether I wanted Rilda 'r not because o' 'em! Now I know they got good stuff in 'em atter I saw 'em fight the way they did today. I jist don't like the way they fight 's all! That's all that's held back me astin' fer Rilda. Atter today I'm astin' to jine your family. I want to be a part of the Dingus family!"

"We'll have to make a bigger bed fer you or put you on the floor and let you sleep until the boys can make a big bed to hold you!"

"Th' floor'll suit us won't hit, Honey," says Sweet William, "until the boys can make us a bigger bed!"

The mules sweat at the load. The wagon creaks over the deep brown crab-grassed ruts beneath the crows, hawks, hot sun and leaves.

MOONIN' ROUND THE MOUNTAIN

I WAS WITH TREECY. We's in her parlor. It was August
and the moon was high in the sky. We could see it from
Treecy's winder. I had my arm around 'er. We watched
the moon together from the winder. We watched it
pass a white cloud on the August sky. I'd never paid much
attention to the moon before. It had never looked as good
as it looked now.

"Treecy, honey," I says, "I've been comin' to see you
fer fourteen years. We've sparked right in this parlor. I've
come to see you every Wednesday night. I've come every
Sunday and stayed over Sunday night regular as the clock
ticks. We've sparked our lives away. I've ast you to marry
me a thousand times. Your answer is always 'no.' I've
never seen you as purty as you are tonight. I do want to
marry you, honey!"

"Yes, Ace," says Treecy, "the moon is purty tonight.
I've never seen it as purty in my life. I'm so lonesome I
want to cry. The wind is blowin' so lonesome-like out there
in the black-gum leaves. But I can't marry you, Ace. You
know the reason why. You won't quit your drinkin'.
There's no use to talk about it."

Treecy looked at me with her soft-blue eyes. Tears
streamed from them. They shined on her cheeks like silver
beads in the moonlight. I just looked at Treecy. She was
growin' a little older. She was gettin' purtier all the time.
I begin to feel like Treecy. The wind in the trees made me

feel lonesome too. The sound of the beetles in the August grass made me want to cry. We heard the love songs of the whippoorwills. I never felt so lonesome in all my life.

"You know I don't love anybody else," says Treecy, "or I wouldn't have courted you all these years. I've loved you, Ace Hatfield. I've thought how nice it would be fer us to marry. We could jine our farms together when we get married. There's just a fence between 'em."

"I've thought of that," I says. "You and your mother livin' over here on Short Branch together. My mother and me livin' over on Duck Puddle. Our farms jinin' at the top of the ridge between Duck Puddle and Short Branch. We could put our mothers under the same roof. I could run the farms. You could run the house."

"I've thought about that too," says Treecy. "I've told you, Ace, I'd never marry you as long as you drink that old rot-gut moonshine. I've told you 'bout it so much I'm ashamed to mention it. I hate the name of moonshine. It got Pap shot. It killed your Pap by degrees. Now it's goin' to get you."

"Treecy," I says, "I've fit agin it hard as any man. I love it better than a cat loves cream. I just can't hep it. I just crave it. I haf to have it. You know I paid that Indian doctor one hundred dollars to cure me. He didn't do it. My poor old Ma has made yarb remedies out'n poplar bark, fern roots, wild-cherry bark, yaller root and the roots of bone-set. It didn't do me no good. Ma made me take the remedy a whole year. Honest, the remedy was worse than the cure. Yet I wasn't cured."

"I'll never marry you," says Treecy, "until your breath stops smellin' like a moonshine barrel. You've come to see me twice a week fer fourteen years and not once have you come when I didn't smell old rot-gut moonshine on your breath. I know about moonshine. I've seen too much of it. I don't want to be pestered with it the rest of my days.

I've prayed fer something to happen to turn you against moonshine. I pray every night fer it to happen. I believe it will happen too."

"Honey, you do love me," I says, "but when women start prayin' fer somethin' to happen it usually does. I'm afraid to go home in the dark. It makes me afraid. Remember I have to pass the Short Branch graveyard. You know that I love you. You know I've had chances to marry other girls. But you are the girl of my choosin'. I want you. I'll never love another girl as I love you."

Tears streamed from Treecy's eyes. Tears streamed from my eyes. I had a little 'shine in me but not enough to make me cry. It was Treecy talkin' to me with soft words that made me cry. Treecy prayin' every night fer me. I'll tell you it hurt me. But I couldn't hep drinkin' moonshine.

"I just got to go," I says to Treecy. "I can stay here no longer. I got to go home." I pulled Treecy over to me. I held her close. I kissed her wet face. I kissed her lips and kissed them as I'd kissed 'em fer fourteen years.

"Good night, Treecy," I says.

"Good night, Ace," she says.

I walked out under the oak tree. I unhitched Moll's bridle rein from the low limb on the blackjack saplin' that stood in Treecy's yard. Moll was a-prancin' under the tree. She'd tramped a circle under the saplin' just the length of the bridle rein.

"Whoa, Moll," I says. "You're wantin' to go home, ain't you, gal?" I jumped into the saddle. I thought about the Short Branch graveyard. I thought about the Hatfield graves there. Grandpa and Pap buried side by side under the oak trees. Moonshine got Pap. Moonshine got Grandpa. Moonshine would get me. It had already got me. I couldn't get the gal I loved. Moonshine stood between us.

I rode down the path from Treecy's log house on the

Short Branch hill. I rode toward the county road that leads over the hill past the graveyard. I'll tell you I felt funny. I felt lonesome. I couldn't keep from cryin'.

"I can't stand it, Moll." I says. I pulled a horse-quart o' moonshine from my saddlebags. I took a big swig. Then I took another. I hadn't rid to the county road until I took another swig. I took another and another. I killed the whole bottle. "Let's go home, Moll," I says. "Let's go past the Short Branch graveyard."

The trees reeled past me. The ground came up and met me. One hand on my bridle rein and one on my .44—I went up Short Branch toward the graveyard. When I got right below the church house, I began to feel funny. I heard a voice. I kept my hand on the .44 in my left holster.

"Ace, oh, Ace," I heard someone say—it sounded like Pap—"Ace, my boy, you are goin' to the dogs. You are on the road to hell and damnation. I'm your Pap—Ace—look over here—I can't leave! I'm bounded by the ground plane. I'm tied to this old world. I'm a spirit."

"You didn't do so well, Pap," I says. "It was from your bottle that I learned to drink——"

"Don't talk to me like that," says Pap—Moll began to prance. She was afraid of Pap's spirit. We had to ride past it. It was under the oak tree just ahead of us—right by Pap's grave—I could see him just as plain as I ever saw him in life. He was standin' there in the black suit we buried him in. His white beard came halfway down the front of his coat. When he talked his chin worked—and his beard moved back and forth.

"Pap, I don't want to shoot at your spirit," I says, "but I will if you don't shet your mouth. I'll let you have six hot bullets right between the eyes——"

"Do better, Ace, my boy," Pap says. "You'll be where I am if you don' quit drinkin' Toodle Powell's moonshine.

I drunk it fer forty years. Look where it has put me. You'll never get Treecy until you do better!"

Moll stopped. She nearly bucked me over her head. She snorted. She stood on her hind feet. "You're scarin' my horse, Pap," I says. "Clear out. Git back in th' grave!"

"Son—your Ma—" Pap started—I couldn't stand it any longer. I pulled my .44 from my left holster. I emptied it right at Pap's white beard. He throwed up his hands. He hollered—I didn't take any chances. I pulled my .38 from my right holster. I started pumpin' the hot lead at Pap's spirit with my .38. He went back into the grave. I spurred Moll in the ribs. "Let's go, Moll," I says. . . .

I don't remember how I got home. I woke up the next mornin' in bed. I thought it was a dream about shootin' at Pap. But both of my pistols were emptied. I had an awful headache. I never told Ma at the breakfast table what had happened. It would have worried Ma. Alf Jackson came down after breakfast. He said he heard a regular gun battle up on the hill at the graveyard last night. Said pistols blazed and men hollered. He ast Ma if she heard 'em. Ma said she didn't.

I went to the barn to feed Moll. She was in her stall. The bridle was on her manger where I always put it. The saddle was in the corncrib where I always left it. I had to ride over on the fur hill and get the terbacker barn ready fer the terbacker. After Moll et, I saddled her, I rid toward the terbacker barn. I had told Elmer Adkins and Flint Woods to be there to help me on Monday mornin'. I didn't feel like work. But I went to work anyway.

Elmer and Flint were there. It took two to hold the crossbars while one drove spikes in them to hold them fer the heavy terbacker sticks. August would soon be gone. I'd haf to cut my terbacker before frost. It was colorin' now. Lord, I felt tough. I had to work. I dreaded it.

"Have a little snort, Ace," says Elmer. "This will liven your spirits." Elmer pulled out a horse-quart.

"It just saves me," I says, "I'm feelin' tough this mornin'."

Elmer took a swig. Flint took a swig.

"Not too much, boys," I says, "we've got a lot of climbin' to do in the barn today."

Elmer could climb like a gray squirrel—a little thin man with big feet and big hands and a round pair of owlish-gray eyes. His black hair stood up like feathers on his head. Flint was a short man like I am—thick through the shoulders with a bull neck and red saw-brier beard on a hard iron-lookin' face. He would drink his horse-quart of moonshine and do as big a day's work as any man. I could drink 365 horse-quarts of old Toodle Powell's moonshine in a year and farm more land than any of the ten men livin' on Duck Puddle.

I was standin' on some loose boards purt nigh at the comb of the terbacker barn. I was lookin' up at the roof. I had my hammer in my hand. I saw somethin' like a black clod of dirt—just 'peared like it leaped at my throat like a bullet. I struck at it with my hammer. I missed it. It dabbed me in the Adam's apple. It socked me like a wasp. I felt the sting. I knocked it off on a plank. I set my foot on it. I smashed it. It was a funny-looking spider.

"I'm hurt, Elmer," I says. "A funny-lookin' spider dove out'n th' comb of the barn and socked me on the Adam's apple. It stung me like a wasp. I feel sick already. Come here—you and Flint." The last I remembered Flint and Elmer were lettin' me down out'n the barn loft with a block and tackle. It just seemed like I went to sleep.

When I waked up I was at the house. The room was filled with people. Treecy was there. She was wipin' tears out'n her purty blue eyes with th' corner o' her apron. Ma was cryin'. Elmer was standin' at the foot of my bed and smokin' his pipe. Flint was standin' beside of him.

"He's opened his eyes," says Treecy. "He's comin' to— Ace is comin' to!"

"He ain't done it!" says old Doc. He was standin' at the side of my bed with a pill bag in his hand. "I'd like to think Ace is comin' to. It's been seven days since that spider bit him. It bit him in a bad place. It's pizened his whole system." Old Doc begin to cry. "Old Ace is a goner, I'm afraid. He's in the same fix as a lot of men I've doctored in my time. He's just come to, to say a few words before he passes on to the Great Beyond."

"You're drunk, Doc," says Flint. "You're on a cryin' drunk! Do somethin' fer Ace. He's revived. Look at his glassy eyes."

"I've revived him, ain't I?" says Doc. "Whose patient is Ace—mine or yours? Who's got this case, young man? My body may look old but my heart is still young. I'm still th' doctor here, I'll have you to know."

I couldn't talk. I tried to speak. Just seemed like I couldn't get the words out. Seemed like my face was bloated and my neck was big as a bull's neck.

Doc sat down in the rockin' chair. He lit a big cigar. Doc's big stummick stuck out in front of him. He was gettin' his breath hard. I could hear him get his wind like a wind-broken horse.

"Can't you pull 'im through, Doc?" says Treecy.

"One chance out'n 999," says Doc. "He's come to that revivin' spell men have before death. He'll speak in the minute. I'm an old doctor. I've doctored fer 61 years among these hills. I've seen this so many times before. It's somethin' us doctors don't have any jurisdictions over. God Almighty intended this revivin' period fer man before he dies so he can make his will, his confessions and speak to his loved ones."

"Do somethin'," says Treecy. "Don't talk like that! Do somethin'. I want Ace to live. I love Ace."

"I can't hep that," says Doc. "I've seen other women's loved ones die. Death comes to all of us. It's not bad. Take it easy. Just to tell you the truth, I'm sittin' here and waitin' fer death myself. I wouldn't take a bit of my own medicine to stave death off. Ace is a goner."

Doc puffed his cigar. Ma cried like her heart would break. Ma's hair is white as cotton. She looked out at my terbacker field on the hill above the house. "What will Ma do if I do die?" I think—"and who will Treecy marry?— I can't die—I haf to live——"

I tried to speak. I tried to say: "Spider bit me." I tried to say: "Have I been in this bed seven days? It just seems like one long night to me. I ain't been in this bed seven days."

"He's tryin' to talk now," says Flint. "Ace wants to say something."

"He wants to speak to his loved ones," says Doc. "Just as I've been tellin' you. Maybe he's got a confession to make!"

"Spiders and snakes," I say—"spiders and snakes—damn 'em to hell—nohow—terbacker—moonshine—spiders and snakes—Pap."

"He's talkin'," says Flint. "He's got snakes in his boots. Spiders in his boots. I know—I've had 'em——"

"I have too," says old Doc—"and I can handle Ace from now on too. I've had snakes in my boots many a time. He's got a chance. One chance out'n 99 now."

"Yes," says Elmer, "I've had snakes in my boots. I've had birds to come down out'n the air and pluck hairs out'n my head to line their nests with when I's gettin' over a big toot."

"Get some moonshine quick, Elmer," says Doc. "Heat it

just as hot as Ace can stand to have it poured down 'im.
Heat a quart—do it quick as you can. Old Ace may pull
through yet. Seven days ain't the turnin' point in a man's
life nohow. It's nine days—then he turns fer the better or
fer the worse."

I watched Elmer run out'n the house. Treecy watched
me. When Treecy looked at me, I looked at her. I just
wanted to pull her down on the bed and love her. I wanted
to kiss her but I couldn't. It just seemed like I was a piece
of lead. I was heavy. I couldn't move.

"My poor Ace," says Treecy—"just to think a little
spider put him in the bed. Strong as Ace is. A spider got
'im. Maybe he'll be planted beside his Pa and Grandpa
among the tombstones in the Short Branch graveyard."

"A spider would get an iron man," says old Doc. "You
let a devilish spider or a copperhead bite you and you're a
gone goslin. I've doctored too many copperhead bites in
these terbacker fields around here. If one was to bite you,
you'd be planted among the tombstones too!"

Elmer run in the house. "I got a horse-quart, Doc," he
says, "of Toodle Powell's moonshine—it's the brand that
Ace drinks."

"Roast it, Treecy," says Doc, "hot as we can get it down
Ace and in two days he'll be a dead man or a well man."

Treecy takes the horse-quart of moonshine into the
kitchen. I couldn't see Treecy come out'n the kitchen fer
the smoke. Doc filled the room with big blue clouds of
smoke. Elmer smoked his pipe. Flint smoked a cigar with
Doc. It looked good to see the boys smokin' again. It hurt
me because I couldn't smoke with them. I remember what
Pap told me on his deathbed about wantin' a cigar and
some licker. I thought about shootin' at Pap's spirit now. I
hated that I'd done it. I thought I might die and hurt Pap.
I had all kinds of wild thoughts. They just came into my
head. I'd try to stop them but I couldn't. Thoughts are

something that you can't stop. They come uninvited to
your head. They knock on the door of your skull. They
open the door and walk in. You've got to let them stay
until they get tired and move out.

"It's ready," says Treecy.

"Did you heat it all?" says Doc.

"Yes," says Treecy, "th' whole quart."

"Pour it all down 'im," says Doc. "Give it to 'im fast
as he can take it. If he won't open his mouth—pry it open
and give him the whole quart. Hurry now! Follow my
orders."

When I waked it was mornin'. The English sparrers were
chirrupin' in the vines around the house.

"Ma," I says, "ain't it breakfast time?"

"Ace," says Ma, "Ace—is that you?"

"Yes—it is, Ma," I says.

"How do you feel, Ace?" says Ma.

"Fit as a fiddle, Ma," I says. "I'm a new man."

"We thought you's a goner, Ace," says Ma. . . . "We've
had a time here. We give you up fer dead——"

"I'm a livin' man," I says.

"A whole crowd set up here with you until three o'clock
this mornin'," says Ma. "Elmer said you took a change fer
the better. Treecy's in the bed asleep now. She's been here
the whole nine days. She's been here waitin' on you, Ace!
Poor girl's nearly cried her eyes out."

"Poor Treecy," I says. "She's th' purtiest woman in the
world. If I could just quit moonshine."

"She is that and more, Ace," Ma says. "She's a woman
fer a livin'. She's a good housekeeper and a good cook. I'll
get you some breakfast, Ace."

Ma went into the kitchen. I got out'n the bed—put on
my clothes. I went to the dresser and looked in the glass
at myself. I wanted to see if I looked bad. I wanted to see
if I looked pale. I couldn't tell. The beard was out an inch

long on my face. There was just a little spot on my Adam's apple where the spider socked me.

"Is that you, Ace?" says Treecy. She came runnin' into the room. Her bright blue eyes looked dim and faded.

"Yes, it's old Ace," I says. "What's left of him!"

"Ace, is it you or is it your spirit?" says Treecy, throwin' her arms around my back and puttin' her clean soft face against my beard.

"Go in my room," I says, "and look in my bed. You'll see that it is empty. Ma is in the kitchen gettin' my breakfast. I'm a well man. Moonshine cured me."

There was a knock on the door. I heard Doc talkin' to Elmer and Flint.

"I'll open the door, honey," says Treecy.

Treecy unbuttoned the door. There stood Doc with his pill bag. Elmer and Flint were with him.

"Come in, boys," I says.

"Now, Elmer," says Doc. "I told you moonshine could put you in the grave or it could bring you out'n it! Look at Ace! Look at 'im, won't you! A dead man yesterday! Took a turn fer life last night—well today—ready to cut terbacker!"

"Can't be his spirit," says Elmer, "with all that beard on his face——"

"Spirits don't hang around th' lookin' glasses," says Flint.

"How are you fellers?" I says.

"Can't complain," says Doc.

"Brought you a quart as a token o' old times," says Elmer, "Here, boy! Put your nostrils above th' bottle neck!"

I took the horse-quart. I took the stopper out. I smelled of it.

"Whew," I says. "Lord deliver me! I can't stand th' smell o' it. Oh, never—never again!"

"Oh, Ace," says Treecy—"oh, my Ace!"

"My Treecy," I says. She jumped into my arms.

"You can't drink it?" she says.

"No," I says.

"My prayers," she says.

"The spider," says Doc.

"A preacher," I says.

"A sixteen-gallon keg at th' bellin'," says Elmer.

"When?" says Flint.

"Tonight," says Treecy.

"Atta boy," says Doc. "He's a well man. Th' Hatfields live on!"

EYES OF AN EAGLE

"Shoot low, Shan," says Uncle Fonse. "Son, you're shootin' over the birds. I've been standin' here watchin' you. Maybe your sights ain't in line."

Uncle Fonse stands under the walnut tree in the front yard and watches me shoot. His great fire-shovel hands hang limp at his side. His graying hair toys with the wind that bends the rose bushes and whispers among the walnut leaves.

"Uncle Fonse," I says, "I believe it's the wind blowin' the twigs the reason I'm not shootin' any better. It's hard to hold on a starling when the wind is movin' a twig. It is hard to hold the rifle to your shoulder and move your bead back and forth as the twig moves with the bird. I've tried too many times and I know."

"It's not hard," says Uncle Fonse looking at me with his gray eagle eyes. "If you can shoot, you can kill a bird at nearly any angle. I know the weight of my gun—the feel of my gun. I know the sights—whether you take fine or coarse bead on different distances. I love to carry my pistol in my hand and fondle it. I love to carry my rifle and to know the feel of it. There's something about a rifle, gun and pistol you get used to. I don't know just what it is. I think I must have been born with a pistol in my hand. Pap always liked a gun so well. He was a wonderful shot."

"Shhhh, be quiet," I says. "A starling flyin' back to the

137

locust tree. I'll get him before he gets into the walls of the house."

I lie down on my belly on the grass. I aim the rifle from prone position. I take steady aim. I fire and the starling falls to the grassy yard with a light thud against the ground. "Got 'im," I says. I push my rifle bolt back—blow the streaming wisp of smoke from the barrel and reload. Uncle Fonse looks at me and smiles.

"I'd never do that," he says. "I'd stand and shoot from my shoulder like a man. That would be too much trouble for me to shoot from that position. I don't like to see you take that much advantage of the birds. I can't help it if they are dirtyin' the walls of my house. I'll haf to paint them again anyway. I'll haf to get a long ladder and go up there and tear the nests out. A spark would set them big nests on fire and burn my house down. I've never seen such nests. Looks like crows' nests all around this house."

There are English sparrows' nests, starlings' nests, wrens' nests, yellow hammers' holes bored through the border boards, one screech owl's nest, a sparrow hawk's nest, and black birds' nests around Uncle Fonse's big house. Aunt Liddie told me to take the rifle and thin them out.

"Don't kill a wren," Aunt Liddie warned me, "nor a song bird of any sort. Get the sparrows, black birds, cow birds, and starlings. Don't kill the sparrow hawks either. They catch the sparrows. Don't bother the screech owls. They are harmless and your Uncle Fonse likes to hear them in the yard trees at night. Don't bother the yellow hammers. They are too pretty to kill. I can't help it if they do bore holes into the walls of the house and lay their eggs and raise their young."

"You don't know what a war there is among these birds the year around," says Uncle Fonse. "They can't get along. They fight all around this house. They fight over the nests from year to year. The yellow hammers bore the holes in the walls and the starlings take their nests. Sometimes the robins try to get them and they do get them. They lay their eggs and it's not long until you see the robin eggs all over this yard. The starlings carry them out—throw them down and break them. The starling is a mean bird. I ain't got a bit of sympathy for it over the way it does the other birds. Pour the hot balls at them, Son! But be careful not to kill the birds your Aunt Liddie don't want harmed! If she finds a dead wren you know what a time there'll be here. She would not have any of 'em killed if they'd behave themselves and act like birds ought to act. Look at that wall, Son! I'm ashamed for my neighbors to come here. They've dirtied it that way this spring."

"That's a shame," I says. "And Uncle Fonse, it seems like when I kill a starling two more come back to take the place of that one. I killed thirty-six yesterday afternoon. Today, it looks like there is a hundred more starlings flyin' around here."

"It's hard for me to raise wheat, here," says Uncle Fonse. "Ain't hard to raise it for my bottoms bring good wheat. But the starlings harvest my crop for me. They eat my mulberrys. They eat my cane seeds. They are the biggest nuisance on the place. In the winter time I have taken a clothes basket and filled it with starlings for pot pies. I've given all my neighbors starlings to make pot pies out'n. I've got as many as 360 in less than two hours, from behind the Virginia creeper vines on the walls of the house and barn. They roost there after the first frost. I'll bet you birds can become a nuisance. They were worse when Pap lived. They harvested his corn for him in the fields. Pap said when Grandpa lived here they were even worse. I can barely remember that. I remember the Kirks shot them for pastime. Pap used never to miss one with a rifle."

"One now," I says. "See him circle back to the locust tree."

"And from that locust tree," says Uncle Fonse, "he flies to the house. Funny about the starlings. The dead limbs on top of that locust tree is where they love to light. I'll bet you cut that locust down and the dead limbs in the top will be filled with BB's and rifle balls. That's what killed the limbs up there. Too much shootin' in that tree. See all the little fine limbs have been shot out."

"I've shot three hundred starlings," I says, "from the top of that tree since I've been here. Seems like I'd rather see a starling fall from that tree as the house-top, mulberry tree or the walnut tree. They are better targets too up there among the dead limbs with the wind around them and the sky above them."

"Son," says Uncle Fonse, "you may be considered a good shot with a rifle around here among these fellars of today— but you wouldn't a got a smell among the old men of yesterday. I ain't sayin' that to be sayin'. I know what I'm talkin' about. I ain't tryin' to run your shootin' down. I'm just tellin' you. I tell you every man used to carry a gun here. Every man used to shoot for pastime. We used to shoot all day on Sunday. It was our life. It was our love. We'd ride our horses out that lane and run at a gallop too —we'd put a ball in every fence post along that fence. That's been forty-five years ago. We'd ride around a big oak that stood out there in the hollow and put six balls— all in a straight circle around the tree—all the bullets a foot apart. My horse loved the crack of my pistol."

Uncle Fonse's gray eagle eyes look at me. He never takes his eyes off'n me while he talks. He talks with his big hands too and he spits bright sluices of amber on the carpet of yard grass. "My people," he says, "moved to this very spot in 1798. My Great Grandpa come here from Virginia. You go upon the hill at Mount Zion and you'll see the graves of my people. We are planted there on that hill."

"I've seen the graves Uncle Fonse," I says, "when I went up there to Sunday School. The Kirks are buried in a long row. I figgered out each generation by the dates on their stones."

"They were the marksmen," says Uncle Fonse—"If those old men could arise they could show you how to shoot. I've seen Pap go up the Tygart River and bark a mess of squirrels many a time. We didn't have a mess of squirrels either unless we got one for each one in the family—Pap and Pa, Sister Emma and seven brothers. Pap would shoot under or over the squirrel—never touch the squirrel—just hit the bark beside it and kill the squirrel. He shot close to their heads."

"Wait a minute Uncle Fonse," I says, "another starling."

I take aim from my shoulder. I steady my rifle—line the sights and squeeze the trigger. I fire—the starling goes down, flapping down through the air toward the wheat field.

"A broken wing, Son," he says. "Not good shootin'. Too bad the young generation can't shoot. But a body can't blame them. They ain't got nothin' to hunt like we had to hunt. We wouldn't waste cartridges on starlings. Ammunition was too high and money was too scarce. Your Aunt Liddie is a good shot. I've bought her a twenty-gauge gun to kill suck-egg dogs with that come here when I am in the fields plowin'. She used to kill them with my pistol. But her eyes ain't good as they used to be. She used to take my pistol and knock starlings from the top of that locust. She stood here on the porch and brought them down. She takes my pistol and shoots down when she see the ground moving up and down. She always gets the baby-handed mole. Moles are bad here to tear up the grass. She used to squirrel hunt with me up the Tygart. That was when she was a younger woman."

"Not many squirrels on the Tygart now," I says. "I

went up that river one day last fall and I didn't see a squirrel. I didn't see any timber for squirrels."

"There used to be a God's plenty," Uncle Fonse says
never batting his eagle eyes. "I'll tell you what went with
the squirrels. They went with the timber. That river used
to flow from a timber country. Never flooded like it does
today. When it did get out'n banks, it didn't get high over
the bottoms. It just got high enough to leave a lot of rich
silt on the bottoms and you talk about corn, wheat, cane
and terbacker—the Tygart bottoms used to grow them. All
you had to do was plant the seeds and knock down the
highest weeds. Today it is another story I ain't got time
to tell. Did you know that river has floated a million crossties besides the saw logs! I used to see drifts of crossties
piled on drifts in that river. That's in the 80's, Son, when
they built the C & O Railroad through here. I had a job
carryin' crossties from the crane that lifted them from the
water to the river bank. I carried them and put them on
flatcars. I'd pick up big 7 x 9 crossties all day long and load
them when I was sixteen years old. I didn't know that was
the last of my squirrel timber. I didn't know then that a
man would ever change. I thought he'd go on forever—
stout as a bull. But time will change a man—I don't care
how damn stout he is."

"Another starling," I says—"I'll get him."

I press the butt of the rifle against my shoulder. I line the
sights on the tiny bulk of black in the top of the locust
tree. I steady myself—squeeze the trigger gently when the
sights are in true line with the bird—"spick," goes the rifle.
The bird tumbles from the tree to the ground.

"Got 'em," I says.

"The best shot you ever made," says Uncle Fonse, "was
the last Sunday morning when you shot that starlin' from
the top of that sycamore tree—that was a good hundred
and twenty-five yards from the house."

"Wasn't a bit of wind blowin'," I says. "My nerves were steady as an oak. It was so far I could hardly see the bird too and I shot from my shoulder."

"I was watchin' you from the winder," says Uncle Fonse —"I saw it all—I told your Aunt Liddie you'd never do it again—only one shot in a thousand. That was a wonderful shot. I had hopes you'd be a good marksman—but when I come out here and watch you shoot now. You ain't gettin' but two starlings with every three cartridges."

The sun is sinking over the sharp-pointed hills to out west. A blue twilight wind hovers over the green wheat fields in the valley—over the big house and the big barn. Starlings chirrup plaintively, trying to get back to their nests in the house. Uncle Fonse stands by me. When I aim my rifle—he squints his gray eye as if he were aiming the rifle. He goes through the tense maneuvers of a man shooting a rifle at a tiny object. He reloads his mouth with bright crumbs of burley tobacco and holds the cud firmly in his jaw.

"I never did tell you," he says, "but I spent five years shootin' in California. I went to San Joaquin Valley in 1901. I tried out for shootin' ducks on Tulara Lake and Summit Lake. I just drifted in there and heard about this place where they wanted good shots to shoot wild ducks, swans, geese and English snipes. There was a Kentucky boy with me. He was from this county. We went there and we stayed. We made us a camp. We killed most of our grub. I liked it so well I stayed five years before I saw my people back here——"

Uncle Fonse looks into blue twilight space toward the range of Kentucky hills. "You know there's always something to call a body back. I was sparkin' the purtiest little red-headed girl you ever saw in California. Her Pap owned two ranches and once he said to me: 'Fonse when you take Arabella, I aim to deed you one of my ranches.' He was

drinkin' when he said it. Arabella had sent me over to the
saloon to get him. We's ridin' back in the two-horse express
wagon and shootin' at coyotes as we rolled along. He had
a .44 and I had a .38. When one popped in sight we made
him dance. A coyote is a smart thing. He'll get out of your
pistol's range and then do a lot of howlin'. Lord, but that
was a great time. I got all the shootin' I wanted. I shot from
September 15th until March 15th. Durin' the summer
months I worked on a ranch."

"Did you like California?" I ask.

"Like it," he says—"Son, it was a man's paradise when I
was there. It was a young and growin' country. For the last
thirty-four years I've laid off to go back. It's a long ways
to California from Kentucky. I'd like to visit the Valley
and see if it's built up any. Guess it has by this time. No
more game like there used to be. When we'd run out'n lard
at the camp—we'd go down to the swamps and kill a wild
hog. We'd skin him and render us some lard. We'd be out
on the lake by four in the mornin' and shoot until two in
the afternoon. Then we'd let the ducks come to the lake
and roost for the night. I averaged nine ducks out'n ten
shots. I made the best money I've ever made. We got $1.50
apiece for cranes; $2.50 apiece for swans; and, from $2.50
to $9.00 a dozen for ducks. It all depended on the kind of
ducks we killed."

"What's the best shootin' you ever did?" I ask.

"I killed seventy-two mallard ducks," he says, "in one
hour and forty-five minutes. I took the buck-eggers. The
shootin' was so fast—so many ducks—I got too excited. My
gun got too hot—I had to dip it into the lake. It was a great
life—Son—a great life, I'll tell you. Now, I'm back in Kentucky—runnin' a farm. But little game here anymore. And
if there was plenty of game here—I could not shoot like I
used to shoot!"

"The Kirks used to be the best shots among the Ken-

tucky hills," I've heard Laff Morton say—Laff would stroke
his long, white beard and say again: "You couldn't beat the
Kirks—bodies of metal and nerves steady as rocks and the
eyes of eagles in their heads. No braggin' about the Kirks
—women and men could all shoot. Kirks about all gone
though—just Fonse left in Kentucky and the game around
him all gone."

"I have seen Uncle Fonse," I says, "kill six teal ducks
when they flew from the flood waters, at six shots. I've
seen him turn his rifle upside down four years ago and clip
sparrows' heads off in the top of the locust tree. I've seen
him take a pistol four years ago and shoot a black thread
in two at sixty paces—a black thread stretched across a
footpath—tied to a stake on each side of the path.

"Take my rifle Uncle Fonse," I says, "and see what you
can do for the starlings. They are tryin' to get back to the
house to nest now."

"Yes," he says, "the dirty things—dirtyin' the walls of
the house and messing up the Missus' porch. Of all the
birds in the world—I've never liked a starling. Maybe it is
because we've had to fight them in this valley—and a smart
bird they are. They used to roost in a little mulberry tree
out there in the yard. I suppose five hundred would roost
in that little tree. One night we planned to sew three sheets
together and cover the top of the tree with them. We got
our sheets ready—set up and waited for them to come to
roost. There was a dark cloud that hung in the North—the
way the rains come here—And don't you know the starlings
did not come. The next morning when we got up the tree
was split open by lightning—what do you think of that?
I say they are smart birds."

"Locust is full of starlings," I says. "Look upon that
dead limb—six starlings."

Uncle Fonse sits down on the stone doorstep. He puts
the rifle to his shoulder. He takes steady aim and fires. The

birds fly away in circles over the house and then fly straight
for the sycamore tree in the wheat field.

"What's the matter with me," says Uncle Fonse. "Guess
it's because I ain't used to your rifle. I don't know the feel
of this rifle. I ain't fondled this rifle like I have my own
guns. But I ought to do better than that. Here comes another swarm of starlings—now watch me!"

Uncle Fonse turns the rifle upside down. He takes aim—
squeezes the trigger.

"Splick," the rifle goes. The birds fly away.

"Shucks," he says—"what's the matter with me? That
hurts every bone in my body."

Aunt Liddie comes out on the porch. "What's the matter, Fonse," she says. "Can't you kill one?"

"I ain't yet," he says—"I've missed two shots. I've missed
them this close, too, Liddie. I think it's because the rifle is
new."

Aunt Liddie looks at me and smiles. The birds circle
back to the locust tree.

"They are comin' back to the house whether or not," I
says. "They must have eggs in their nests."

"They ain't comin' back if I can help it," says Uncle
Fonse.

He lifts his rifle to his shoulder. He takes careful aim—
slow aim. He fires. The starling tumbles from the top of
the locust tree. "Ah," he says, "I've got the range of the
rifle now. I'll show you how to knock them."

"Did you ever think, Fonse," says Aunt Liddie, "that
you can't expect to shoot like you used to shoot? You are
not young as Shan. Your eyes ain't what they used to be.
When you read the paper now you have to wear glasses."

"Didn't do it," snaps Uncle Fonse, "until I was sixty-one.
I can shoot with Shan any time. Ain't I seen him missing
one starling after another all evening! What do you think
I am? A dead man in the grave? I'll show you just because

that tree fell on me—didn't make me a walkin' corpse. I'll
show you!"

Uncle Fonse aims at another starling. His broad shoulders
are turned toward us. His big rough index finger fills the
trigger guard on the rifle. We watch him aim—slowly—
slowly, the trigger is squeezed. The rifle barks and the starlings fly away. "I'll be dogged," says Uncle Fonse—"must
be bad lightin'—the sun has gone down, but it is very quiet
since the wind has laid. I ought to have knocked that bird.
I believe it's the rifle—believe the sights have been twisted
some way."

"Maybe so," I says, "I've handled that rifle pretty rough
here lately."

"I never handled a gun that way," says Uncle Fonse. "I
took care of one just like it was a child. I always loved the
feel of a gun. You boys of today don't love your guns like
we used to."

The starlings circle back to the tree. Between Uncle
Fonse and a white sky—pretty as a picture, is a row of
starlings lined on a dead locust limb. "I'll pick one off'n
there," says Uncle Fonse. He takes aim and fires. The birds
fly away. "I pulled the trigger too soon. That's why I
missed. I got too anxious. Just as I pulled the trigger the
birds flew."

Aunt Liddie shakes her head. Uncle Fonse can't see her
shake her head.

"Fonse," she says, "I wish you and Shan would thin the
starlings out. They are ruinin' my house. I'm ashamed for
people to come in here. I have to scrub the back porch
every morning. It's a sight how dirty starlings can get. It
nearly works me to death to clean after them."

"Don't mind the cartridges, Uncle Fonse," I says. "I've
got another box when you shoot them. Shoot all you
please."

"It hurts me to miss so," says Uncle Fonse. The birds

come to the tree and he shoots. He misses. They come again and he shoots and misses. They keep coming and he keeps shooting. He doesn't kill a starling. They are trying to get to the house. They whiz into the tree like bullets and Uncle Fonse shoots bullets at them. He misses and he misses. He never makes another hit.

"Must be the lighting," he says disgustedly. "Surely I can't miss like that. The moon is comin' up now. Guess I'll quit for this evenin'." Uncle Fonse hands me my rifle. He gets up from the stone step and walks slowly into the house. He doesn't talk. He doesn't smoke a cigar as he usually does while he reads the paper. He will not talk to me and Aunt Liddie. He looks at the paper and doesn't say a word. He thinks that we think he is reading the paper. We know that he is not. We can see from the side of the paper turned toward us that he has the paper upside-down.

"I'm gettin' a drink of water," I says, "and I'll turn in. I'm a bit sleepy!" I carry my rifle on my shoulder to the kitchen. Aunt Liddie follows me to the kitchen. As I lift a dipper of water to drink Aunt Liddie whispers in my ear: "Your Uncle Fonse is hurt. He can't stand to miss a shot. He's been a wonderful shot but he ain't got the eyes he used to have. He'll be pouty for a week over this. He'll say your rifle wasn't any good. He'll say the lighting was bad. He don't want to believe he is slippin'. He don't want to think that time has slipped up on him—that he is gettin' old."

"Aunt Liddie," I says, "I'll tell you. Don't mention it to him, please. But Elmer and I were shootin' at walnuts the other day with him. We threw them up for each other and we'd crack them in the air. Both of us were ahead of Uncle Fonse—he first blamed the rifle. I winked at Elmer—we started to missin' the walnuts on purpose. Uncle Fonse got ahead. He was the happiest man I ever saw. We let him keep the lead. 'I'd begin to think,' he says, 'my eyes weren't

what they used to be. But now I know they are.' I know he
has been a better shot than I am now or ever will be—
but I can beat him now. I have to let him beat me."

"I know I can't shoot like I used to shoot," says Aunt
Liddie, "but I accept it. I know that I am older than I once
was—my eyes are not as good and my nerves are not as
steady. Where I used to take one shot with Fonse's pistol
and kill a suck-egg dog—I've got to take three shots sometimes now before I get him. Sometimes, I miss a mole under
the ground rooting up my grass. But when I miss I shoot
again. If I miss the second time, I just keep shootin'."

I go upstairs to my room. I put my rifle in the corner
and go to bed. From my upstairs window, I can see the
little Mt. Zion church house on the hill. The moonlight
floods the valley like bright daylight. I can see the white
tombstones in a long row where the Kirks are laid to rest.
I can see the green stools of roses there and the green carpet of myrtle.

"Uncle Fonse," I think, "with his broad shoulders, his
fence-post arms and his big hard fire-shovel hands—fingers
almost too big to go under the trigger guard of my rifle;
Uncle Fonse with the elongated gray eyes sharp and steady
as an eagle's eyes. There are not many men in Kentucky
today like Uncle Fonse. He is one of the best shots in the
State of Kentucky for his years. There on the Mt. Zion
hill lies the dust he was made from, pioneer dust that
cleaned the valley and built the turnpikes and the railroads;
dust that was powerful in its day—that lived, breathed air,
saw sunsets, cleared the wilderness and barked the squirrels; dust that helped to build a nation—now eternally sleeping under the quilts of myrtle, dirt and winds—gone, gone,
as the Red Man, the giant trees and the wild game and the
topsoil of the land.

"God's little two acres of slope there," I think, "holds
millions and millions of dreams that will be hidden eter-

nally; the long shots that were made with the long hunting rifles; the fights with the Red Men now sleeping in the valley below them—whose bones work up from beneath the plows that plow the empty fields each spring; bones that are scattered all over the bottoms; bones that slip into the Ohio River each time a part of the bank slips into the river —bones—bones—bones—the valley of bones; the valley of dry bones and of lost dreams of the long huntin' rifles; the blinded eagle eyes in the quilts of dust; gone, gone, gone forever—eternally sleeping while we with the lesser eagle eyes plod the earth above them and plow into their dreams; while the roots of our corn and wheat spring from their bosoms.

I get out of bed, walk barefooted down the wide carpeted stairway, go quietly through the front room—ease the front door open so as not to make a sound for Uncle Fonse is a light sleeper. I walk out across the porch, across the yard to the back of the house. I look over the bank where I threw the starlings. I pick up six dead starlings with dew shining on their glossy black wings. I carry them to the locust tree and drop them one by one to the grass. I leave them shining in the moonlight.

The sun rises a ball of fire in the East—reflects purpling strips on the quiet river waters. Aunt Liddie pounds on the floor beneath me with the end of the broom to wake me. I roll out of bed, dress, walk downstairs and walk out to inhale a breath of April air from the yard shrubbery and sweet-scented tender April grass.

"Uncle Fonse! Oh, Uncle Fonse, come out here," I holler.

"What's the matter?" asks Uncle Fonse running from the house like something desperate has happened.

"Look under this tree," I says. "I know I didn't knock these starlings out of the locust. I shot mine and threw them over the bank."

"I thought," says Uncle Fonse, "that I wasn't makin' so

many misses. It was that dad-durned twilight last night. A man can't shoot in the dark, Son, and find the birds. I didn't think I was gettin' that bad. I'll go in there and show these birds to the Missus."

Uncle Fonse gathers the birds covered with dew from beneath the locust tree. He walks around the house, to show Aunt Liddie the birds. "I'll show her," he says. The sunlight floods down upon him—the bright golden sunlight of another day.

THE BLUE TICK PIG

RAGWEEDS ARE SMELLY on a hot day. You try pullin weeds for the pig and you will know that the hot sour smell will fill every air sack in your lungs. But that is what the pig likes. It likes ragweeds, pulsey, careless and horseweeds. But horseweeds are down by the river and who's going down there and cut horseweeds with a butcher knife and carry them across one's hip and under one's arm onehalf mile for a blue and white spotted pig that looks like a bluetick fox hound? One has to think an awful lot of the pig to do this after one has chopped weeds in the corn all day. Pulsey and careless are down in the corn field. A body could pull careless all day and not have an arm load. Pulsey is too flat on the ground and it is hard to stoop over and pull it. A backbone cracks like a broom handle if it would have to bend over all day and pull pulsey. That is why it is better to pull the ragweeds from behind the wellbox for the pig. They have to be cut out of the yard anyway. Just as well pull them for the pig.

Pa named him. Called him Blue Tick soon as I packed him home that day. I worked one day for Cy Shelton, pullin' tater onions and carried them to the crib loft to dry. When the sun went down and I started to go home Cy Shelton said to me, "Do you want the quarter for your day's work or would you like to have a pig?" I had never seen the pig, but I says, "I'll take the pig."

So we went out at the pig pen. There was fourteen pigs

in a straw bed on the north side of the rail fence in a corner. The sow was fightin them and they were fightin the sow. "Here is the pig," Cy said, and he handed me the runt pig by the ears and it was squealin. The sow jumped up and boo-booed at us two or three times when Cy was balanced on the rail with the pig by the ears. Soon as he straightened up his back and handed me the pig, the sow laid back down on the straw and the thirteen pigs went to nudging her for more milk.

I put the pig in my overall pocket. And Cy said, "Watch and don't smother it. That pig ain't big as a house rat, remember. I been a little afraid a hog-pen rat was goin to git it sometimes when it got away from the sow. It's the runt. It can't get any milk from the sow. I knowed we'd have to raise it by hand. We don't have time to fool with raisin a pig like that. The runt usually makes the best hog. It will do it nine times out of every ten. Take care of that pig and you'll have a hog there someday."

W'y of course I'd ruther have Blue Tick as a quarter. A quarter will only buy me two yards of muslin at the store to make me a shirt. It will buy Pa three pokes of Red Horse chewin tobacco. It will buy three pounds of sugar. A quarter is just what they need at home. They use quarters too often. Now I have the pig. The pig is mine. Someday it will grow to be a hog and then I couldn't put it in my overall pocket. It would rip it then from corner to corner. Think of a big hog in my pocket! I have a rat-sized blue pig with white spots on it. The path is just two miles home. And when I get there I'll give the pig milk. I hope it lives till I get home. If it lives till I get there then it will live to be a hog.

"Less why didn't you take the quarter instead of bringin that runt pig back here? That is like Cy Shelton to cheat a child. If he'd fool with me two minutes I'd take that pig back over there and make him eat hair, eyes, blood and all raw as a turnip. Got you over there to work and pammed a pig off on you that is not worth a dime when you was to get a quarter. A runt pig! A day's work gravelin out tater onions and carryin them to the crib loft on a hot July day! Takes advantage of my child with a runt pig for a day's work! Come on, let's take that pig back."

"Pa, I wanted the pig. I wanted to raise it. I asked Cy Shelton to take the pig instead of the quarter."

"You did, huh! Well, why did you do it?"

"Well, I go out and work for a quarter. I bring it home. You take the quarter down to the store and you buy salt, sugar, tobacco—You buy cloth to make the baby a dress. I don't get anything. The quarter ain't nothing to me. It is something dead. It is just like a rock. Now I have somethin that's mine. If it only lives to be a hog. Then look what I'll have. Now it is like a little mouse sleeping here in my pocket."

Pa got over his mad spell. But he wanted the quarter I was to get for my day's work. He wouldn't have the pig. He says it looks like a blue-tick hound did that he used to own. He said the blue-tick hound was a jim-dandy possum dog, the best that this county ever saw. So, Pa calls my pig, Blue Tick. Pa says, "That Blue Tick pig you got out there at the barn. It takes more time to feed it than it is worth."

I tell Pa, "W'y I don't mind runnin down a goose a-pullin a tail feather out a quill to fit a bottle stopper for Blue Tick to put his little long rat-like mouth over and draw cow milk from the castor-oil bottle. But I washed the bottle clean. I'd do anything for Blue Tick. I don't mind. When I'm out workin in the field and the dinner bell rings, I jump over corn rows and furrows and stumps to get down to the house and feed Blue Tick. Murt Hensley told me to keep him on the same cow's milk. And I have done it. I've had him on old Pansy's milk ever since I got him."

Pa saunters out to the little pen I have him in by the
wood shed. He stands by the pen and he says, "Someday,
and that not before very long, that pig is coming out of
there. Mind what I tell you, them little foot-high boards
ain't goin to hold that pig. W'y it's big as a possum. You
feed Blue Tick good or he'd be comin out of there now. It
may be he is too fat. Look at his little belly skin. Tight as
a drum, ain't it?"

And I say to Pa: "Pa, he's drinkin from a bowl now. I
can't feed him from the goose quill. He's cut teeth and he
bites the goose quills in two after he has drained all the
milk through them. He just whales in and bites the quill
in two."

Well, I'll cut these ragweeds from behind the wellbox for
Blue Tick. I won't have to cut them Saturday when we
clean the yards. I'll have them cut already. Blue Tick likes
ragweeds.

I would go to the river and knife down some horseweeds
for Blue Tick, but it is too far and I am too tired. We have
worked like mules in the corn today.

Blue Tick ain't tired as I am. But Blue Tick is hungry.
He is always hungry. I believe Pa likes Blue Tick now.

I'll bet he wouldn't take a quarter for him. He wanted
to take him back to Cy Shelton. But he wouldn't want to
take him back now. Pa wants him more than I do.

I know what Pa wants with him. He wants to kill him
for meat late next spring about March. That's the idea Pa
has in his head. But I can't stand to see him killed. I'm not
goin to have Blue Tick killed. The sun is hot. The ragweeds smell. They go down and open up every air sack in
a body's lungs. The scent is almost strong enough to knock
the air sacks out of a body's lungs.

II

The potatoes are all dug now. The turnips are pulled.
The corn is cut. Summer has gone. Autumn is here. There
is nothin growin now. Everything is dyin. See how the dead
leaves fall from the trees. The cows have been brought in
from the high hill pasture and turned in on the meadow
weeds that have grown up after the last cuttin. Nothin is
growin now unless it is the meadow weeds. There are a lot
of ragweeds down there and some horseweeds around the
edges in the rich ground. Autumn is here. Nothing but
weeds are growin. The mules run in the lot, the cows run
on the meadow. The fattenin hogs have a rail-fence lot.
But Blue Tick is fenced in a plank-fence square.

Since he got bigger I put one plank all the way round
his four-plank pen and made it higher. Now Blue Tick is
a shoat behind planks that will not let him see out and the
barn-shed roof will not let him see up. So I'm going to ask
Pa if he will let me turn Blue Tick out and let Blue Tick
see so he will know more than he does.

Blue Tick was once a pig. He ought to see the stars, for
even a pig likes to look at them. And now he is a shoat. He
ought to eat green ragweeds in the meadow. He ought to
have something besides middlins and cracked corn mixed
with milk in a bowl. He needs to root down in the pasture
where the greenbriers are and find the knots on the greenbrier roots. Shoats like them after they learn to root down
with their noses and get them. Blue Tick is big enough to
do all this and that poor shoat has never seen the stars. W'y
he'd learn to play if he could just get out of that pen. He'd
never even want to go back and look at that pen. He'd
learn to chase a dead leaf as a hound dog chases his tail.
He'd learn to run and play before bad weather comes. He
ought to be out where he can root up greenbrier roots and

find chestnuts and walnuts and pieces of coal and hard slate
to munch over.

"You can turn that pig out," says Pa, "but if it starts
rootin up this yard I'll put ten rings in his nose. You remember that. I won't have my meadow rooted up by that
pig. Pigs are hard on grass when they once get a taste of
the sweet roots that lay a little ways under the ground."

I took the hammer and I hit the planks. The same nails
that I drove in to hold Blue Tick in the pen will screak
out of the little two-by-two willow posts and let Blue Tick
go free again. Hear the hammer hit the planks and hear
the nails loose their holds in the willow wood. Blue Tick
goes free again as he was the day I found him in the lot
with his mother. But he was too little to know he was free
then. Now is the only time in his life he has ever been free.
He walks out of the pen. Then he runs back into it.

Blue Tick is afraid of the wind. He doesn't know it is
something that he can feel and can't see. He is afraid of
the ground. He steps like a person barefooted in sticker-
weeds. He is afraid of a cornstalk. Blue Tick is afraid of
the shadow he makes in the autumn sunlight. He sees a
tree, but he cannot tell how far away the tree is when he
walks toward the tree. He hits the tree with his head.

He will learn soon to judge how far away in the wind
the tree is. He looks up at the sky and he grunts. And when
he sees a bright leaf fall from a tree he runs. Blue Tick is
afraid.

Yesterday when the cool wind was messin with the
greenbrier tops I saw Blue Tick messin with their roots.
He was goin down with his nose in the soft new-ground
earth. He must have loved the smell of the soft sweet dirt.
I stood and watched him. And then I said to myself, "I'm
glad he's found the greenbrier roots. I know now that he
will not have to have ten rings in his nose. He won't root

up the meadow grass after he has found the brier roots, for the brier roots are sweeter than the grass roots. Shoats like them better too."

I'm glad that Blue Tick has learned how to miss a tree. He walks past them now. He never hits one.

He is no longer afraid to step on the ground. He is not afraid of a leaf. Blue Tick is not afraid of anything. He is a pretty shoat now. His hair is not dirty any more. There is no mud on it. He is clean as the dead leaf because he sleeps with the dead leaves.

III

Autumn is fading into winter. The brown world is changin to drab. The trees stand leafless in the wind. The cows have been brought from the meadow and turned into the woods pasture. They can browse among the dead leaves. They can sleep under the pines at night. They can sleep among the greenbriers or they can come to the sheds and sleep on the straw. It is up to the cows. The wind sighs among the greenbriers and the bare tree tops.

Blue Tick is growin. He drinks skimmed milk from a wooden trough now. I made the trough out of a hollow chestnut log. I sawed the ends off and nailed boards over the ends. The milk water-soaked the wood and it is now swollen. There is not a crack for the milk to leak out. Blue Tick knows I feed him. He follows me about over the barn yard. He goes with me when I take the mules to haul a load of fodder. He goes with me to clear ground. He goes with me everywhere I go. He goes like a dog and when Lead goes with me to the field, Blue Tick goes along and trots beside of Lead. But soon Blue Tick pants. He gets tired climbin hills. And Lead trots along without drawin a heavy breath. Lead does not like Blue Tick and he snaps at him when he gets close. Blue Tick would be friendly with Lead.

Pa says, "I don't want to get that pig in no bad habits like you have the turkey gobbler and the rooster."

And I say to Pa: "I didn't get that turkey gobbler in no bad habits. He took up that fighting himself. I didn't teach it to him."

Pa says: "The next time that turkey flogs one of the children I'm going to catch him and put his head across a block of wood and use the ax on his neck. And the very next time that game rooster flies in my face when I go to feed the mules I'm going to break his back with a ear of corn. A body can't feed for having to fight the fowls."

And I say, "I did not get that rooster to fightin either."

Pa says: "Ain't I seen you go out there o' a mornin to feed the hogs and you'd crow and get him started after you all riled up and you'd run and he'd hit you and you'd run and by doin that you got him so bad we can't live for him tryin to take the place. Now don't get that shoat Blue Tick to fightin. If you do, pon-my-words, I'll dash his brains out with a hammer."

When I milk the cows Blue Tick comes up and I milk warm milk from the cows' teats into his mouth. He opens his big mouth and his big white tongue covered with warm sweet milk foam looks like a white ear of corn. Blue Tick likes the milk I milk into his mouth from the cows' teats. I know that I'm not going to have him fightin. Though he did bow up to Lead the other day when Lead snapped him through the ear and left a tiny hole. Blue Tick follows the cows when he is not with me. He loves the cows nearly as much as he does me. He follows them all day long in their rambles through the winter woods and to the waterin hole. At first they were afraid of Blue Tick, but anymore they like him and they smell of his nose and snort and he smells of their noses and yawns. I watched them yesterday up on the hill by a chestnut log. The sun come out and the sun rays hit the dead leaves and made them warm. The cows laid down and Blue Tick laid down with them. He got right up close to the cow's spine and just stretched out so lazy-like in the winter sun that a body would a thought him dead. The cows laid there in the winter sun and chewed their cuds and Blue Tick laid right there with them like he was a cow too. When they mooed, he boo-hooed. They all slept there in the sun long as it lasted and when the sun went behind a rift of snow clouds they all got up and came over the hill to the barn.

IV

Winter has gone rapidly. The snow and ice are leavin the hills now. The hens scratch among the cornstalks in the barn lot. Birds are coming back. The English sparrows have never left the barn. The house wrens have come back to the rag sack in the smoke house where they had a nest last year and year before last. Green tips are appearin on the greenbriers that Blue Tick did not root up with his nose to eat the warts on the greenbrier roots.

Pa says: "Don't believe I'll kill that hog till next fall. Shame to kill him now and him lean as he is. That frame will hold six hundred pounds of meat."

And I'm so glad Pa feels this way about it. But Pa ain't got no right to kill him a-tall. He is my hog. I paid the quarter for him when he was about the size of a mouse. But look at him now! He grows faster than a elephant. His back looks like the winter-colored bluff over there when the sun comes out on the spots of white dead grass. Part of him is bluish like the dirt. Then there are the winter white spots of dead grass in the sunlight.

Now the cows go out to nibble on the greenbrier sprouts. Blue Tick goes with them. He follows them through the woods and sleeps with them under the pines. He is gettin big like a cow. He comes in with the cows and when I milk

them he comes up close for me to squirt milk onto his
pretty tongue. He opens his mouth anymore and comes so
close I have to soo-soo him back. But I sit on the stool chair
and milk the cows and give Blue Tick good warm cow
milk and it goes fine for his supper and good for his breakfast on the cool spring mornings.

v

It's a funny thing. I met Enic Stubblefield down there
this mornin by the gate and he said his cows had been
milked. And our cows had been milked the same mornin.
It is a strange thing. He said that his cows' teats looked like
they had been scratched by the briers and my cows' teats
was the same way. It is a funny thing. I'll tell Pa about
somebody milking our cows. I think I know who it is.
Estille Tentress was expelled from school last year for
slippin down in the pasture and milkin Charlie Penning-
ton's cow. He was caught right in the act. He milked the
cow in his dinner bucket and turned the milk right up and
drunk it. We was right there hid in the bushes, me and
Uncle Urban, and saw him do it. He is the one right now
milkin the cows and I'll tell Pa. Didn't get a pint of milk
this mornin from Pansy nor a half pint from Star and Roan
put together. He couldn't drink all the milk. He's sellin it.
Estille Tentress is a bad egg around where there is cows.
He likes sweet milk and their one cow can't give enough
milk for twelve children.

This is Ham Flemington. Here he comes, squat and
ducky, black mustache, gorilla-armed, big hands and mush-
room face. He comes up the path. He says, "Somebody is
milkin my cow."

And I say: "Somebody is milkin all three of my cows.
Didn't get a quart of strippins from all three cows this
mornin."

"Who's doing it?" Ham says.

"I'd love to know who is doin it," I say. "I'd like to sprinkle them with shot."

"If I find out I won't sprinkle them with shot. I'll take it to the Law and let the Law sprinkle them with shot."

He passes goin to town "Fencerail" Isaac Keen. His arms dangle at his side. He comes up and says, "Where is your Pa, son?"

And I says, "Pa is over on the hill clearin ground."

"Did you know somebody is milkin my cows? I turned them in the woods pasture that jines your field. Well, somebody got all the milk. There was slobbers all over my cows' teats. They was rough like a brier had scratched them."

Now here comes Pa from the clearin. "Tin Purvin come over there where I was workin and said two of his cows that run in the field next to our pasture had been milked and the two cows that run in the northside pasture had not been touched. Tin said this same thing happened once before when he was a boy. But he said Mike McGan found out what it was. He said he watched his cows one whole day and nothin bothered them. It was the second day round yonder back of that piney pint, the old cow was pickin up next to a rock cliff and a big cow snake crawled quietly from behind the rock and wound his body up like a corkscrew till he got his mouth over the cow's teat. At first she kicked a little. She mooed and looked at the ground and booed. Then she went on pickin grass and that snake milked every teat she had and then lit right on the other cow and milked her too. And when he got through he was all bloated up and he just rolled up and went to sleep there in the sun. Then Mike said that he shot it with a double-barreled shotgun right between the eyes and made shoe strings out of its hide."

Fain Wimpler comes down the path. He says: "Gentle-

men, don't think I'm tellin you a ghost story, but I went
down to the barn last night to milk my cow and somethin
big as a white calf tore out of that barn—tore two planks
off and got away. It had my cow tied down and her teats
was wet with slobbers. I never saw anythin like it in my
life. I throwed the milk bucket down and whistled for my
dogs, but they was both gone after a fox. I was so skeered
I couldn't whistle until it had time enough to get over the
hill."

VI

Today I take the rifle. Pa takes the shotgun. We go with
our cows to the fields. If it is Estille Tentress, we are goin
to find out. If it is a cow snake, we are goin to get it the first
cow he corkscrews up to. Blue Tick goes with us. He roots
alongside the cows and eats the blades of sweet grass where
he can find them. He roots up the greenbrier wart roots
and eats them. He is big like a ram now. He trots along
with the cows and Pa says, "Don't reckon it could be that
hog suckin the cows, could it?"

And I says: "Why no, you know it is not Blue Tick
when he comes right in with them every night when I milk
them. I been around him all the time and I never saw a bad
pass out of that hog. Never. Who ever heard tell of a hog
suckin a cow anyway? I never did in my life. Did you?"

"No I never did, and, son, I'm fifty-six years old. I've
heard of cow snakes, but not hogs."

The sweet wind of spring shakes the long blue hairs on
Blue Tick's hocks. The leaves, thin, and light-blue green,
swish in the pretty spring wind. Flowers grow by the roots
of the beech trees. They are windflowers and bloodroot
flowers. But Blue Tick cannot see when a flower is pretty.
All he is lookin for is the taste. He nibbles down the flowers and chops them in his long shoe-like mouth. Then, to
think Blue Tick would bother one of the cows. He just

don't remember his mother. Maybe he thinks a cow is his mother. I'll bet that is it. Over the winter dead leaves they go and through the little blotches of green grass. They cross the creek and they drink the clear cool creek water. Then up the next bluff and through the wild ferns and the flowers.

All day we follow our cows. The sun is gettin low in the late March skies. The wind is blowin among the green grass and the windflowers and the bloodroots. The wind is blowin through the green pasture leaves and the light green pasture grass. The sky, too, is blue as water-over-June-gravel. The cows trail the path home. Blue Tick trails the cows and we are next in line with gun and rifle.

The stars come out. The whippoorwills call. It is time for the whippoorwills. It is spring. Blue Tick comes into the barn lot with the cows. Lead comes to the barn lot to lick the old skillet we feed the kittens foam from the fresh milk in. Lead snaps at Blue Tick and Blue Tick bows up his side like a fish as if to say, "Come on, you hound dog, and I'll let you feel one of my tushes." As we are busy milking the cows, Blue Tick and Lead begin to quarrel.

Ham comes over and he says, "Followed my cows all day with a shotgun across my shoulder and I never saw a thing." While Ham is still here Isaac comes over. "Followed my cows the God-blessed day. Never saw nothin but a blowin viper snake and a couple of crows. Funny thing about the way our cows all got milked one night."

Then comes Tin: "Boys, never saw a thing all day and I followed my cows with a automatic pistol. I aim to light right into it with hot lead if powder will burn and the trigger will squeeze."

Fain Wimpler comes up to the milk gap and says: "Never seen a thing today, boys. Never seen a thing."

Tonight the moon hangs in the sky like a wisp of dead poplar leaves. I can look out from my window to the barn.

The ground is light as day. I can see the old dead potato
tops from last year's harvest. I can see little green bunches
of grass. I can see the stakes where we heated water to kill
the hogs. I can wonder about the cows. I see them goin
back up the trail, Pansy in front, then Roan and then Star.
Blue Tick is followin Star up the trail. I don't believe it is
Blue Tick suckin the cows. Surely he doesn't know how.
I get up and put on my overalls and shirt. I slip downstairs.
The moon is pretty tonight. I go out across the chip yard,
past the barn and through the barn lot and alongside the
rail pig pen. Then I follow the trail up the hill path, the
way Blue Tick followed Pansy, Roan and Star.

And now I come upon them. They do not see me. I
watch them lyin in the moonlight not far in front of me,
beside a dead chestnut tree top. Blue Tick is sleepin alongside one of the cows. He sleeps beside of Roan. If he is
milkin the cows I'll see. The moon is comin down through
the thin leafed spring tree tops. I stretch out flat on my
stomach. I do not make a sound. The wind blows over me
and shakes the thin leaves on the sour-wood sprouts.

And now Blue Tick wakes from sleep. He nudges Roan
like he was a young calf. He is suckin the cow. It is Blue
Tick. It is Blue Tick. He is a smart hog. He has never done
it before us. I know now what the ghost was Tin saw. I
watch Blue Tick. The cow does not care. The moon shines
down on them. There they are stretched side by side. Blue
Tick is big like a cow. Pa will kill Blue Tick when he finds
this out. I cannot stand to see him killed. Why did I ever
milk milk into his mouth on the cold frosty mornings?
Why did I ever, for even a hog will learn. The turkey
learned to fight. The rooster learned to fight. The hog has
learned to take the milk himself from the cow instead of
having it milked for him.

I go down to the barn and get some corn. I come back
and toll Blue Tick away. He goes back to the cows. So I

throw down so many rails and drive the cows through to the old house under some apple trees. I drive them in the house. In goes Blue Tick with them. I throw down the ear of corn. Blue Tick is eatin. While he is eatin I drive the cows out of the house. I bar the door. Blue Tick is in a big hog pen, one that will hold him. I drive home the cows.

VII

The young rabbits hop across my path. It is early mornin —no sign of sun yet. The thin leaves on the trees stir in the mornin breeze and the dew of the mornin hangs to the leaves. It is early. It is breakfast time. The house is close. Just one more fence to cross and the old orchard and then the house. The door is open. Panels have been knocked out. I'll look for the tracks. Here they are—down the path toward Liam Galligher's barn—it is just under the hill. And Liam owns the place we live on. My heavens!

Under the pine trees I run. The rabbits can get out of my way or stay in my way. If the rabbit has made the third grade in school he has learned that man desires blood—that man is a killer. Look at Pa wantin to kill Blue Tick—and he will kill Blue Tick because he sucks the cows at home and the neighbors' cows. I'm running fast. I am afraid that Liam will kill Blue Tick. Listen—Listen! I hear! I hear! Here comes Liam up the path ridin a sorrel pony with a blazed face. "I caught the thief," he says. "I got him. It is a hog!"

"My hog," I say. "Yes, my hog—you didn't kill him, did you——?"

"No I didn't, for that is the first time I ever heard of anything like that in my life let alone seein it—But it is the truth. I went over to the house and got my wife. She said that she's never seen anything like it in all her growin up and that if ever her Pap did he'd never said anything about it. So I just drove the cow out and worked him through the partition into the log barn and fastened him in a mule stall. That will hold him. I've just started to tell the neighbors that I got the cow snake and he is a hog after the milk that has been milkin their cows."

"Don't tell Pa. He will kill Blue Tick."

"No, he must not kill a hog like that—He is too smart to kill. We'll take that hog to the Fair over at Turnipseed and get a decent price for him. That is a curiosity that all the people in the country would like to see. We'll crate him up and put him in the spring wagon right now if you want to and take him to the Fair if it would be all right with your Pa—Reckon he'll care?"

"Blue Tick is mine—not Pa's. I raised him from a mouse-sized pig. I don't want him killed."

"It would be a shame to kill him. Get on this pony behind me. We'll load him up right now and take him to the Fair and tell about him after he is sold. We'll haul him there in the spring wagon."

The crate is made. We put it in the stall where Blue Tick is. We toll him into the crate. We nail up the end. We open the double door and pull his crate with a mule to the shed. Then we hoist him up to the low joist with a four-strand rope pulley and a mule. We shove the spring wagon under the crate. Then we let the crate down in the express. We have Blue Tick ready for the Fair.

The road is dusty and it leads to nowhere. Turns, willows, creeks — horseweeds — curves—ditches—sandpiles. House by the side of the road. Willows by the road. Chip yards beside the road. And the village at the end of the road, maybe. But the pony is hitched to the express and we move though the pony does have a load, a hog, a boy and a man. And the end of the road and here is Turnipseed and the Fair grounds.

Mr. Hix the manager says: "That hog won't suck no cow. I been at this game of buyin three-legged chickens, and two-headed calves and six-legged cows and three-eyed heifers for a long time—But in all my experiences have I ever seen a hog that would suck a cow. I'll tell you what I got to have is a cow and if that hog sucks that cow I'll give you four fifty-dollar bills for that hog. If he don't suck the cow you get him off these grounds and do it quick."

"It's a go," says Liam.

A boy with a green shirt and a white necktie with tattooed arms brings the cow from a barn. And when we let him out of the crate and put them both in the tent he bows up to her side and boo-boos. Then he starts to milk the cow and she starts to kickin. But finally she lets him have his way, for he puts his head under her flank and there is not much she can do about it for she cannot kick him. "That beats any novelty I've ever seen in my day in the show business. Here, young man, are your four fifty-dollar bills. And here's you a ten smacker, Mr. Galligher, for having sense enough to haul a hog like that to the Fair instead of butchering it. It is the biggest find I have had in many a year. Hang around and watch people flock in at a quarter a whack to see this tonight. I'll have four hundred people in here this night."

And I have four fifty-dollar bills. I can buy pounds of sugar now and calico shirts and overalls and shoes. But I'm not goin to buy anything like that. They'll go. One thing will stay and that is land. Nothing can change it much or hurt it a great deal. I'm goin to buy that forty acres of Priam Hamilton. He wants $175 for it. Then I'll have $25 left.

And as I ride back in the spring wagon with Liam and the moon comes down above our heads and falls on the little pretty green willow leaves alongside the creek—I think of the land I'll own and the willow trees I'll have on my place. Trees will be mine and the wind will be mine that passes over my place. The moonlight that falls on it will be mine.

I'll own the big trees and little trees and I can own ducks
and chickens and turkeys on my place. The sky above it
will be mine while it floats above my place.

And then Blue Tick was gettin so big and would have
made so much meat for us—But how in the green world of
spring could I stand to see them boil water to scald Blue
Tick with—shoot him between the eyes with a rifle and
scald off his hair and scrape him like a turnip! Then hang
him up and slit him open with a knife—How could I stand
to see it after I raised him on a bottle, to go and look at his
big, pretty, white, clean, sweet-smellin body when he was
hangin to a gallows with a stick run between the leaders
under his hind legs and fastened over the gallows and red
blood dripping from the end of his nose.

WILBURN

I followed Wilburn through the woods. I heard the pheasant drumming among the cool green hills where the crow flapped his wings and caw-cawed to another crow. The hawk sailed above easily in the air. The buzzard circled higher in the sky above the green hills. "Watch the cattle now," Wilburn said. "Don't you come too close where that ox can get his big foot on you. It will just be too bad. Stay clear of that ox."

I followed Wilburn and his team of cattle down the lonely cattle roads where the giant trees are hauled from the high boney hills.

When I went home I said: "I am Wilburn." I got a stick and I said: "Whoa back, whoa back there, Buck! Whoa back, whoa back there, Berry!" I used my stick. I tapped gently at first. Berry would not mind me. Then I hit a little hard and then I hit a little harder. I said: "That Berry is a good ox—good as there is in these log woods or any log woods."

When I saw Wilburn going to town with a turn of corn on his back, I filled a flour sack with sand and put it on my back. I said: "I am Wilburn. I am going to the mill today with a turn of corn."

Mom said: "No, son—you are not Wilburn. He is another man. You are yourself. You are Shan."

"I look like Wilburn then, don't I?" I asked Mom.

Mom nodded 'yes' with a smile.

"I'm growing up to be a man like Wilburn some day and have a big lot of foxhounds and drive a lot of cattle," I said. "I'm going to be big as Wilburn. I'm going to plow the land with a big team of cattle like Wilburn does. I'm going to follow behind the big plow and hear the roots popping and see the stumps roll out. I'll see the cattle get down on their knees and pull the stumps out of the earth. I'm going to be a man like Wilburn."

When we cut the logs to build our new house, we had a house-raising. Pa invited Wilburn to come. Mom and the neighborhood women fixed a big dinner for the men out under the pine tree. The women set two big tables of food they cooked under an open fire. The men lifted the big logs and skidded them up poles onto the square pen of pine, poplar, oak and chestnut logs. They lifted a big house log, upon the skids. Two men pulled the log with a rope from one corner of the house and then from the other corner. Wilburn was one who pulled with the rope. When the corner of the long house log was pulled upon the frame of logs, Wilburn hollered, "Steady, men, steady!" Wilburn took his ax and started notching the log. The chips flew, one chip, two chips, three chips! Wilburn bit his lips and showed his snow-white teeth. The chips flew faster.

"Much of a man that 'Wilburn' is," one of the men said on the ground below.

"Powerful as an ox," said another.

"Watch him use that ax, won't you. Never was a man as powerful. I wish I were a man powerful as he is with a double-bitted ax."

I saw Wilburn standing high on the house in the sunlight. I could see his face shining. I could see him in the wind. I heard Mom say to one woman: "My boy wants to be like Wilburn. He wants to drive cattle like Wilburn. He wants to carry a turn of corn to the mill like Wilburn. He tries to walk like Wilburn and act like Wilburn. He follows Wilburn all day in the log woods."

II

Wilburn's Uncle John stayed with him. He was a tall man with a white mustache that covered his thin lips. He was bent nearly double with age. He walked with a big sourwood cane. He wore a big black hat that he had worn for years. He wore a big brown overcoat in the summertime. He wore it when he delivered milk in the little town two miles away. When I met him in the road, he took a path around through the brush. He muttered strange words to himself.

Wilburn's Aunt Laura stayed with them. They lived in a log shack under the apple trees and the pear trees and below a mountain spring. The white thunderhead clouds swelled mountain-sized in the sky, above their shack. The slopes around their shack were desolate, sawbriar-covered and forgotten. Laura had had her back broken. Her hair was white with age. She crawled and swept the cabin floor. She crawled and fed the chickens at the edge of the porch. Laura gave me sweet apples when I walked across the mountain to their shack with Wilburn.

The woods were green in April. White clouds floated over the green woods and a yellow moon hung in the blue sky. There was fragrance in these April woods, flower, and vine. The fragrance made me drink deep breaths of April air into my lungs when the fox horns were blowing. There was music in the barking of hounds as they topped the piney points close behind the fox. "Listen to old Bess," Wilburn said. "She's shore driving that fox! Listen to that gal speak, won't you!"

Wilburn laughed in the moonlight under the fluffy green of April. The stars and the moon were in the tender April

sky. Life was just kind to Wilburn and me. The green trees
gave their April fragrance and the flowers were in bloom.
There was music of the barking hounds. It was sweet to
our ears as the wind that made music through the pines the
night long.

My dog, Scout, came up and took the lead. He was
closest to the fox. It was sweet music to hear Scout barking
around the mountain slopes in April. I watched Wilburn.
He looked at me—his eyes shining in the moonlight. He
would laugh and show his white teeth like a row of big
blackberry petals. "Wait a minute and old Bess'll be right
there in the game," said Wilburn. "If old Bess don't, old
Sooner will. It's time for old Sooner to open up there. Ain't
done nothing tonight."

These were great nights in the woods with Wilburn
when our hounds ran the fox. Great nights under the millions of white stars—high, high, high over the bony ridges
where the foxes have their holes under the great rocks and
where they raise their young. Great nights under the green
trees with Wilburn in April when life was young. Great
nights, great nights, never were there nights like these.
"Don't you sprawl out there on that damp ground," Wilburn said. "It will give you the rheumatics."

I got up and brushed the dead leaves from my back. I
felt stiff and cold. I rubbed my eyes. Wilburn had a little
fire made of sticks. He was hovering over the fire and
throwing the brands up in a little center-heap. Blue thin
blazes were streaming to the April wind. I shall remember
these nights with Wilburn—nights, nights, nights—nights
of hound-dog music and the stars and the wind.

III

Wilburn plowed his corn on the mountain slope across
the hollow. I was plowing corn now on the other side of the

hollow. "I'll beat you to the top of the mountain this time," Wilburn said. "I've got the prettiest corn I've had in years." His corn was dark waving corn.

It had pushed from the rank earth and the black earth-loam into the wind, the sun and the rain! Wilburn plowed an ox with a mule's collar on him upside down. The ox wore the same harness a mule wears. He was a giant ox and he pulled the cutter plow through the earth and tore out the stumps in the corn rows. I saw Wilburn behind old Berry. "Boy, that old Berry is one more ox," Wilburn hollered to me. "Watch me tear out these stumps. Watch him, won't you, boy. Just watch him."

Wilburn laughed and showed his teeth. His lips tightened when the plow hitched on a stump and the plow handles jabbed Wilburn in the ribs. The crows flew out of the green woods caw-cawing until they saw us. They caw-cawed more than ever then and flapped furious wings back into the green timber. Wilburn followed Berry—the black earth rolling over at his feet. The furrowed earth was the sweet-smelling odor of spring and growing corn. There was the smell of tender sprouts that shoot from the earth after the first spring rains. There was the smelly smartweed that grew from the new-ground ash-heaps where the brush had burned. "Are you going to fox-hunt tonight?" I asked Wilburn.

"Suits me," said Wilburn. "I'm a little sleepy though."

"Oh yes," I said. "You were out last night. I heard your horn. I heard one of your dogs howl to answer your horn."

The spring passed. It flew into summer and the crops grew. Summer on the earth is the productive time for man. Summer is the time for men to make bread—the passing, passing summer days under the golden sun of summer and the white rain drops that moisten the lips of trees, plants, vines and flowers. Summer is the trail of beauty, growth, and fragrant smells of devil-shoestring blossoms, corn silks,

and corn tassels. Summer is the trail of time, beauty, and
eternity.

IV

The icy winds came and one by one we went to bed. A
sheet of snow covered the bony-scarred acres. "You've
got that new disease that is sweeping this land," said Dr.
Sellard. "It is the influenza."

We were all in bed. There was not one of us able to help
the other. The beds were filled. There wasn't anyone to
cook, cut wood, milk the cows and feed the cattle.

"Doc, as you go over the hill," said Pa, "you tell Wilburn
to come over. Tell him we are sick. Tell him we are all
down sick in bed."

"This new house with the open cracks is enough to kill
the last one of you," said Dr. Sellard. His lean shriveled
hands helped his thin lips speak these words as he left the
house. He walked across the chipyard through the snow
and climbed in the saddle slowly. The horse had his tail tied
up in a knot to avoid the slush-snow and the mud. He
trotted slowly down the bank toward town.

"I'm afraid of this disease," said Wilburn. "I've come to
do all I can for you. I've come to help you and if you all die
guess I'll die with you. I don't want to die."

Wilburn came to my bed with medicine. He brought me
buttermilk to drink. He waited on seven of us. He cooked
for us, swept the house, milked the cows, and cut the wood.
From my bed I could hear the barren oaks stiffly screaking
in the wind. I could hear the winds in the pines and the
lonesome 'oo–oo.' I could hear the foxes bark on the hill
above our barn when they came to get our chickens that
roosted in the barn stalls.

Wilburn worked night and day. "Shore you're going to
get well," said Wilburn. "None of you's going to die."

We did get well. We got out of bed one by one and

hovered before the big blazing log fire Wilburn had built. "I tell you," said Pa, "Wilburn is the finest man that ever put his foot on shoe-leather. If it hadn't been for Wilburn what would we have done? Tell me another man like Wilburn? The hills don't have them."

V

The skies above us were April skies again. White clouds sailed over the blue skies like ships on a blue sea with their sails filled with wind. The trees leafed again now. Spring was here and we were proud to be alive. Spring was here and we plowed the rugged slope on one side of the hollow while Wilburn plowed the rugged slopes on the other side. We fox-hunted again together and breathed the fragrance of the spring wind deep into our lungs. We breathed the mountain air from the hollows and the high hills. We heard the music of our own hounds. We heard a great symphony of music of hound dogs' barks—the sweetest symphony in the world. "Oh, listen to old Sooner," said Wilburn. "Ah, he shore is driving that fox tonight! Listen to 'im, won't you! Just listen, Shan." Wilburn sat by a fire made of sticks and leaves and laughed.

The crops grew again from the land. Crops come and go as the seasons come and go. When spring comes winter goes on a long voyage. It is something apast. It is a rotten leaf. It is a lost season cast upon the winds of time, that will never come again. It is a piece of time that we have lived, that we have lost, that will not come again.

VI

Pa walked across the pasture hill. It was a day in June and the white thunderheads went out to space. Pa stepped over the rail fence, took his handkerchief from his hip pocket and wiped his bacon-brown neck. Pa walked across the sheep pasture to the house. "Say, did you know Wilburn is sick," said Pa. "He's down in bed. He's got a pain in his side." Pa was troubled. He walked to the well. He drew a bucket of water from the well. Pa took the dipper from the nail on the well-gun and drank a dipper of cool water. His Adam's apple worked up and down with each swallow.

"I want to eat an early supper and get back over to see Wilburn," said Pa as he put the dipper back on the nail. "It's a funny thing. Laura had the Doctor with him. The Doctor said he'd haf to be operated on."

"Wilburn sick?" Mom asked. "He saved this family that cold winter when people died of the influenza. I've often said if it hadn't been for Wilburn we'd all've died. He cooked and waited on us and saved us when people were afraid to come here. People were afraid of the influenza as they were of death when it first broke out here among the hills. Wilburn was not afraid. We cannot do enough to save Wilburn."

"Wilburn is afraid of a hospital," said Pa. "He's never seen a hospital. He's afraid to go."

"I was just thinking," said Mom, "if there isn't someway to save him without taking him to the hospital."

"He has to be operated on," said Pa. "That's the only way on earth to save him. Dr. Sellard says he has to have his appendix out. He's waited too long already."

"Get him off to the hospital then," said Mom. "He's one of the best men that ever stepped his foot among these hills. No wonder all the boys want to be like Wilburn. I hope Shan will be the man someday that Wilburn is now."

VII

The Doctor looked at Pa. I looked at Wilburn lying on the wooden bed. He was writhing in pain. His voice was softer now. He did not laugh like he did when he heard our fox hounds running. He did not talk like he did when he drove the big oxen over the timber road. He didn't look like the man that followed Berry behind the plow in spring and turned the black-loam over. He lay on the bed. His great liquid eyes moved slowly in their walnut sockets. His lips had grown pale. "My corn is getting weedy, Mick," said Wilburn to Pa. "I wish I was well to plow and hoe my corn. I don't want to go to the hospital. I haven't got the money to go. I don't want to borrow it. And who'll care for my fox hounds when I am gone?"

"Don't worry about the money," said Pa. "We'll take care of your corn and see about the dogs."

Wilburn nodded with a smile that he would go. They carried him on a pair of bedsprings down the rocky mountainside where the ambulance could reach him. They opened the ambulance doors and put Wilburn in the ambulance. The motor droned and the wheels rolled slowly down the crooked road. "I'm afraid," said Pa as he watched the ambulance move slowly down the rough road. "I believe Wilburn won't come back a living man."

Men from the hills gave money. Many gave a dollar; some two dollars; and a few gave five dollars. Many children gave all they had to give, a dime, a quarter, half dollar! This was for Wilburn's doctor bill and to send him to the hospital.

"Have you heard from Wilburn?" Laura asked me when I passed the shack. "I'm afraid for Wilburn. The dogs howled for Wilburn last night. Bess and Sooner howled all night." Laura wiped the tears from her eyes and brushed back her snow-white hair from her face. John walked around the house with a big overcoat on and it was July. He cut the wood for Laura. He milked the cows and slopped the hogs.

"Tomorrow, Laura, we are going to hoe Wilburn's corn," I said. "I've just been around and notified the neighbors. The corn is getting weedy. We'll clean the corn tomorrow. I'll bring the mule and haul you some stove-wood soon as we plow the corn."

"It's so nice of you," said Laura. "I just couldn't believe we had friends to do as you people have done." She wiped the tears from her eyes.

"Look what Wilburn did for us," I said. "We never had anybody to do as much for us as Wilburn did. I've tried to live like Wilburn and be like him all my life."

I didn't want the weeds to take Wilburn's corn. I didn't want Wilburn to die. I would miss Wilburn. I would miss seeing him in the chipyard cutting stove-wood. I'd miss hearing Wilburn speak. I'd miss hearing his big laugh. I'd miss him in the cornfield. I'd miss him fox-hunting on the ridges. Wilburn must stay here. He must stay here forever. It would never look right unless I could see Wilburn standing at the woodblock under the sweet-apple tree by his log shack.

VIII

Twenty men gathered to hoe Wilburn's corn. We took twenty rows of corn at a time. It was hot. The sun burned our backs. The weeds wilted and dried in the sun. The field was sprinkled with workers all working, working for Wilburn.

The clean corn below us waved in the wind. When the weeds wilted and dried in the sun, the corn was left clean on the loam-land. The corn was left clean to silk and tassel. It was Wilburn's corn. Above this cornfield were the woods where we fox-hunted. "Twenty rows of corn at a through," said Uncle Hankas, "and this cornfield surely fades." High noon and we climbed to the top of the hill. Wilburn's corn had been hoed clean as a pawpaw whistle. "A crow would have to carry his grub over this field of corn," said Uncle Hankas.

Each man carried his hoe across his shoulder. We walked the ridge road to the divide. Men were wet with sweat. We parted on the ridge path and went to our homes for dinner. We could hear our dinner bells ringing over the land. We could smell the growing corn. We could feel the hot blistering wind. We could hear the crickets singing. We could see the grasshoppers dancing in the sunlight.

"He didn't make it," said Pa. "I've just been to town to see. Wilburn died last night. He called for you, Shan, before he died." Pa shed tears. He wiped the tears from his eyes with his red bandana. "Ah, how I will miss Wilburn," I said.

"Never was a better man than Wilburn," said Mom. "Guess poor old Laura will die when she hears about Wilburn's death."

IX

The horse with the spring wagon rolled up the mountain slope to haul Wilburn away. I went in the house to see Wilburn. He looked as if he were asleep and he would wake soon. I had seen him look this way many a night in April under the green oaks, asleep in the moonlight. It seemed to me that he was not dead. He could not be dead. He was just asleep under a green tree in April. People about the house were crying. Pa was a strong man but Wilburn's death made him shed tears. I did not shed tears. I thought of him as just being asleep and that he would soon wake up and we would fox-hunt again. I did not follow the wagon to the grave on the hill. I knew where they would bury Wilburn. His grave would be at the other end

of the ridge where we fox-hunted. That was where they
would lower Wilburn into his eternal bed. It was not the
place for Wilburn's bed. He ought to sleep in his cornfield where he could hear the fox horns blow and where
the barking of the hound dogs would be sweet.

Now when I pass Wilburn's shack at night, I think,
"What if I meet Wilburn. Wilburn cold, cold, cold,
sleeping on the other side of the hill under a quilt of
sawbriars and dirt away from where the fox horn's blowing and the hound dogs barking. If I meet Wilburn I will
tell him, 'Old Sooner is too old to run the fox now, Wilburn. Bess is white with age. She can barely walk out to
meet me when I pass your shack. I often see Laura, Wilburn. She is very old but she still crawls and sweeps the
floor and cooks for John. She weeps for you, Wilburn.
We miss you, Wilburn. Laura gave me your horn and your
gun. I have them. She wanted me to have them. I'm keeping them for you."

I am afraid to cross the hill at night. I am afraid to meet
the man I wanted to be. I think, 'What if he would meet
me on the path and laugh and shake my hand and ask me
how I am. What if I could see that same old smile and
hear that same old laugh.' I am afraid at night when I pass
Wilburn's shack. I always hurry toward home. Wilburn's
shack is east of my shack. I hurry toward the sunset.

FERN

"When we were boys in the mountains
And she was a girl from the hills—"

WE SAW THEM BRING HER. We stood on a pasture hill in August crabgrass to our knees and watched the mules pull the express through the soap-stone mud below us. Don said to me, "That's them moving in ain't it Stephen?"

Mom told us that morning we would have newcomers in the old Callihan house. And she said they had a sick girl. Mom said she had the consumption and they was going to haul her into the Hollow on a cot. How Mom got the news I don't know but I think Fannie Price told her at a quilting. She was hauled in on a cot in the back of the express. Just her face showed from under the quilts.

Don and me went down to see them unload her. The mules was tired and a-panting. They'd done hauled one wagon load of furniture in from the station and then they went back and got Fern. I saw them lift the crazy-patched quilt off'n Fern's face—it sorty covered up part of her face. Don and me stood off about fifty feet in a patch of briars. When we saw Fern Don said, "Stephen, let's move in a little closer. She's pretty as a doll."

I thought Fern was the prettiest girl I ever saw and I didn't like it because my brother Don thought she was pretty. It looked like to me he could have thought Grace Livingston or Mary Sparks was just as pretty but he didn't.

He thought Fern was pretty because I thought she was pretty.

"Come here," Fern said to me, and I thought I'd break my neck getting through the briars by the Irish-tater patch down to the wagon where Fern was. Don followed me. He went along too. It was me the one she wanted. I walked up to the wagon.

"Fern is my name," she said to me, "what is your name?"

"My name is Stephen Ensor. That's my brother Don. I knowed your name was Fern before you moved here. Mom was over to Fannie Price's to a quilting and found it out someway." And I looked at Fern and she looked and looked at me. I knowed it was me she liked instead of my brother. But Don just stood there and looked on at Fern in the wagon-bed.

Fern's Pappie and Mammie worked and worked unloading the furniture and putting it in the house and the mule-driver Tobbie Spry helped them too. They lifted dressers and tables and chairs and carried them into the house. They carried baskets of dishes in the house and stone jars and willow baskets and all the things that a family has when it moves. They turned the chickens out of the crate and let them run around the house. It was a awful lonesome place there. Fern in the bed. I wanted to ask her if she could walk but I darst not to ask her. Wind blowed through the rose briars and the apple tree limbs and the corn-tassels over in our corn on the hill.

"Ain't you got no brothers and sisters to play with," said Don.

"No I am the only one," said Fern. "If there's anymore to my family I don't know about them. I am the only one. They ain't my Pappie and my Mammie there. They just keep me. My Pappie and Mammie are dead. They've been dead a long long time. I can remember when Mammie died. It was in the fall-time. Winds blowed the dead leaves down off some rocks back of the house and they pitty-patted on my window panes like bird claws. Pappie died when the buds were swelling in the plum trees back of the chimney. I remember it well as if it had been yesterday. The Doctor said if he could pull him through the spring till the leaves quit putting out, then he would be all right till the leaves started to fall again. But they didn't pull him through. He's got what I got. I must a-got it from him."

"Would you like to have one of the red apples out'n the top of that tree," I said to Fern.

"Yes," said Fern, "a real mellow apple is the only kind that I can eat." And don't you know before I had time to pick up a rock Don run under and shook the tree and grabbed a mellow apple from among the briars and the weeds and brought it out to Fern. He beat me. I just let him do it. Don is my brother and a year younger than I am. He is sixteen and I'm seventeen. Fern is about as old as I am.

"How about me coming over to see you, Fern," I said as I heard our dinner-bell ringing us to dinner.

"Come anytime you can," said Fern, "I get so lonesome here flat on my back with nobody to talk to. You come too Don. Both of you come over when you can come and you don't live so far away across that little hill when I can hear your dinner-bell."

"No it's just a little ways across the hill over there and we can come over a lot of times to see you," Don said.

Well I looked at Fern as we left. Her cheeks was the color of a first-ripe plum and her face was white nearly as the petals of a blood-root flower. Her hair was gold-colored like love vines and about as curly as any hair I ever saw. It laid down over her shoulders. If she'd just not asked Don back. I knowed Don liked her same as I did. I could tell the way he watched her and when she laughed Don

just stood and eyed her. She had teeth whiter than the chalk
we used at the blackboards at school.

"I think she's the prettiest girl I ever saw," Don said as
we were tearing through the briars and grapevines to get
home for dinner. Mom rung the bell again for us. I heard
her holler and tell Martha to go to the field after us. We
wasn't in no cornfield chopping weeds. We wanted to see
the newcomers move in. We get enough of chopping
weeds from April till August. We get awfully tired of
chopping weeds before school starts. We hurried to the
house—run in carrying our hats and we run in the wrong
way. We came through by the pig-pen when we should
a-come through by the smoke-house.

"Where you boys been," said Mom eyeing us over her
glasses.

"We been out there behind the barn seeing if them
possum grapes was getting ripe——"

"Now you know them grapes don't get ripe till 'long
about October," said Mom. "You've been over there to the
Callihan house where the new people are moving in today."

Of course I up and told the truth. It's hard for a body to
go on lying when he is already caught. A body ought to
make good preparations to lie. I ought a-knowed them
grapes didn't get ripe till October but then I didn't think.
I was thinking about the girl I saw. I was thinking about
Fern. But Mom didn't do nothing to us. She sent us back
to the cornfield out by the smoke-house this time and told
us to get the crabgrass chopped out that evening. That
crabgrass was enough for ten men to dig out in one half a
day. But we worked like mules. We went and come
through the field. Sweat streamed from Don's nose like a
sluice of water falling from a rock. We got it chopped out
all right and we come in home and done up the work.

Well that night I watched Don and he watched me. He

said, "Stephen, are you going over to the Callihan house to see Fern." I pretended like I didn't hear him but I'd made up my mind to go and take her a bunch. I never had picked flowers for a woman in my life.

I slipped down by the creek and I got a armload of milk-weed blooms sort of a brindle-colored and I shook the bees out 'em good so one wouldn't sting Fern. I got some butter-cups down in the swamp shaped something like little shoes and I got some iron weed blooms and mixed 'em all up to a right pretty bouquet and then I slipped around back of the barn and took over the bank to the Callihan house. Well, I went down to the house and knocked on the door and Fern's step-Mammie opened the door and here was brother Don a-settin' right over by the bed where Fern was a-lay-ing. He had brought her a pretty bunch of goldenrod and I'd forgot about seeing it turning down on the point where the persimmon sprouts bend over the road.

Fern looked at me and laughed. I'll declare I thought she had the prettiest teeth I ever saw in my life. There she lay in the bed—moonlight come in at her winder and fell all over her bed like sunlight. Didn't need a lamp. It was the harvest moon. I just wanted to ask her right there to marry me. But here was Don with Fern too. Don has light hair—almost as light as Fern's hair and I guessed I was out of place with my charcoal-black hair. But I loved Fern. I knowed I did. Me and Don was boys from the mountains and Fern was the girl from the hills. She said, "You boys just tickle me to death." She looked right at Don. I didn't like it. Don always just spoiled everything for me. He got the best candy at home and the best clothes and he always put in just like he did with Fern.

"Where did you come from, Fern?" I said.

"I come from the coal-mining deestrict," she said.

And then I said, "Who was your Pappie and Mammie, Fern?"

And Fern said, "Shhh—" holding her finger over her mouth and pointing back to the kitchen. There was her step-Mammie back there a-rolling biscuit dough and looking over her specs at us with a big kind of calf eyes. She was a woman I just didn't like at first sight. She wore a big bonnet with slats in the front of it and she went around over the kitchen like a mouse. I saw her Pappie out cutting stove-wood by the rose bush and he was tall like a bean-pole with a yowe neck and a little face that had a sharp-pointed nose stuck on it like a mud-dauber's nest stuck on a old washpan. I just didn't like them and Don didn't either.

Well, we had to go that night. I remember leaving as well. It comes to me fresh as a buttercup in the dew. Fern lifted her poor skinny hand from under the quilt to me. I wanted to squeeze it. I was afraid to. I was afraid of breaking a bone in her hand. I didn't want her to reach that same hand to my brother Don but she did. The moonlight fell across the floor and I remember Fern said, "I wish I was strong like you boys for just a week. I would love to get out with you and get mountain tea from the knolls. I would love to go up in the high hills where the lambs are all the time baaing to their mammies. I would just love to run with the wind and pick the flowers and climb grapevines and gather wild grapes. We'd have the best time together—take the dogs and watch them track the rabbits. We'd watch the leaves fall from the persimmon tops to the ground. I do love persimmon leaves."

Well, she just talked on and on. I felt so sorry for Fern. She was so pretty and had to lay in the bed all the time. Just think of it! Don and me—we didn't get to lay in the bed of a morning much as we wanted to lay in the bed. I thought about the leaves falling as me and Don went back to the house. If Fern could just pull through when the leaves fell then she'd live till the leaves begin to bud anyway.

Don and me went over the bank and past the barn home. We went by the moonlight. It was smeared over the weeds and the woods like a big white wind. I just hoped and prayed Fern would get well enough for me to marry her. Just get out and walk like I could and she'd be a angel pretty as she was. Why she's prettier than any girl in the Hollow. I thought about her all the way back. I could just hear every word she said just as plain as if she was saying them. I could see her lips bend when she laughed and I could see her pretty teeth. I could see her hair curled like love vines down over her shoulders and out on the quilt— two big long braids of it. I wanted to marry Fern. I didn't talk much to Don going back. He didn't seem like the brother that he'd always been—helped me in fights and helped me to hoe corn and all. It just seemed to me that he wasn't no kin to me.

When we got in the house the lamp was still burning and Mom and Pop was sitting up talking. I heard Mom say 'Don' and then she said 'Stephen' and then 'Fern.' And I knowed she was talking about us. Well I didn't care long as Mom didn't say anything about Fern. I heard Mom say to Pop, "Them boys of ours are losing their heads over the sick girl over the hill. Fern is her first name. God knows her last name. She's been sick all her life with consumption. They can't fall in love with the poor girl. They mustn't do it. They's too many well girls and big and strong that can use a ax or a hoe. And just think they both are fond of her. I was talking to her step-mother. She said they'd been coming around to see Fern. I guess the woman I talked to was her step-mother. Nobody can tell much about that family."

And Pop said, "I heard she wasn't any kin to them. That her Pappie was a miner and left enough insurance money for somebody to take care of this girl when he died. Her Mammie died first. Then her Pappie. That is the way I understand it and this couple are taking care of Fern. I

don't know what her name is. I never learned. But that
poor girl can't get well. She can't walk again. She is a
pretty girl in the face. She is pretty as them Gordon girls
used to be. You remember they just looked like flowers in
bloom all the time. Their Pap was some kind of a preacher
till old Henry Thomas caught him in his meadow one night
stealing grass and then he give up preaching. But he worked
around someway and got a insurance policy out on all his
eleven children. One died every year. Beat anything I ever
saw. The prettiest nine girls you ever saw—the two boys
were not much to look at. Well, the old man outlived
them all. Looked like ever since I was a boy that he had one
foot in the grave and the other foot ready to slide in. But
the old man is going to outlive some of us younger bucks.
When the consumption gets hold of a pretty girl it takes
her nearly every time. Look at that poor girl."

And I just thought, "Yes look at that poor girl. I can't
take her flowers the next time. What could I take her? I can
just see her on that bed. It is her home. All the moonlight
she can get is through her window. I wish she was just
well. I'd take her to church and the square dance if I could
get away from my brother Don— We'd go along under the
tall poplar trees and through the old apple orchard to
church and see the stars shine down from the sky on our
heads. We'd have a good time together—I'd be hers and
she'd be mine. No one else could have her. No one could
get her. She would be mine much as my ears are mine."

August started going in a hurry. Just seemed to me like
it slipped by. The butterflies left the milkweeds and the
ironweeds and the wild geese began to holler and honk
from the sky. The leaves began to turn. The goldenrods
got yaller as gold over all the pasture fields. The creeks
sorty hummed along over the rocks and dwindled and left
sulphur on the bedrocks. Falltime would soon be here. And
I'd heard Fern say she'd like to see a snake. Well I took old

Satan out to the sweet clover and he runs a snake like a rabbit. I heard him hit a trail and I saw him sniff and jump back and I got me a club and followed him up. The black-snake quiled. I put a forked stick over the back of his head and he fit like a copperhead. I reached down and got him. I took him over to show him to Fern. And who do you think I found already at Fern's? Don was there and he had caught a big flat-headed copperhead and they was whispering so Fern's folks in the next room wouldn't hear what they was saying about the snake. I just took my little blacksnake and slipped it loose in her room. Don killed the copperhead and throwed it into the hogs. They'll eat all of a copperhead but its head. We talked to Fern that night and talked.

Fern's step-mother set in the front room beside her man and I could see they wasn't the love between them they was between me and Fern. They set in the house and quarreled with one another. And I said, "I'll never quarrel that way with the woman I love if I ever get to marry her." And Fern she looked with her mellow blue eyes and laughed and laughed. She must a-knowed I meant her. Don never said a word. He was there with his good gray pants on and his blue shirt and white tie and Sunday shoes.

The sun was shining down hot that Sunday. I went to see Fern. I went alone. The grasshoppers buzzed on their little short wings from one bunch of broom sage to another. I picked one up and he spit tobacco juice on my hand. I took him to Fern. I picked her some goldenrod and some blue-beggar lice. I knocked on the door and Lizzie Shacklesworth told me that they'd killed a big blacksnake behind the meal-barrel. She said it must have come out of the rocks back of the house and I said I guessed it did. I went on in the house to talk to Fern. "The poor blacksnake had to be killed," she said. I gave her the grasshopper and the goldenrod. She took them and thanked me.

"Poor thing," she would say to the grasshopper and handle him like he was made of glass. He didn't even spit on Fern. She'd a-liked him better if he had. He got loose from her white hand and jumped all over the bed. I caught him and gave him his freedom to the wind and sun. Fern told me to. The August sun rays filled the room and the scent of the corn come through the window and Fern said, "I love the smell of corn and hot weeds. The country looks so lazy now. I would love to ride over the countryside and see the corn and smell the pines and the cockleburrs and the smartweeds."

I said to Fern, "Would you ride on a sled behind our mules? If you will we can take you over the old timber roads and through the briar thickets and the cornfields and the pastures."

"Oh, I'll be tickled to death," said Fern, "I just can't wait to take the trip. For soon the leaves will begin to fall and that is the time of year I always dread. I'd rather see the snow fall. I'd rather see the big white flakes of snow hit against my window pane. Seems like the flakes of snow are so lazy unless there's a winter wind behind them. And the little snow-birds play out among the dead weeds. The flakes look like a clean bed in a new snow— White sheets spread over the hills. I do love the snow. I don't like to see the leaves fall."

We geared the mules that morning, Don and me. We curried them till they looked fresh and we put tassels on their harness and hitched them to a sled. We made the sled to haul corn from the rough ground. We put a featherbed tick on a set of springs in the bed and a couple of feather pillows and a sheet to go over Fern. We got in the sled and drove across the hill. Her step-mother Lizzie didn't want to let her go. But finally she let us have Fern. We told her we would take good care of Fern. Lizzie ought to a-knowed that.

I helped carry Fern and put her in the sled. Don and Lizzie and me carried her. She was light as a feather. She wasn't anything but skin and bones. I thought of the bones I'd seen out on the pasture hill among the dog-fennel when I helped carry Fern to the sled. When we carried her to the sled she laughed and said, "Feel the wind with your fingers." And she held her bird-claw fingers out to the wind. She laughed and looked up at the sky and at the trees turning brown.

Don drove the mules and I set back beside of Fern. Don set on a seat in front and he would say, "Get up there, Barnie. All right, step up there Jack. Whoa, Barnie—not so fast around this place boy—not so fast." Well the sled moved just as easy over the ground. If there'd just been a little snow. But this was about the last of August. Fall was just getting into the wind. A body could just barely feel it.

Fern looked into the sky and she saw a flock of wild geese in the shape of the letter L honking their way across the country—high in the bright air of August. The road we took led us through a pasture—here was a lot of iron weeds and milkweeds. The bees were sorty buzzing around some old wilted petals and the honey bees and butterflies was working on the blue sandbriar blossoms. Fern would say, "Oh, look at the wild geese. I wish I could fly like the wild geese—just go forever and forever in the high blue air." And Don said, "Yes and come down to get something to eat and a man laying in the brush for you with a double-barrel shotgun or a pump gun or automatic. I'd rather be old Don driving these mules as to be any wild goose that ever trailed the sky."

The old fields just smelled of dying weeds and flowers. We drove down past Shelton's polebean patch and they was late—pretty blooms was on the vines and Fern wanted a bean vine with the blue blooms on it. Don stopped the mules and I got the vine for Fern. She put it up to her

mouth and tasted of the vine and smelled it and played with
it like it was a doll. I couldn't keep from thinking about
old Lizzie that kept Fern and what she told her about Don
and me coming over there and disturbing Fern of her rest
and keeping them up so they couldn't get their rest at night.
Why she told Mom that she went to sleep one day when
she's a-getting dinner and fell against the stove and burnt
her hand. She said we's the cause of it for we had kept her
up the night before. She said we was plum crazy about
Fern and she was getting plum crazy about us. That was
good news to me if it had just been me and not "us."

We passed Shelton's house—the old log house in the
Hollow with the well by the smoke-house and the well-
sweep with the water-bucket jingling on it in the wind.
Fern laughed and said, "Why I never saw a contraption
like that in my life." I got out and drawed a fresh bucket
of water and showed her how it worked. Then I give her
a drink out of the water-gourd hanging on a peach tree
sprout. She drunk the water and said it tasted better than
any water she'd tasted in a long time. Little drops of sweat
were breaking out around her forehead. Her hair was pretty
curled across her shoulders and her head propped up so she
could see.

We left Shelton's house—went down past the potato
patch and under the beech trees and up the Hollow to the
left. Going up the Hollow was kindly, like going up a big
green tunnel. On both sides the wind blowed the big clouds
of green beech leaves and oak leaves until they looked like
the sides of two fat mules in the harness, pulling hard and
getting their wind hard. We could hear the squirrel 'yow-
yow' at us thinking he was safe among the green leaves
around a hole in a hollow beech tree. Fern had us stop the
mules so she could hear the squirrels bark. Daisies just lined
our road and the meadow queenslace was filled with grasshoppers and bumblebees. Fern would grab for the grass-

hoppers and I told her to be careful she might likely grab a bumblebee and get her little hand stung. Don wanted me to drive but I wouldn't do it. I wanted to set back and talk to Fern.

Fern had us stop the mules by the creek and let them wind a little bit. The sweat broke out around their collars and their flanks begin to foam up with sweaty suds a little bit. We stopped where Fern could see the minnows in the creek playing around in the sunlight waiting for a bug to fly in the hole. Don jumped out and caught a grasshopper and throwed it in and a whole bunch of minnows went right in after him and he was too big for them to swallow. Well, a big old sunfish swum out from under the bank and swallowed the grasshopper and went back. Then Fern said to Don, "You didn't have any right to do that. Didn't the grasshopper have a right to live same as the minnows?" And Don said, "Don't hogs and cows have the same right to live as you and me but don't men kill them and eat them? Ain't it the way of all life—the stronger devours the weaker." And Fern up and said she didn't like it at all. But there wasn't anything we could do about it.

The mules rested up and we went upon the ridge past the coal mines. We drove right around the road to a entrance of a mine. Sulphur water run out of the mine and it had a cool smell. It run over blue slate bottom. There was blue stacks of slate piled up and a old rusty coal buggy setting on the old rotted track. There was a stack of old dull picks stacked up against the coal buggy. We saw a rat run out of the mine. And Fern said, "My father used to work in the mines. I barely remember it."

We drove on around the hill—around the old rutted coal road where the wagons used to creak with their heavy loads. The shoemakes looked so pretty in the sun. Leaves a-turning to gold and red. You know a shoemake is the first to turn in Kentucky. Seems like they get ripe before their

time. They are the prettiest things when they do turn—
they reddened a whole hill and just to see the goldenrods
blooming among them on a old poor hill like this one is
where was passed the mine. The hickory leaves were sorty
turning—the lower leaves was.

We topped the ridge again. The ridge road is a old road
the old settlers used to use. Big trees shade it. Big oak trees
with initials carved in their bark and we saw the chimney
rocks of a lot of the old settlers' houses that time and wind
and the rain had destroyed. Some of the old logs was left
among the briars. A lizard would bob his head up to catch
a fly. A red wasp would buzz over. A crow would fly over
caw-cawing to his mate. Birds would sing from the ridge
trees. We saw a gray squirrel run up a tree and flip his tail
at us and bark. We went out the ridge under the shade of
the tall trees. We could see the Hollow below us—five or
six miles of a big string of blue with a little stream of water
down in the middle and blotches here and there that looked
like blood. This was where the shoemakes were turning.
And Fern looked up through the green roof above our
heads and she said, "You know I wish that I could live forever. I do love life. I'd hate so to leave it." Tears stood in
Fern's blue eyes. The big white clouds floated above us in
the August sky. I could see them floating over above the
green clouds of leaves.

We just had to pass it. There wasn't any road around the
old graveyard where the dead of the Hollow's sleeping.
There it was spread under the oak trees. White stones here
and there. Iron fences around a bunch of graves. Lizards
running up and down the white stones and around over
the trees and the iron fences hunting for flies. And who
knows how many copperheads down among the old rose
bushes and the flowers in that graveyard. The wind kindly
blowed lonesome over the place and the green leaves

flapped in the wind. More tears come to Fern's eyes and we moved on.

We told her after we got by that the dead from our Hollow—most of them slept on this high hill overlooking their country of oaks and pines. And Fern said, "I'd rather be buried there as any place I've seen. It's so lonesome there. But it is so peaceful and so quiet." We drove on around by the sulphur springs—saw the red water oozing out from among the ferns—the water that is supposed to extend life. Don got out and made Fern a poplar leaf cup and dipped her a drink of water. She drunk the water and made a face. She said it tasted like rotten eggs smelled.

We went down another shady hollow—under the dipping limbs of the oaks and through the ferns and the wild alum in bloom. We could smell the scent of rotted logs and the moist hot smell of the pea vine under the trees. The creek murmured like a song over pieces of rotted logs and big rocks and over little gravel shoals. Birds fluttered in the green leaves above our heads and sung little songs about the summer passing. We come to our cornfield and a whole army of blackbirds had gathered there ready to go south. Then we turned up over the hill—along the bluff newground corn. It was all tasseled and eared out and smelled sweet as sugar in the wind. Bumblebees were hissing around its tassels.

We got back to Shacklesworth's and pulled up in the yard. Lizzie come out to help us carry Fern in. I could see she didn't like it because she'd gone out with us. But we took good care of her. And she said, "I've seen so much today. I've seen so much. I wish I could see it all over again." We helped carry Fern to her bed—all three of us carried her in the house and put her back in the bed that had been her home and was again. She'd been out of it only a few hours.

Old Lizzie Shacklesworth told all over the county that

we had come in and got Fern and took her ridin' against
her wishes and Fern hadn't been well since. She said she
wanted us to stay away from there. She never told us but
she told Ester Hix and Ester told Mom at church about it.
I went back just the same but didn't stay long at a time.
Fern asked me to come and talk to her. She had crocheted
a bedspread and she had pieced a quilt since she had been
sick. She said if anything happened to her she wanted Don
to have the quilt and me the bedspread.

Time come slowly on like a ox walking up the road.
More leaves began to fall. Falltime was drawing near at
hand when all the leaves would be swept off with the fall
winds and rains. Mom went over to Shacklesworth and she
said Fern was getting weaker. She said she could tell by
the rose-flush on her cheek. She said it wasn't natural. She
said it was death-like and it kindly made me feel sad. Fern
was too pretty to die like a flower before the frost. I
wanted to go back and see her. I didn't like Lizzie Shacklesworth because she'd talked about us. I couldn't trust her
face. She had a sneaking look like a sheep-killing dog.

I can never forget that night with Fern. I just went in to
see her anyway. Lizzie and her man was a-setting by a little
fire. Not much of the heat was getting into Fern's room.
I set in the chilly room and talked to her. The moon looked
big as the bottom of a dishpan in the pretty October sky
and it was copper-colored as a bright new penny. The
moon's rays flooded the pasture right out from the house
till it looked bright as day. We could see the persimmon
trees that looked like they growed into the sky. They was
upon the hill above the house. The cows stood under the
persimmon trees on the late pasture. White clouds sailed
across the autumn sky. The katydids sung down in the
cornpatch and the beetles boomed all over the yard. It was
awful lonesome. And a whippoorwill struck up a mournful
tune by the milkgap. I thought it was too late for whip-

poorwills in October. I just had to tell Fern I loved her. I remember what she said, "What is the use for you to love a butterfly that cannot stand the winter ahead—a butterfly pretty as it is must die when the leaves fall and the frosts and snow come. I'm something like the butterfly—here today to bloom and tomorrow—I don't like to talk about it. There's no need for me to pull your black hair up to my face and love you— There is no need for me to love anyone. I can't. I'm denied what other strong normal healthy girls are privileged to have. They don't know how fortunate they are—born into a world with normal strong healthy bodies. It means more than all the riches in the world. It means all. You never know until you experience what I have experienced."

There was graveyard silence in the room. Tears come to Fern's eyes. I could see them in the moonlight. They come to my eyes but I didn't want Fern to see them and I brushed them out when she looked out at the window. I didn't do much more talking that night. I wanted to cry. If I could have I thought, and that would be all that could save Fern, the falling leaves—I'd put them back on the trees around the house. I just couldn't stand to see Fern go. I run back home that night. I was afraid. I was afraid that I would see a ghost and it would tell me that Fern was going to die.

I didn't go back to see Fern for a few days. Heavy rains fell. Clouds raced near the mountain tops like a pack of thin-bellied hounds after a fox. Winds come in big torrents and whistled through the woods and swept the leaves from the trees like first frosts trims fodder of its blades. The air become damp in the mountains. The land smelled sour. The dead leaves smelled sour.

Mom come from church and said Minnie Chatsworth said that Fern was a lot worse—said she was sorty sinking since the bad weather come on. She told it at the dinner table and Don never said a word. Pop said, "Brief is the

destiny of human life. And not for long is any of us granted
to tread the grass. Youth—youth—they have to die same as
the old. Death is something the young fear and there's
nothing the old can do about it."

Days passed and Don and me hauled in the corn and
sprouted the pastures. We never saw Fern. I couldn't stand
to see Fern and think all the time that would be the last
time I saw her. We cut the stove wood and ricked it for to
season a few days before we hauled it to the woodshed. We
cut the cane wood and cut and shocked the sorghum cane
before the frost hit it.

We drove the mules in and fed them their dinners and
went to the house to get ours that day in October. It was
a chilly day. The sun was a little fainter than it had been
in the sky. The days had begun to get shorter. We could
feel winter coming in the wind. The trees had lost nearly
all their leaves—the poplars, elms, shoemakes and sassafrass
was stripped bare. When we set down and put our feet
under the table and smelled the steam coming off the hot
soupbeans and hot corn bread, Mom said, "Do you suppose
they don't have a fire for that poor girl across the hill, cold
as it is. I ain't seen no smoke come from over there today.
Always before I could see it cloud up above the poplars
back of the barn. I ain't seen no smoke from over there for
over a week."

When we went back to get the mules after dinner I told
Don I'd step over and see Fern. He said he'd go with me.
We went over the hill back of the barn under the poplar
trees, down through the blackberry briar thicket and into
the yard. The house was silent. No one seemed to be stirring in it. There wasn't any smoke coming from the
chimney's throat. The windows had boards nailed over
them.

I knocked on the door. Nobody answered. "Let's tear
the door down," said Don, "this looks awful funny to me.

Move out and never say good-bye. Move out with a girl nearly ready for the coffin. Let's crash the door in. We can fix it back."

"Suits me," I said to Don. "Let's get a fence-rail and lunge it against the door." We found the butt of a water-soaked hickory log at the edge of the clearing the fire didn't burn. We carried it to the house. We got together with our weights and the weight of the log and let the door catch the weight. The nails pulled loose from the boards and the lock flew unfastened. We walked in. It's a funny feeling to go into a house nailed and barred when you expect something. Somebody might step from behind the door and crown you with a broom handle or a coal pick. Well, we found most of the furniture left in the house. Was they all dead? What was the matter? No life stirred. The door between the living room and Fern's room was closed—barred with nailed-on boards. We went back and got our log, swung against it with all the weight in our bodies and crash come the door. We walked in.

Here was Fern in bed. Looked like she was asleep. I said, "Fern, wake up!" She did not move. I said again, "Fern, wake up!" She did not move. The rose-blush had faded from her cheeks. They was white as chalk and her lips were blue. Her lips were curved with about a half-way smile and her pretty teeth showed between the edges of her blue lips.

"She's dead," says Don, "dead sure as the world. Can't you smell her?"

"I can smell something like a store-house smells when you first open it of a morning," I said. "I been thinking it's the house I smell."

"It is poor Fern," said Don. "They've let her stay here and die. The money they got for keeping her I guess has run out and they have gone. Wonder if she was dead when they left or they let her stay here and die?"

"It does not matter," I said, "since she is already dead. Let's tell Mom. Go get her and I'll stay here till you come back."

"All right."

When Don went out of the house to get Mom I walked up to Fern and touched her face with my hand. It was cold as clay. Tears streamed from my eyes. Poor Fern. Don and me was the best friends she had on earth. I liked Don now since he had been a friend to Fern. I was jealous of him though he was my brother. It is quite natural for a man to be jealous of the woman he loves.

I tried to lift Fern. Her body was still. Her blue eyes stared sightless from their dark sockets. They was set still as a picture under glass. I couldn't lift Fern. Maybe I was scared. No, she was stuck to the bed. I hated to uncover Fern. But I was curious to see if she was tied in the bed. I threw off a quilt. No she wasn't tied down. She was stuck to the bed. The slats of the bed had stuck into her thin body. The bed tick had rotted where she laid on it without attention. Maggots were working around the slats.

"No wonder she died," I cried out to the empty house, "no wonder Fern died. She died from the want of attention and that old scalawag and buzzard spread over the county Don and me was keeping her up and that was against her health.

Pop come back with Mom and Don. He brought his rifle and a plowline. He brought a cur dog that would run a human being like a polecat. I could see he was quivering when he come into the house.

"Come and see what killed her Mom," I said.

Mom come back to the bed. Mom ain't like a lot of women. She won't scream. She's been to about every sick bed in the neighborhood and every death. She never said a word.

Pop said, "Take her to the house and prepare for a nice

burial. I'm after the Sheriff and then we're after the killers. I never did trust them people. It was always a funny set-up to me. Nothing like this can be done in Kentucky and get by with it. They'll be swung to a limb or burnt at the stake." He walked out of the house, down the path toward Fieldsburg. His steps were fast. The cur dog, Satan, followed him.

Mom, Don and me carried Fern to the house and put her on a clean bed. Don got on a mule and aroused the neighbors as to what had happened. The house was crowded with women that afternoon. Men went with rifles in droves toward the town. Many had plowlines. I saw Lester Fields in one little crowd of men. His eyes fairly danced. His mustache drooped. He did not speak. He had a rifle on his shoulder.

That afternoon women made a robe for Fern and washed her and put her in it. She was cleaner than she had been now. Her face was clean, her blond curled hair brushed back. She looked like an angel in death. She lay on the bed in the backroom and people went and looked at her when they wanted to—they came out of the room shedding tears. The girls went down in the hollow and gathered wreathes of the blue-sand-flower, goldenrod and farewell-to-summer. They laid the wreathes around the room and on her bed. There was the scent of flowers around Fern that I remember and her at peace on the bed—she, in death so much like an angel.

Pop come in at dark when people had come in to set up and the rooms was filled, the lamps filled with kerosene, the wicks trimmed and lighted. The yeller light flushed on the tear-stained silent faces.

"They caught 'em in Gatesville and got 'em in a good jail there till the mob can't get 'em," said Pop. "If they'd a-been around here and could a-been found, they'd a-been dangling right now from a limb on a tree, plugged as full

of holes as a water sieve. The Law says they'll give them a
fair trial when they done confessed the money they got for
keeping her run out and they went out and left her living
—let her lay there and die. Hell's too good for such people.
That's why we have powder and lead and plowlines and
trees."

People kept coming that night. The miners come in. You
can tell a coal miner at a glance, blue-bud around his
knuckles and fingernails, shoulders stooped and his face a
blue-pale. I remember what Link Harvest said, "I'd be
ashamed to meet my God if I'd let two people commit a
offense like this and get by with it." Luke James spoke up
and said, "We are human beings in the mountains. When
one of our crowd gets wounded we don't rush in and kill
the wounded one like a bunch of ants, but we avenge the
death of one of our people— One that has met with such
horrible death as this girl. We dynamite the jail or they'll
be given the extent of the Law." His lips trembled as he
spoke.

"They pretended to be her friend," said Lem Hackett,
"when all the world they wanted was a little bit of money.
That won't do them any good in Hell. God save us from
our friends. We can take care of our enemies."

There was the autumn moon in the sky that night. Moon
rays danced on the window panes and flickered through on
the white sheets on the bed. There was the wind outside
that kept ravishing the old half-stripped trees and the brown
hills like crows ravish a cornfield. There was the silence
of death in the room where Fern lay dressed in the white
robe the women of the Hollow made for her. There was
the sweet smell of the wildwood flowers, flowers prettily
outlined in the moonlight. There was the silent crowd sitting in the front room, in chairs on the beds with sorrowful
faces. The tiny red flames crackled the wood in the big
fireplace.

There is just something to human beings—a strange something. They fight each other and kill in the mountains but
in a case of death they stand side by side, solid as the hills
for each other with chains of friendship eternity cannot
break.

The sun was bright and red next morning. Six men went
to scoop out a grave for Fern. We told Pop what Fern
said when we hauled her past the pioneer graveyard on the
ridge overlooking the country. Pop said, "Well, she'll be
buried there." There wasn't any need to buy a lot. People
just go in a graveyard in the hills and find a place and bury.
They don't have to fool with buying a lot and staking it
off. Lots of times they bury a stranger in a family lot. It's
always understood that the space around a family lot belongs to that family and is not interfered with. Five men
went to the barn and took good seasoned poplar lumber
and made a coffin. The women lined it.

That afternoon we hauled Fern to her last resting place.
We couldn't get there with a wagon or express. We hauled
her on the sled that she'd been there on before. We went
past the sulphur spring. Don drove the mules. The crowd
followed. It was the biggest crowd that ever attended a
funeral on the ridge. People came from all over the countryside. The preacher preached a long funeral under the shade
of the graveyard trees. Nearly every person on the ground
shed tears. I saw Fern there the last time and I cried, "Why
did Fern have to die?"

She was lowered into that earth that had soaked the blood
of our fathers and that earth the bones of our fathers had
fertilized. A ravishing wind of autumn whipped through
the trees in the graveyard, crying for more leaves from the
bare twigs and muffled the words of those below.

BETWIXT LIFE AND DEATH

"HEP ME IN AT THE DOOR, Lonnie," says Grandpa to Pa. "Don't be so slow about it. My breath is gone. It jest keeps gettin' shorter. I can't get enough wind to keep me goin'."

"I told you, Pap, about goin' out on a mornin' like this," says Pa. "It's zero weather. Snow is on the ground. The frost is siftin' through the trees like corn meal through a sieve."

Pa took Grandpa by the arm. He hepped him up the steps. Icicles were hangin' to his beard. His beard was whiter than the icicles. It was white as the snow that lay on the January hills. Grandpa's hands were shriveled like a sleepin' black snake is shriveled under the dead winter leaves.

"Take me to the bed, Lonnie," says Grandpa to Pa. "I'm blind as a bat. Think it was th' sun shinin' on the snow that caused it. I looked at the hills for the last time. I looked too long. I'm goin' to leave 'em, Lonnie. It will be jest a matter of time. I'll pass to the Great Beyond before sundown."

"Maybe not, Pap," says Pa. He led Grandpa to the feather bed in the front room.

"Here, Pap, is the bed," says Pa, "now lay down and take a nap and you will be all right!"

"Yes," says Grandpa, "I'll be all right, Lonnie. I'm goin' to take a long nap. I'm goin' to take a long trip. I've got a lot I want to tell you. Bring you up a chear and sit down. I want to talk to you. I've jest finished the deed. I've worked on it all last year. I've jest got it finished in time."

Grandpa grunted as he talked. His long white beard fell down across his vest. His shriveled hands looked blue. Grandpa laid and looked at the ceilin'. He talked fast as his breath would let him talk.

"I got my deed writ out before you got your corn gathered, Lonnie," says Grandpa. "I'll tell you, Lonnie, you can't get no place in this world and let your corn stand out and take the weather until January. A good farmer has his corn in the crib before Christmas. Never but once in my life did I miss gettin' my corn in before Christmas! Your Ma was sick then. I had to wait on her and do all the work. I's just eighty then. You're a young man with health in your body, yet you let your corn stand out in the shocks and the mice eat it. You're a young man at sixty-five!"

"Pap, you ain't had no business being out on a cold day like this," says Pa. "Out without socks on your feet and your shirt opened at the collar!"

"I've done it all my life, Son," says Grandpa, "cut timber that way when the weather was twenty degrees below zero. It ain't hurt me yet. If the good Master had seen fit to let me live four more years I would a-been on His footstool five-score years. He calls for me to come home. I am goin', Lonnie, before th' winter sun sets in the cloudy sky!"

It hurt me to hear Grandpa say this. He'd lived with us since I could remember. Wind blowin' over our house top made a wild sound. Just seemed like it was the lonesomest sound I ever heard. Frost flyin' through the bare treetops and the sun shinin' and the hills looked like big mountains of shinin' silver.

"I'm deedin' you the home place, Lonnie," says Grandpa. "I'm deedin' Jim, Mart, Steave, Cy, Ambrose, and Alf a farm apiece. I didn't have a farm for Liz and Nance. Their men can take care of them. I want the name of Grayhouse to go on. I'm deedin' all my children's children a hundred dollars a piece. I don't want them to save it nohow! I don't want 'em buyin' cattle, sheep, and hogs with it. I am makin' it plain in my will that I want them to buy clothes with it. I want them to come dressed to my funeral! I've got the dresses marked in the 'Wish Book' that I want my grand-daughters to buy! I've deeded you boys my saddle horses. No better in the land, Lonnie. I want you to ride to the funeral on these horses. I want the saddles shined. I want the bridles shined. I want the horses to look like they did when I took care of 'em!"

"Will we have time to do this, Pap?" says Pa. "Can we get Jim here from Oklahoma? He's down with the fever you know!"

"I want you to wait until he gets well," says Grandpa. "Keep me here at th' house until the girls can buy their dresses and the boys buy their suits o' clothes! Set a day and bury me. Let it be in the spring when the wild roses begin to bloom in the fence rows! I've never dressed fine enough while I lived. You boys never did. I want my grandsons and granddaughters to dress while they live. I want them to look like they've just come out'n a bandbox."

"I'll try to carry out your plans, Pap," says Pa. The tears streamed from Pa's eyes. Pa wiped his beardy face with his hands.

"Try to carry them out," says Grandpa—"you must carry them out. I am dyin' now. I want you to say you will carry them out!"

"I'll carry them out," says Pa. "I'll do just as you say!"

"Put me in the coffin that I've made," says Grandpa. "Put me up in the garret of this house. I want to stay here long as I can. I was born and raised in this house. I was married in this house. I raised my family here and I will die here before the sun sets today. There will surely be room up in the garret for my coffin until spring! Keep me until

Jim gets over the fever and can get here from Oklahoma.
I know it is a fur piece he has to come. Be sure to give him
plenty of time."

"I'll do it, Pap," says Pa. "I'll do just as you say."

"Have a settin' up a night a week and let the young
people come here and have a good time," says Grandpa.
"I didn't have enough of a good time when I was a little
shaver. Pap worked us too blasted hard. I want my grandchildren to have a good time. That's about all I can think
of, Lonnie, just now. I hear the death bells! Have a good
time, take care of the horses and hold to the land. I've got
it fixed so it can't leave the name of Grayhouse. Let the
children enjoy themselves—I'm goin'—on my long trip!"

That's the last Grandpa said. He went to sleep. Died just
so easy. I watched Grandpa die. Pa stood by and saw the
last breath leave 'im. Grandpa was layin' across the feather
bed in the front room. Pa wiped the tears from his eyes.
He walked out'n the room. "I can't stand it," says Pa—"just
to think Pap changed that way in his old days. I wonder if
he was in his right mind."

"Yes, Grandpa was in his right mind," I says. "You know
he was in his right mind. He worked until last year. The
last thing he did was cut the brush from the fence rows.
It took him a year to make the deed. He had so much writin'
and so much figurin' to do with all his land, horses and
cattle. He had so many to give it to. Grandpa just sees
what he's missed in life. He's missed a good time and a lot
of fine clothes. I'll take my hundred dollars and buy clothes.
I'll dress fit to kill. I'll get me a girl and I'll do some sparkin'.
Worked here all the time and I never go anyplace!"

"It'll be all right I guess," says Pa. "Pap jest never teached
us like that. He used to make us work. He used to say, 'If
you spare the rod you'll spile the child.' He ust to get us
out'n bed at night and whop us. W'y he's done more work
than any man I know among these Kentucky hills. He's

got the land bound up until we can't sell it. We haf to deed it to a male heir by the name of Grayhouse."

"Now you know he's in his right mind," I says, " 'r he wouldn't a-done that."

"Son, get on the mule," says Pa, "and go over the deestrict and norate that Pap is dead. When they come tonight we'll read parts of his will and explain to the people that we'll put him away now and bury him later in the spring. We'll bury him when the girls have time to buy their fine clothes and Brother Jim gets over the fever and can get back here from Oklahoma. Th' other children can get to th' funeral anytime."

"All right, Pa," I says, "I'd better tell Ma to come home from Sister Rachel's. I'll tell her Grandpa is dead."

It was a cold time. I saw the sun goin' down like a fadin' ball of fire over the hills beyond Little Sandy River. "Just as Grandpa said," I thought. "Said he would be a dead man before the sun got down."

I remembered hearing Grandpa say, "When a child is born it is a sunrise. The sun goes up over the sky through the long day. That is a lifetime. Then the sun sets. Man is dead. His work is done."

The wind nearly took me out'n the saddle. The frost flew into my face. It made tears come to my eyes. The wind stung my face. I felt the sting of cold chillin' th' blood in my veins. I rode to every house in the deestrict. I told them to come tonight to the settin' up. When I told Ma that Grandpa was dead she wouldn't believe me.

"W'y he et two eggs for his breakfast, seven biscuits, milk gravy and bacon like he's done for the past thirty years," says Ma. "He drunk two cups of strong black coffee without sugar or cream in 'em." Ma hurried home. Sister Rachel come with her.

When people come to our house through the flying night frost they would say before they got beside the fire

to warm, "W'y I'm surprised about the death of Doug
Grayhouse. I've been seein' him goin' over the farm every
day. It is a big surprise."

They would ask what Grandpa had done with all his
money, his land and his fine saddle horses. Pa would tell
them he willed it to his children and his money to forty-
nine grandchildren. He would tell them he didn't have
enough to will to his thirty-six great grandchildren or his
five great-great grandchildren.

The first night we sung a few songs. Brother Combs
preached a few words. The neighbor men dressed Grandpa
—put him in his weddin' suit and put him in the wild cherry
coffin he had made. It had been seasonin' fifteen years up
in the garret. Pa, Brother Raymond, Uncle Cy and Uncle
Alf carried it down from the garret. Grandpa was laid
away in his coffin.

"It bothers me to know," says Pa, "how I'm goin' to
keep Pap up there. It is all right to keep him up there now
in this cold spell. But what will happen when th' spell
breaks?"

"I'll tell you how they kept my Pap for forty days,"
says Washington Nelson. "They put his coffin in a big
box and put salt around it. Had about a foot layer of salt
all around the coffin. It preserved Pap all summer!"

"Then that would preserve Pap until spring wouldn't it,
Wash?" says Pa.

"Oh yes," says Wash. "Ain't no danger o' nothin' when
you got a foot of salt around the coffin. You could keep
'im five years up there in the garret like that."

"Then tomorrow we'll make a big box and put Pap's
coffin in it," says Uncle Cy. "We'll haul out about ten
barrels o' salt from town and put around 'im. That will
keep 'im until spring."

The crowd didn't do a lot of laughin' and talkin' until
we got Grandpa carried up in the garret. Then the women

went to talkin' to one another like nothin' had ever happened. They shook hands and talked about knittin' socks, piecin' quilts and plaitin' rugs. The men talked about farmin'.

Oh, sometimes someone would say: "Doug Grayhouse was a good man. He'll be missed in th' deestrict."

"The Lord kept Doug Grayhouse here for a long time. Must a-had a purpose in mind when He done it."

Just the old people would say things like these. The young people acted just like Grandpa wanted them to act. They had a good time. There was a lot of sparkin' goin' on among us. Gracie Thombs come. I liked her looks a lot. Cousin Willie Grayhouse, Uncle Cy's boy, watched her too. I could tell that he liked Gracie. He tried to set next to her. I got the closest. It pleased Gracie a lot to watch both of us tryin' to get the closest to her.

January was a cold month. Snow laid on the hills. The wind whipped through the lonesome oak tops. It made the sound of a mournful turtle dove. When I heard the wind in the oak tops above the house, it made me feel sad. When I heard the wind in the pine tops I wanted to cry. It made me think of Grandpa. I'd think about Grandpa up in the garret with all that salt around 'im. I'd wonder if Grandpa was a spirit, flyin' about the house like a night owl. I thought he might be a screech owl in one of the oak trees in our barn lot—sittin' there in the cold with his feathers all ruffled up. I'd think Grandpa might be a spirit you couldn't see—that he might be goin' through the big rooms of the house my Great Grandpa built. When I heard the wind I was scared to death. I couldn't help it. It brought Grandpa back to me. I was afraid to go upstairs to bed and to think that Grandpa was only a floor above me. One night I dreamed he come to my bed and patted me on the head. I choked until I couldn't speak to him.

Pa would get Grandpa's will and read a little bit of it

every day. Pa would put the will in the trunk after he read awhile in it. Pa would wipe tears from his eyes. "I'll tell you, time changed Pap a lot," Pa would say. "I never thought a man could change so after he reached ninety. Every time Pa started to write a sentence in the will he would say: 'Betwixt life and death, upon this footstool.' Then Pap would go on and bring out what he wanted to say. He wants the young people to come here once a week until he's buried. He wants them to play *Skip To My Lou*. He wants 'em to even have dances! He wants them to drink if they feel like drinkin'. Pap's will even sounds crazy in places! I will do just what I told Pap. I told him on his death bed that I'd see that what he wanted was carried out. I don't like to do it. But I'm afraid Pap will come back to me and haunt me if I break my promise. I look for him every mornin' when I get up to build a fire at four o'clock. Pap allus got up when I got up to build a fire. 'Early to bed,' he allus said, 'early to rise, makes a man healthy, wealthy and wise.' "

"Yes," says Ma, "we want to do everything your Pap wanted. If we don't, this house will be haunted eternally. Doors will fly open. There will be knockin' on the walls. A red dog will run over top the roof. There will be noises like somebody ripping off the shingles. Do everything Pap Grayhouse wanted you to do. I don't want to spend the rest of my years in misery. I'm scared to death now to think that I live and work beneath 'im. It's hard for me to believe he's up in the garret awaitin' burial when the wild roses begin to bloom in the fence rows!"

Pa got a letter from Uncle Jim's boy John. He said he was glad to get his hundred dollars that Grandpa had willed him. Said he would strut out in new clothes now. Said he would show the girls in Oklahoma a good time.

"If Cousin John can show the girls in Oklahoma a good time," I thought, "then I can show the girls in Kentucky a

good time. I'll show one a good time. I'll show Gracie
Thombs a good time. If Cousin Willie Grayhouse hadn't
got a hundred dollars too! If Grandpa had just left him
out'n the will! But Grandpa hadn't! I'd just haf to fight it
out with 'im! I'd get Gracie Thombs!"

We had the settin' up every Friday night. That's the
night Grandpa said for us to have it in his will. He said if
we had it on Saturday night, we could only stay up until
twelve. After that was Sunday and we broke the Sabbath.
Said for us to have it every Friday night and stay up all
night if we wanted to. Grandpa said we wouldn't do much
work on Saturday anyway since it was so close to Sunday.
Said since he'd grown older and a little wiser, that he believed people ought to take Saturdays off anyway. Said
too much work and not enough play made "Jack a dull
boy." Then, think of Pa thinkin' Grandpa was not in his
right mind when he wrote his will! It hurt me to think Pa
had said these words. Pa just hadn't lived as long as Grandpa! If Pa ever lived that long he might agree with Grandpa's
will. My young days would be over then. I wouldn't
care about dressin' in good clothes, sparkin' girls and
dancin' all night.

We had four settin' ups in January. Gracie was there
every time. We played *Skip To My Lou*. I skipped with
Gracie. Cousin Willie got mad. He'd break in every time
he had a chance. "I'm as good a-lookin' as you," I thought.
"I'm as old as you. Why ain't I got the same chance as you
to get Gracie? She smiles at me more than she does you.
She skips with me more. Why don't you take Murtie Perkins and let me have Gracie Thombs? Murtie loves you.
You won't pay her any mind. People are talkin' about the
way we're fightin' over Gracie, and Grandpa a corpse up
in the garret!"

We had four times as many young people at the last
settin' up we had in January as we did the first one. Young

people heard about what Grandpa had said in his will fur and near. They come in droves. Some of them didn't know Grandpa and they didn't know us. They didn't have any-place to go among the hills in the winter time and they just come to the settin' up. They joined in our games. They had a good time. The winter nights didn't get too dark for them. The roads didn't get too muddy or too long and the snow didn't get too deep. The young people come.

* * *

It was in February that I fell deeper in love with Gracie Thombs. I begin to think I couldn't do without her. I could shet my eyes and see her standin' before me. I could see her purty brown curly hair. I could see her blue eyes. I could hear her laugh. I could feel the touch of her hand like I felt when we were skippin'. I was in love with Gracie Thombs. Cousin Willie's Ma told my Ma that her boy Willie was wild about Gracie. Said she wished there was some way to stop the settin' ups. Said they'd become a nuisance and the whole country was talkin' about them. Said they was talkin' about the way the young people were actin'. Ma told Pa about what Aunt Emma had said.

"I can't hep it," says Pa. "I can't hep how much the people talk. They will just haf to talk. I've got to do what I told Pap I would do. He is up in the garret. Maybe, Pap hears every word I'm sayin'. I hope Pap does. I can't go against a promise I made 'im on his death bed. I'll do what I promised Pap I would do no matter if I don't believe in the foolish idears Pap got in his head after he passed ninety. I'll do what I promised if it does go against the grain. I don't want Pap's spirit to follow me and haunt me in this house the rest of my days. I don't want to ride one of Pap's fine saddle horses to Pap's funeral either. I know the other boys won't. It will look funny to see seven of us boys on

seven thoroughbred horses ridin' to our father's funeral
but we'll haf to do it."

At the settin' ups in February we had a few dances. We
had Willie Sizemore's jug band. We stayed up nearly all
night long. What a time we had! I wanted to see Friday
come all week. Pa worked us so in the fields. "Children
you can frolic on Friday night but remember you are
under my thumb durin' the week. Now forget about Friday night. Bend down on your hoe handles. Bend down
on your ax handles. Bend down on your mattock handles.
Spend a little elbow grease! You're drivin' me crazy talkin'
about Friday night!"

Just like January, we had a cold February. The heavy
snow laid on the ground. Just seemed like it loved the
ground so much it would not leave. The deep snow and the
cold wind held back the old people. They wouldn't come
to the settin' up. A lot of them thought Grandpa was out'n
his mind when he made his will. "W'y old Doug Grayhouse
was a fine man. He was a Christian man. What got into
him in his old days—after he passed ninety that he wanted
the young people of the hills to leave the plow and come in
every Friday night and kick up their heels at a shindig
under his dead body! Peared like he wanted to be where he
could hear their love makin'. Peared like he wanted to be
where he could hear the old dance tunes and the clickin'
of their brogan heels on the puncheon floor! You can't
tell about people! That's the strangest thing I ever heard
of here among the hills! Wants to wait until the wild roses
bloom in the fence rows before they bury him. Wants to
wait until Jim gets over with the fever in Oklahoma."

It was the last of February when we heard from Uncle
Jim. "I'm out'n bed now," he said in his letter, "but my
hair has all come out. I hate to come home without hair
on my head. I know it will come back in a few months'

time. I hope I'll have hair on my head by the first of June! Don't bury Pap before I get there. I ain't seen Pap for forty years. I want to see him no matter if he is a corpse. It will be a great day for me. I'll get to see all my brothers and my sisters and all of their children. It will be like a family reunion."

We had to get the corn ground turned in March. The snow melted and left the hills and we had worlds of work to do. The snow had laid on the ground too long. We had our terbacker beds to burn and sow. March nearly worked us to death. We had corn ground to get ready. Stalks and sprouts to turn under so they'd be mellowed for the corn roots. We had fences to mend so we could turn the sheep and cattle in the pastures. We had sassafras sprouts to cut out'n the young wheat before they got so tall they'd shade the wheat. Everybody worked along the Little Sandy. All the boys and girls in the deestrict were workin' but they found time to come to the settin' ups. They come in from the fields tired and they went away rested.

* * *

April come and we had the fences mended. We had the sheep in the pastures. We had the cows on the grass. We had the thoroughbred horses on grass. We had the sprouts cut from the wheat. We had most of the corn ground turned. We had the terbacker ground ready. We's just gettin' along fine with the work. The birds come back to build in the boxes Grandpa had fixed for 'em. When I'd see the wrens comin' back to the coffee sacks filled with rags in the smoke house, I'd think of Grandpa. He'd fixed the rag sacks for them and a lot of tin cans and water buckets he'd hung up for them to build in. The wrens and the martins would fly about the house and barn. They'd light on the comb of the house. I wondered if Grandpa could hear their footprints above him on the clapboard roof. I had a lot of thoughts like this. Pa must a thought a lot too. He'd stand and watch these birds buildin' their nests. Grandpa loved the birds. The birds loved him. They would fly down from the top of the house and barn and eat bread from his hands.

The oak trees leafed out. The wild rose vines leafed along the fence rows. Great masses of 'em leafed along the roads that led over the place. I wished Grandpa could just be back for a day in the spring and walk over his farm here among the Kentucky hills. I know he'd like it! I could just see him now walkin' along lookin' at the oaks when the buds started swellin' and sap come back to their veins. I could see him lookin' at the wild rose stems along the fence rows. I could see him take his mattock and cut the sprouts from the fence rows and leave the wild rose stems stand.

"It takes clean fence rows to make a purty farm," Grandpa used to say. "Wild roses look good along the fence rows in June."

I'll tell you I was glad to see spring come back. I was glad to see the creeks fill with blue waters from the high hills. I was glad to see the little lambs taggin' after their mammies. I was glad to see the horses run and kick up their heels. Grandpa used to like to watch them. "That is the young life in a horse that makes him kick up his heels," Grandpa used to say. "He will slow down soon enough. It all comes betwixt life and death."

I was just glad that spring had come. I wasn't scared like I was last winter. Ma wasn't scared half as bad to hear a wind rustlin' among the tender leaves on the oak trees as she was to hear a winter wind moan through the bare limbs on the oaks and whistle among the corn stubble in January.

I could see Gracie Thombs pass our house now. She was barefooted goin' to the store. I'd see her takin' a basket of eggs to the store. She was so purty. She was just like the spring. It made me love Grandpa more than I ever did. Just think if it hadn't been for Grandpa's will I'd never got to a-been with Gracie every Friday night! The young couples almost doubled in April. They heard about the big settin' ups we's havin'. They flocked from every hollow among the hills. "If th' crowd keeps multiplyin'," says Pa, "I don't know where we're goin' to put 'em. It's two months yet before we can bury Pap accordin' to the last words in his will. Pap's got that will worked out wonderfully well. He didn't spend the last year of his life for nothin'."

* * *

It was in May. The wild rose buds had started to swell. The corn was peepin' through the ground on the high hill slopes. The lambs were gettin' big enough to eat grass. We had started settin' terbacker plants. "The time is gettin' near," says Pa, "that we bury Pap. I hate to see my father go under the green grassy ground. I guess the ground will be good as the garret. But seems like when we have put him under the ground we have lost him. When we have him in the garret, it seems like he is closer to us. But I'll be glad to see Pap put under the ground. The crowds at the settin' up are gettin' too big. It's the talk of this county and the wind forever blowin' among the tree tops and keepin' your Ma scared to death. It is a great worry to me. I didn't know what all was in that will when I made the promises to Pap on his death bed last January."

It was in May when all of Grandpa's grandchildren got their hundred dollar checks to buy their fine clothes. I'll never forget when I got mine. Grandpa said in the will: "Don't write the checks out to my grandchildren until May. I want their clothes to look good at my funeral." He went on and said a lot more about how to take care of the clothes before the funeral and atter the funeral, he would advise us to take care of our clothes, yet he didn't care if we plowed in our new suits since they belonged to us, we could do as we pleased with them.

When Ma opened the "Wish Book" she turned the pages where Grandpa had turned the corners down. In his will Grandpa said: "In the 'Wish Book' you will find the dresses I want my granddaughters to wear at my funeral. They are the prettiest dresses I have found in the whole book. They are plenty long and decent." Ma read what it said about these dresses that they should be worn at night to parties and dances.

"I can't understand," says Ma, "what got into your Grandpa's head. Have you to wear dresses that girls wear to dances at his funeral. But they are long and purty and I guess they are all right. You will haf to dress like your Grandpa requested in his will."

The girls ordered their dresses. The boys ordered their suits. I got me a gray suit with a blue pin stripe runnin' up and down it. I'll tell you it was a beauty. I got a pair of shoes, socks, striped neckties and a dozen shirts. I spent every cent of my hundred dollars for clothes just like Grandpa requested.

"When Cousin Willie thinks he'll out-dress me for the funeral," I thought, "he'll be mistaken. I'll show him who'll look the best to Gracie on Grandpa's funeral day!"

We'd had the second settin' up on the second Friday of May. There was some crowd. The house was so full part of us had to dance in the yard. We tied lanterns up among the oak limbs and went on like we'd done since last January. The Sizemore band played and we danced on a platform built o' planks. I danced with Gracie. I forgot Grandpa was up in the garret. I forgot how scared I was last winter when the snow was heavy on the ground and the wind made such lonesome sounds among the oaks. The wind made purty rustlin' sounds now among the green leaves on the oaks. I forgot about thinking Grandpa's spirit might be in a screech owl that roosted in the oaks in our barnlot. I forgot what Grandpa had said about the wild roses in the fence rows. I forgot everything about Grandpa when I danced with Gracie. If it just wasn't for Cousin Willie Grayhouse, everything would have been all right.

Maybe Cousin Willie didn't like me. Maybe he hated me more than I hated him. I didn't know. I didn't care. I had my mind made up if he fooled with me I'd beat the face off'n him. I told him that one night at the settin' up when he jumped in and danced with Gracie. He had the impudence to say: "The time will come when we'll fight this thing out. We'll fight to a finish. One of us has to conquer the other. The one who whops gets Gracie."

"Cousin Willie," I says, "I'll take you up on that. I'll fight you tonight. I'll beat your damned head into the ground."

"I don't want to dirty my new suit of clothes tonight," says Cousin Willie. "It's the first time I ever wore a long suit of clothes, I don't want to ruin 'em on you."

"I've got on my first long suit of clothes," I says. "It's the first time I've ever wore long clothes. But I'll ruin my suit to beat you up."

"I've got more sense than to fight tonight," says Cousin Willie. "Wait until I'm in my old work clothes. Then we'll just see who gets Gracie."

I took a swing at Willie. The crowd come in and stopped us. I would a hit Willie right there. I couldn't hep if it was at the settin' up. I couldn't hep it if Grandpa was right above us. My blood was riled and I'd a-fit Cousin Willie Grayhouse all over the hill. I was in love with Gracie. I'd got so I didn't care who knowed it. I was a little bashful at first. But that wore away. Now I had my new suit of clothes and I wasn't goin' to be out-done by a first cousin. I didn't like Willie. He had the same blood in his veins that

I had but that didn't make no difference. I'd taken enough off'n him. I wasn't goin' to take any more.

"I believe there's drinkin' goin' on at the settin' ups," says Pa, one mornin' at the breakfast table. "There's a lot of glass laying around all over this yard. It looks like broken bottles to me. If I find bottles of licker out there I don't know what I'll do!"

I thought Pa might pour the whiskey out. I told the boys about it. We worked out a way. We tied the horse quarts of whiskey up in the oak trees by the necks. Pa would never find them then. When we wanted a quart one of the boys went up the trees and cut the string and brought back the quart. One night Pa and Ma were out watchin' us dance. They stood under the oak. They heard the wind blowin' the bottles together.

"Listen, Gurtie," says Pa, "that's the funniest sound I ever heard made by the rustlin' o' leaves in th' wind. It may be Pap's spirit over here. He might be sorry for the rope he's given these youngins. They've whopped the older folks from the settin' ups!"

Ma never said a word. She just looked at Pa. Then she watched us dance. The platform was so full we barely had room to dance. It looked like we's goin' to haf to build another platform.

*   *   *

It was on the first day of June when Pa got a letter from Uncle Jim. "I'll be home June 10th for the funeral," Uncle Jim wrote in his letter, "have everything ready. My children have their clothes. They can hardly wait to come. I dread ridin' a thoroughbred saddle horse to Pap's funeral. Pap must not have been in his right mind when he put sicha foolishness in his will. That don't sound like the Pap I had. He used to make me read the Bible two hours every Sunday before he'd let me go to the river to swim."

"Wait until he reads Pap's will," says Pa, "he'll find that Pap changed his mind atter he passed ninety. He'll be surprised at Pap's will. He'll see what a time I have had to see that Pap's will was carried out as Pap wanted it done. I'll never see that another will is fulfilled. It's had me worried to death. From last January until this June has put ten years on top my head. I'm ten years an older man."

We had our last settin' up the first Friday in June. I'll tell you the house was full and the yard was full. We had our dances goin' and all kinds of games. We had our bottles up among the green leaves on the fruitful oaks. I danced every dance with Gracie. Cousin Willie was so mad at me he could bite a spike nail in two. He acted like he wanted to fight me all night. Our settin' up didn't end until the moon went down in the mornin' and the roosters had started crowin'. I just wondered what Grandpa thought about the good times we's havin' now. I believe if Grandpa knowed how much better our good times was a-gettin' he wouldn't a-been buried until summer was over—maybe not until snow fell again. I was havin' the best time I'd ever had in my life. But it was time for the funeral now. Our good times must come to an end. Three more days and Grandpa would be under the ground. I'll never forget takin' Gracie home Saturday mornin' atter th' last settin' up. I come back along the fence row just as the sun was gettin' up—while the dew was still on the weeds. I never saw wild roses purtier in my life. I never saw the place as purty. Terbacker was lookin' so good in the long curved rows around the high hill slopes. The corn was gettin' up to a mule's knees.

"Grandpa picked a purty time to be buried," I thought. "He couldn't have picked a purtier time in Kentucky!"

I wish you could have seen the crowd at Grandpa's funeral. It was like a homecomin'. I met my first cousins in Oklahoma. I'd never seen them before. Pa shook hands

BETWIXT LIFE AND DEATH

with all his brothers. I saw my sisters among the twenty-
seven granddaughters of Grandpa's. All the girls were
dressed in long dresses that swept the ground. They wore
white slippers and golden slippers. The dresses didn't have
any back in 'em. I'll tell you they looked good.

"It's a funny idear of Pap's," says Uncle Jim, "about the
girls wearin' sicha dresses to his funeral. I guess if he wanted
it—we haf to abide by his will."

"Yes," says Pa, "his will has been properly carried out
and we can't afford to break it now."

The girls didn't have nary two dresses the same color.
Grandpa's twenty-two grandsons were dressed fit to kill.
"I wish Grandpa," I says, "could be here and see us now.
He would be proud of his blood kin. He would see us
dressed fit to see the President of the United States."

The grave had been dug two days before. The wagon
and the mules were waitin' to haul Grandpa to his last
restin' place. We hadn't carried him down from the garret.
It was a crazy thought, I guess, but I thought: "What if
Grandpa is not in the garret. Wouldn't it be a joke? What
if Grandpa had come to life and got out and slipped away?
What if Grandpa had become young again?"

Pa, Uncle Jim, Uncle Cy and Uncle Alf went up in the
garret and let him down with ropes to the upstairs. They
took the coffin out'n the box of salt and carried it downstairs. Pa looked a little shaky when he started to take the
screws out'n the coffin. When he raised the lid he says:
"Pap's just as natural as he was the day we put him in
here."

We marched past and looked at Grandpa for our last
time.

"Looks just like he did before I went to Oklahoma,"
says Uncle Jim. Uncle Jim had his hat off. I couldn't keep
from looking at his head. I'd told Gracie about Uncle Jim

losin' his hair when he had the fever. I saw her lookin' at Uncle Jim's head too. The hair had sorty come back.

You should have seen us as we went to the graveyard. The mules and wagon were in front with Grandpa. Pa and all his brothers were on Grandpa's thoroughbred horses. They rode up next to the wagon. The horses pranced and twisted and stood on their hind feet. Then all of Grandpa's granddaughters and grandsons come next. Then the rest of the kinsfolks. Then there was a whole army of young couples that had been comin' to the settin' ups. It was the biggest funeral we ever had at Oak's Chapel. Brother Combs preached Grandpa's funeral in the chapel. Sister Reeves played the organ and we sung a lot of songs. I was with Gracie. Cousin Willie sat right over from us. He looked at us all the time Brother Combs preached the funeral. I thought he was goin' to try something just by the way he looked.

It was when they carried Grandpa out'n the church house, many of Grandpa's friends carried wreaths of flowers to put on his grave. There were many wreaths of wild roses. . . . When they started to put them down by the side of the grave one rolled off'n the pile. I picked it up and put it back on the stack. Cousin Willie reached down and fixed it on the stack another way. It was right in front of all of our people and a lot of our neighbors. Then Willie looked hard at me. He was just mad because I was with Gracie. I tried to punch him in the nose and Uncle George held me. Uncle Jim grabbed Cousin Willie. "You can't fight here, boys," says Uncle George.

We stood and looked at one another all the time they's lowerin' Grandpa in the grave. Before they got him down, while Uncle George and Uncle Jim were watchin' Grandpa lowered with the check lines, I lunged at Cousin Willie and give him a haymaker on the chin. He sprawled on the ground in his new suit of clothes. He got up and come at

me again. The second haymaker I handed him, he stayed
on the ground.

"Stop that fight George," says Pa. He come runnin'
over.

"Ain't no fight to it," I says, "I hit Cousin Willie and
he hit the ground."

"It's awful," says Uncle Cy, "you boys fightin' at Pap's
funeral. I'd be ashamed."

Cousin Willie was down on the ground moanin' and
goin' on. Cousin Willie was cussin'. He wouldn't a-done it
but he's out'n his head.

"Let 'em fight," says Uncle Ambrose. "It's a good sign
that the Grayhouse blood ain't losin' its color."

"Come on, Gracie," I says, "let's go home."

I took Gracie by the arm. Aunt Emma was fannin' Cousin
Willie when I left. The crowd was divided. Part o' 'em was
standin' around Cousin Willie while the rest o' 'em watched
th' men lower Grandpa into the grave.

SAVING THE BEES

"Come over here, Shan," says Big Aaron to me. "I've got something I want to tell you." I walk over across the creek to a rock cliff. Ennis Shelton, Little Edd Hargis and Dave Caxton are standing beside of Big Aaron Roundtree. Big Aaron is smoking his pipe. Ennis, Little Edd and Dave are smoking home-rolled, hawk-billed cigarettes.

"Now, Shan," says Big Aaron, "we are going to save the honeybees in this country. We are going to try to free them. The honeybees don't have liberty anymore. Look up in your yard! Your Pappie has six stands of them back of the woodyard. Look at the stands of bees my Pappie's got—twenty-six of them over on the bank from the house under the pines! Look at the honeybees that old Willis Dials has! Look at the bees Kenyons have upon the Old Line Special. Look at the bees Uncle Fonse Tillman's got and old Warfield Flaughtery! Boys, we've got to do something about it! Are you willing to jine us, Shan? If you tell anything it won't be good for you! If you are ever caught saving bees and you are whipped because you won't tell on the rest of us—you let them whip you until the blood runs out—and you never tell! Can you be that kind of a soldier?"

"I can," I says. "I'll do all I can to save the bees. We ain't going to take my Pappie's bees, are we?"

"We are going to take your Pappie's bees and my Pappie's bees," says Big Aaron. "We don't have any respect for any person's bees. We are going after all of them. We are going to take the bees back to the woods. We are going to set them free. It is a big job but we can do it. Every man must fight to the last. He can't get cold feet. If he is shot at—he can't let that bother him. He must grab the bee stand and run anyway. The bees must be put back in the woods—let them grow wild again. It's got so in these parts you can't find a wild bee tree anymore. It is a shame to coop bees in boxes and sawed-off logs and make them work their lives away for a lazy bunch of people. We won't have it!"

The water drips from the roof of the cliff. It drips on my ear and tickles it. The ferns hang over the front of the cliff. There is a pile of ashes on the floor of the cliff with burned-brown rocks around the ashes. There is a wire wrapped around a splinter of rock above and hangs above the ash pile. It has a hook on the end of it to hold a pot. There are chicken feathers around the rocks. Back in one corner of the cliff is a .22 rifle. Beside the .22 rifle is a .32 Smith and Wesson pistol. Beyond the drip of water is a big pile of dry oak leaves.

"Boys, this cliff can be our home," says Big Aaron. "It is our hide-out. We can work from here when we are saving the bees. We can have chicken any time we want chicken. We can have honey any time we want wild honey. We can have Irish taters and sweet taters any time we want them. Show me a house here that ain't got a tater patch beside of it. We have a cup here to catch our water from the drip in this cliff. We have a good oak-leaf bed. All five of us can sleep in the oak leaves with our guns beside of us. This cliff is back from the road and the ferns nearly hide the front of it. It just looks like the green hillside. No one would know that a cliff is here unless he would come over here, push the ferns back and look in. If he ever does that he'll be batted in the face so hard he'll never do it again."

"When will we meet, Big Aaron?" asks Ennis Shelton.

"Be here tonight when you see the moon come above the pines on the Flaughtery hill," says Big Aaron. "You be here, Shan. Don't pick up no stranger and bring 'im along either. You come straight to the cliff. All of you boys be here on time. It is in the light of the moon now and the moon ain't goin' to waste no time nohow gettin' to the top of that pine thicket on the Flaughtery hill."

"We'd all better be gettin' home to get our suppers now," says Dave.

Big Aaron hides the pistol and the rifle in the leaves. He walks under the cliff—pushes back the ferns and sticks his head out. "Everything is clear, boys," he says. He leads the way out. We follow Big Aaron. He is sixteen years old. He has big arms and a big bull-neck. He can pull the plow in the field like a horse. His hands are hard as rocks. He has a heavy beard on his face. He is the stoutest boy among the Plum Grove hills. He can lift 7 x 9 crossties and load them on a jolt wagon. He can shoot a sparrow's head off with the .22 rifle from the top of the highest tree. He says he can save all the bees among the Plum Grove hills.

I leave the boys at the forks of the road. I go up the creek home. I eat my supper, carry in stove wood, kindling —draw up water for the night from the well under the oak tree. I milk two cows and strain the milk into the crocks on the big flat rock on the smokehouse floor. I am ready to go to the cliff. I turn to walk away. "Where are you goin' Shan?" asks Pa.

"Fox huntin'," I says. "I'm goin' out with Big Aaron Hargis to hear his hound pup run."

"Just like me," says Pa, "when I was your age. I loved to hear hounds. Go out and lay around all night on the cold ground. That's the reason I'm so full of rheumatics today. But you go on and live and learn like I have. I still love to hear the hounds."

I walk down the hollow to the big road. I turn down the big road—down to the big sycamore. I look up the road and down the road—I cannot see anyone coming. I run across the rocks at the foot of the bluff. I run down behind the trees. I climb up the little path to the cliff. I can hear voices within. I climb up—part the ferns—the boys are all under the cliff. I look toward the Flaughtery hill—the big moon is coming up behind the trees. Its face is red—it is blushing like a young boy that watches things from behind the trees.

"You're here," says Big Aaron. "Now Shan Powderjay—remember if you ever tell anything, the rest of us will down you and cut your tongue out. That is the jail sentence for a tattle-tale among us. We have a job to do and we must do it. You fellars follow me tonight. We're goin' after Willis Dials' bees. I've been past his house today. I know where he keeps his bees. I know a little path that leads up the bank to the bee gums. You fellars just follow me."

We follow Big Aaron down the hollow. We do not go along the road. We follow the creek bed. We wade the water. We come to the big white oak at the forks of the W-Hollow and the Three-mile road. We take to the hill. We follow a fox path over the hill to the Old Line Special railroad tracks. We can see the big log house upon the bank above the railroad track where Willis Dials lives. "See the bee gums in the front yard, boys," says Big Aaron. "There are five of them. There are five of us. The bees ain't working now. Stick little pieces of wood in their holes so they can't come out. Lift them easily. You won't get a sting. I'll get the first bee gum. You just watch me. Do as I do."

Big Aaron slips up the bank. He takes little sticks and stops the two little holes where the bees come out of the gum. Then he lifts the gum to his back. He walks down the bank. No one whispers. Each of us stops the holes where the bees come out with little sticks. We get our bee gums on our backs— We follow Big Aaron up a little path to our left around the Plum Grove hill. After we get away from the yard—a dog comes out and barks. He barks and barks. "Don't be afraid, boys," says Big Aaron. "He ain't no bitin' dog. He's one of them barkin' dogs that never bites. Come on with your bees."

"Lord, but this is a heavy load, Big Aaron," I says. "I don't know whether I can carry it or not. Sweat has popped out all over me."

"You ain't no man," says Big Aaron, "if you can't carry a bee gum loaded with honey and bees." My bee gum is a cut of a hollow log with boards nailed on the top and bottom. It is black gum and it is heavy.

"I'm about all pooped out with my load too," says Dave Caxton. "Sweat is streaming in my eyes until I can't see the path. I'm wet as a river with sweat."

"Follow me," says Big Aaron. "I've got the heaviest bee gum of all you. I got a cut from a hollow beech-log. It's the heaviest wood in the world. I'd hate to think I couldn't carry one cut of a saw-log." We follow Big Aaron down the cow-path and up the Jackson hill. We follow slowly to the top. We are getting our breaths like spans of mules pulling a jolt-wagon load of crossties out of W-Hollow. Big Aaron reaches the top. He sets down his bee gum. "Here's the top, boys," he says. "Now we'll smoke before we go down the other side."

We reach the top of the hill. We put our burdens down. The bees are mad within the gums. If they could get out they would sting us to death. But we have them fastened in behind the little sticks. We roll our cigarettes in brown sugar-poke paper. We fill the papers with crumbled, home-grown tobacco. Dave takes a dry match from his hatband. He strikes it on his teeth. He lights our cigarettes. We stand in the moonlight and pant and blow smoke toward the red-faced moon. The cool wind from the high hilltops hits us. It dries our sweaty clothes. It cools our faces.

"Let's finish our job," says Little Edd Hargis. "How much futter we got to go?"

"Just under the hill," says Big Aaron. "I've got the place picked. It's safe for the bees."

We throw down the stubs of our cigarettes. We twist the fire out'n them with our shoes. We pick up our stands of bees. We walk down the hill behind Big Aaron. We walk down to a locust thicket. There is a groundhog path back under the locusts. Big Aaron bends down and walks back this path. We follow him back to a little open space where he puts the bees down. "Ain't this a safe place for the bees," says Big Aaron. "Look what a purty place for them! See, I got one bee gum here already. I got one of Pap's and brought it here. He ain' missed it yet."

Big Aaron has come already and put rocks down for us to put the bee gums on. He has made foundations for many stands of bees. We place the bee gums solidly on the rocks. "When you get 'em fixed on the rocks," says Big Aaron, "jerk the sticks out and come away and leave them. They'll think they are at home in the morning. They'll work just the same as they've always worked. They are at home out here. They are away from everybody. They have come home to the hills where they used to be."

We place the bee gums on the rocks. We slip the sticks out of the holes. We slip back down the path—over the hill to the hollow. We cross the creek, climb the bluff to the rock cliff. "We are back home," says Big Aaron as he goes under the curtains of ferns to the good leaf bed. Big Aaron sprawls out on the leaves. Little Edd puts the .32 on a shelf of rock. Dave unstraps his rifle. He lays it on the shelf of rocks. We sprawl out for the night. "Our work is done for tonight," says Ennis. "I'm glad it's done too. I looked every minute to see fire flash from a gun when we's getting them bees. It ain't safe where there's a lot of house dogs around."

"Don' talk about it now," says Big Aaron. "You'll get me skeared after it's all over. Forget about it now. Our night's work is done. Go to sleep and dream."

I dreamed that Willis Dials saw me steal his bees. I thought he run me with a corn-cuttin' knife. I was just keeping out of his way. He was just barely touching me with the knife but I would jump out of his reach. His little black eyes looked like balls of fire. He had a pipe in his mouth and his lips were snarled. When he struck—I jumped and the knife just touched me. I could feel blood running from my face and neck.

"Get up all of you," says Dave. "It's Sunday morning —hear the Plum Grove church bells ringing. Get out'n that drip of water Shan. You've rolled over under the drip. Your shirt is wet." Dave laughs and laughs.

"That made me have bad dreams," I says. "I thought Willis Dials was after me all night. He was cutting at me with a corn knife. I could feel the blood running down my neck and face."

"Well, boys," says Little Edd, "we had a good fox chase last night. Let's all go home to breakfast."

We crawl out of the cliff—walk to the forks of the road. We part at the forks. I walk up by the sweet-tater bottoms to the house.

"Your Ma left breakfast on the table for you," says Pa. "She's gone to Sunday School. Hurry up and eat breakfast and help me do up this work. You can tell me about your fox chase then."

"All right, Pa," I says.

I eat my breakfast. I walk out where Pa is. I help him milk the cows and slop the hogs. I tell Pa about the big fox chase we had. Pa says he must have slept like a log for he didn't hear the hounds and that he always listens for them.

233 SAVING THE BEES

I tell him if he didn't hear them it was his own fault for our hounds really put the fox over the hills.

When Mom comes from Sunday School she says: "Mick, did you know somebody took all of Willis Dials' bees last night? Took five stands from him. Said he saw them leaving with them. Said he shot five times. Said they had a wagon over on the road and loaded the bees on the wagon and run two big black horses hard as they could tear up the road with all his bees in the back end of the wagon. Preacher preached this morning about it. People are coming in here and stealing honeybees! Did you ever hear of sicha thing?"

"Must a-been hard up for honey," says Pa. "I'm forty-five years old and I never heard of people stealin' honeybees out'n a yard. I've heard o' men findin' bee trees on another farm and slippin' in and cuttin' 'em without permission—but I never heard of thieves brazen enough to walk in a man's yard and carry his bees to a wagon! I don't know what this world's a-comin' to——"

"It ain't comin'," says Mom—"it's goin'—and to the Devil it's goin' fast. We ain't had sicha thing to happen at Plum Grove for years. Betsy Roundtree was talkin' about it as we come back across the hill. She says she puts the fear of God into Big Aaron. I tell her I know that my boy will never steal—never—whatever he does that's onery—stealin' won't be a part of it."

Everybody talks in the community about Willis Dials losing his bees. We hear about how Willis shot at them— how they took to the wagon and drove the big black horses up the road—their feet striking fire from the rocks. We hear all sorts of tales. We do not talk about it. We listen to the others talk. I go to Prayer Meeting on Wednesday night at Plum Grove with Mom. Big Aaron is at Prayer Meeting. He comes to me and says: "We fox-hunt to-

morrow night. Be at the cliff by moonrise. We go to
Flaughtery's tomorrow night. We got to get his bees. He
ain't got but four bee gums. Ain't much but enough to pay
us for our trouble."

Thursday night we call our dogs—meet at the crossroads.
The dogs take to the hills to start the fox. We go to the
cliff. When the hounds are bringing the fox across the
hollow by Warfield Flaughtery's house and his dog runs
out and barks at the fox hounds, we slip upon the bank
back of Warfield's house—we plug the bee gums with
sticks. We load them on our backs. We walk away. Little
Edd carries the pistol and the rifle. We walk down the
creek to the big sycamore, then we turn to our right. We
walk up under the pines where the moonlight falls almost
as bright as daylight. We put the bee gums down to rest,
wipe sweat and smoke. We roll our cigarettes in the brown
sugar-poke paper. We smoke and sit silently under the
pines in the moonlight. We get up, twist the fire out of our
cigarette stubs with our shoes. We move across the hill to
the place under the locust thicket where we keep our bees.
We place them securely on the foundation rocks—pull the
plugs out of the holes. Warfield Flaughtery's bees now
have their freedom. We go back to our cliff for rest. Big
Aaron gravels some of Warfield's sweet taters from the
ridges in the bottom by the sycamore tree. We stick the
taters in the ashes under the cliff. We build a fire over
them. We lie down on the leaves on the far side of the
cliff for a little rest. The fire will burn down—the embers
will roast our taters. When we awake, our breakfast will be
ready. We'll eat a bite of breakfast and go home. We know
our Paps are listening to our hounds bring home the fox.

"Breakfast, boys," says Big Aaron—"wake up to a good
sweet-tater breakfast."

I watch Big Aaron rake the roasted sweet taters from the
ashes. He peels the bark from one. He eats the golden-

colored roasted sweet tater. "Better than honey," he says—
"you fellars get up and taste o' one."

I get up from my bed of leaves. Little Edd, Dave and
Ennis get up. We get roasted taters from the ashes—peel
the bark from them. They are warm and sweet. "I read,"
says Big Aaron, "where George Washington's soldiers et
roasted sweet taters and went barefooted at Valley Forge
in the winter time. I'd hate to think I couldn't stand as
much as they could stand. People just don't know what
good grub George Washington's soldiers had to eat. I ain't
gone barefooted in the winter time but I've gone in swim-
ming when I had to cut the ice and that didn't bother me
a bit."

"That ain't nothing, Big Aaron," says Ennis—"we've all
done that. Talk about something we ain't done while we're
here at the breakfast table."

"We ain't got my Pap's bees and Shan's Pap's bees," says
Big Aaron—"but we will get them if we keep our health.
Boys, we'll hear a lot about somebody's getting Warfield's
bees. Just say we saw that team of black horses goin' out'n
the hollow about twelve o'clock— Say we saw the driver
slapping the horses with the lines."

"That's it," says Ennis. "He's the man Willis Dials saw
gettin' his bees."

"It'll be a joke about how many liars we have at Plum
Grove," says Little Edd, "if they ever find our bees. They'll
know then about the black horses." Little Edd talks with
his mouth filled with sweet tater.

"It's time boys we's getting home," says Dave. "I've got
to work in the terbacker field today."

Big Aaron picks up the sweet-tater bark. He puts it in a
little pile and covers it over with leaves. "Remember," says
Big Aaron, "we meet here Saturday night at seven o'clock
—rain or shine or no moon. Now we must all get home
and help our Mas and Paps." Big Aaron sticks his head

out from under the ferns. He crawls out. We follow him down the bluff—across the creek and up the road. At the forks of the road I leave them. They go up the creek and I go up the Right Fork home.

"Now, Mick," I hear Warfield say, "my bees are all gone. All four stands are gone I tell you. I've found tracks down to the road—a lot of big tracks and little tracks. I can't track 'em no further. I heard dogs barking last night. The fox hounds run the fox right across by my barn. My dog barked and barked. I never thought anything. Now my bees are gone."

"Shan, Warfield lost all his bees last night," says Pa.

"Yes," says Warfield, "I lost my bees. Just keep bees to get honey for Ma and me. We live alone around there and ain't never had anything bothered in the last sixty years. I'll tell you the world is going to hell. I never heard of thieves taking bees before."

"W'y Mr. Flaughtery," I says, "we were back on the ridge last night and we heard a man driving in the hollow. When we walked down to the beech-tree footlog we saw a pair of black horses hitched to a wagon—the driver stood up like a ghost and whipped his horses with the check lines. We saw the fire fly from their hoofs as they left the hollow."

"The same damned thief," says Warfield, "that got poor old Willis Dials' bees. Old Willis wasn't seeing things. He actually saw the thief. I heard that Willis stung him with a few shot. I heard Sol Perkins found blotches of blood on the turnpike. Looks like if that thief got hot lead once he'd be afraid he's going to get it again."

"You can't lock from a thief," says Pa, "and you can't bluff one with bullets. You just haf to get 'im. Put him under the sod is the only cure."

Warfield goes home. I go to the cornfield with Pa. I think about when Saturday night comes. "What if someone

shoots me? What if someone shoots Big Aaron? I don't
want to sleep under no ground. I want to live. Maybe, we'll
make it somehow without getting shot."

It is Saturday night. I call Pa's hound dog and my hound
pup. I walk down the Right Fork to the hollow. I turn
left, walk down the road to the sycamore tree. The dogs
leave me and take to the hills. I walk across the creek,
climb the bluff up to the cliff. I hear voices. The boys are
waiting on me. I crawl under the ferns to the big room
under the cliff. The lantern is dimly burning.

"We have a hard piece of work before us tonight, Shan,"
says Big Aaron. "Uncle Fonse Tillman has one bee gum.
He has it around from the house, chained around a big
beech tree and the log chain is padlocked. We haf to have
that stand of bees. I've brought a cross-cut saw and a meat
rind. We'll grease the saw until you can't hear it run—saw
the tree off above the bee gum and slip the chain over the
stump. We'll fool the old boy. It's a prize bee gum. He ain't
robbed it for four years. He's afraid of his bees."

"We ain't afraid," says Little Edd. "I'm beginning to
feel like I'm a man if I am shot tonight."

"Let's go," says Big Aaron. "Don't anybody talk. Shan,
you help me saw the tree down. You are tall and you can
reach above the bee stand and saw and it won't tire you."

We follow Big Aaron out of the cliff. We follow him up
across the hill back of the cliff. Big Aaron follows a cow
path to the top of the hill. We see the fox hunters' fire on
the ridge. Big Aaron cuts down under the hill through the
briars and brush—we follow him—we cut back up to the
ridge road on beyond the fox hunters' fire. We walk down
the point to Uncle Fonse Tillman's little log house. Big
Aaron leads us to the beech tree. He runs the meat rind
over the saw. We start sawing. The saw slips through the
wood like a mouse slips away from a cat. There isn't a
sound you can hear ten steps away. "The chain takes up a

lot of the sound," says Big Aaron. Our saw eats through the green beech tree. It falls through the night air with a slash— not a dog barks at Uncle Fonse's house. We lift the padded log chain up over the clean smooth-topped stump. Little Edd plugs the bee gum. Big Aaron puts it on his back. We walk back over the hill to Big Aaron's Pap's house. I carry the log chain and the padlock.

"I know Pap's bees," says Big Aaron. "I know where he keeps every stand. We haf to work all night, boys. I'm going to carry two light bee gums at one load. You boys can take one apiece. We can carry all of our bees at five loads."

"You can't carry two stands at one load," says Ennis.

"The hell I can't," says Big Aaron. "You ain't never seed me really put my strength out. I can just about carry three to the top of that hill over yander."

We chain two stands together for Big Aaron. He picks them up with ease. He walks away. We plug our stands of bees. We walk down the hill to the road. We climb the hill under the pines. We rest on the ridge and smoke. We pick up our loads and carry them down under the hill to the locust thicket. We place them securely on the foundation rocks. We take out the plugs. We walk back the little path that leads us to our city of bee gums.

"Now boys," says Big Aaron, "we got four loads to carry from home and a load of bees over at Shan's Pap's place. It will take us all night to do this. We'll haf to work fast. We can't walk across Warfield's tater ridges at the bottom by the sycamore tree. We'll make a path and they'll track us. We'll come up the hill at a different place every time. Let Pap track us down to the road. There's a lot of wagon tracks. He can't go no further."

We follow Big Aaron. We carry the second load. We carry the third load. We carry the last load. We carry away all the bees that Alec Roundtree has. "This will hurt

Pap an awful lot," says Big Aaron, "but he has hurt the bees an awful lot. He went into the wild woods and took them from their homes in the trees. Now we take them back and leave them in the wild woods—a place so wild the hoot owls holler in the daytime."

"It's two o'clock in the morning," says Ennis, "and daylight comes soon. Do you suppose we'll have time to carry Powderjay's bees away before daylight?"

"We got two hours," says Big Aaron—"I can carry them away by myself in that time. Come on you fellars. You ain't no tireder than I am. I'm goin' to bring two stands over this time. I'm taking the log chain to wrap around them. Shan you lead us the best way to your bees."

We walk up the hollow with our plugs to stop the holes. Our bees are beside the road. We just walk along—our dogs are running the fox. There is not a dog at the house to bark at us. We plug the bee stands. Big Aaron chains two together—loads them on his back. We get a bee gum apiece and we follow Big Aaron. Little Edd carries the pistol in his hand to shoot if we see somebody coming up the road. "Little Edd, just shoot to skear 'em a little," says Big Aaron. "Put the bullet fairly close and they'll tear out."

We hurry down the road. We cut across the meadow beyond the big sycamore tree. We take to the pine woods on the hill. The moon is down, down. The way is dark. We follow Big Aaron up the hill. He sweats and groans beneath his load. We reach the top of the hill. We are wet with sweat. We are tired out. "Last time tonight," says Big Aaron. "Let us have a good smoke."

"Who—who who are you?" says a voice near by. We never move. We do not speak.

"Who—who who are you?" says the same voice.

The wings of a big owl swoop over us. We can feel the cool air from its wings.

"Did you ever hear a hoot owl speak that plain?" says

Big Aaron. "My heart was in my mouth. I thought it was Pap. I thought we's goners. Lord, but how thankful I am. Let's get the bees over and put them with the rest of the bees. This will make us forty-two stands of bees." We pick up our loads again. We walk over the hill to the locust thicket. We place them securely on the foundation rocks. We unplug the stands and walk down the little path we have worn under locust trees.

"Let's all go home and go to bed," says Big Aaron. "Remember we saw that team of horses about twelve o'clock again last night when we followed the fox hounds from the Flaughtery Ridge to the Powderjay Ridge. All tell the same tale. We're going to hear about this and not from Sunday School. Pap will be one mad man in the morning."

I leave the boys at the forks of the road. I am so tired I can hardly get home. I worked all day in the terbacker field—I carried bees all night. I am tired. I can sleep all day if there's not too much war going on in the hollow. I walk home—barely crawl to my bed upstairs. I just get my shoes off and fall across the bed. I'm all pooped out. "Lord," I think, "I'm glad I didn't get shot. I'm thankful to the Lord and I would pray to Him but I've been out taking bees and the Lord wouldn't listen to my prayers." I fall asleep.

"I'm robbed, Mick Powderjay," I hear Mr. Roundtree say. "They got my bees last night. Seventy-five gallons of honey stole from me last night. Lord, how I'll miss that seventy-five dollars! Took every bee gum I had—stripped me clean."

"Well I'll be damned," says Pa—"I never noticed that. All my bees are gone too. Look up there won't you! I'm robbed too! My God—look won't you! Thieves have come right inside my yard and took my bees!"

I get up—put on my clothes and go down. I walk out where Pa and Mr. Roundtree are standing. "Pa, did you say somebody got our bees last night?" I says.

"Look for yourself," says Pa. "I couldn't believe my eyes when I first saw it. Got all of Alec's bees last night."

"What?" I says.

"Yes," says Alec, "I've got Big Aaron out tracking this morning. Said he saw a span of black horses leave the hollow last night about twelve o'clock. Said the driver was layin' the buckskin to 'em and the fire was flyin' from their hoofs! Said the driver was leaning back and holding the check lines like a tall ghost."

"I saw it with my own eyes too," I says.

Uncle Fonse Tillman comes down the hill. He walks with a cane. He comes down to our yard—just ripping out oaths and cavorting. He waves his cane into the air. "Some thief got my only stand of bees last night," he says. "I had them chained to a beech tree. They cut the tree and slipped the chain over the stump—took chain, padlock and bee gum. I'll kill him if I ever find him. I'll kill all the thieves connected with it." He pulls a long blue forty-four from the holster and twirls it.

"We ought to swing 'em to a limb," says Pa, "if we can get 'em. We'll take the span of horses to pay for the bees."

Pa, Uncle Fonse and Alec Roundtree swear and stomp the ground. Pa puffs a cigar faster than I ever saw him puff one before. "A damn dirty shame," he says. "I've lived here all my life and this has never happened before. Somebody from a-fur has to come in to steal our bees."

Big Aaron comes up the road. "Pa," he says, "I've tracked them to the road. I see fresh wagon tracks. I can't track them no further."

"They're gone," says Alec Roundtree. "All my bees are gone."

"Mine too," says Pa.

"And my bee gum, log chain and padlock's all gone," says Uncle Fonse Tillman.

"I've said," says Pa, "you can't lock against a thief. The best way is to fill his hide so full of lead it won't hold shucks."

I walk out across the yard with Big Aaron. "We meet at the cliff next Tuesday night," says Big Aaron, "to set the last of the bee gums free. We're going up the Old Line Special to Kenyon's place. I've looked the place over. I've got the plans. We'll set them free."

"I'm getting afraid," I says. "Look at these men. Listen to them cuss and watch them stomp their feet!"

"Yes, Pa smiled when he cut down the wild bee trees," says Big Aaron. "He can't remember how the bees stung him trying to keep him from robbing them and taking them out'n the woods. Now Pa cusses around because they have gone back where they belong. Shan, you be ready Tuesday night. All this will blow over—besides, we're goin' beyond the Plum Grove hills to get these bees. We're going up the Old Line Special!"

Tuesday night I walk down to the cliff. Everywhere we go we hear wild tales about people's seeing the bee thieves—dressed in white—driving big black horses. People shooting at them and they were hit by bullets and there was blood along the road. We laugh about it. We know what big lies can get started while we work to save the bees.

"Now boys," says Big Aaron, "we go to Jake Reek's place. He has a handcar beside the Old Line Special. See he is a track man and uses the handcar. He has it padlocked but there's a crowbar there. We can pry the chain off. We can put it on the track and ride up the rails to Kenyon's. They live beside the railroad track. We can put the bees on the handcar—come down to Plum Grove in no time and carry the bees back on the hill."

"That is great," says Ennis. "We'll get to ride the hand-car. Won't that be fun!"

"It won't be fun goin' up the Old Line Special," says Dave. "We haf to pull uphill. But comin' back we can coast all the way to Greenupsburg. Just turn the levers loose and let 'em work up and down—just watch that one don't crown you on the head."

Big Aaron leads the way. We follow him to Jake Reek's house. We walk down the path to the railroad. The hand-car is settin' beside the railroad track. Big Aaron goes over in the weeds. He comes back with a crowbar. He put it behind the chain and yanks against it with all of his strength. The lock flies open.

"Let's set 'er on the tracks, boys," he says. "Let's go to Kenyon's place and get the bees. The bees are in the orchard way out in front of the house."

We lift the handcar on the track. Little Edd hunkers down. He takes care of the .22 rifle and the .32 pistol. Big Aaron and I pull on one side—Ennis and Dave pulls on the other. The wheels grind against the rails. The cool wind hits our faces. We are off up the two streaks of rust—around the curves hard as we can go—into the Minton Tunnel—through it like a flash—out into the moonlight on the other side.

"Boy, I'd like to own a handcar," says Dave, "and just go places on it. I like a handcar. It's a lot better than walking over these old hills. I don't mind to free the bees when we can go like this. Come on and let's use more elbow grease."

"Just as you say," says Big Aaron. "Everybody pull and let's travel."

"Ah, where you goin' on the Blue Goose?" a man hollers to us.

"Don't answer him," says Big Aaron. "People over here

go on this handcar after the Doctor. He thinks somebody is sick. Just keep pulling."

We don't answer.

"Pow. Pow. Pow. Pow." His gun barks at us. "Pow. Pow. Pow." The bullets wheeze all around us.

"Cut down on 'im Little Edd," says Big Aaron. "He's started this with us."

Little Edd empties the .32 pistol at him. We hear him run to the bushes screaming.

"You's nipping fer 'im Little Edd," says Dave. "Good work, boy. When they start this shooting with us we're ready."

Little Edd holds the rifle ready if he shoots again. I stop pulling the handcar to reload the pistol.

"I'll get 'im with this rifle if he tries that again," says Little Edd. "I'm a dead-eye Dick with a rifle."

Now we pull up to a switch and a big white house on our left.

"Right here," says Big Aaron. "Take it easy now, boys. Get the plugs, Dave, and let's go over and get the bees."

We walk over under the apple trees. We plug the stands. There is not a whisper. Every man knows his duty. He picks up a stand of bees. He carries them to the car.

"Three stands left," says Big Aaron. "Shan, you and Dave come with me to get them."

We walk back under the apple trees. We start to pick up the bees. The house dogs let out a yell. We grab the bees and run to the handcar. We put them on. Kenyon's door flies open. A man stands in the door—dressed in white. He turns an automatic shot gun loose at us. The bullets fall like rain. We crowd on the handcar. We start moving and little Edd brings down a dog with the first crack of the rifle. He shoots at the other dog—he whines, yells and runs to the house. "Just skint him," says Little Edd. "I'll plug that door the fellar's just closed."

"Don't do it," says Big Aaron. "This is a gun country—
more than the hollow we're from. Let's go down the track
—pump the handcar even if it is down hill. Go faster than
the Old Line Special's No. 8 ever pulled her passengers."

We turn the handcar loose. You can hear it a mile riding
the two streaks of rust. "Pow. Pow. Pow." Somebody
shoots from the bushes. Little Edd empties our .32 at the
sound of the pistol. We keep moving. A bee stings me on
the leg. One stings Big Aaron. They are stinging all of us.
A plug is out of a hole or a bullet plugged a hole in one
of the bee stands.

"We'll be there in a few minutes," says Big Aaron. "Just
keep going until we get in front of Jackson's." Before we
get to Jackson's I get nine bee stings under my pants leg.
Big Aaron gets six, Dave five, Little Edd thirteen and
Ennis don't get a sting. We pull down to Jackson's—put
the brakes on—slide the car forty feet on the rusted rails.

"Off everybody," says big Aaron. "See the bees coming
out at the side of the bee gum. That fellar back yander put
a hole through the bee gum with a .44. Glad it was the
bee gum and not one of us. We are safe. We'll leave that
stand here and take to the hills with the other seven."

"Dave, you can carry two, can't you?"

"Yes," says Dave. "I'm scared to leave that'n. Rope two
together for me."

Dave takes two stands. Big Aaron takes two. The rest
of us take one each. We go up the Jackson hill. We walk
fast in the moonlight. We walk up the hollow, twist to our
right until we come to the locust thicket. We put the bee
stands solidly on the rocks—pull out the plugs and leave the
bee city.

"Forty-nine stands now," says Big Aaron. "Just lost one
stand. We'll never do nothing with them now. Let's run
back to the handcar. We may be able to get the car back
to Jake Reek's place. If it wasn't for all the bees on it we'd

take a ride tonight on that car. I do love to ride it."

We run through the brush like a pack of fox hounds. We follow Big Aaron. He leaps the briars and brush and we leap them and go under the fences. We go back to the handcar. Big Aaron kicks the stand of bees off. There's not many bees in the stand. They are all over the handcar. We get on the handcar and start back up the track. We pull hard and fast through the tunnel—over to Jake Reek's place. The bees sting us. We do not care. We have the handcar back. We pull it from the railroad track—put it where it was—fix the chain and padlock back just like they were. We walk over the hills home and rub the places where the bees have stung us.

"It's all over now, boys," says Big Aaron, "for we have saved the bees. Any man that tells gets his tongue cut out by the roots. Now go to your homes. We won't meet at the cliff until all this trouble blows over. Now let's all play mouse and go to his own house."

"Shan," says Mom, "did you hear about somebody gettin' the handcar over at Jake Reek's place? Said there was a swarm of bees on it the next morning down around the cogs. Said when the men started to pull it, the bees nearly stung them to death. Said a lot of wild men had the car out riding it and shooting at men along the road. Shot Mel Spriggs in the leg. Said he hid in the brush and plugged one or two men as they come back. Went up the road and got all of Kenyon's bees. Said Mr. Kenyon pumped lead at 'em until he's black in the face. Said he really filled 'em with shot but they just kept going."

"Lord," I says, "what else is going to happen around here?"

"I'll tell you what's a going to happen," says Pa. "We've got the thief. Enic Spradling was squirrel hunting around on the Jackson place the other day. He found forty-nine stands of bees. It tallies all but one stand. We've lost fifty stands. You wouldn't believe old Jackson would take all them bees, would you? Well, he has."

"Why he's a sick man," says Mom. "I heard he had the consumption."

"If he's got any consumption," says Pa, "it's the corn-bread consumption. We can't get him on a bee thieving charge. The Government's got him. Got him for selling moonshine whiskey too. W'y he's a bad man. Old Judge April-May-June (A.M.J.) Canter is going to put the cat on him. He'll be on the next soldier train that goes to Atlanter, Georgia. You're going to have to go over there and get our six stands of bees someway. Alec Roundtree is going to send Big Aaron after his. This has been a hard thing to believe. Old Lonesome just sit over there on the hill and acted like he didn't have a bit of life in him. Look what all he's done. Just turned out bad in the deestrict. Let this be a lesson."

"All right, Pa," I says. "I'll get Big Aaron. We'll go for the bees."

"Don't forget to look for Uncle Fonse Tillman's log chain and padlock either," says Pa.

"I won't," I says. "I think we'll be able to find it."

HAIR

IF YOU'VE NEVER been to Plum Grove then you wouldn't know about that road. It's an awful road, with big ruts and mudholes where the coal wagons with them nar-rimmed wheels cut down. There is a lot of haw bushes along this road. It goes up and down two yaller banks. From Lima Whitehall's house in the gap it's every bit of a mile and a half to Plum Grove. We live just across the hill from Lima's house. I used to go up to her house and get with her folks and we would walk over to Plum Grove to church.

Lima Whitehall just went with one boy. I tried to court her a little, but she wouldn't look at me. One night I goes up to her and I takes off my hat and says: "Lima, how about seeing you home?" And Lima says: "Not long as Rister is livin.'" Lord, but she loved Rister James. You ought to see Rister James—tall with a warty face and ferret eyes, but he had the prettiest head of black curly hair you ever saw on a boy's head. I've heard the girls say: "Wish I had Rister's hair. Shame such an ugly boy has to have that pretty head of hair and a girl ain't got it. Have to curl my hair with a hot poker. Burnt it up about, already. Shame a girl don't have that head of hair."

Well, they don't say that about my hair. My hair is just so curly I don't know which end of it grows in my head until I comb it. I've prayed for straight hair—or hair of a different color. But it don't do no good to pray. My hair ain't that pretty gold hair, or light gold hair. It's just about the color of a weaned jersey calf's hair. I'll swear it is. People even call me Jersey.

There was a widder down in the Hollow and she loved Rister. Was a time, though, when she wouldn't look at him. She was from one of those proud families. You've seen them. Think they're better'n everybody else in the whole wide world—have to watch about getting rain in their noses. That's the kind of people they were in that family. And when a poor boy marries one of them girls he's got to step. They are somebody around here and they boss their men. So Rister James went with the woman I loved, Lima Whitehall, when he could have gone with Widder Ollie Spriggs. Widder Ollie wasn't but seventeen years old and just had one baby. Rister was nineteen and I was eighteen. Lima was seventeen. If Rister would have gone with Widder Ollie it would have made things come out right for me. God knows I didn't want Widder Ollie and she didn't want me. I wanted Lima. I told her I did. She wanted Rister. She told me she did.

Widder Ollie was a pretty girl—one of them women that just makes a good armful—small, slim as a rail, with hair pretty as the sunlight and teeth like peeled cabbage stalks. She'd have made a man a pretty wife. She might not have made a good wife—that's what Effie Spriggs told me. Effie is John Spriggs' mother and Ollie married John when she was fifteen. Effie said Ollie broke a whole set of plates, twelve of 'em, on John's head over nothing in God Almighty's world. And he just had too much honor in his bones to hit a woman with his fist. He just stood there and let her break them. And when she got through, John was kind of addled but he got out of the house and came home to his mother Effie, who is Widder Effie here in the Hollow. (She tried to pizen her man, but he found the pizen in his coffee and left her.) Widder Ollie went to live with Widder Effie later. They had a plenty—a big pretty farm down in the Hollow, fat barns, and plenty of milk cows. They were kindly rich people with heads so high you couldn't reach them with a ten-foot pole.

Widder Ollie, as I said, wouldn't look at Rister at first. She laughed at him when he used to hoe corn for her pappie for twenty-five cents a day. She made fun of poor old Rister's snaggled-toothed mother and said she looked like a witch. She laughed at Rister's pappie and said he looked like old Lonesy Fannin. That was an old bald-headed horse-doctor who used to go from place to place pulling the eye-teeth out of blind horses, saying they would get their sight back. And she said all the children in the James family looked like varmints. She'd laugh and laugh at 'em and just hold her head high. Then suddenly she was after Rister to marry him. But that's the way—pride leads a woman to a fall. And after she gets up, with a little of the pride knocked out of her, she's a different woman.

But I didn't blame Rister for not wanting her when he could get Lima. Lima was the sweetest little black-headed armload you ever put your two eyes on. I was in the market for Lima the first time I ever saw her. And I guess that was when we were babies. But I didn't know how to get her. I think I was a durn sight better-looking boy than Rister. It's funny how a woman will take to an uglier feller that way and just hold on to his coat-tails whether or not. Hang on just as long as she can. I always thought the reason Lima did that was because she knew Widder Ollie wanted Rister. And if there'd a been another girl around in the district in the market for a man *she* would have wanted Rister because Lima wanted him and Widder Ollie wanted him.

But nobody was after me. I was left out in the cold—just because of my hair, Mom always told me. Mom said I was a good-looking boy all but the color of my hair, and

women wouldn't take to that kind of hair. Of course, it
don't matter how ugly a man is, his Mom always thinks
he's the best-looking boy in the district.

II

I used to go down past Lima's house last June when the
roses were in bloom, and the flags. Them blue and yaller
flags just sets a yard off and makes it a pretty thing. Now
Rister never saw anything pretty in flowers. He never saw
anything pretty in a woman's voice or the things she said,
or the shape of her hands. He would watch a woman's legs
—and go with them far as he could. He was that kind of
a feller. I knew it all the time. I'd pass Whitehall's house.
It would be on a Wednesday when Mom would run out
of sugar or salt and I'd have to get on the mule and go to
the store and get it. Rister would be down to see Lima on
a weekday. Now God knows, when a man is farming he
don't have no time to play around with a woman like a
lovesick kitten. He's got to strike while the iron is hot.
If he don't he won't get much farming done. When I saw
Rister and Lima I reined my mule up to the palings. And
I started talking to them as if I didn't care what they were
doing. But I did care. I says: "How you getting along
with your crop, Rister?"

"Oh, pretty well," he says. "Nothing extra. Terbacker's
getting a little weedy on me. Too wet to hoe in it today.
Ground will ball up in your hand. Too wet to stir the
ground when it is like that."

Well, I knew he was a lying. But I never said anything.
I know when ground is wet and when ground ain't wet.
I'd been out working in it all morning. It was in good
shape to work. Rister used to be a good worker. But you
know how a man is when he gets lovesick after a woman.
Take the best man in the world to work and let him get

his mind on a woman and he goes hog-wild. That was
the way with Rister.

While I was there looking over the palings, Lima went
right up into his arms. He kissed her right there before me.
Mom always says a woman that would kiss around in front
of people was a little loose with herself. Well, I would
have told Mom she lied about Lima if she'd said that about
her to my face. I just didn't want to believe anything bad
about Lima. I wanted her for my wife. But, men, how
would you like to look over the palings from a mule's back
and see your dream-wife in the arms of a man bad after
women—right out among the pretty roses and flags—and
her right up in his arms, her arms around his neck, and
his arms around her waist pulling her up to him tight enough
to break her in two. And he would say to her: "Oo love
me, oo bitsy baby boopy-poopy oo?" And she would say:
"I love U, U bitsy 'itsy boopy-poopy oo. I love my 'ittle
'itsy 'itsy bitsy turley-headed boopy-poopy oo." God, it
made me sick as a horse. It's all right when *you're* loving
a woman. It don't look bad to *you*. But when you see somebody else gumsuck around, then you want to get the hell
out of the way and in a hurry. It's a sickening thing.

I reined my mule away and I never let him stop till I was
a mile beyond the house. I went on to the store and got
the sugar. That was Wednesday night and Prayer-Meeting
night at Plum Grove, so I had to hurry back and do up the
work and go to Prayer Meeting.

I'm a Methodist—I go to church—but God knows they
won't have my name on the Lamb's Book of Life because
I saw the fiddle, play set-back, and dance at the square
dances. Some of them even say terbacker is a filthy weed
and none of it will be seen in heaven. Some won't even
raise it on their farms. But I go to church even if they
won't have me until I quit these things. I just up and go to

see and to be seen—that's what we all go for. It is a place
to go and about the only place we got to go.

I hurried and got my work done. I put the mule up and
fed him. I helped milk the cows. I slopped the hogs, got
in stove-wood and kindling. I drew up water from the well—
got everything done around the house and I set out to church.
Well, when I got down to Whitehall's place, there was
Lima and Rister. They were getting ready to go. I gave
them a head start and followed after. But I hadn't more
than walked out in the big road until here come Widder
Ollie and that baby of hers. He was just big enough to
walk a little and talk a lot. We started down the road. I said
to Ollie: "Rister and Lima's just on ahead of us."

And Ollie says: "They're on ahead? C'mon, let's catch
up with them. Take my baby boy, you carry him awhile."

So I took her baby and started in a run with her to catch
up with Lima and Rister. You know, a woman will do
anything when she loves a man. I could tell Widder Ollie
loved Rister. She was all nervous and excited. She had her
mind set on getting Rister. And when a woman has her
mind set on getting a man she can about get him. That
made me think if she could get Rister I'd have a chance
to get Lima. That was the only reason I'd be carrying a
widder's baby around. I had heard that baby was the
meanest young'n in the world. Now I believed it. It had
been spiled by them two women—its mother and its grand-
mother. He would kick me in the ribs and say: "Get up
hossy! Get up there! Whoa back, Barnie." And when he
would say "Whoa back" he would glomb me in the eyes
with his fingers like he was trying to stop a horse. Then
he would say: "Get up, hossy, or I'll bust you one in the
snoot." And then he started kicking me in the ribs again.
I was sweating, carrying that load of a young'n and keeping
up with Widder Ollie. I felt like pulling him off my back
and burning up the seat of his pants with my hand.

We saw them—Rister had his left arm around Lima's back and she had her right arm around his back. They were climbing up the first hill, that little yaller hill on this side of the haw bushes. It was light as day. The moon had come up and it lit the fields like a big lamp. Pon my word and honor I couldn't remember in all my life a prettier night than that one. You ought to have seen my corn in the moonlight. We had to pass it. I was glad for the girls to go by it and see what a clean farmer I was and what a weedy farmer Rister was. Not a weed in any of my corn. Pretty and clean in the moonlight and waving free as the wind. Lord, I felt like a man with religion to see my corn all out of the weeds and my terbacker clean as a hound dog's tooth—my land all paid for—not a debt in the world —didn't owe a man a penny. Raised what I et and et what I raised. All I needed was a wife like Lima. She'd never want for anything. And I thought: "What if this baby on my back was mine and Lima's? I'd carry him the rest of my days. I'd let him grow to be a man a-straddle of my back. But if I had my way now, I'd bust his little tail with my hand."

We got right up behind Rister and Lima. And they looked around. Widder Ollie had me by the arm. I had her baby on my back yet. God, it hurt me. But I held the baby while Lima won the battle. You know women are dangerous soldiers. They fight with funny weapons. The tongue is a dangerous cannon when a woman aims it right. We just laughed and talked. We just giggled before Rister and Lima got to giggling at us. I was afraid they'd laugh at me for carrying the baby. They went on up the next hill —us right behind them. We went past the haw bushes and on to church. We just laughed and laughed and went on crazy. That baby on my back, a-making a lot of noise. We went up the hill at the church and the boys said: "Look at that pack mule, won't you?"

Well, to tell the truth I'd ruther be called a pack mule
as to be called Jersey. So I just let them whoop and holler
to see me with Widder Ollie and carrying her baby. Everybody out on the ground laughed and hollered enough to
disturb the Methodist Church. Church was going on inside.
But there was more people out in the yard than there was
inside. They could see more on the outside than they could
hear going on inside. I just wagged the baby right in the
church house. Everybody looked around and craned their
necks.

Rister and Lima acted like they were ashamed of us.
Tried to sidle out of the way and get us in front so they
could dodge us. But we stayed right with them. They set
down on a seat. We set right beside them as if we were all
together. People looked around. I had Widder Ollie's boy
in my lap. He tried to hit the end of my nose. I had a
time with him. I could see the girls whisper to one another.
They watched us more than they did the preacher. He
was telling them about widders and orphans. He was
preaching a sermon on that. Rister would flinch every now
and then. He wanted to be on another seat. But he couldn't
very well move. So he just set there and took it. And I
took it from that young'n. But I thought: "There'll be the
time when I come back to this church house with a different woman. I'll come right here and marry her. It will be
different from what they see tonight."

III

We set right there and listened through that sermon.
Boys would come to the winder and point to me from the
outside—being with a widder woman who hadn't been di-
vorced from her man very long. Boys around home thinks
it's kindly strange to go with a widder woman—but I don't
think so. They say a body is in adultery. But when two

can't go on loving each other and start breaking plates—
twelve at a crack—it's time they were getting apart. Especially when two has to go through life tied together when
the mother-in-law tied the knot. I just felt sorry for Widder
Ollie. She had always loved Rister and would have married
him to begin with if it hadn't been for that mother of
hers telling her so many times that she got to believing it
that she was better than any man in the Hollow.

Well, they got us in front coming out of the church
house. I thought we'd better take advantage of getting out
first. So we took the lead going back. Boys just giggled
and hollered at me when I come out of the house with the
baby on my back. I didn't care. I was seeing ahead. So we
just went out the road. The moon was pretty on the fields.
A thousand thoughts came into my mind. I didn't want
Rister to have Lima. I loved Lima. God, I loved her. Widder Ollie said to me going home: "Don't think it has done
much good for both of us tonight. We'll have to think
of something different. I love that boy till it hurts. I could
love him forever. I can't get him: Lima don't love him.
She holds him because I want him. That is the way of
women. You want what you can't get. When you get
what you want you don't want it. I have always loved
Rister. But my people wanted me to marry John. I married
him. My mother married him. Life is not worthwhile without Rister. And here you've been out carrying my baby
around and letting people talk about you so you could
help me get Rister and you could get Lima."

That was right. Life was not fair. The night was so
pretty. The moon above my clean corn. My house on the
hill where I would take Lima. I needed a wife. I wanted the
woman I loved. I loved Lima Whitehall. And when we
passed her home I wouldn't look across the palings at the
roses. I remembered the week-day I passed and saw Rister
out there with her. I just took Widder Ollie on home. And

when we got to the gate I said: "Widder Ollie, I am Rister kissing you. You are Lima kissing me. You are Lima for one time in your life. I am Rister one time in my life. Shut your eyes and let's kiss. Let's just pretend." So we did.

Then I started on the long walk home up the branch. I had to pass Lima's house. Moonlight fell on the corn. Wind blew through the ragweeds along the path. Whip-poor-wills hollered so lonely that they must have been in love with somebody they couldn't get. I went in Lima's yard to draw me a drink of water. And right by the well-gum stood Rister and Lima. They weren't a-saying a word. They didn't see me; I didn't let myself be known; I just stepped back into the moonshade of one of the yard trees. I just stood there and watched. Lima went into the house after kissing and kissing Rister. When Lima left, Rister stood at the well-gum. He looked down at the ground. He kicked the toe of his shoe against the ground. There was something funny about the way he was acting. He kept his eye on the upstairs winder in that house. It had one of them pole ladders—we call them chicken ladders—just one straight pole with little tiny steps nailed across it. It was setting up back of the house—from the ground to the winder.

Then, suddenly, Rister let out one of the funniest catcalls you ever heard. It would make the hair stand up on your head. It wasn't a blue yodel, but it was something like a part of that yodel Jimmie Ridgers used to give. He done it someway down in his throat. It started out like the nip-nip-nipping of scissor-blades, then it clanked like tin cans, then like a foghorn, way up there high, then it went like a bumblebee, then it rattled like a rattlesnake, and ended up like that little hissing noise a black snake makes when it warns you. I never heard anything like it. If it hadn't been for me knowing where it had come from I'd set sail off of that hill and swore it was a speret that made the noise. Rister gave the catcall once—held his head high in the air—

no answer. So he gave it again. And from upstairs came the answer—a soft catcall like from a she-cat. So he takes right out in front of me and runs up that ladder like a tom and pops in at the winder.

I thought I'd go home and get the gun and come back and when he came down that ladder I'd fill his behind so full of shot it would look like a strainer. Then again I thought I'd go over and pull the ladder down and make him go down the front way. God, I was mad! But I didn't do neither one. The whole thing made me so sick I just crawled out of the moonshade and sneaked over the hill home. I didn't know what to do. It just made me sick—sick at life. I just couldn't stand it. I couldn't bear to think of Lima in the dark upstairs with Rister.

I thought about taking the gun and going back and blowing Rister's brains out when he came back through that upstairs winder. I could have done it—God knows I could have done it. But they'd have got out the bloodhounds and trailed me home. Lima would have known who did it. I thought there must be a way for me to get Lima yet, and for her to come to her senses. But then I thought they are up in that dark room together. Lord, it hurt me. Pains shot through and through me. Life wasn't worth the pain one got out of it. I had something for her—a farm, a little money, clean crops, and plenty of food for cold days when the crows fly over the empty fields hunting last year's corn-grains. Rister didn't have nothing to take a woman to but his father's house, and den her with his own father's young'ns.

I went upstairs and got the gun from the rack. I put a shell into its bright blue barrel. Just one shell for Rister. I would kill him. Then I put the gun down. I would not kill Rister. I could see his blood and brains all over the wall. Old Sol Whitehall would run out in his nightshirt. He would kill Lima if he knew. And I wouldn't get Lima. It

is better not to let a man know everything—it is better to
live in silence and hold a few things than to lose your
head and get a lot of people killed. I put the gun back, took
the shell out of it, and set it back on the rack. I went to
bed. But I couldn't sleep. I could see Lima and Rister in a
settee in the front yard, kissing. I could hear that catcall.
I memorized it. I said it over and over in bed. It came to
me—every funny noise in it. I called it out, several times.
It made the hair stand up on my head. It waked Pa up and
he said: "I've been hearing something funny in this house
or my ears are fooling me. Funniest thing I ever heard.
Like a pheasant drumming on a brushpile. Goes something
like a rattlesnake too. I can't go to sleep." But Pa went
back to sleep. I kept my mouth shet. I just laid there the
rest of the night and thought about Rister and Lima.

I didn't eat much breakfast the next morning. I went out
and got the Barnie mule and I started plowing my terbacker. I couldn't get Lima off my mind. I prayed to God.
I did everything I knew to do. And it all came to me like
a flash. It just worked out like that.

So I waited. I just waited about ten hours. I plowed all
day, worked hard in the fields. After I'd fed the mule, et
my supper, done up the rest of the work, I slipped back
up the path that I had come over the night before.

All the lights in the Whitehall house were out. The ladder was up at the winder at the back of the house. Everything was quiet. The old house slept in the moonlight. The
hollyhocks shone in the moonlight. Old Buck came around
and growled once or twice. But he knew me when I patted
his head. He walked away contented. Brown, he was, in
the moonlight—like a wadded-up brown carpet thrown
among the flowers

I held my head in the air, threw my chin to the stars, and
gave that catcall—just as good as Rister gave it. Lima answered me from upstairs. The dog started barking at the

strange sounds. My cap pulled low over my funny-colored hair I climbed the ladder and went in through the winder. The dog barked below. I was afraid. If Sol Whitehall found me there he would kill me. But I had to do this thing. I just had to.

Lima said: "Oo bitsy 'itsy boopy-poopy oo. My turley-headed baby boy."

I kept away from the streak of moonlight in the room. . . . Well, no use to tell you all. A man's past belongs to himself. His future belongs to the woman he marries. That's the way I look at it. That's the way I feel about it. This is a world where you have to go after what you get or you don't get it. Lima would not stand and say: "Here I am. Come and get me." No. She couldn't say it long as she was free—free without a care in the world. If she was like Widder Ollie, she'd be glad to find a nice young man like me even if I did have hair the color of a jersey calf and so curly you couldn't tell which end grew in my head. I know that much about women.

When my hat come off in the moonlight upstairs Lima just screamed to the top of her voice. Screamed like she had been stabbed. I made for the winder. She hollered: "That hair! That hair!" She knew who I was. I went out of that winder like a bird. I heard Sol getting out the bed. I landed on soft ground right in the hollyhock bed, as God would have it. I took down over the bank—circled up in the orchard through the grass so they couldn't track me. I hadn't got two-hundred feet when I heard Sol's gun and felt the shot sprinkling all around me in the sassafras like a thin rain falls on the green summer leaves.

I went on to bed that night. I dreamed of Lima. I loved her. I didn't care about Rister and his past with Lima. The way I looked at it, that belonged to them. A girl has the same right to her past that a boy has to his. And when a man loves, nothing matters. You just love them and you

HAIR

can't help it. You'll go to them in spite of the world—no matter what a man has done or a woman has done. That's the way I look at it. Be good to one another in a world where there's a lot of talking about one another, a lot of tears, laughter, work, and love—where you are a part of the world and all that is in it and the world is a part of you. I dreamed about Lima that night. She was in my arms. I kissed her. She was in the trees I'd seen in the moonlight. She was in the wild flowers I saw—the flowers on the yaller bank. She was in my corn and my terbacker. She was in the wind that blows. She was my wife. She wasn't Rister's. She was mine. I loved her.

IV

Well, August ended, and September came along with the changing leaves. Then October when all the world turned brown and dead leaves flew through the air. The wind whistled lonesome over the brown fields. The crows flew high through the crisp autumn air.

The months dragged by. We went to church, but I barely ever spoke to Lima or to Rister. I went with Widder Ollie sometimes. People were talking about Lima. People understood. A woman, with her crooked finger over the paling fence, said: "That poor Lima Whitehall was raised under a decent roof, and in the House of the Lord, a church-going girl with as good a father and mother as ever God put breath in. And look how she's turned out. You just can't tell about girls nowadays. They'll fool you—especially when they run around with a low-down boy like Rister James. Curly-headed thing—everybody's crazy about his hair. Look at that bumpy face and them ferret eyes and you'll get a stomachful, won't you?"

And the woman driving home from town with an express and buggy said: "You are right, Miss Fairchild. It's

them low-down James people. That boy. He ought to be
tarred and feathered, bringing a poor girl to her ruint.
She's a ruint girl. Never can stand in the church choir anymore with the other girls and play the organ and sing at
church. Her good times are over. That James boy won't
marry her now. They say he's got to dodging her. Poor
thing."

So I went to Widder Ollie and I said: "Everybody's
down on old Rister now. You ought to go talk to him. He's
down and out. Now is when he needs help. You know
what they are accusing him of. I guess it's the truth. Wait
till after I see the baby and I might take Lima and the baby.
Be glad to get them. If I do, you can grab Rister."

"I'll do it," said Widder Ollie. "I'll spin my net for him
like a spider. I'll get the fly. I love that boy. I love him.
He's got the prettiest hair you nigh ever see on any boy's
head."

The land was blanketed in snow. The cold winds blew.
Winter was here. We heard the people talk: "W'y, old Sol
Whitehall's going to march that young man Rister right
down there at the pint of his gun and make him marry
Lima. It's going to be a shotgun wedding. Something is
going to happen."

The talk was all over the neighborhood. Everybody in
the district knew about Lima. It is too bad when a girl
gets in trouble and everybody knows about it. Around
home she can never get a man. She's never respected again.
For the man it don't matter much. He can go right back
to the church choir and sing when they play the organ.
Nothing is ever said about the man.

"I won't marry her," said Rister, "and old Sol can't gun
me into it. I'll die first. I'll go away to the coal mines and
dig coal till it is all over. I'll go where Widder Ollie's pappie is—up in West Virginia."

So Widder Ollie goes to West Virginia after Rister has

been there awhile. She leaves her boy with her mother and
she goes to stay awhile with her pappie. I thought that
was the right move. It just looked like everything was coming nicely to my hands. I had worked hard. I had prayed
hard. I had waited. It was time to get something. But what
a mess. What a risk to run over a woman. How she had
suffered. How I had suffered. The lonely nights I'd gone
out to the woods—nights in winter when the snow dusted
the earth—when the trees shook their bare tops in the wind
and the song of the wind in the trees was long and lonesome and made a body want to cry—lonely nights when a
body wondered if life was worth living—white hills in the
moonlight—the barns with shaggy cows standing around
them and sparrows mating in the eaves. Life is strange.
Lima there, and the Lord knew what she'd do the way
people were talking in the district. I was just waiting to
see. It would soon be time.

The winter left. Birds were coming back from the South
—robins had come back. And Rister was gone. Rister was
at the mines—had a job—making more money than he'd
ever made in his life. He wasn't working for twenty-five
cents a day no more. He was working on the mine's tipple
for three dollars a day. He was wearing good clothes. He
was courting Widder Ollie right up a tree. And he had
her up the tree-a-barking at her like a hound-dog trees a
possum.

The days went swiftly. April was here—green in the hills
and the plow again in the furrows. Mom was there that
ninth of April. She was with Lima. Doctor so far away and
hard for poor people to get. Lima came through all right.
She had the baby. Mom came home the next morning—I
was waiting to see. She said: "It's got that funny-colored
hair—that jersey hair with two crowns on its head. But
it ain't no Harkreader. It's the first time I ever saw any
other person but a Harkreader have hair like that."

I never said a word. I was so happy I couldn't say a word. I had the almanac marked and it had come out just right. So I up and went down to Whitehall's to see the baby. I went in by the bed. I reached over and picked up that baby. It was my baby. I knew it. It was like lifting forty farms in my hands. I kissed it. It was a boy. I never lifted a little baby before or never saw a pretty one in my life. But this baby was pretty as a doll. I loved it. I said: "I'll go to the store and get its dresses right now, Lima."

And she said: "W'y, what are you talking about?"

"Look at its hair," I said. "Only a Harkreader has that kind of hair. You know that."

Fire popped in her eyes—then tears to quench the fire. They flowed like water. "When you get out of bed," I said, "we'll go to church and get married. We'll go right out there where we went to school and where we played together. We'll forget about Rister."

She started out of the bed. I put her back. When a girl is down and out—a girl you love—a girl who is good and who loves as life lets a woman and a man love—I could shed tears. I could cuss. I could cry. But what I did was to run out and chop up that settee. I dug up the green sprouts of the flags and the roses. My daddy-in-law, old Sol Whitehall, ran around the house on me and yelled: "What the devil are you doing? Am I crazy to see you in my yard digging up my flowers?"

And I said: "You are crazy, for I am not here, and you are not Sol Whitehall. You are somebody else."

I dumped the flower roots over the palings. I left Sol standing there, looking at the wind.

I ran toward the store. I said to myself: "I got her! I'll plow more furrows. Clear more ground. Plant more corn. I'll do twice as much work. I got her! And I am going to get my boy some dresses. Hell's fire! He's greater to look at than my farm!"

I got him the dresses. I ran back and told the preacher to be ready soon. She must be mine. And when I got back with the dresses my pappie-in-law said: "And that scoundrel—married. Rister married to Widder Ollie Spriggs. Damn him to hell! God damn his soul to hell and let it burn with the chaff!"

But let them talk. Let them talk. They'll never know.

We went to the church. We were married there. Made Lima feel better to be married there. I could have been married in a barn. Would have suited me.

You ought to see my boy now. Takes after me—long jersey-colored hair. He's my image. He don't look like his Ma—not the least. He's up and going about.

Rister's back home now. He works for Widder Ollie and her mother. They all live in the house together. Everything came out just fine. We went to church together the other night, all of us. Rister and Widder Ollie walked behind. We went into the church house carrying our babies. I know people thought I was carrying Rister's baby, and that he was carrying the one I ought to carry. The Widder Ollie's brat was digging Rister in the ribs and saying, "Get up, hossy. Get up, hossy, or I'll hit you on the snoot."

And he'd have done it too, if Rister hadn't stepped up a little faster. That kid is twice as big as he was the night I carried him. Ollie says he won't walk a step when she takes him any place. Makes Rister carry him everywhere. People look at us and grin. They crane their necks back over the seats to look at us all together again. Ollie understands. Lima understands. Rister don't understand so well.

And we go back across the hills shining in moonlight. Summer is here again. Corn is tall on the hills. Then I hold my head in the air, throw my chin to the stars, and I give that strange catcall once more. Rister looks a little funny. He understands now better than he did.

VACATION IN HELL

YOU KNOW HOW IT IS HERE among th' hills. A body's got to make a little money. I've been makin' mine diggin' coal. I make enough durin' th' fall after th' crop's gathered in to buy my youngins some winter clothes and shoes and pay my taxes. I get five cents a bushel fer diggin' th' coal and wheelin' it out where th' jolt-wagons can get to it. I can dig about thirty bushels o' coal a day on an average. That makes a dollar and half a day and honest to God that ain't to be laughed at in times like these. It's better 'n cuttin' timber fer fifty cents a thousand, or hoein' corn fer seventy-five cents a day or doin' gin work fer some farmer fer fifty cents a day.

Lefty Weaver dug coal with me. Lefty and me's been buddies a long time. Atter we'd gather our crops we'd go back to th' coal bank over on Rufus Pratt's place and dig coal together. We allus worked as buddies. I'd hep Lefty gather his crop and he'd hep me. Old Lefty was as good a worker as ever God put breath in. He fit his work. Warn't no standin' back and shirkin' when Lefty took holt o' a thing. When he lifted he didn't stand and holler and grunt like a lot o' fellars. He lifted hard enough to bust a gut. That was Lefty. It took me humpin' all day to do th' work that Lefty done. I shore to God worked to do my half o' work. I jist wouldn't let Lefty out-do me.

Atter we'd worked out in th' fields and farmed all summer, w'y, Lefty called goin' back to th' coal bank a vacation in hell. Th' bank we dug coal from warn't th' best bank Rufus had. He's got four coal banks on his place. But we warn't steady diggers and Rufus give us th' bad bank. It may not be so bad but it got a bad name when th' Right Entry fell in and smashed Sid MacCoy and Lief Porter. It jist got a couple o' fellars is all. That give it sorty a bad name. Th' roof on none o' Rufus Pratt's coal banks ain't any good. It's a brittle rock roof. Got to keep it posted all th' way in. But 'pears like th' roof above our vein o' coal is rottener than any th' roofs.

It was jist two weeks ago. Sall got my breakfast and I drinked a couple o' cups o' good hot black coffee. I was dressed in my bank clothes, and Lord but they's cold in th' December wind when I got out and started down to Lefty's. I hurried down th' path to Lefty's. He'd had his breakfast and was ready. We struck off down th' road to th' mines. It was so cold and our old bank clothes was filled with mud and kindly damp to be wearin'. But we didn't mind that. We jist hurried to th' mines. It's allus warm in th' mines o' a winter time you know. Water a runnin' out and rats livin' back there jist as warm and comfortable.

We put our coal forks and picks and shovels in th' coal buggy. We refilled our lamps with carbite, put in a little water and turned th' little wheel to get th' spark. "Kaflunk" and pop went th' fire and lit our lamps. Then we bent over sorty behind th' buggy and shoved off back to a mile under th' hill. Lefty's big shoulders and mine together nearly spread across some th' nar places in th' coal bank.

"Lefty," I'd say, "you beat anybody diggin' coal I ever saw. Jist lay there on your side and prize around with a crowbar or two a little bit and durned if th' whole vein don't tumble down fer you. In this hard diggin' durned if I don't believe you can dig fifty bushels a day." Lefty'd jist laugh and th' little carbite flame would flicker from

his lamp. We could tell when a hot wind was pressin' to
th' front o' th' bank. Th' flames on our carbite lamps
'peared to be tryin' to pull away from th' lamps and get
back out'n th' mines.

"A lot o' seeps comin' through here," says Lefty, "we
must be under that damned sag. We'll need a lot more
posts. We'll haf to take a couple o' days off and do a lot o'
postin'. If we don't this damned roof goin' to come down
shore'n God made th' lumps o' coal. I seen a big rat runnin' out'n here t' other day."

I says: "Lefty, so much o' this bank postin'—havin' to
go out and cut tough-butted white oaks fer posts and
haulin' 'em here to th' coal bank—then cartin' back and
settin' 'em up—it's that what cuts our average o' coal
diggin' down. And look at all th' bone and slate we got
to cart out and dump over th' hill."

"I know," says Lefty, "but that ain't it. We got youngins
at home. We got a wife ain't we? And wouldn't this be a
deep damn grave? All th' tombstones we'd have would be
th' saw briars above us, th' green briars, th' tough-butted
white oaks and th' rocks! If this entry'd ever fall in I'll be
damned if I'd believe anybody could find us where we are
now. We've got this hill filled up with enough big holes
fer a hundred moonshine stills and a thousand foxes to
den in. Th' foxes 'll get it if th' moonshiners don't beat
'em to it."

It's th' truth that I allus thought o' Sall and my seven
youngins when I's back under th' hill. But look at Lefty—
he had eleven youngins! Would have another one right
soon. Lefty'd have a round dozen! What if th' hill was to
get 'im? What if th' hill was to get me? What would his
Murt and my Sall and all our youngins do without us? I
jist hated to think these thoughts but sometimes I did
think 'em. I'd think 'em as I come in behind th' buggy
shovin' with all th' strength I had. Sometimes I'd haf to

brace my feet on one o' th' little crossties in th' track and shove with every ounce o' weight and strength I had.

"See that rat," says Lefty to me, "there he goes! Yander, see 'im! That's th' sign o' a bad roof Hargis. We'd better do some mine postin' tomorrow. We can't go on too fur. I believe we're under that damned sag. It's that big saddle down in th' ridge—dangerous as hell too. We can't tell exactly how we're runnin' with this entry."

I tell you old Lefty's really shovelin' down and prizin' out th' big lumps o' coal. I's loadin' 'em and takin' 'em out'n th' buggy and dumpin' 'em fer th' jolt-wagons and th' teams. By noon I'd shoved out five buggy loads o' coal. Not quite ten bushels to th' buggy. But we'd been doin' good work.

"There goes another rat," says Lefty. "I seen its eyes. Runnin' out'n here."

"Th' moonshiners 'll have a lot o' company when we leave this mine," I says.

"When we leave this mine," says Lefty, "it'll be too dangerous fer th' rats."

"You're about right," I says, "men stay longer in these mines than the rats."

"Th' rats can live a lot easier than men," says Lefty, "they ain't no law to keep them from pilferin'. Jist too bad when they get caught."

"I never liked a rat until I come here," I says. "I didn't know there's one good thing to be said fer a rat. But there is one thing. He warns us when there's danger in th' coal banks. We can see 'im runnin' out. I jist often wonder who warns him!"

"He's more ust to th' ground than we are," says Lefty, "allus lived in a hole in th' hill, under a smoke house, cellar or a hogpen!"

"We jist been in a hole fer ten years," I says.

"We ain't no rats neither," says Lefty, "but if we'd

lived back under th' hills all our lives and was born back here, w'y, we'd be changed a lot. You jist think what if a man never saw daylight and worked back here all his life in this night. What would happen to 'im! Jist ast a few o' th' old coal diggers! W'y, he'd get like a varmit. His eyes would get afraid o' th' light. He'd be afraid o' th' light."

"Another rat," I says, "see 'im. Look—watch 'im! There he goes! Where's all th' rats a-comin' from nohow?"

"Don't ast me," says Lefty, "you know as much about 'em as I know. They jist live back in here where it's good and warm is all. They live back here like we do."

Lefty was down on his side diggin' coal. I was jist over on th' other side from Lefty. I was diggin' with a short handled pick. Th' coal it 'peared like was comin' out so easy.

It jist seemed to me like I wasn't diggin' coal. It 'peared to me like I'd been diggin' coal. No, I was not diggin, coal. I was gatherin' peaches. It was July. Th' sun was hot. My how th' sun did come down. It was almost too hot to get my breath. I'd take a big willer basket and walk up th' ladder into th' peach tree. I'd reach up and pick th' peaches. I'd put them in my basket. Th' basket was heavy to hold. Th' leaves on th' peach tree were thick and th' wind was smothery. It was hard fer me to get my breath.

I'd put th' big peaches in th' basket. Once I started to take a bite off'n one and I saw a green snake on a peach tree limb. It was lookin' right into my eye. I jist took aim at 'im with th' peach and drawed back my arm and let th' peach fly. I took th' green snake right above th' eye. He jist bent double like a measurin' worm and tumbled down out'n th' tree. I couldn't see where he hit on th' ground fer I's up in th' peach tree and there's a lot of green wilted leaves below me.

I picked th' basket o' peaches and went down th' ladder

with 'em. It was a ladder like we got at home fer th' chickens to walk up in th' oak tree to roost. It bent a little with
my weight. Th' peaches was awful heavy. But I helt it
against my hip and helt to th' ladder with th' other hand
and I got down all right. I dumped th' basket o' peaches
in th' barrel that Sall had used to sulphur apples in. I jist
didn't like th' smell o' th' durn sulphur. But I poured th'
peaches in th' barrel and went back up in th' tree atter
more peaches.

I started to take a bite off'n a big ripe peach. I jist looked
up in time. It was a durned big stripped-tail spider. He
had big hard shiny eyes that looked like agates in th' sun.
He's shinin' his two eyes on me right in th' wilted leaves
in th' peach tree top. They looked like flashlights after
dark. "God," I says to myself, "what's it all about nohow? A body pickin' peaches and can't get to take a bite
o' one o' 'em."

I took th' big ripe peach and I cut drive at that spider's
eyes. I took one o' 'em casouse. Th' ripe peach jist splat-
tered all over th' spider's face. Th' last I saw o' 'im he's
goin' down through th' peach tree limbs a wipin' th' mushy
peach from his face with one o' his long hard legs. He was
a monstrous spider. About as big as a quart cup I'd say.
But I hit 'im in a touchy spot when I plugged his eye. He
fell fur below me. I never saw 'im hit th' ground. It was
too fur down out'n th' tree.

"Now," I says to myself, "I'll take me a bite o' peach."
I pulled me a big peach and started to take a bite. I jist
looked in time. It was that durned green snake again. He
was right on th' limb in front o' me a-lickin' out his tongue.
Fire was dancin' in his eyes too. He was mad. Ripe peach
was smeared all over his head where I'd hit 'im before. I
didn't know whether to hit his big open mouth with my fist
or to hit 'im with another peach. He was at close range. I
didn't take a chance with my fist. I jist drawed back and I

let 'im have it. Th' peach jist smashed over his face and eyes and he tumbled out'n th' tree like a stuck hog.

"I got 'im this time," I says, "now I can eat a peach in peace."

I reached up and pulled me another peach. Jist as I got ready to take a bite I looked up and seen th' spider. He whetted his front legs across each other and they made a racket like rubbin' two files across each other. He'd cleaned th' peach I'd hit 'im with off'n his face. It was clean as a chip chopped from a tree. His eyes were big and shined like two silver dollars at me. He'd come back to get a bite o' me. Lord, I've allus been more afraid of a spider than I have o' a man. I know how they'll jump twenty feet to bite a body. I intended to get 'im before he got me. I jist drawed back my arm and I cut drive so hard with that peach at his head that I had to hold to a limb to keep from fallin' out'n th' tree. I busted 'im right between th' eyes and he jist crumpled up like a green leaf scorched by fire—jist wound up like a ball and tumbled out'n th' tree.

"I got you this time," I says, "you damned stripped-tail thing!"

I picked peaches and put 'em in my basket. I jist about had all th' peaches I could carry down out'n th' hot tree. Lord but it was hot up among th' leaves. Jist once in awhile I could get a breath o' wind. I believe it was th' hottest smothery day I ever saw. I'd pick th' peaches fer Sall and then I'd go back to th' coal bank and dig coal. "There's something funny about this," I thought, "I dig coal in th' fall and winter and here I am pickin' peaches fer Sall to can. Maybe it's a dream." Then I thought: "It can't be a dream. Here are th' peaches and here am I up here in th' tree. Right here is a good peach. I'll reach up and get it and take a bite!"

I pulled th' peach down. It had big red spots on it that colored it like a body's cheeks when th' winter wind stings

'em. I was jist ready to put my mouth over th' peach and
bite out a hunk when I looked upon th' limb above me and
here was that snake and spider. Both side by side. They'd
doubled teamed on me. They'd got together down on th'
ground. Now they'd come back up in th' tree to fight me.
"I know this tree," I says to 'em both. "It is my peach tree.
It is up on th' hill above my pasture field. This peach tree
is th' big tree that allus bore so many peaches. It's th' one
in th' low swag by th' old rotted white oak stump. It's my
tree and by-God I'll defend it. No snake nor spider can run
me off'n my own premises."

They jist looked at me. I didn't expect 'em to speak.
Who ever heard o' one speakin'. They jist bite a body 's
all. "If I hit one o' 'em," I thought, "th' other'n bite me
shore as God made th' peaches. I'll jist get down out'n th'
empty tree and let 'em have it. I've got th' peaches. They
have th' tree." I jist went down th' ladder and th' last I
saw o' 'em they's settin' upon th' limb like two chickens
gone to roost. Eyes a shinin't like silver dollars.

I dumped th' basket o' peaches in th' barrel. I hated to get
close to th' barrel fer I smelt th' sulphur. I'd haf to tell Sall
about th' snake and th' spider. She wouldn't believe me.
She'd say that I'd been dreamin'. I'd ast 'er why she give
me th' old sulphurin' barrel to put th' peaches into. I'd
have a good'n on 'er! I jist laughed and laughed. But I'd
picked th' barrel o' peaches. I's wet with sweat a-doin' it
too. Now I'd light my pipe and have a smoke.

I set down on th' ground. I's purty tired-out. I pulled my
homemade terbacker crums from my pocket and I put a
handful in my pipe. I's tampin' 'em down with my finger. I
heard somebody comin' over th' hill talkin'. It was right
back o' my peach orchard. You know where that patch
comes around th' hill. I never heard as much laughin' in all
my life. Sounded like a whole crowd o' men. I felt in my
pocket fer a match but I couldn't find one. I says: "It's all

damned funny. It's jist like I was when I's a boy. I ust to
dream I's tryin' to make water. I'd get about ready and
somebody's face would pop up. Then I'd run someplace
else and get behind th' sprouts. I'd get ready again and
somebody'd slip up on me. I never could find a place. In th'
mornin' I'd wake up with a big wet place in my bed—a big
yaller circle on th' clean white sheet.

Then Mom would come 'n say: "Why can't you wake
up? You big Lummix! Jist lay there and sleep and float th'
bed off! Look at my sheet now! It'll be a purty thing to
hang out on th' clothes line to dry and all th' neighbor
wimmen and th' girls to see! What can I tell them! Hargis
floated th' bed away again last night." This must be a dream
too. I couldn't eat a peach fer a snake and a spider! A spider
big as a quart cup! Huh! I couldn't smoke my pipe fer I
couldn't find a match!

"But it's not a dream," I says to myself, "here's my peach
orchard. It's in June. It has to be June. I'm gatherin'
peaches. Here's th' green leaves wilted in th' sun. Right
over there is th' big beech on th' pint. Yander is th' big
poplar on th' knoll. Right over yander is my house. I can
hear somebody comin'."

When I turned my head around to look th' way I heard
th' voices I seen four men comin' down th' hill. They's
laughin' and talkin' and havin' a lot o' fun. Jist layin' th'
talk off with their hands. They's comin' right down th' path
toward me. I didn't know a one o' 'em. They's smokin'
cigars and pipes and makin' merry. Big puffs o' smoke were
circlin' above their heads.

I says: "Howdy, fellars! One o' you ain't got a match
have you?"

"Ain' that funny," says a big freckled-faced fellar with
horse-teeth.

Then they all begin to laugh. They'd bend over and pat
their knees and laugh.

"He wants a match," says a little sawed-off dumpy fellar with black hair combed straight back over his head.

"What do you know about 'im wantin' a match?" says a tall bean-pole boy with a red face and little mouse teeth. "Jist to think he wants a match."

"Yes," says a big barrel-bellied boy, with red hair and bird-egg blue eyes, "th' poor fellar wants a match. Ain't one of you fellars got a match? Don't you see he's got his pipe filled and wants to smoke? Say, open up your hearts and give th' poor fellar a match. Ain't you wanted to smoke and didn't have a match?"

Then they bent over and laughed again. The fat boy with th' bird-egg eyes jist shook all over when he laughed. "Wants a match," he'd say. Then he'd laugh. "What do you know about that! Ast me fer a match. He don't know who I am?" Then he bent over and laughed again.

"Hep yourself to th' peaches boys," says th' bean-pole fellar.

"Don't mind if I do," says th' fat fellar. "Old Hargis don't know who I am. He ust to know me! I know him don't I? Sure, I do. I'd know 'im anyplace."

I says: "How do you know my name? I've never seen you anyplace. I don't know you."

Then all the men laughed. "He don't know you," says th' sawed-off dumpy fellar with th' black hair. "You'd better tell 'im who you are."

"Do you remember th' time your Pap had that little bottom in tame huckleberries below th' old Koonse Saw-Mill?"

"Yes," I says.

"Do you remember beatin' up Austin Finnie?" he says to me.

"Yes," I says. "And his brother Jim come over and put a shiner under each one o' my eyes!"

"That ain't got a thing to do with it what brother Jim done. I am Austin Finnie!"

"W'y, you've been dead fer twenty-six years. You are buried at Three-Mile Hill."

"You jist think I've been dead. I've been alive fer th' first time in my life. Nothin' to bother me now. Nothin' to worry me. I thought I'd come over and bring th' boys to welcome you home. Welcome you to your new life!"

"I'm not dead," I says. "I know damn well I ain't dead. I'm a livin' mortal. This is my peach orchard. These are my peaches. Up in that peach tree is a spider and a snake."

"Yes," says Austin, "they are there. That is right. So am I over at Three-Mile Hill too. Jist a part o' me that don't amount to a damn. You didn't know me because I was a boy when I left here."

"Allright," I says, "I still don't believe you're Austin Finnie. I believe I'm dreamin'. If you're Austin Finnie show me where that tree fell on you and run a limb into your right lung that killed you."

"Allright," says Austin, and he jerked his shirt open and showed me th' big pink scar.

"Good God," I says.

"You don't know th' fellars I got with me either do you?"

"W'y I don't know none o' you fellars. You've jist told me you's Austin Finnie and showed me th' scar where th' tree fell on you. Th' Austin Finnie I knowed was jist a boy fourteen years old when th' tree fell on 'im."

"Well I've had to grow up damn it," says Austin. "I couldn't stay fourteen forever. Don't you know that!"

"You don't know me neither," says th' tall bean-pole boy. "You ought to."

"No," I says, "I don't know you."

"I'm your brother Wilburn. Jist growed a little is all."

"You don't look like me," I says.

"Of course not," says he, "you take atter Ma's people and I take atter Pa's people."

"My brother Wilburn died when he's eight years old. It was twenty years ago. I can't remember 'im very well."

"I'm Wilburn Dixon. I've jist growed a little 's all. I run around with th' fellars from right around here. You know these two fellars too, Brother Hargis. Buster Broughton, you remember 'im. Died with th' measles in 1914. Pert Rister died with th' fever in 1916."

"Durned if I don't believe I know old Buster," I says, "I thought your coal-black hair and eyes I'd seen sommers before."

I shook his hand. I says: "I'm glad to see you again. Now I'm beginnin' to believe you boys. My new-found Brother Wilburn and my old friend Pert. Let me shake your hands. Boys I'd a-never knowed you!"

"Of course not," says Buster, "we've all growed so. But you've thought a lot about us since we've been gone. That's why we've come to welcome you. Thought we might have a card game or something to show you how glad we are to see you."

"We's jist funnin' with you about th' match," says Pert Rister.

Brother Wilburn, Buster and Pert jist bent over and laughed and laughed.

Austin looked at me with hard eyes. He didn't laugh. He hadn't got over th' beatin I give 'im when we's boys. It allus bore on my mind atter he died. But he ought to forget. We's jist boys then.

"You said you wanted a match," says Pert Rister, "I'll give you one. I ain't got a match but I'll get you some fire."

He just cracked his hands together and a blaze shot up. They all 'peared to vanish in smoke. I never seen which way they went. Nearly all th' peaches had been taken from my barrel. Th' snake spread its thin hard lips up in th' tree and grinned at me. Th' spider's eyes got brighter. They had their heads close together and looked down at me. That was th' last I remember. I was awfully hot.

I wanted to sleep. Th' air got so hot and smothery. I was so wet with sweat. My clothes were wet as water could make 'em.

Then I thought I's in th' bed. Don't remember how I got there. I thought it had all been a dream. Now I was in th' bed with Sall. I thought I had th' kivers wrapped around me and I couldn't get no breath.

Then I got my head out and got a little breath o' fresh air. Then I went to sleep—gradually—a smothery, sweaty, sort of sleep with a heavy quilt upon my back.

Th' next thing I remember was I woke up on t'other side o' th' hill. I was layin' on a quilt on th' ground.

I says: "What's happened?" Sall was beside me cryin'. She says: "Don't you know, Hargis? Honey, don't you know th' mine caved in? They've had to dig you out?"

"Am I hurt," I says, "have I got any bones broke?"

"Ask no questions," says Sall, "but lay right still under th' blankets."

I never saw so many people around th' old mine. But there was a new entry now. It was on t'other side o' th' hill. When th' coal bank caved in it just dropped down.

Where th' earth dropped down all th' other miners dropped a hole straight down. We's nearly to th' top o' th' ground fer we's runnin' under th' saddle o' th' hill and th' roof was brittle.

"A big piece of rock," says Sall, "was all that saved you. It fell and you fell beside it. Th' roof come down and th' big rock by your side helt it up and made a little room fer you. There was a crack that went down through th' ground to you. Jist looks like th' Lord was with us."

Murt is cryin' as she comes over th' hill and I say to Sall:

"What about Lefty?" Murt comes from th' entrance o' th' coal bank on t'other side o' th' hill—she hurries down through th' corn-stalks where th' corn was cut last fall. Th' mud is shoe-mouth deep. Th' sun has come out and melted th' frozen ground.

"He's dead," says Sall. "They took him out at th' main entry. Th' big heap o' dirt fell between you. It got Lefty. Couldn't take 'im out from this side. Lefty is dead."

"Oh he's dead, he's dead," says Murt, wringin' her hands and a cryin'. "Lefty is dead. Lefty is dead."

"Carry me up some, you fellars," I says, "and let me look at that hole where you dug me out." Steve Morton, Shucks Pennix, and Eb Flannery, and John Stableton took a corner apiece o' th' bedsprings I was layin' on and carried me up where I could look over. Lord, I jist couldn't believe I'd been dug out'n that hole. No wonder I's meetin' th' dead and smotherin' pickin' peaches.

I says: "Sall, how long have I been under this hill?"

"Two days, Honey," she says. "Monday night when you didn't come home I knowed something was wrong. So I run down and told Shucks Pennix. He went to th' coal bank and took a crowd o' men. They begin to hunt fer you and found th' coal bank caved in. Th' men know about th' roof. They found th' entry you's in and it was caved in so they come outside and walked over th' hill and found th' slip. One crew o' men dug all night down through th' slip. One crew o' men worked from th' other side o' th' hill. They went back through th' main entrance and dug from th' other side. Then a shift o' men relieved each crew th' next day. Four shifts o' men have been workin' to get you out. About th' time they got you out, they took Lefty out dead from th' other side."

"I'd like to know what's th' matter with me," I says. "Can't move my arms and legs. 'Pears like my breath is short too. I believe my slats are all caved in."

"That's it, Honey," says Sall, "and your spine fractured. Doctor Norris was right here when they hauled you out'n th' hole. You got both arms broke, and one side o' your ribs caved in. But that's all right, Honey. He says you'll live. Look at poor Lefty! Look at poor Murt!"

"I envy Lefty," I says. "Fellars carry me over th' pint on t'other side o' th' hill and let me see old Lefty."

Th' boys took me away from th' deep-deep rabbit hole they dug me from.

They carried me on th' mattress springs over th' muddy ground where I could see thousands o' tracks in th' mud and th' corn-stalks was all mashed down and th' sprouts skint. I tell you it was good to feel th' winter wind against my face and feel th' Kentucky sunshine again. I's jist a old wreck.

My body would never be again what it had been. Th' boys carryin' me'd say: "Be careful now. Don't slip and fall with 'im. Take it easy. Ground is slick from thawin'."

All that stuff atter I'd been under tons o' dirt and rock and got out a livin' mortal to spend th' rest o' my days in bed or in a swing built to th' jist like old Ephraim Potts did th' time he got his back broke.

There was a big crowd standin' around th' main entrance o' our coal bank. Lefty'd jist been hauled out'n th' mine a little while. He was layin' on th' coal-buggy. Th' buggy was holdin' a different load o' coal.

His face was bloody. His old dirty overalls was a red color now. They'd been soaked in Lefty's own blood. Murt come back across th' hill with Sall. She's leanin' on Sall's shoulder and cryin'.

I jist laid on my bed and looked at Lefty. It hadn't been very long ago that he was a powerful man. He could dig more coal than any man I'd ever seen go into th' mines. But he wouldn't dig any more coal. He didn't know what it was all about now.

His big body was layin' upon th' buggy like a big lump
of red-painted coal. He had th' look o' pain on his lips jist
like he'd been shovin' his whole weight against a buggy
load o' coal stuck on th' track. His shoulders looked nearly
as wide as th' coal-buggy and his powerful big muscled legs
fell limp over th' end o' th' buggy. Lefty, my old buddie
was dead.

I says to Sall: "I envy Lefty."

"You ought to thank God," says Sall, "that you got out
alive. Lefty is dead."

"I got out jist a hull o' a man," I says, "jist like a holler
oak. Th' heart o' me is gone, I'm no more. I'll haf to go
through life like this. I'll never be th' same. Lefty missed
all o' this. He's better off in th' long run."

It took eight men to carry me home. Four carried me
until they got tired. They walked along and rested while
four more men took me and carried me apiece. I took my
last look at th' old hill that had been a killer o' men. Th'
roof over th' coal was brittle. That had caused it all. Men
feared but they went back and dug th' coal. They had to
have money. They had to live.

"It don't matter how many posts a body sets under a
roof like that," says Shucks Pennix, "that roof is liable to
fall any time. Lefty and Hargis had th' worst coal bank o'
th' bunch. But th' other coal banks are jist about as bad!"

I never talked. I jist listened. Sall walked along and
looked at me and kept th' blankets tucked around my bed
so th' cold winter wind couldn't blow under. I saw th' big
heap o' yaller dirt in th' field where they'd gone down and
got me. It looked like a big yaller chimney standin' out
there in th' cornfield. I looked at th' winter oaks standin'
along my patch so silent and contented and waitin' fer th'
spring.

I was goin' home now. It jist didn't seem right that I'd
been away from home a couple o' days and nights. It

seemed like I'd jist waked up in bed atter a night o' sleep.
I jist thought: "Wonder if it ain't that way fer Lefty?
Jist waked up atter a night o' sleep. But Lefty ain't broke
up like I am. Lefty is better off. I hope he is. Old Lefty was
a good worker. But we won't dig no more coal together
from under this old hill."

I couldn't wipe th' tears from my eyes. Sall would walk
along and wipe 'em off. She knowed why I shed 'em. She
didn't say anything. I didn't neither. Th' men kept walkin'
along with me. I wanted to say but I didn't: "It's my last
vacation in Hell. Jist to think about all th' wild dreams I
had! That snake and that spider! I can see 'em yet! Gettin'
so hot too! Gatherin' peaches!"

I says: "Sall, you got all that sulphur barrel o' peaches
I've picked fer you canned yet?"

"What peaches, Honey?" she says.

"I've been pickin' peaches fer you and a stripped-tailed
spider and a big green snake tried to run me out'n th' tree.
I picked a whole barrel fer you and th' sun was so hot. I
thought I's goin' to die. I wanted to smoke and couldn't
get a match to light me pipe!"

Atter I told Sall this I laughed. She says: "Oh, yes—I've
got 'em canned." She thought I's talkin' out'n my head.
Th' men carryin' me begin to look funny at one another
and shake their heads and nod.

They thought I's out'n my right mind and all done fer
but I warn't. I'd get all right. I'd be like th' big silent oaks
they's carryin' me under. I'd jist haf to stand and wait th'
long winter through fer th' spring.

WHIP-POOR-WILLIE

YOU'D KNOW HOW HARD it was to get married if you wasn't a very good-looking fellar with only one eye. That is the way it is with me. There's not but two eyes among the three men in our family. Not enough eyes, I'd say. Pa's just got one eye. Got hit in the eye with a rock and lost it. Was born with two good eyes. And I was born with two good eyes, too, but I got one shot out at church one night. Brother Edd was born with two good eyes till his wife shot 'em out with a double-barreled shotgun. We need more eyes in our family. It's been hard for me to get a wife. God knows I've worked hard and skimped and saved to get a little ahead so I can get a wife. I got a farm to take a wife to. I've raised enough good barley and sold it, and calves, hogs, corn, milk, eggs, cream and butter and young calves. W'y, I've saved my money so some woman would pick me up for a man that would make her a living, instead of starving to death. But it's my looks. Women just won't come close to me. I know I need a glass eye but I just ain't put out the money for one yet.

I had been out cutting brush on the hill. Was burning a terbacker bed. Had worked hard, and when I went to the house that night I never was so surprised in my life. I walked in, and there stood one of the biggest birds I ever laid my peepers on. And Pa—poor old Pa—he turns his good eye up to me and I turns my good eye up to him. It's his right eye that's good and my right eye that's good and

283

when we look toward one another—w'y our heads are kindly squared around. And Pa says: "Gibbie, meet Willie Showwalter."

And I says: "Sure glad to meet you, Willie."

"Champion boxer in the Navy for two years," says Willie. "And I come back here and got tangled up with a skirt. You know old Locum Hunt's girl Daisy—well, I jumped the broom with her and since old Locum lives in one of your houses, I'd like to rent that log house down there by them two graves."

"W'y, I got that old house rented to Widder Ollie Sperry," I says. God, I didn't want him in my house. I saw that right now.

"No you ain't," says Pa. "Widder Sperry was out here and she said she was going to rent a house closer to town where she could get family washings to do and not have to carry 'em plum across that hill."

I never said a word. I was afraid to say anything. You ought just to see Willie Showwalter. No wonder he whipped everything in the Navy. W'y, his arms are big as our gate-posts and woolly as a strawberry patch. And durned if he doesn't have them mean, slate-colored snake-eyes—narrow, bean-slit eyes. His hair has two crowns in it. That is a sign of a man that will kill you. So I didn't take no chances on a fellar like him. I just broke out and said it too soon: "The house is yours on condition that we draw up a article in the words of writing and that you give me half and I furnish everything. I furnish you the house, the garden, and cow pasture free for two cows. I furnish you seed corn and the mules and plows and hoes, and you do the work. This will be the nature of the word in the writings."

I spoke before I thought. I only thought there on the floor: "What if he hits me in the other eye? What if he ups and pops me with that other fist? W'y I would be as blind as my brother. I'd go crazy, for I'd never learn to pick the guitar and saw the fiddle like my brother Edd has to pass the time away. It would kill me to keep away from my work—couldn't get out with a hoe and cut weeds. I just couldn't stand it to be blind. I'll let him have the log house to live in. I want to keep my other eye." That's why I let him have the place. Poor old Ma setting in front of the fire smoking her pipe. She never said a word, for she likes Locum's wife Effie—that's Daisy's mother. Ma just set there and pulled long draws of smoke from the tiny pipe-stem and blowed the smoke in the fireplace. Ma and Effie kindly had it fixed up for me to marry Daisy once, and she went back on me. Just because of my looks.

Oh, but if you could just see Daisy, you'd want her on your place to live, just to look at her if nothing else. W'y it done me a lot of good just to think about that girl. I used to just think if I had her for a wife—pretty as she was— hair the color of ripe wheat-straws and eyes as blue as clear summer skies, hands that are too pretty to put in dish-water— Oh, but she's one of the prettiest girls I ever laid my eye on. Just to watch her walk and see her pretty figure. I always wanted that girl for my wife. I can't help it if I am ten years older than she is. Ten years don't stand in any man's way between him and the woman he loves. And the only thing now that stood in the way was her marriage certificate to that big brute of a Willie Show-walter. W'y I'd heard a lot about the Showwalters. Never heard any good about them either. They's always fighting somebody or fighting among themselves, making moon-shine whiskey on other people's farms, for the Showwalters never owned a place. And just to think that big ugly brute could come right on one of my farms and steal the prettiest girl my renters had. I ought to a done had me a glass eye made and I would a had her. I'm as good-looking as that brute—champion boxer of the Navy my right eye! What good's that going to do him and her when he starts plowing these old hills to make a living! Never will forget when that big devil left our house. He was barely low enough to miss the top of our door. He just filled the door of our house. And he married a little woman and a pretty woman —fair as a white hollyhock.

It was March. I'll never forget it. Time was here when a body got the smell of the wood-smoke in his craw and the call back to the plow. I know I got the smell of the cornfields in my craw. I wanted to start the plow and smell the dead leaves, the greenbriars, the corn-stalks and the oak sprouts and sassafras sprouts burn before me. I wanted to see the brush-pile flames and see the furrows roll. I just wanted to get Daisy off'n my mind. I remember how Willie and Locum went off our hill that night. Had the lantern lit. Of course Willie didn't need it with them snake-eyes of his'n. But Locum's like Pa. He's getting old and can't see none too well nohow. I remember how the wind hit against the poplar twigs by the pigpen. I remember there's the first green we see from our house every spring. It's the poplar twigs by the pigpen.

Pa comes upstairs where I started pulling my britches off to get in bed, and he says, "Son, I thought that was the best thing to do. Give that fellar a trial on the farm just because of poor old Locum, Effie, and little Daisy. Been your farm for the last ten years. As well as I could see his eye, I didn't like the looks of it. Looks to me like a bad egg. I thought we could handle him. Got some pretty good law in the county now, and if he just starts anything, w'y we'll have the law on him."

"That's not what I'm worrying about, Pa. I don't believe we ought to have let him have had that place. It's going to cause trouble." I didn't tell Pa that I was in love with Daisy. You know, Pa just thinks I never love a woman because I live with him and Ma and I'm past thirty years old. Pa thinks my days for dreaming of a woman are over. But believe me they are just beginning. I never wanted a woman any more in my life than I want one now. I just lay here in the bed and look out over my fields in March—covered with starlight—and pine to have a woman to sleep right here on my arm and enjoy life with me.

But we got Willie on the place now. We got the articles fixed up. Uncle Mel was witness and Locum was a witness. They signed them. All set for the big year and a big crop. Redbirds back to the poplar twigs. Spring just around the corner. The sweet smell of the green leaves coming back to the elm-trees and the poplar-trees. The woods filled with wild flowers and ferns. Oh, it makes me want a wife more than ever. Even the birds have wives, the rabbits, the black snakes. All of them have wives. And here I am among people—but women just don't take to me.

Spring here, and Pa says: "If that Willie Showwalter is any account to work, it will be the first fellar that's ever come back to the hills from the Navy that's worth a damn to work."

Willie said, before he moved in the log house below us, he'd put a roof on the kitchen if I'd rive the boards. He said he'd clean off the bank above the house so if the fire got out it couldn't get down to the house when they were away and burn the house down. There's Freed Pennix's crazy boy been setting fire out in the woods to watch 'em burn. I didn't want to take no chances. So I put this in the article.

"Just been down to the house," says Ma, "to see how Daisy is fixed. I'll tell you it is a plum sight to see how little that girl is making out on. A old stove that wouldn't burn good dry locust stove-wood. Got a old bed that her Ma give her. A old broom that she made herself by tying broom-sage onto a nice, straight stick. That's all they got that I saw in the house, besides some old boxes and a few old plates, knives, spoons, and saucers and a water-bucket and a gourd dipper. Looks to me like she driv her ducks to a bad market by taking that thing."

Ma was a little out'n breath and wheezing a little after climbing the hill in front of our house and sucking on that old pipe of hern. I never said a thing to Ma, but I thought a whole lot I didn't say. I know Effie wanted me to marry Daisy, and Ma wanted me to have her, and if that fellar just fools and fiddles around and moonshines, Pa'll help me put his big brute frame off'n this place, because Pa is a saved man.

I was down on the hill and I wished you could a seen that big devil plowing. Lazy as a elephant going around the bluffs in the April sunlight. Poor little Daisy, right out there with him. Her right up there in front of the mules a-cutting stalks and sprouts. Her pretty little self right out in the hot sun, working for that man. That's the way of a woman, they say, when she loves a man. She'll die and go to hell for him. He never has a fault to her. And if he ever does anything, w'y somebody else is the cause of it. W'y, I'd give everything that I own if I had a dough-beater pretty as Daisy who thought that much of me. A woman pretty as Daisy to just love me to death. I hid in the brush and watched them. I looked with my good right eye through the brush at them. He plowed awhile and then he went up to her—she threw down the hoe. He kissed her and kissed her, and she kissed him. And when she kissed him, I prayed to God in the heaven above that he would die and fall right in his tracks and I could just run down out'n the bushes and grab her and she'd love me just like she was loving him. But God wouldn't answer no such prayer as that. Praying for a man to die so I could get his wife.

Just to think, I can do about anything else that I want to do, get about anything else that I want to get—yet, I can't get the woman I want. I fooled around until she fiddled away from me—the woman I loved—one right here on my farm. She just happened to be at Plum Grove church one night and this bird was there and full of licker as a dog-tick—saw Daisy and broke his neck to come home with her. Met her right about where I lost my eye. Right at church. Oh, I'll never get over losing that eye. Never put another quarter in the collection plate since. I figure that they owe me. I figure that somebody owes me for that eye. Old Willie didn't go with her but a few times till he was bringing her around the road with his right arm plum around her and she had her left arm part of the way around him. They'd listen to the whippoorwills sing. Come right under them tall sycamores below Locum's house and they'd stand there in that dark puddle of night where the moon couldn't shine and they'd spoon and spoon. She just fell in love with him. That's all there is to it—him a good-for-nothing lazy devil with a woman in every port, and me come to her with clean hands and a loving heart and couldn't get her. That's a woman for you, but it didn't keep me from loving her. I just loved her to death, in my own mind, and dreamed that she was in my arms every night.

Pa passed their house a lot. I was afraid if I went past there too much I'd be tempted to say something about love to her—it in the spring and me dying for love. So I just thought the best thing for me to do was to stay away. Of course I slipped around and peeped through the bushes once in a while to watch them work. W'y half the time he'd be stretched out on a quilt under the shade-tree, and she'd be working hard as she could work. She'd be hoeing corn. She'd always take the lead row of corn on that big thing. She could do more with a hoe than he could. And he never did clean off the bank back of the house. That

was in the article in the written word. But he just didn't
do it. I believed what Pa told me about these boys coming
back from the Navy.

"Pa," I says, "we got a white elephant on our hands.
That Willie Showwalter won't work. W'y he ain't even
cleaned off that bank back of the house. He's not any
good."

"Got to take it easy, Gibbie. If we don't, we're liable
to have a lot of trouble with that fellar. He's been looking
around for somebody to fight him at the County Fair. We
got to watch that fellar. He's liable to take foul-holts on
us because we got a little bit a land. When you get your
hand in the lion's mouth, get it out easy as you can.

"I believe," says Pa, "that fellar's making moonshine on
this place. He's making it on my farm or your farm, one.
I'm going to find out, and if he is, there's going to be a
time. I'll clean this hollow out. I can't help it if he has been
in the Navy. When a McDuggan gets his dander up, w'y
it don't make no difference if the whole American Navy
is before him."

Pa ran in the house and got the gun. He went around
through the pasture like a man going to kill a squirrel.
W'y he went around the hills that were in timber and took
the gun barrel and parted the sprouts under the tall trees
looking for the still. Says Pa: " 'Pears like I've been smell-
ing moonshine right early of a morning when I feed the
hogs. 'Pears like it comes on the first morning wind." And
Pa hunt all over the hills for a still. Used to Pa wouldn't a
done a thing like this. Pa's saved and is trying to live a
better life. His church don't believe in music, guitars, paint,
powder, or whiskey. It don't believe in having your fingernails all dolled up. It's the Church of God. A lot of people
call 'em Holy Rollers, but they're a different brand alto-
gether.

Pa came home and he says: "W'y I've looked every-

place. I can't see a sign of a still. W'y, you can't fool me
about a still. I used to make moonshine myself. I just
thought he was making moonshine the way he slept around
of a day out under the shade-trees while his pretty little
wife had to hoe the corn. And one day I come along and
found her plowing. He was under a apple-tree at the end
of the field fast asleep. And I just went over and kicked him
in the seat of the pants, and I says: 'What do you mean
letting a woman plow and you asleep with a nice little
Christian woman as you've got. Can't be a word said about
her but what is a good word.' And he waked up and rubbed
his eyes and says: 'Just sleepy, Mr. McDuggan.' And I says:
'Sleepy, hell. First time a woman has ever plowed them
mules since the day they were born. Now you get your
onery tail up off this ground and get a hold of them plowlines or I'll have you arrested for vagrancy.' I don't care
how big he was. Don't care where he had been. He took
me at my word. He got right up and took a hold of that
plow, and his wife was ashamed to let people know just
what a damned onery thing she got."

"You sure he ain't moonshining?" I says again to Pa.

"Quite sure," says Pa. "He just ain't worth powder and
lead to blow out his lights, when it comes to work. I told
Locum that this morning. Locum said if his crop got too
far in the weeds that him and the boys would go in for a
day or so and dig him out. Said he could see now that Daisy
had driv her ducks to a bad market. Too late now to cry
about it. Said he didn't believe in second marriages, and
since she got her tail end blistered, she'd have to set on the
blister. He said he didn't believe that Willie was making
moonshine. Said he was getting a lot to drink from some
place. Come in and raised a fuss with Daisy. Poor little
thing. Her only sixteen and married to that thing."

I just come in one saying: "Yes, I wanted to wait till
she was seventeen or eighteen. It just didn't pay me to wait.

If it was to do over again, I'd marry her at fifteen. Before she had time to know just how ugly I was. Let her marry me before she ever got out and saw a lot of men."

Ma don't believe in second marriages for anybody. It don't make no difference to Ma how big the blister was the first time—she always told my sisters they had to set on it. If the blister was big as a frying-pan, they had to set on it. I had it made up in my mind if Pa got him for making moonshine and they sent him to the pen, w'y then if Daisy wanted a divorce she could get it. That was lawful ground. It looked like the quill was going to split sooner or later and I wanted it to so I could get Daisy.

"Just married her," says Lottie Starbuck to Ma, "to get what he wanted. Just the way of a man. He wants what he wants and when he gets it he is through. The way of that big onery devil. That's the way they say when a man stays in the Navy four years. W'y I wouldn't marry a man that come out'n the Navy for nothing on earth. No matter if his head was strung with gold. Just to think of him fooling with women in Chinee, Ja-pan, and all them low-down strollops in Africa and South America—not our kind of women—w'y the cross-eyed, cotton-headed hellions, and then a coming back here to a decent woman. No wonder they're never satisfied. Poor girl of Effie's married to that low-down hellion. W'y I live around the pint close to his mother's. She says he's no account to work. And you know when a mother confesses that her son ain't no good to work—then, he really ain't no good to work. She says he's been onery in the Navy. Said it was the Navy, though, that ruint him."

Ma just draws in a puff of smoke and blows it out again. I like to see old women smoke their pipes, but I don't like to hear them gossip about another man, even if I don't like the man. Even if I do want his wife. It's a sight to hear Lottie go on about poor old Willie. Much as I'd like to

hate him, I feel sorry for him now. She just tells Ma everything right in front of me. W'y Lottie lost her man about
two years ago. Her comb has been red ever since.

"I was talking to Locum," says Pa, "and Locum said that
Willie said he just wouldn't plow corn any more in this
drouth. His little wife out there plowing again. That big
strollop laying up there in the shade. Said he'd quit work
until it rained. I'd like to know just when that fellar ever
begin work. W'y he's too lazy to ever start it. He married
that woman just to let her make him a living. And she's
from a working family and will very devilish near do it."

Oh, but it nearly broke my heart to think about her
marrying Willie Showwalter, the great champion of the
American Navy. It just killed me to think about a woman
pretty as she was getting hitched up with a rascal that had
a woman in every port. You know how that burns a man
up. If Daisy ever gets free from that prize-fighter of hern,
I'm going to have me a glass eye made, shore as God made
little green persimmons.

I thought all the time that love-quill would split wide
open. I didn't think that Daisy could stand it on and on
forever. She couldn't stand to set on that blister big as a
frying-pan. I looked out the front door by the pigpen and
here come Effie and little Daisy right behind her. They
were walking fast.

"Something must be wrong," I says to Ma, Ma a-setting
by the fireplace a-wheezing on her pipe—no fire this time
of summer, but it's a habit Ma's got, setting by the fireplace
in winter or summer and hovering over it like a chicken
with dropped wings.

"Guess somebody's sick," says Ma.

Well, they come right up in the front yard. Effie was
barefooted, with a big chew of terbacker in her mouth,
a-spitting bright amber through the cracks in her teeth.
I could tell she was mad as a hornet.

"I says," says Effie to Ma, "Daisy, if you can't live with
that thing any longer we'll get the Law. We'll see that
you can get a divorce from that thing. W'y just pick up
and leave her when he wants to. Just up and goes and
never says 'yea' nor 'nea.' The biggest feeling thing I ever
saw. All time wanting something to fight. I says to him this
morning when he passed the garden—says I—'Big boy, if
you want something to fight, come in the garden. I'll use
the hoe and you use your fist.' Believe me he made hisself
scarce down the road. Oh, I was in the mad enough to a
bit ten-penny nails in two. I just shook. Just to think how
hard it is to raise a decent girl these days and then let her
marry a thing like that. W'y it's the talk all over the neighborhood, so Lottie told me, that all the women were saying—he just married her to live with while she's young and
pretty. Now he's tired of her and he's off to another
woman. I'll kill him with a garden hoe if the Law can't do
nothing about it. I'll kill him, I'll kill him." Effie's hands
quivered, and tears streamed from her eyes. I never saw
her so mad. Well, Ma stopped smoking long enough to
wipe the tears out of her eyes.

"Ah, ah," says Ma, "men have a good time when you
come to think about it. The woman has all the trouble—the
biggest part of it. I've often wished I was a man so I could
get in the Navy and go to all parts of the world. I don't
blame a man for being in the Navy. I would go, too, if I
was a young man. Look at us, Effie. Never hardly in our
lives without a nursing baby or carrying a baby to give it
birth. I don't doubt it's the best thing she's not married.
Ain't going to have a baby are you, Honey?" says Ma,
turning to Daisy who is behind Effie, crying.

"No," says Daisy, sniffing the tears from her cheeks.

"W'y that big capon can't get a girl with baby. He's
been ruined in that Navy, Lottie tells me. Had a lot of bad
diseases. She'll never have any babies unless she gets 'em by

some other man. Oh, but she's got a blister big as a half-bushel basket to set on."

"After you raise your children you don't know what you've raised," says Ma. "Look out there setting under the pine-tree. Look at my Edd with his eyes shot out. Blind as a bat. Out there listening to the wind blow through the pine-tops and listening to the birds sing. Look at this boy Gibbie. My best boy. Got his eye shot out at a Methodist Church. You'd think a boy was safe around there, wouldn't you? Look at my man. Got one of his eyes knocked out in a rock fight. Just sometimes wonder if people wouldn't be better off if they'd never be born. Look at my girls. Raised under a decent roof. Look what happened to Clara. Look what happened to Arabella and Flora. My worst girl got the best man. You just can't tell about these things. Clara and Arabella were lucky to get a man at all. Now they got big houses of little brats to raise up and give 'em pecks of trouble. It's just that way with a woman. She don't have any sense long as she's a-bearing children. The Lord made her like that. And if she don't have no children, she'll never love her man. God made woman to want to bear children for the man she loved. And after she gets old as I am, she just wants to set around and smoke her pipe and think back about the children. Don't matter what they've done —murdered, stole, shot, thieved, hung on the gallows—they are all good children because they are her children. That's the way with a woman's life."

Ma just talked and smoked her pipe. I tell you—not because Ma's my mother—but Ma knows a lot. She can tell young girls a lot. She's not a fool. Ma's been around among the women a lot, too.

I tell you while Ma was talking I just stood and looked at Daisy. I wanted her right now. Just because I only had one eye was no sign I couldn't get babies. I tell you my heart just melted. If I could help Daisy get her divorce,

I would do it. I would spend one of my farms to get her
free from that big brute. It would be heaven here on my
farm if I just had Daisy. Summer about over, but love in the
fall with her would be just as great as it would have been
in the spring, when the birds were choosing mates, and the
snakes and the terrapins. After this drouth we had a little
corn and milk-cows. We had hay to cut and put in the
barn-loft and a few blackberries canned and some apple-
butter made and three big hogs to kill for our meat and
lard. Oh, but we could live. Thoughts ran through my
mind like wild ducks fly through fall skies.

"Well," says Effie, "I wonder if you know a good truth-
ful lawyer we can get that Willie can't offer ten dollars
more to and bribe. He might act fair. And he might not,
if he thinks Daisy wants another man. You just can't tell
about a family like them Showwalters. Don't think God
would hold it against her if she got out and got her a decent
man to live with—one that hadn't fooled with every old
strollop in the country—one that could get her a child. I'm
hunting a lawyer this very morning. Going to town to get
one to get Daisy free."

"I'll help you get a lawyer," I says, "a lawyer that understands young life. He's not been married very long. Has a
young wife. He'll understand. It's Jake Landon. You can
just tell him all your troubles. Don't have to be ashamed
about it. Walk up and tell him. We went to school together,
and that boy's a poor boy. Worked hard for his education.
He'll be as reasonable a lawyer as you can find in Green-
briar."

"Thought we might get the divorce a little under fifty
dollars. Maybe we might get the young man down in his
price. We're going to get it—though, if we have to hull
walnuts at fifty cents a bushel and pay forty dollars for it.
That'll be only eighty bushels of walnuts. My, but our

hands will be so stained with walnut stain that coal oil and lye soap won't never take it off."

"Oh, but," I thought, "Honey, it's never going to make you hull eighty bushels of walnuts. I'll see to that. Sweet little Daisy with the prettiest hands in the world. I'd see it'd never cause her all that trouble. The trouble would be in the church when Daisy got ready to marry me—her second man, and her first one living. Old women going around and talking about when the first one of us dies, that one goes to hell for living in adultry. Good Lord, I'd soon die and go to hell and live in heaven awhile on earth. I'll take my heaven on earth before I'll take my hell. That's the way I feel about it. Old women going around and putting that out."

"Come on," says Effie, "let's get to town—come on, Gibbie, and go with us. We want you to take us to the lawyer Jake and tell him we are good to pay."

"I don't want to go, Ma," says Daisy in a low, soft voice. "Willie ain't bad. I don't want to go see a lawyer. No sense paying a lawyer."

"I'll take you there," I says, "and I'll stand good for your cost of the suit if you want the divorce."

"Come on then," says Effie. "You don't want to be married to that big brute." And we started around the ridge. Daisy held back a little, and Effie led the way—barefooted, with a new cud of terbacker in her mouth, just a-spitting and mashing the briars flat with her big bare feet. I kindly hated to go to town that way and have people staring I used to be in high school with. But then I looked at Daisy with my good eye, and I thought: "You're worth having anybody to stare at me. You're worth my farm and Pa's farm and all the timber on them."

"Now," says Lawyer Jake, "to rush this case up—charge him with cruelty. Get your divorce on that ground. We can rush it right through for you. No children on the road are there?"

"Don't know if there is or not," says Daisy.

"He means, Honey, you are not going to have a baby, are you?"

"Not to my knowings," says Daisy.

"Not by that capon she's married to. Been in the Navy and galavanted around with a bunch of fureign strollops——"

"Well," says Lawyer Jake, "we'll get the ball rolling and get your divorce by the time summer is over."

Well, we's soon back home. Had all the business fixed up it took to get a divorce. Back out home and soon as she got the divorce, I planned to ask her to be my darling bride.

"Got every little thing fixed up, Ma," I says.

" 'Pears like," says Ma, "you're a taking a lot o' intrust in that gal—a gal that's right now living in adultry. I'd rather not see you marry at all as to live with her and die first and go to hell. I'd rather see you live alone the rest of your days as to marry her. What does the church say about it? What does Brother Issiac Flint say about it? W'y it would ruin all of us if you's to marry that gal and bring her in here. W'y you can't tell what that Willie Showwalter will do. No more pride in that family than to live off the Government and drink unstrained cowmilk warm from the cow's sack—then you play the second fiddle to a man like that—you'd have to law all your farm away before the thing is over. If you marry her and get blistered, you'll have to set on the blister if it's as big as a nail-keg."

Lord, the whole thing was right up to me. I've been a good Methodist, but the Methodist Church and all the winged Brethren can stay out'n my love affairs. It's none of their business if my wife's been married five times before she married me. When a man loves a woman he loves her. That's the way I feel about it. You durn tooten.

"W'y we just let that boy have the house down there because he married your girl, Effie," says Pa. "That's the only reason. Didn't think about him turning out like this. W'y they tell me he's been about every place in the world."

"That's right," says Effie. "He's been too many places and has galavanted around with too many loose women. He come up the other day—the sneaking thing—and told Locum to tell me that I could have all their garden stuff but five bushels of Irish taters and a bushel of sweet taters. Said he wanted to sell that many and get him a few dollars to get on the road again. Said he wasn't through seeing all this old world. Said he wanted to see the Pacific Ocean again—said he wanted to fight in the ring again before he got too old to take it. Said he didn't want to sweat around on all these old hills and hoe corn and bring up a family— I told Locum—no use for him to talk about a family—and him like a bar-hog. And I'd take all the house plunder, for I'd put it in the house for them—I'd take the chickens, for I hatched the eggs for them under setting hens and give 'em to 'em just for the raising. I give 'em two of our old spotted sow's last litter. I'd take them back, for they belonged to me. But he could dig the taters—we'd give him that much to get rid of him."

I just up and went down to the house where they lived. I thought I'd see Daisy there working around the house— moving her furniture or the chickens—or cutting weeds in the late garden corn. I went through the woods. And when I got on that hill right above the garden—w'y, sure enough, I saw her in the garden just a-digging away. She's a good girl to work. That's all she knows—is work. I thought now would be the time to pop the question to her. So I slips down through the bushes—down to the end of the garden— around past the willows by the end of the creek. And I run right up to her—put my hands over her eyes and I says: "Who is it?" And she didn't guess. And I says: "Guess."

And she says: "G-G-Gibbie." And I says: "Right you are, Sugar Babe." And she just acted like a little girl that's never been kissed. God, I just grabbed her right in my arms and it was heaven to hold her in my arms and to love her on my own big farm—on my garden premises. I squeezed her hard enough to crack her tender little ribs. I was afraid of breaking one. "It's the first time a girl's been in my arms in five years, Honey," I says to her. "God, I love you."

About that time, just like a thunderbolt out of the quiet heavens, a whippoorwill says: "Whip-poor-willie. Whip-poor-willie. Whippoorwillie. Quit. Quit. Quit." Just right in broad daylight. And I let my loving holts go on her and I says: "W'y that's funny, a whippoorwill a-hollering this time o' year, in the middle o' the afternoon." And she looked up at me with that pretty little mouth and a queer little smile and says: "I think it's funny, too." And I went back to love her and it hollered again. Every time I started to kiss her, w'y it started hollering—a funny thing. I remembered the place here was hanted. A woman lived here once, so the story goes, and she had a mean husband—so she fixed her little children (three of them) and her lazy man a good dinner and went upstairs, tied a sheet around her neck and to the bedpost and jumped out the winder. She hung herself. Now a headless woman can be seen here at this house—and something that goes like all the dishes falling out'n the safe—something like a wolf on the roof has been seen with a big mouth and white teeth tearing off the shingles. I just thought it was that hant. I run down toward Daisy's Pappie's house at the lower end of the farm. We just left the hoe there in the garden.

Summer leaves turned into brown—autumn kept coming on. Sweet-tater vines turned black. Corn was shocked. Cane was getting ripe to make in lassies. And don't you know that man of hern didn't leave.

Effie says to Ma: "W'y he comes down at the end of

the lane and sings so Daisy can hear him. Gets a little closer
every night."

I just couldn't believe it. I was going to see Daisy on
Sunday, Wednesday, and Friday nights. Them was my
courting nights. A day between for sleep. When I'd see
Daisy, I could tell she had been crying a lot of times, and
I'd say: "W'y Honey, what's you been crying about,
lovey?" And she'd say: "It's because I love you so." And
I'd just grab her with loving holts and squeeze her fit to
die. I'd love her and she'd just cry and I'd call her my
Honey. And she'd cry that much the harder. It was just
hard to tell about her.

It was on Tuesday night, and I ups and goes down to
her Pappie Locum Hunt's place. I just couldn't stay away.
It wasn't the right night, but I went anyway. The trees
were so pretty on my farm and the corn in the shock. I do
say I have a pretty farm to take a woman to. All I need,
as I have just said, is the glass eye. When I passed the house,
I saw Effie standing in the yard, barefooted and squirting
terbacker—arms folding. She's a-watching Daisy a-going
down the road just as you'll watch a turkey hen to her
nest. And I was watching her, too—only Effie didn't see
me, but I saw Effiie, and Daisy didn't see neither one of us.
Daisy was going right toward that whippoorwill. Leaves
falling now, and when the leaves fall in Kentucky, it is late
for a whippoorwill. Daisy just kept going, and I just kept
follering her. "Whippoorwillie, whip-poor-willie." And
Daisy made a dive right in the tall bushes. She threw her
arms around that big brute's neck, and she says: "Oh, my
poor Willie. Oh, I have not whipped poor Willie—I've not
whipped poor Willie—all last night when you sung it on
t'other hill it run through my head like blazes of fire."

And he says: "My ittle Oochie-Boochie." And she says:
"My ittle Oochie-Boochie-Poochie." I thought I could love.
But the way they loved was a lesson for me. God, it was

sickening. I just couldn't stand it. I says: "Hell with a glass
eye for any woman. I'll just do without the damned eye.
Poor old Ma—poor old Ma—she's all right." And I just left
them there, loving in the bushes, and Effie right below
them, squirting terbacker juice between cracks in her teeth
—with a great big half-moon smile on her lips and her
hands folded with that "come and get me, Honey" look in
her moonstruck face. God, I took through the bushes
home. I says: "I'll sleep in my own bed. See the moonlight
on my fields myself. I'll not get that damned glass eye. No
skirt can make me do it. You can't tell no more about a
woman than you can the wind or a mule. The wind blows
no certain way—the mule has no set time to kick."

SIX SUGAR MAPLES ON THE HILL

I WAS A-HELPIN CHARLIE MEADOWS cut Cy Thombs' saw-timber in Bee Tree Hollow. I'd been a-helpin Charlie cut timber all winter. It was February and we'd just about finished timber-cuttin when a big man crawled like a lizard among the tree-tops to our shanty. We'd just gone to the shanty to get our supper.

"Howdy, boys," he said. "Looks like somebody's slayin the trees in Bee Tree Hollow. I had an awful time gettin up here to you."

"Yes, stranger," said Charlie, "we've laid many a tree on the ground since we started this job last November."

"My name is Alex Pratt," said the strange man.

He reached me his big hand. I shook his hand.

"My name is Adger Holmes," I said. "I'm glad to know you."

"I'm Charlie Meadows, Alex Pratt," Charlie said.

"Glad to know you, Charlie Meadows," Alex Pratt said. He shook Charlie's hand.

Alex Pratt stood before us and twisted the long ends of his black mustache with his gnarled fire-shovel hands. The veins stood out on the backs of his hands the color of dead winter ragweed stems. Alex's steady hawk-gray eyes beamed like sunlight into my eyes. I stood before the shanty door with my double-bitted ax in my hands and a cross-cut timber-saw across my shoulder. I had a pint of coal-oil in my hip pocket.

"That aint somethin to drink you've got there in your pocket, Adger Holmes?" he ast me.

"Nope, it's not," I said. "It's coal-oil we use to cut the resin off'n the cross-cut saw when we saw the white-pine logs. It's either we use coal-oil or meat-rinds to grease the saw and meat-rinds are too greasy to carry."

"Never heard of that before," Alex Pratt laughed and slapped the tops of his boots with his big hands. He bent over and laughed and laughed. The big muscles worked in his neck when he laughed.

"You aint cut much timber, have you?" Charlie ast Alex.

"Nope, I aint," Alex said. "I never was much good with an ax. When I use a double-bitted ax, I allus stick it too fur in the tree. When I start to pull it out, I break my ax handle. I can sink the ax to the eye every time I strike. That's why I've come to your shanty this evenin. I heard you fellars were the best axmen in Elliot County. I've got a job fer you when you finish."

"When this job is over I'm goin to leave this shanty-life," Charlie said. "I'm goin back home on Sand Suck Creek to my wife. I am goin home to farm. I aint wantin another job."

"What will you be doin, Adger Holmes?" Alex turned to me and ast.

"I'll be out'n a job in three days," I said. "I'll be on the road lookin fer somethin to do. What is the nature of the work you want done, Alex?"

"I've got seven acres of new ground to clear fer ter-backer," he said. "There's a lot of work to be done on this new ground. It is kivered with tall saplins. The tops of these saplins are held together with wild grapevines. It's awfully hard clearin. I want to put a good man on this job."

"Do you pay by the day'r by the acre?" I ast.

"Ten dollars an acre."

"That's good money," I said.

"Yes, the regular price fer clearin land in Elliot County is six dollar an acre and you keep yourself. I'll give you ten dollars an acre and your keeps."

"It must be hard clearin."

"It is," he said.

"I'll take the job," I said. "We'll finish this timber-cuttin job in the next three days. You can be expectin me."

"I live the last house up Whipple Tree Hollow," he said.

"Whipple Tree Hollow." It flashed through my mind what Pa told me before he died. That was when I had a home with Pa. That was before I started roamin over the country huntin a home, a lackey boy here and a lackey boy there. That was before I'd had a hundred different jobs in a hundred different places and I found them all about the same.

"Your mother," Pa told me before he died, "is buried in Whipple Tree Hollow. She died when your only brother was born. He died with her and they are buried together under the sugar maple at the west end of a field that is north of the house. I left six sugar maples on this hill when I cleared it fer a crop. Your mother worked in this new ground with me. Each spring I tapped the maples and got sugar water. We made maple syrup and maple sugar. I'd love to take you back there, Adger, and show you so you'll know where your Ma and brother are buried. I set a bunch of blade-grass at the head of her grave. I guess it's dead now—has been whopped out by the briars and sprouts —but the large field rock that I put at her head and the small one I put at her feet ought to be there if the land aint been plowed again."

II

Alex Pratt lumbered off'n the steep bluff below our shanty. He held to the sprouts as he went down to keep

from fallin. He dug his boot-heels into the new-ground
dirt so his feet wouldn't slide from beneath him. I was
silent. I couldn't say anything. Just the faint recollections
I had of Ma and Pa and Whipple Tree Hollow come back
to me.

"Why are you so silent, Adger?" Charlie ast. "Are you
mournin because this timber-cuttin job is over and you'll
haf to hunt you a new home?"

"It's not that," I said.

I cut wood fer the shanty fireplace and carried two
buckets of water from the spring at the roots of the big
beech tree atter I broke the ice. While I got in the wood
and water, Charlie baked our cornpone, fried our taters,
bacon and eggs. We et our suppers and sat before the fire
and smoked our pipes.

As I smoked my pipe, I could see Ma. I could barely
remember her. I tried to go back and remember all my
mind would let me. I could see the slat bonnet over her
crow-black hair. I could see the bonnet strings tied in a
bow under her chin. I could see the white dress with the
black dots that she wore. I could remember followin her
and holdin to her dress tail when she walked up the
furrowed new-ground hill with Pa to hoe terbacker.
I could see her sun-tanned face and her blue eyes—and the
way she laughed, I couldn't forget.

As I looked into the blazin shanty log fire, my memory
was clouded; yet, I could see distantly the six sugar maples
on the hill. I followed Ma and Pa to them the spring before
Ma died. I remember they gathered maple 'sugar-water'
from these trees. I gathered little rocks from the new
ground and piled them under the sugar maple while Pa cut
his and Ma's initials and a heart around them. I could barely
remember the log shack at the foot of the hill. I remember
goin in at the front door and runnin across the puncheon
floor to the back door.

I couldn't forget the day when Ma was silent and the neighbor women dressed her in a new dress and put her in a box the neighbor men made at the barn. I remember I wanted to see my mother and baby brother but one of the women took me out under a plum tree and give me a 'purty.' It was a ripe red plum. I played with the plum and laughed when she talked to me. And that afternoon they carried the box up on the hill. That was the last I remember of Ma.

"I can't stay in Whipple Tree Hollow any longer," Pa said. "I'm goin back to Big Sandy to my people." We left the green terbacker growin on the hill. Pa bundled all the clothes we had. I rode down Whipple Tree Hollow in front of him on the mule's back and led our cow with a long rope. We went to Big Sandy and lived with Grandpa and Grandma until they died and Pa died. They died just a year apart and I was fourteen then. I went out to find a place to work fer my clothes and keeps. My home has been where my hat is.

III

I made one-hundred and seven dollar out'n my timber-cuttin job. It was a lot of money to have when I said good-by to Charlie Meadows and went to live with Alex Pratt and clear the seven acres of new ground. I found Alex's place just like so many other places where I had lived. I slept on a shuck-bed upstairs and I had grub to eat that would stick to the ribs. I had to have grub that stuck to the ribs when I used my ax.

I started clearin new ground February 14th. Snow was fallin in a steady white downpour among the tall leafless saplins. It was tough clearin. But I had my good ax. It was my friend. I loved the weight of it. I loved the feel of it. It slayed the saplins fer me. I used a grubbin hoe fer the briar clusters and a mattock to dig the wild grapevine stools

out by the roots. When Sundays come, I tramped over
Whipple Tree Hollow tryin to find the six sugar maples
on the hill. I couldn't find them. It had been thirty years
since we'd left Whipple Tree Hollow. Land can change
in that time. New crops of trees can grow and the old
fields grow up in brush, briars and trees. I looked fer some
sort of a sign to show that we had once lived on Whipple
Tree Creek but I couldn't find it.

It was the middle of March and I was clearin high upon
the hill. I found a big sugar maple. I looked at its bark. It
had been tapped long ago.

"This surely can't be the hill," I thought, "that Pa and
Ma had in terbacker. This can't be the hill where Ma is
buried. This can't be one of the six sugar maples where
Ma and Pa gathered maple 'sugar-water' to make maple
syrup and maple sugar."

I was cuttin a cluster of green briars beneath this sugar
maple tree when I found a little pile of rocks under leaf-
rot loam. I remembered pilin the rocks beneath this tree
when I toddled atter Pa and Ma when they went to gather
the 'sugar-water.' I examined the bark carefully and found
the initials "M. H." and "E. H." These initials were fer
Willie and Elizabeth Holmes. They were Pa's and Ma's
initials. They were inside a heart that Pa had cut on the
tree. I remember the day he cut them with a white bone-
handled barlow knife. I had found the hill where my
mother and my baby brother were sleepin.

I didn't go out among the saplins and hunt Ma's grave.
I just waited until I cleared the saplins. I would find it then.
One day atter I finished work, I walked down to the foot
of the hill. I found the plum-tree stump where the neighbor woman give me the 'purty' plum so I wouldn't cry
fer Ma atter they put her in the box. The plum tree was
dead. Only its stump remained. I looked fer the place
where the house ust to be. I tramped among sawbriars

and sprouts. I kicked up dead-leaf loam with the toe of my brogan-shoe. I found the foundation rocks.

Somethin come back to me. I was a little boy again. I was goin in at the shack door. I could see my tall mother in a white dress with black dots in it. She wore a slat bonnet on her head. Her bonnet strings were tied in a bow knot under her chin. Her face was sun-tanned. I listened to her laugh. I sat in a deep study until the March wind chilled my blood.

"This is not a house," I thought. "This is a place where a house ust to be. It is a house in the wind now. It has wind doors, wind walls and a sawbriar floor. This is a place of desolation. I am the only one who remembers now. I can remember there was once love here, there was laughter here—there was happiness. Now it is a house in the wind. It is a place of desolation. Dreams, love and laughter are kivered with sprouts, briars and last year's leaves."

Atter I finished each day of work, I walked down off'n the hill and sat on a corner rock of this old log shack. I felt it was my home. It was a house in the wind but the only dreams I had of my mother were here. Her dreams, her laughter, and the color of her clothes were here. I pretended this was my home.

IV

"I've been seein you sittin over there every day on a rock," said Alex. "You remind me of a settin hen on eggs. You aint tryin to hatch a rock, air you, Adger?" Alex slapped his boots with his big hands and laughed.

"That aint funny, Alex," I said. "That spot of ground is dear to me."

"Why?" Alex ast. His face changed when he spoke.

I didn't answer. It was a long story to tell and I didn't tell him. He thought I was actin lonely-like. He ast me if my bed wasn't good and if my keeps were all right. I told him my bed was better than most beds I'd slept on and my keeps were good.

I was clearin around the hill slope toward the west. I cut saplins from around four more sugar maples. The bark on these maples was scarred with auger holes. I had only one more maple to find. I just about had my clearin done.

I can't tell you how I felt when I cleared the saplins from around the sixth sugar maple on the hill. It was a big twisted sugar-maple with rough gnarled roots that hooved above the leaf-rot loam. Under the shadow of its long limbs, I found a bunch of blade-grass. Beside the blade-grass, I found a big rough headstone. Below it, I found the footstone partly kivered with leaves and dead briars. "It's Ma's grave," I wept.

It was the memories that come back to me. The place was smooth as a floor. It didn't look like a shovel had ever lifted this dirt and the tall fine body that gave life to me was hidden here with her laughter and her dreams. I didn't cut saplins that atternoon. I fixed Ma's grave. I shaped a mound over her and fixed her headstone and the footstone back just as Pa had placed them. I loosened the dirt around the bunch of blade-grass. When I went home to supper, I didn't tell Alex Pratt about Ma's grave.

v

By April 1st. I had the saplins, brush and briars cut and piled in brush-heaps. I left the six sugar maples on the hill. I had done all Alex ast me to do except he said fer me not to leave a tree. It would shade his terbacker. I was ready to leave Whipple Tree Hollow. I was ready to find a new home.

"I'm done, Alex," I said.

"You've not finished," Alex said. "You were to cut every tree. You've left six big sugar maples on the hill to shade my terbacker. You'll haf to cut them trees first."

"You'll haf to cut 'em," I said. "I aint cuttin 'em."

"You won't get your money until you do. It was in the contract that you were to cut every tree on that hill and pile 'em in brush heaps."

"I aint cuttin the sugar maples."

"Why aint you?"

"Memories," I answered. "Somebody had tapped 'em in time. They have made maple syrup from them. They have made maple sugar. There are two persons' initials cut there with a heart around 'em."

"Don't be batty, Adger," he said.

"I aint batty," I answered. "I found a grave under one too. I fixed the field stones back at the head and foot like they ust to be. I just don't aim to cut them trees if you never pay me. I believe ghosts will come back and hant anybody that cuts 'em."

"I don't aim to pay you until you cut the maple trees. It is accordin to our contract. I am an honest man, Adger Holmes. I've never beatin a man out'n a penny in my life. It would hurt me to owe a man and not pay him."

"You won't pay me," I said, "because I don't aim to stick my ax in the sugar maples. They are people to me. They are my friends."

"You air batty, Adger. You've been cuttin sugar maples fer Cy Thombs. You've cut thousands of sugar maples and now you won't cut six. I aint heerd you talk about ghosts comin back and hantin you over the maples you have cut."

"I won't cut 'em," I said. "You can keep my seventy dollars. I can live. I've got a little money. I'll be on my way. I'm goin West. I hear it's a great country fer a man."

VI

I carried my turkey of clothes tied to my ax handle across my shoulder. I went to Dry Fork. I bought me a john-boat. It was April and the weather was good. I went down Dry Fork to Little Sandy River. I went down Little Sandy River to the Ohio—down the Ohio to the Mississippi —down the Mississippi to the Missouri River. I went up this river until I was tired of rowin a boat. I sold my boat and I started workin from farm to farm across Missouri. I was in Nebraska, Kansas, Oklahoma fer six years. I got homesick fer Kentucky's mountains. I started back to Elliot County the way I'd come. I started back in a john-boat. I was all summer gettin back.

The leaves were fallin when I got back to Elliot County. I was glad to see Kentucky again. I was walkin down Sand Suck Creek on my way to Whipple Tree Hollow. I met Charlie Meadows.

"Glad to see you, Adger."

"Mighty glad to see you, Charlie."

"Guess you've heard about Alex Pratt, aint you?" he ast me.

"I aint heerd about 'im. I've been in the West fer the past six years. I aint heerd nothin from the old county."

"He sent his boy Oscar over here lookin fer you. Oscar said his Pap was in bed—said he was a pile of skin and bones. He said it was all over the debt he owes you. He's about to worry hisself to death."

"I'll get over on Whipple Tree Hollow to see Alex," I said.

I left Charlie Meadows and hurried down the mountain path with my turkey over my shoulder. I hurried around the mountain slopes and across the hollows. I wanted to get there before sundown.

VII

"Howdy, Adger," Alex said soon as I walked into his room. He reached me his long bony hand from under the quilt.

"What are you doin in bed, Alex?" I ast. "You was a well man and strong when I left here."

"Where have you been, Adger?" Alex ast.

"In the West."

"We've looked everywhere fer you," he said. "I'm about gone. If you hadn't come back, I'd a-died."

"What have I got to do with your dyin?" I ast.

"I'm an honest man," he said. "When I owe a man, I haf to pay him. Somethin has hurt me deep inside the past six years. When I got up in the mornin before I got bed-fast, I'd look over yander on the hill. I'd see the six sugar maples and I'd remember you. I'd remember that I owed you seventy dollars. You know I was a powerful man when you worked fer me. I weighed two hundred and forty pounds and I wasn't fat. I've lost twenty pounds a year. I don't weight but one hundred and twenty pounds now. Soon as I pay you the seventy dollars plus six per cent interest fer every year I've owed you, I'll get all right."

Alex's jaw-bones looked like they'd cut through the skin any minute. His glassy eyes were sunk in his head. His mustache was white and thin and stuck out like a two-year-old's horns. His fence-post arms were thin as ax handles.

"Here's your money, Adger, with six per cent interest fer six years," he said. Alex pulled a sock from under his pillow. "I've kept it fer you. I've never put a plow in that land. I was afeard to. I thought you had a reason fer not cuttin the sugar maples when I saw the scars and initials on the trees. That grave skeered me too. I remembered what you said about the hants."

"I need the money," I said. "Thank you fer it."

"You've saved my life by comin home," he said.

"Home," I said. "This is my home. I wanted to return to these sugar maples on the hill. I've thought about them while I was in the West. I'm glad you've never cut them."

THIS IS THE PLACE

UNCLE MEL'S BREATH IS A LITTLE SHORTER than it used to be. He is puffing, puffing like wind rattling the dead leaves on the January white-oaks. He moves along the path, pulling his gigantic frame, his muscular two hundred pounds of muscled clay—his bald head with its fringe of graying hair—glistening in the sunlight—his arms at the old magnificent swing—like the pendulum of a clock, that old faded blue shirt, his faded blue overalls that always look clean on Uncle Mel, with one suspender over his shoulder —the other swinging loose—his giant hands flexibly attached to his huge hairy arms—lumbering along over the narrow path—squeezing between the trees with his broad shoulders, under a Kentucky sun, under the Kentucky skies—and on the hills that gave him birth, clay for his gigantic frame— and food to nourish his strong body and give him his great strength to throw the green crossties on the wagon and lift one end of the small saw-logs.

Uncle Mel walks down the hill—down the path past the strawberry patch. He takes the lead—his eyes, black as midnight, gleam brightly in the sun. They flash at the trees that Uncle Mel has seen so often—the tough-butted white oak trees on the steep banks below the strawberry patch— the land too rough and too steep for Uncle Mel to clean of brush, briars and sprouts for strawberry land. "Well, if I could recall the years," says Uncle Mel, "recall the years and had a new pair of legs. I'm like the apple on the tree. I'm getting ripe. There's a few soft specks in me. When the apple gets ripe it's likely to fall." Uncle Mel walks on out the path—out past the old logs left at the edge of the strawberry patch to burn on April nights and May nights and fill the heavens with smoke to ward off the frost that kills the strawberries. Ah yes—you are not fooling Uncle Mel. He always has strawberries. Uncle Mel knows how to handle the frost that kills the young berry in the blossom. In front of us is the little knoll with the grove of tough-butted white oak trees—with thousands of sagging branches that sway with the wind-seeded Johnson-grass where men would love to roll and drink a keg of cool beer.

"This is the place," says Uncle Mel, "right here. You see this is a real place for all of us to be buried. Here is a good place for us to be reunited in the end—reunited for the long sleep." Uncle Mel stands beneath a branch-entangled white oak tree—the sun is high now. Uncle Mel is looking at the sun. "You see the sun comes over from the east. It goes down quietly in the west. It does not leave a path. It goes the path of wind and sky. That is the way we are in the end. The sprouts will grow on our farms. We'll go over as the sun—come to a quiet setting on this little knoll. There'll not be any path in the end. The sprouts will come up here—they will cover this hill unless countless generations of our kin are born in this hollow and live here—that these hills are to breed Sheltons and Powderjays forever and take back their dust in the end."

We are the blood of hill people. We have always been hill people—back, back, back, back, for so many, many, many long years that the hills have become a part of us, in our brain and the dirt of the hills is the clay of us—the mood of the wind in the pinetops and the sawbriars are the mood of us—the freedom of the woods, the wind and the skies—quietly, quietly, quietly, with little change. We have come the paths of the rocks, the eternal rocks, and

the clouds that float above our land—and the trees that
grow upon it. We have come a long path down—long,
long, long. The hills have claimed our dust—Cold Harbor
has claimed it, Virginia has claimed it, Gettysburg has
claimed it, Big Sandy has claimed plenty of it—enough for
a fertile acre—Antietam has claimed it and the hills of West
Virginia and North Carolina—France has claimed it, and
Flanders and Bull Run. There has not been a lot that we
have owned to hold our dust—we are lone sleepers under
the skies that float above the backbones of hills—under the
skies that float across America—Kentucky holds our dust,
bushels of it—her trees have grown from the strength of it
and her wild flowers have blossomed from it.

"Yes," says Uncle Mel, "we could all get along here
very well I think. Your Pa being a Republican—that will
be all right then. We can sleep under the same cover."
And then I could say to Uncle Mel: "It will be the first
time the Sheltons and the Powderjays ever agreed on
politics. It will be when we are all sleeping together in this
silent city that we have planned—where we perhaps will
not have the croaking frog to tell us spring is here and the
crow building in the pines. Lord—Lord—Lord—I have
heard Republican and Democrat—until I am sick of it all—
down from 1854 the taut lines have been drawn—it will
soon be the hundredth year if the two parties last that
long. What does it matter? It should not matter in a graveyard—it should not matter when we are dust—when we
have at last come under one cover on a land that is our own
at last."

"I used to have a funny notion about where I would
take my rest," says Uncle Mel. "I never said anything
about it. I used to think I'd like to dig my bed down in
the ridge of rock that is the line between your Pa's place
and mine—where that pizen vine is and them initials cut
all over the rock at that little sand gap—then I thought the

sides of that rock would crumble off and I'd be in there and they'd crumble right down to me—expose me. Then I thought that rock would be too hard to sleep on. I've thought a lot about my bed here lately and I believe this is the right place for all of us."

"The Powderjays are about all gone, Uncle Mel," I say, "they sleep other places and under different skies—they sleep on the river from whence they came—the Big Sandy. You know why we got to this country—why we came to the hollow years ago—and we have lived here ever since in this small world. There are not many of us to come to this knoll—my brothers ought to be here. Don't you think we should bring their dust back from the low-hills on the other side to this west side? Grandpa don't own that land any longer over there—it is in the hands of strangers now —only a few rusted wires keep the cattle off the ground where they sleep."

"Just them two boys dead—let me see—isn't that right? Not one of my eight dead, not Jan's seven, nor Jake's nine —and let me see—one of Mammie's fifteen died when she was a little thing—buried on Trip Creek—all ought to be brought back—all of them ought to be brought into one family instead of sleeping on so many hills that other men own—not that it matters—for the dust of them will sprout wild flowers and trees and corn, my son. But that dust will rise you know and we need to be on the same hill where it will be a family reunion in the flesh—we can be together and then we will be able to tell who is right in this world and who is wrong. We can have a lot to talk about then— a lot my son, a lot."

Uncle Mel stands under the white oak tree. He looks up through the tangled branches moving in the wind—his bald head gleams—shines where the sun plays through the openings between the branches and leaves bright criss-crosses of sunlight on his head. Uncle Mel moves his hands when he talks—a giant man standing in the rays of the setting sun, Uncle Mel speaks: "Never was in the whole Shelton race of people where a man killed a man. We have had fights but we have never killed a man. See the prints of boot-heels on my temples! That's where they stomped me when I was a boy—old Jim Fonson's boy—stomped me —got me down. Thought they had me killed. I got up and I followed them. They went on laughing. The other fellow who helped do it was Ron Green. Two of them on me. Busted a bottle over my head and left me. I was drunk. They were not near as drunk as I was. I never forget it. They've stayed out of my way all of these years. That happened when we were boys. I could break either one of them in two. We have killed in wars—but never a fight— man to man. Pap got knocked out once for an hour or two. Went in a coal bank to get a man. It was dark in there and Pap walking in against the dark—the man could see Pap for he was against the light. So, he took Pap in the head with the coal pick. Got the scars on his head yet. He never went in any more coal banks to get a man."

Uncle Mel stands and he looks over the fields. The wind blows with a scent of sweet smells from the cane heading in the sun and the tasseling corn. It is good wind to breathe. Uncle Mel breathes it and he talks: "No my son—the Sheltons have loved books. They have been book people my son. W'y my Grandpa, old Percy Shelton, used to have a big room of books—big stacks of them and he read and preached all the time. Before he died when he was past four-score year and five he walked five miles and preached four hours. The old men said it was the best sermon he ever preached. He was a dead man the next day. When a man started anything in his church—he went back and got him. He had order and he preached. He was a officer in the Union Army, my son—and his son, your Grandpa, turned against his own father for the South. And when he cast his

first vote my son—Grandpa was there with a withe—and he
made Pap haul his coat—Pap hauled his coat and he said:
'You can lick me Pap but I'll vote the way I see fit.' And he
saw fit, my son, to vote the Democrat ticket—the only way
to vote my son. It stands for the poor people—it is the right
ticket my son. That is why I say your Pa is wrong. You
can't tell him that for the Powderjays took after the old man
Powderjay who fit in the Union Army. That ruint the
whole family on down even among you boys—my own
sister's boys.

"I can see the silent city here—the grass among the ridges
—the old rose bushes that will grow here among the lichen
stones. That will be forever—oh so many, many years—that
will be so many years that there is no need for any one to
count—the oaks will have grown taller and their branches
spread more as to keep out the sun and the myrtle will
blossom with tiny blue blossoms—it will climb over the
mounds and around the roots of the trees—the lichen stones
where the Powderjays and the Sheltons will have at last
come to dust—all joined under the same cover—the Kentucky earth—sleeping, sleeping, sleeping—where there is no
noise save the tinkling of the sheepbells on the hills, the
love calls of the whippoorwills, the katydids—and the wind
blowing through the seeded grasses. The Blue and the Gray
will have at last come together—quietly in the dust side by
side—and who will remember then among the generations
unborn where the Democrats among us sleep and where the
Republicans sleep? And who will remember then about the
dreams of two families—about the great strong man Uncle
Mel—his strength of muscle and his clearness of mind—his
old fields where he had in corn where timber grows tomorrow? Sawbriars trail over the thin banks of sterile earth—
ah, then, who will remember the millions of dreams of those
who sleep in the silent city and whose blood goes on and
on—blood that is American—cradled in the laps of Amer-

ican hills, under American rocks and American skies. And
shall they who pass by laugh and say: 'There's the dust of
yesterday—old dust sleeping with cornfield stones to take
their names and numbers—old, old, old—ancient dust—dust
of America—sleeping—wonder if they await a day when
they'll pop from their graves like young rabbits from a
nest!' "

If Uncle Mel could just hear them and answer he would
say: "You damned right we'll come popping out 'n here.
The whole dad-durn push of us. That's why I walked out
on that summer day—or was it spring—what does it matter
now—that's why I told that college boy of my sister's that
day that we ought to all be buried together—that boy got
a lot of sour pudding stuck in his head at college. Got to
doubting until I got hold of him and showed him some
light. I says to him: 'W'y look at the butterfly in spring
how it wakes up in heaven. Comes from the tomb—the stout
cocoon. Look at the flowers how they bloom in spring and
the great magnificent earth—how it has its seasons and how
it works right on the dot. Bound to have order back of
that.' So I took my watch and I says: 'Son look at this
watch. You see it don't you. See how it runs and keeps
time to the second. If there wasn't somebody back of that
watch in Switzerland—a God of that watch—its Creator—
how in the hell could it keep time, son? Now how can the
time of this world click like it does—got to have a Creator
son—got to have a Master.' And you can laugh all you want
to laugh but when that old trumpet blows you'll never see
such strings of Sheltons and Powderjays coming from
under the cover—all right here together under these trees
where it will be cool and the blossoms of the myrtle will be
sweet to smell. I hope resurrection will be in June. That's
the month I've always loved.

"And to think, here on this hill—this little hill where life
goes on quietly and undisturbed save by the wind, the

sheepbells, the whippoorwills and the katydids—I shall sleep beside of my brothers, my sisters, my mother and father and all my uncles on Mom's side of the house—the big Shelton uncles and all their children. It will cover the knoll already—the generations already living if they were all dead —and there are the generations unborn to be brought here in the hollow to this silent city—where there is not a silent city nor has there ever been as far as we know and can trace—it might have been in the dim years past—but we do not know—we do not find their shin bones working out of the earth nor their elbows—it is a land that gives birth to men who live and die here and are hauled away to some other place to sleep where there is more noise.

"It does not matter so much about dust," says Uncle Mel, holding to the twig of a white oak. "Our dust sleeps during a winter waiting for the trumpet just like this oak tree will sleep during this winter when the sleet covers its bark. We'll sleep just like one night. Then we'll all wake up and be our natural selves again— Now our dust doesn't matter. I never could see why people cried and went on so over a man when he died. Let him lose a leg in the lumber woods and have that leg buried they never thought about crying. Just went on and buried that leg and forgot about it. One of his arms the same way—both arms and both legs. You'd never hear a lot of crying and going on. But let the man die—the whole of him—and then you'd hear them crying and going on. What I never could understand why we grieve over the whole and never say 'scat' about one of the parts. It never matters about our dust so we all get close and can be together and give the old timers a surprise when we all get out 'n the bed."

"And what do we do while we are waiting—while our dust is sleeping the long night," I say to Uncle Mel, "in the narrow confines of our small world—in the village of this silent city of Powderjays and Sheltons with our in-laws plus that have come to sleep beside their wives." "My son," says Uncle Mel, "we shall go on living in the same way we lived here—only we'll be light as the wind. We shall be as we have been—have the same color of hair, shapes of noses, the same voice—we shall run with our old company—I expect to have my farm here and do the things as I have always done. How can that which is the real Mel Shelton die? It can't die. You can't take a hammer and beat it to death even if you beat my head off. The real Mel Shelton will be here. You can't kill it. It was not born to die—only the husk that encloses it was born to die. We are going to bring all these husks right here and crib them."

"Then I shall have the dust of my brothers brought here," I says to Uncle Mel, "though I hate to disturb them after they have slept these years on the low hill beyond the hollow. And I shall have their dust planted on the hill that will enclose our dead—the hill that overlooks the cane patches and the corn fields—beneath our skies at home—among my blood kin—not among the strangers on another hill—away from the rest of us." And then I think: "Wonder if we shall know when spring comes, Uncle Mel? Wonder if we can tell if it going to rain by our rheumatics bothering us a little and our hair standing on its end? Ah—wonder, wonder—and if we can feel the roots of the white oaks as they expand by the new rich dust we give them—that strength that belonged to the big Sheltons and the tall Powderjays—that which was American dust—gathered from the thin earth of Kentucky clay banks beneath her wind and her suns—blest by Kentucky's fruitful crop years and her lean years—Democrat dust and Republican dust—Methodist dust and Baptist dust—ah, the long years, the lean years—all in a night of peaceful sleep—maybe, we shall welcome after a hundred years of living and loving life and the earth—the wind, the sun, the moon and the trees on the Kentucky hills—and Uncle Mel says we shall not die. Uncle

Mel will not die. He is a Shelton and the Sheltons often have their way—wonder, ah wonder if even about Death and the silent city where no man speaks—but where we sleep—sleep, night and the winds of destiny that speak not to us but pass over us and mourn through the warm nights of spring when the whippoorwills call—ah too, of another generation—speak of love, of life and of living. But we speak not at all—the ghosts of us light as the wind and the wind with the identity of us stamped invisible—laugh to the wind and walk through the corn fields at night when a pretty moon is in the April sky—we laugh and speak to each other on the same old mountain paths. We cannot die. You cannot take a club and kill us. You might beat off our husk but the real of us is here—it will not die—not even when the smell of summer—the ripened corn and the heading cane with its white-dotted stems—all of the smell shall pass over it—the luscious sweet tang of scented wind from the growing summer and the creepy night of sheepbells tingling on the hills will mingle with the ooze of night wind in the green weeds and the foxglove on the bluffs—ah not when the winds of autumn sigh for those gone and forgotten—sigh for us with the mixture of wind in the dead grass and the hanging leaves—we who have been dead so long and sleeping on the hill, cold, cold, cold—sleeping on the hill, where the snake creeps by and the lizard crawls on the tough-butted white oaks and the old blue demijohns that hold the clusters of odorless sweet williams and percoon blossoms shriveled to tiny wisps—and the wild Indian turnip's white blossoms—ah, the lizard crawls and the lizard never speaks. We never know of expanded roots and whispering trees and grass and roses—and the roots of myrtle never whisper to us or hold a fragrant bunch of myrtle blossoms to our noses—we who have loved life, fought, kissed, played, worked, loved and hated—we who have been a stream of life—a constant flowing river toward the

sunset—we who have tramped the hills and had no home
and died and were buried among the ribs and thighs of hills
—and now we have a home—a bed for a long rest in the end
while hither thither on the roads of destiny—blown by the
strange winds of time."

"We must go my son," says Uncle Mel, "the sun is going
down in the west. It will be time for me to get home and
do up the feeding. Got four hogs to feed and a couple of
cows to milk." And we start toward the house—down the
hill among the black oak stumps—the graveyard of a gigantic forest, long dead and forgotten. Peach trees with well
pruned tops and healthy coats of bark, row crookedly the
rugged hill to the west. "My trees—see them—I believe in
fine orchards and clean corn fields." And then Uncle Mel's
garden with the rows of palings and the jars that hang on
the palings—the goose-neck hoes that lean against the palings—"My garden is clean. I keep it clean. I work it clean
as I read a book clean—one that I love—I read my Bible
clean."

Ah, I could tell Uncle Mel what I once heard a preacher
say: "Ah that old man—that old bald headed Shelton—he's
an infidel. Fixes the Bible to suit himself. Twists it around
him with a lot of crazy beliefs. He's standing in the way
of many with his set idears on the Bible. He says we are
wrong. He never comes to church. I have seen him out
sauntering through the woods at night—ah, strange man
that he is."

"And son," says Uncle Mel, "remember this my son.
Live, live your life till you will not fear whatever that is to
come. Live so that you can look any man in the face. Be
as solid as a hill. Pay your debts when you can—if you can't
tell your creditor you cannot. And remember my son, there
is not a substitute for sweat. There is not a substitute for
honesty—live, live and tend the earth and know the spring,
the summer, fall-time and the winter. Know the seasons and

when to plant as your people before you. Live by the square. Die by the square. Remember my son, shrouds are pocketless."

Ten thousand stars are in the sky—a blue sky above the clouds of fluttering leaves that whisper to themselves and to each other—and beneath the clouds of leaves there is darkness. "Do you need a lantern," says Uncle Mel, "going up the holler? We stayed over there too long. Here I am after dark doing my work up." "I can make it all right, Uncle," I says. "Eyes of the owl—can see at night—could feel my way up that hollow." And I know Uncle Mel I think as I stumble up the hollow. "Late doing up his work. W'y he takes spells and reads a book clean before he cleans the corn. He keeps the weeds out 'n the book instead of the corn. Haven't I seen his corn get mighty weedy—then out of a clear sky he would come and work from daylight till dark—work until it was clean as a hound dog's tooth—ah, that is Uncle Mel."

"Shrouds are pocketless," keeps drumming in my head—over and over again as the leaves whisper to each other and to the wind, "Shrouds are pocketless." And the wind moans through the leaves above my head—wind that is blowing across Kentucky and sweeping on to some destiny—or not to a destiny at all—winds of the broad America—that strike her rugged, hiss and moan with the jagged hills piercing the side of the wind—ah, the great expanse of America under the cold blue American heavens illuminated with millions of stars that shine upon an earth that is both cruel and kind —an earth that is American—an earth that is mine and that has given me the flesh I have on my bones—an earth, the rugged, jutted, cruel earth, kind earth, that will give me a knoll to sleep in—a silent city that will hold the dust of my kin under the same cover—in the same great bed—under the roots of the white oak trees—ah, an earth that is mine forever where the winds will sweep over me and utter

strange sounds that I shall not hear while I'm asleep beside
of Mom and Pa and Uncle Mel and all of my kin that walks
the hills today and generations of kin unborn—ah, that we
are American—forever, American. And Uncle Mel would
say: "W'y sure we'll pop out 'n the graves Americans and
Democrats and Republicans—Baptists and Methodists."

The boys carry Uncle Mel off the hill—Lon and Will,
shoulder him and carry him to the foot of the hill and to
the house. "I tried to keep him from going to the field this
morning," says Aunt Vie, "but you know how your Uncle
Mel is. He just tore up the place and said the crabgrass was
taking the corn. He was out at daylight this morning with
his hoe. He's been staying in and taking care of the garden
and doing the work around the house. But he had to get
out—so I saw them carrying him off the hill this morning
at ten. It scared the life out 'n me. He's been such a strong
man——"

The Sheltons have been a strong race of people. But the
strong have to die same as the rest of the weak—all have
to bow to the inevitable—strong as Uncle Mel must bow.
"Yes," says Lon, "I was working right behind him. He had
the lead row of corn when he fell. He fell hard as a tree.
I heard him lumber on the ground. I turned and I saw him.
I hollered to Will—and he come and got an arm under
each leg and I got him by each arm. I tell you Pap is heavy.
He was a load from that hilltop. We had a time walking
down hill with him—down the path to the house. He has
never spoken since—fell at work this morning at ten. You
can go in and see him—he's in there on the cot."

"What did the Doctor say?" I says, the tears streaming
from my eyes—and I thought: "The mountains of fine men
must slumber to some destiny—ah whither wind that moans
above the seeded grass—ah whither is your destiny? Where
is the home of man—the long, long home and the journey
thereto?" "The Doctor says," says Lon, "for us to call

Den, Mack, Jake and the girls. He says it is a stroke. And he won't say much more."

I do not want to see him now—my Uncle lying there on the couch in quiet sleep—he who was a mountain of a man when we walked to the top of the hill and surveyed the bed —he who wished for a new set of legs and many more lives to live on earth—how could I stand to see those hands— those giant hands that felt the ax, the maul, the cross-cut saw, the plow handles and the wedge and hoe—how could I stand to see them silent—those great hands where streams of blood once rushed in channels—hands that cleared the fields and built the houses and farmed the land, dug the coal from the groins of the hills—those powerful shoulders still now and the eyes that scanned the strawberry fields with- ered and dull in their sockets—great dynamic wells of energy that ceased to flow—his words—his millions of words that shaped his dreams—ah, I couldn't stand to see him now —his silent lips and quiet hands. "These hills will call for him," I thought, "or they'll rebuild his kind. His fields will want him back—his mules and his hounds. The birds he fed will miss him at the wellgum and the quails that come down off the hill and ate with his chickens. His trees will miss him —his peach orchard to the west of the house and the apple orchard will miss him—and his bees— And we shall think of him tomorrow and our kin might remember him awhile until they pass quietly too—and generations unborn will probably hear of Uncle Mel. Whither, ah whither the winds of destiny? And where is the home of man—that long, long home—that faraway somewhere and the long journey thereto?"

That stream of life has journeyed long under the spa- cious skies of America—over the mountains and among them. It has flowed—a river through the beauty of the green slopes of spring—the lilting beauty of the poplar leaves and the poplar and beech—it was a surging stream of spring, of

clean blue mountain water—and the summer where it
flowed, through growing fields of grain and the ripened
fields of golden wheat—over the hills and through the vales
of smelly flowers—it has come a long way to its home—
that great river of life—and it flowed through autumn—the
winds of autumn mixed with the sweetened odors of dying
leaves and shriveling petals—under the naked trees and over
the rifts—multi-colored carpets—whither, ah whither strong
river to your destiny? To what dark winter is a portion of
the waters left? And the great swirl of water keeps moving
—ah, even through the night the great stream of life keeps
moving on through a channel strong to bear the surge of
wild waters, strong surging waters against the wind, time
and tomorrow.

Yes, the green leaves will come in the spring and the
grass spring anew. Life will come back to these hills in
spring. Winter is for the long sleep and the dream and
forgetting the season past. Life will come back to the
flowers of spring and they will bloom anew in a spring
paradise. Life cannot die. You cannot take a stick and beat
it to death. The butterfly will awake from the cocoon—and
find himself in a heaven of green clouds—in a flowery paradise—to loiter in the wind and find the smelly flowers. "Ah
whither, oh whither, oh man, and to what destiny? Is it the
roots of the tree, the blades of grass, the leaves of the
grapevine? Is it cold, cold, cold lying on the hill forever
beneath the cold millions of stars that are forever American
—sleeping, sleeping, sleeping, oh man where the winds of
destiny moan over the seeded grass and whisper words you
cannot hear nor understand—something about the corn and
the sweat of man and maybe the substitute for sweat, the
substitute for the clay that made him—ah, man is strange
and into what river and to what destiny? To what great
sea of destiny does the river of man flow? You can't kill
me. I won't die. You could take a club and beat me to

death. You could beat off my husk and bury it under the white oaks—yet the real part of me would still be here. It will not die."

Ah spring and hence the many, many years—long, long, long years of bright blue lilting winds of April stirring the early tender thin-green on the trees and the bright polli-nated wind of summer and fluxions of yellow sunlight on the blackberry briars—ah spring and hence the many, many years—the long, long, years—the dead specks of autumn leaves blown on the strange silver winds of time—neither here, nor there, nor anywhere—autumn sawbriars whose leaves turn multi-colored in the sun and the naked stems of the briars that cut and scar across the ancient mounds— the carpet of dead leaves there above the myrtle and among the lichened stones—ah, whither that fertile husk—that off-bearing of the great river—ah whither to what destiny? And why does the green sprig of acacia speak to the wind, and what does it speak—about the breaking of the cocoon? Or that of man?—whispers to the wind strange words while the winds sweep over to their destiny without mutter-ing the strange syllables, the sounds of words.

Whispers the sassafras sprout maybe, or the lizard on the old blue demijohn: "The Sheltons and the Powderjays sleep here. Under the seeded grass, the lichen stones—the myrtle vines they rest. All come home at last—no more for them the distant hills, the Big Sandy, Gettysburg, Cold Harbor, Flanders, Virginia, France. They have come to sleep under the tough-butted white oak roots in the hollow where once there was no graveyard at all. They made the graveyard here—planned it. Took the dust from this hollow—used it for a space of time. Then, like good neighbors they brought what they had borrowed back and gave it to the neighbor they borrowed it from—Sheltons and the Powderjays and their in-laws and next of kin—all sleeping here—tall Powder-jays and mountain-of-men Sheltons. See the pieces of broken dishes and the bottles on their graves—the cornfield stones, and the white stones that give their names and numbers here——"

The seeded grass waves in the wind. The oak leaves flutter dryly in the summer heat—maybe it is in June. The oak leaves whisper, see—say so many foolish things. But that will not matter in years hence—if you could only see us Powderjays and Sheltons breaking from our silent city —here on this hill where it is a good place to drink a keg o' beer—here on this seeded grass beneath these white oak trees— Ah, Uncle Mel—big as he ever was right back—still a Democrat and Pa still a Republican and Ma and Grandpa Shelton and the balance of the Sheltons—and the thin tall Powderjays coming to life again after their brains have grown brittle and their blood ceased to flow through old veins—back again and rested and ready for another life—a longer life—for anything beneath a hundred years is not time enough for a Powderjay—to live, and love, and fight, and curse—and clear the land and build the houses and the bridges—the railroads and turnpikes and fight the nation's battles—under the skies that are American.

If you could see all of us Republicans, Democrats, Methodists, Forty-Gallo Baptists, Hard-shelled Baptists, Free-willed Baptists, Primitive Baptists, Regular Baptists, United Baptists, Missionary Baptists, Union Baptists, Independent Baptists—all of us out 'n the graves a shaking hands and asking the other how he is after the long night o' sleep and how much land he expects to tend this year— How he likes this part o' life called sleep and how glad he is that he's born into this world—so full o' surprises, and life and death —how great it all is—and how much fun it will be to live it all over again—to fight, to love, to live and die—and pay debts and make debts and buy land—the freedom of the earth, and wind and skies—all under the skies American— the expanse of eternal skies upon the earth—all, all, all, flesh and blood and sleep and graves and all, American.

LOVE

Yesterday when the bright sun blazed down on the wilted corn my father and I walked around the edge of the new ground to plan a fence. The cows kept coming through the chestnut oaks on the cliff and running over the young corn. They bit off the tips of the corn and trampled down the stubble.

My father walked in the cornbalk. Bob, our Collie, walked in front of my father. We heard a ground squirrel whistle down over the bluff among the dead treetops at the clearing's edge. "Whoop, take him Bob," said my father. He lifted up a young stalk of corn, with wilted dried roots, where the ground squirrel had dug it up for the sweet grain of corn left on its tender roots. This has been a dry spring and the corn has kept well in the earth where the grain has sprouted. The ground squirrels love this corn. They dig up rows of it and eat the sweet grains. The young corn stalks are killed and we have to replant the corn.

I can see my father kept sicking Bob after the ground squirrel. He jumped over the corn rows. He started to run toward the ground squirrel. I, too, started running toward the clearing's edge where Bob was jumping and barking. The dust flew in tiny swirls behind our feet. There was a cloud of dust behind us.

"It's a big bull blacksnake," said my father. "Kill him Bob! Kill him Bob!"

Bob was jumping and snapping at the snake so as to make

it strike and throw itself off guard. Bob has killed twenty-
eight copperheads this spring. He knows how to kill a
snake. He doesn't rush to do it. He takes his time and does
the job well.

"Let's don't kill the snake," I said. "A blacksnake is a
harmless snake. It kills poison snakes. It kills the copperhead. It catches more mice from the fields than a cat."

I could see the snake didn't want to fight the dog. The
snake wanted to get away. Bob wouldn't let it. I wondered why it was crawling toward a heap of black loamy
earth at the bench of the hill. I wondered why it had come
from the chestnut oak sprouts and the matted greenbriars
on the cliff. I looked as the snake lifted its pretty head in
response to one of Bob's jumps. "It's not a bull blacksnake,"
I said. "It's a she-snake. Look at the white on her throat."

"A snake is an enemy to me," my father snapped. "I
hate a snake. Kill it Bob. Go on in there and get that snake
and quit playing with it!"

Bob obeyed my father. I hated to see him take this snake
by the throat. She was so beautifully poised in the sunlight. Bob grabbed the white patch on her throat. He
cracked her long body like an ox whip in the wind. He
cracked it against the wind only. The blood spurted from
her fine-curved throat. Something hit against my legs like
pellets. Bob threw the snake down. I looked to see what
had struck my legs. It was snake eggs. Bob had slung them
from her body. She was going to the sand heap to lay her
eggs, where the sun is the setting-hen that warms them and
hatches them.

Bob grabbed her body there on the earth where the red
blood was running down on the gray-piled loam. Her
body was still writhing in pain. She acted like a green-
weed held over a new-ground fire. Bob slung her viciously
many times. He cracked her limp body against the wind.
She was now limber as a shoestring in the wind. Bob threw

her riddled body back on the sand. She quivered like a leaf in a lazy wind, then her riddled body lay perfectly still. The blood colored the loamy earth around the snake.

"Look at the eggs, won't you?" said my father. We counted thirty-seven eggs. I picked an egg up and held it in my hand. Only a minute ago there was life in it. It was an immature seed. It would not hatch. Mother sun could not incubate it on the warm earth. The egg I held in my hand was almost the size of a quail's egg. The shell on it was thin and tough and the egg appeared under the surface to be a watery egg.

"Well, Bob, I guess you see now why this snake couldn't fight," I said. "It is life. Weaker devour the stronger even among human beings. Dog kills snake. Snake kills birds. Birds kill the butterflies. Man conquers all. Man, too, kills for sport."

Bob was panting. He walked ahead of us back to the house. His tongue was out of his mouth. He was tired. He was hot under his shaggy coat of hair. His tongue nearly touched the dry dirt and white flecks of foam dripped from it. We walked toward the house. Neither my father nor I spoke. I still thought about the dead snake. The sun was going down over the chestnut ridge. A lark was singing. It was late for a lark to sing. The red evening clouds floated above the pine trees on our pasture hill. My father stood beside the path. His black hair was moved by the wind. His face was red in the blue wind of day. His eyes looked toward the sinking sun.

"And my father hates a snake," I thought.

I thought about the agony women know of giving birth. I thought about how they will fight to save their children. Then, I thought of the snake. I thought it was silly for me to think such thoughts.

This morning my father and I got up with the chickens. He says one has to get up with the chickens to do a day's

work. We got the posthole digger, ax, spud, measuring pole
and the mattock. We started for the clearing's edge. Bob
didn't go along.

The dew was on the corn. My father walked behind with
the posthole digger across his shoulder. I walked in front.
The wind was blowing. It was a good morning wind to
breathe and a wind that makes one feel like he can get
under the edge of a hill and heave the whole hill upside
down.

I walked out the corn row where we had come yesterday afternoon. I looked in front of me. I saw something.
I saw it moved. It was moving like a huge black rope winds
around a windlass. "Steady," I says to my father. "Here is
the bull blacksnake." He took one step up beside me and
stood. His eyes grew wide apart.

"What do you know about this," he said.

"You have seen the bull blacksnake now," I said. "Take
a good look at him! He is lying beside his dead mate. He
has come to her. He, perhaps, was on her trail yesterday."

The male snake had trailed her to her doom. He had
come in the night, under the roof of stars, as the moon
shed rays of light on the quivering clouds of green. He had
found his lover dead. He was coiled beside her, and she
was dead.

The bull blacksnake lifted his head and followed us as
we walked around the dead snake. He would have fought
us to his death. He would have fought Bob to his death.
"Take a stick," said my father, "and throw him over the
hill so Bob won't find him. Did you ever see anything to
beat that? I've heard they'd do that. But this is my first
time to see it." I took a stick and threw him over the bank
into the dewy sprouts on the cliff.

UNCLE JOHN, THE BAPTIST

"JASON, I WANT YOU to get the mules harnessed this mornin," says Uncle John. "See that the check lines are polished and there is a bright red tassel on Jack's bridle and one on Bess's bridle. See that the harness is clean and shiny, that the express wagon is clean. Put a doodle of hay in the express bed for the youngins to sit on—"

"All right Pa," says Jason, "I'll see that it is done." Jason picks up his cap and walks toward the barn.

"Mollie," says Uncle John, "fetch a song book here. I want to sing and get worked into the spirit."

"All right John," says Aunt Mollie. Aunt Mollie is a big woman. She is not very tall. She can stand under Uncle John's outspread arm with plenty of room to spare between her head and Uncle John's arm. She is heavy and broad. She is not tall and bean-pole skinny like Uncle John.

Aunt Mollie brings the song book to Uncle John. He sits reared back in a hickory-backed, split-bottomed chair. "Read the lines of the 'sparrow song' for me Mollie," Uncle John says. "I will sing them. I want to get revived in the spirit before we start. I want this to be the greatest association we've ever had."

"All right, John," says Aunt Mollie.

She gets the songbook from the dresser drawer. She walks like a turtle—slowly she walks—brushing back with her fat chubby hand her graying, loose-flung hair. Aunt Mollie walks back from the dresser and sits down beside of

Uncle John. She turns the well-worn pages of the hymn
book in the sparrow song. Aunt Mollie reads,
Why should I feel discouraged, Why should the
   shadows come,
Why should my heart be lonely, And long for Heaven
   and home—
Uncle John looks toward the stained newspapered roof
ceiling, pats his big feet on the rough plank floor, claps
his big fire-shovel hands and sings these words. "Glory!"
he says when he finishes singing them. "Glory to God,
Mollie! Read me some more."
   When Jesus is my portion? My constant Friend is He;
His eye is on the sparrow, And I know He watches me.
"Glory, glory," says Uncle John. He looks to the ceiling,
pats his big brogan shoes on the floor and claps his hands
and sings the words Aunt Mollie reads.
   "The sweetest words ever writ," says Uncle John. " 'His
eye is on the spar, And I know He watches me.' Read me
more of the Word, Mollie."
Aunt Mollie reads,
   I sing because I'm happy, (I'm happy), I sing because
I'm free, (I'm free), For His eye is on the sparrow, And
I know He watches me. Amen.
   "Amen," says Uncle John, then he begins to sing, clap
his big hairy hands and pats his big brogan shoes on the
hard plank floor. His eyes look up at the ceiling and his
lips spread apart, show Uncle John's new set of teeth that
are white as a young hound-dog's teeth.
   "I've got the mules ready, Pop," says Jason. "I didn't put
any feed in the express though."
   "Amen," says Uncle John. "Glory to God, Jason. My
mules won't haf to have feed. There'll be Baptist corn for
my mules and Baptist grub for my family all along the
way to Mountain Chapel. Glory to God!"
   "John," says Aunt Mollie, "we can't take all the children

with us. The express wagon won't hold them. What are we goin to do?"

"Goin to do?" repeats Uncle John. "We're goin to take half of 'em this year to the Association and take the other half next year. Let Erf, Rodney, Lizzie, Arabella, Porter, Manley, Felix and Shan go. Jason, Mel, Young Johnnie, Dixie, Pert, Violet and Lucretia can stay this year and we'll take them next year."

"I ain't going, Uncle John," I says, "I don't want to go."

"Young man," says Uncle John, "you are goin. You are a young man out in sin. When Aunt Mandie Chapman heard that Baptist sermon on the radio and shouted all over the house and out in the yard until her ticker nearly stopped —didn't I hear you laugh about it atter we carried her in the house and put her to bed? You are goin with us. I aim for you to see somethin that will rile your spirit. Shan you've been born, bred and fed a Methodist on your Pap's side of the house. That's what's the matter with you!"

"Don't pay any attention to Pop," Jason whispers to me. "I believe Pop's goin chicken-brained on the Free Willers. He fights all the rest of the Baptists. Says the Free Willers are the only people on earth that's right with the Lord. I tell him there'll be a lot of people in Hell then. He gets mad at me. Just sits and sings all the time. He tries to pull all of us into the church. He just wants to get up to the Association to show his new teeth."

Uncle John takes Aunt Mollie by the arm. They walk out to the express wagon—big short Aunt Mollie and tall beanpole Uncle John. "Six feet and seven inches tall," says Uncle John. "Every inch a Free Willer and every inch the Lord's."

Uncle John helps Aunt Mollie into the express wagon. Aunt Mollie plumps down on the express wagon seat. The wagon springs gave down six inches more. "Two hundred and sixty-five pounds of Baptist," says Uncle John. Uncle

John climbs up and sits down by Aunt Mollie. "Load in the straw youngins," he says. We climb in the express-bed —Erf, Rodney, Lizzie, Arabella, Porter, Manley, Felix and I. "All loaded?" asks Uncle John.

"Yep," says Erf.

Uncle John lets down the brake, shakes the polished check lines. "Git up," he says. Uncle John looks back at his other seven children. "Don't worry children," he says, "the rest of you can go next year. Be good children and keep the work done up until we get back."

We get seated comfortably in straw as the express wagon rolls down the hill. Over the roots of the giant oak trees, over the two curved paths cut by the bright steel jolt wagon tires and the narrow express wagon tires. The mules step briskly in the bright air of the August mornin over the dusty Ohio lane.

The express wagon rolls down the highway. Uncle John holds the lines in his hand.

"It's great to be a saved man," says Uncle John, "and to be the right kind of Baptist. The Devil is standin at the top of the ground waitin for the wrong kind of Baptist—that kind that tries to pick our churches to pieces."

Uncle John slaps Jack and Bess with the black-polished leather check lines. The steel tires on the wheels grit on the sun-blistered asphalt. Uncle John sits up straight on the front seat with the brake in one hand, the glossy-black check line in the other. Uncle John, the tall beanpole man is so tall that he looks like a man standin up in the express wagon, drivin the mules.

"Children," says Uncle John, "we'll soon be in the old country and the mules will find soft dirt roads to set their hoofs down on."

We go down the main highway, speedin along, our express wagon loaded—people passin in fast automobiles and stickin their heads out from the car windows to look at us.

"Let the heathens rubber," says Uncle John. "If they once get the old time Free-Willer Baptist salvation, they'll know what happiness is. They'll stop their rubberin at everybody that passes."

We come to Dartmouth, Ohio—automobiles, street lights, streets thronged with people. The mules jump stiff-legged, rear against the breast yoke but Uncle John holds them with one hand and the brakes with the other. We sit in the express and watch the people watchin us. We go up Main street. People honk their cars to get past us but Uncle John holds our side of the street and we keep movin toward the east end of town.

"Thank God," says Uncle John, "we'll soon be to the ferryboat. When we cross the river we'll be in Kentucky, the home of real Baptists. I'm gettin happy now. I can feel the spirit movin me."

Uncle John's face changes as we roll down the river bank and onto the ferryboat. "See them hills over yander, children?" says Uncle John. "Ain't good to grow corn but there's more among them than corn. You children will soon know what I'm talkin about."

The mules prance, rear up on their hind feet and slobber at the mouths. The red tassels wave in the Ohio river breeze as the ferryboat chug-chugs its way across the silver ribbon of water.

"Sixty cents," says the ferryboat collector. "Twenty cents for team, wagon and two passengers—five cents apiece for the youngins. Ain't none hidin in the straw there?"

"Nope," says Uncle John. "Brother, I don't do business like that. I left the other half at home." The little short man with the thick dirty hands and the striped hawk-billed cap laughs like Uncle John is tellin him a joke. He takes the dollar bill and hands Uncle John forty cents in change.

The mules are glad to get off the ferryboat and start

up the river grade with us. They strain on the steep grade with us—cars behind us hootin their horns for us to move faster. As we top the bank, the cars whip past us—drivers crane their necks from the cars and look mean at us.

"In God's country now," says Uncle John. "It's a poor country but it's God's country. . . . Every blessed rock, tree and shovelful of dirt was blessed by the Lord."

Uncle John's new teeth clatter in his mouth when he talks. They are white and glistenin behind Uncle John's thin brown lips. His lean jaws move like the sides of a bee-smoker puffin in and out.

"John," Aunt Mollie asks, "how far do we aim to get today?"

"Halfway mark," says Uncle John. "We'll get to Gadsen today and camp in the grove. We may get a little futter."

"Where are we goin to eat dinner and feed the mules, Pop?" Erf asks.

"Don't worry about that son," says Uncle John. "We have stations along the way. Our first stop will be Station A. It will be at Argill. We'll stop at Brother Laff Mitchell's."

We roll along over the Kentucky road under a blisterin sun. We cross the Sandy River, drive through Goodletsville, turn to our right toward Argill. "When we get to Argill," says Uncle John, "we'll be on the horse-and-buggy road all the rest of the way, thank God."

"I'm hot as a roasted tater back here," says Erf. Erf wipes the sweat from his forehead with his index finger and slings it on the dry straw. We laugh and talk to each other and listen to Uncle John holler "Bless the Lord," every time he speaks to Aunt Mollie or the mules. The sun is gettin high in the sky. It is noon and we'll soon be to Argill.

"Well children," says Uncle John, "here is Argill. And over there is Brother Laff Mitchell's. We'll soon be eatin good Baptist grub with our feet stuck under a Baptist table."

"I can really put the grub away," says Manley.

"I could eat sassafras leaves," says Porter, "let alone chicken and dumplins."

"Welcome, welcome, Brother Fonson," says Brother Laff. "Have been expectin you all mornin. Knowed you had to come a fur piece from Ohio. Get out all of you— we'll take care of your mules. Come get your feet under the table."

"Praise the Lord, Brother Laff," says Uncle John gettin out of the express and helpin Aunt Mollie out. We jump down from the straw like chickens turned loose from a coop.

"Just like Heaven will be, Brother Laff," says Uncle John. "We will drink water from the rock and feast on milk and honey." Aunt Mollie, Uncle John and Brother Laff walk down among the tables and we follow them. We find seats and start eatin. "Brother John," says Brother Laff, "the grub has done been blessed."

"Praise the Lord," says Uncle John.

We finish our dinners and light our pipes and cigars. There are clouds of tobacco smoke, hand shakin and shouts of "Praise the Lord" among the people. Then we start hitchin our mules back into the jolt wagons and the express wagons. We load in and the long train of teams start movin out the lane back to the main road.

"It's great to be among your own people," says Uncle John. "I'm a happy man to be among my own kind."

We ride along the snake-curved road beside of Sandy River. There are clouds of dust that swirl from our train of wagons as we move toward Gadsen. The sun beams down on us, hot enough to set fire to the express-bed of straw.

"God's country," says Uncle John, "Praise the Lord. Look at these hills! Here is the home of our Free Willers. Heaven will be like this—plenty to eat, wagons loaded with happy hand-shakin people, all goin some place."

"Sun down," says Erf, "I can say 'Praise the Lord' for that. I've melted down ten pounds this afternoon."

"Gadsen," says Aunt Mollie. "We're gettin near our old stompin grounds when we get to Gadsen."

"Yes," says Uncle John. "I can see the grove. See the people there. It looks like Heaven more and more."

I can see mules, horses, jolt wagons, buggies, express wagons and surreys and people just throng the grove. Our long train starts moving into the grove across the dusty lane. Men show us where to leave our wagons.

"Pull your mules' harness off and leave it by the wagon," says a beardy man with big thick hands. "Turn your mules in that forty-acre cornfield with a crick o' fresh watter runnin' acrost it. A good place for them to eat and sleep."

"Praise the Lord, Brother Thirkettle," says Uncle John. "Forty acres of Free Willer Baptist corn fer a good span of Baptist mules."

"You see Brother Fonson," says Brother Thirkettle, to Uncle John, "we Free Willers have good hearts in us. Brother Willie Higgins just turned his forty acres of corn over to the Baptist mules and horses. It's all the corn he's got too."

"Station 'B'," says Uncle John. "And the people keep comin'. Plenty of corn for our teams and good grub for our people. Watch the busy women workin to feed us! Now Brother Thirkettle, where will we sleep and how will we sleep?"

"Each flock in its own pasture," says Brother Thirkettle to Uncle John. "We'll pass quilts and pillows around to you in a few minutes. You and Sister Mollie can sleep in your express wagon and let your youngins sleep on the ground. People won't get in the wrong pastures here. If they do, they won't be welcome in any pastures in Heaven."

"Glory," says Uncle John. "You are right, Brother!"

We go to the table and eat again. We help ourselves to

the good grub. "I'm gettin too full," says Erf, "and I ain't stirrin around enough. I feel stuffed like a frog. Too much grub and too much ridin."

Uncle John and Aunt Mollie eat their suppers. Uncle John gets their quilts. He spreads one on the straw and keeps one to spread over them. We get our quilts. We put one on the ground and keep one to go over us. Porter, Manley and I sleep together; Rodney, Felix and Erf sleep together and Arabella and Lizzie sleep together. The ground is covered with quilt pallets. Lightnin bugs flit above us. The horses whinny in the forty-acre cornpatch and the mules bray. There is talkin to each other from one pallet across to another. There is talk about corn, mules, children, crops and the Free Willer Baptist Association.

The dawn breaks. Uncle John gets up like he does at home. "Go to the cornpatch and get our mules, Erf," he says. "We must get on our way while the dew has laid the dust. Had a good night's sleep. Praise the Lord."

Everybody starts waking up when Uncle John gets up and starts talkin. Women start makin hot coffee. People start washin their faces in a little stream of water and in washin tubs and dryin on hand towels fastened to the trees. They start gettin ready for breakfast and for the journey to Mountain Chapel.

Erf brings the mules to the wagon, harnesses them. We sit down to the table for bacon, boiled eggs, fried chicken and coffee. We eat breakfast, load in the wagon and start for Mountain Chapel. Wagons follow us and many remain in the grove, the drivers and their loads of people still asleep under the quilts.

"The next stop will be our last," says Uncle John. "When the sun is high, we'll be rollin into Mountain Chapel." Uncle John sniffs the early mornin wind as we move toward Mountain Chapel.

We move over the dirt road, around the curves, under

the green tunnels of leaves where the treetops overlap over
our heads. We dash across creeks and go up hollows. Little
clouds of dust rise behind us as our big mules pull our express wagon along.

"We'll soon be there," says Uncle John. "My heart is
in my mouth. I feel the spirit movin me. I can feel it in my
bones. Praise the Lord!"

We drive up a long hollow to a grove of beech trees.
We find mules and horses tied to the trees, wagons here
and there.

"We're at Mountain Chapel now," says Aunt Mollie.
"I used to come to Baptist Associations here when I was
a little girl. I met John here—drinkin, cavortin and cussin,
and he had an old gun on 'im."

"Yes," says Uncle John, "but I've changed since them
days. I've whopped the Devil and the Spirit of the Lord
has moved me to be a happier man."

Uncle John stops the mules. Erf unhitches the mules and
snaps their bridle reins to beech limbs. We walk toward
the sound of a preacher's voice. His husky voice is echoin
against the rock cliffs on the fern-covered bluffs.

"Brother High," says Uncle John. "I know that voice.
Clear as a bell with a true ring like a good foxhound's
bark."

We walk among people tradin horses. "Great horse-
tradin goes on here durin the Association," says Uncle
John. "Just can't trade within two hundred yards of the
preacher."

The men are runnin old bony plug horses and scrubby
long-haired mules up and down the road, spurrin 'em and
usin the rawhides. We see men with foxhounds, possum
hounds, shotguns and pistols tradin under the beech trees.
We see crates of chickens, geese, guineas, turkeys, sows
with pigs, bar hogs, boars, cows, calves, steers and bulls,
ewes, rams—everything that a man trades on in Cantell

County. We walk across the tradin ground to the head of
a little stream. Here the head o' the hollow is shaped like
a horseshoe. People are sittin under the trees on rocks, on
the ground, on half-split logs. Down below them is a big
platform built of logs—built like a house, five logs high
and covered with a puncheon floor. Across this are logs
split in two and held up by huge blocks of round trees.
Men with long beards are settin on these seats sayin "Amen"
to the "word" Brother High is preachin.

"Amen," says Uncle John, walkin up to the platform.
"Praise the Lord."

Uncle John walks up the steps onto the platform. He
greets each brother while Brother High beats his fists together and preaches the "word." Uncle John sits down on
a split log, claps his big hairy hands and pats his brogan
shoes on the puncheon floor and sanctions all Brother High
says. Uncle John looks like he is standin among the elders
on the platform, he is so tall.

Aunt Mollie sits on a rock in the beech tree shade. We
plop down on the ground and wallow like chickens in
the sand. We are tired of ridin on the straw in the blazin
sunlight. Women and men pass baskets of grub around to
us. We help ourselves and listen to Brother High. Brother
High wipes the sweat from his long locks of hair and from
around his high collar.

"I know John is nearly starved," says Aunt Mollie. "John
has to have his grub at twelve o'clock."

"Yes," says Erf, "Pap's gettin holler as a gourd. I can tell.
Look how wild he's lookin out'n his eyes."

"Now Brothers and Sisters," says Brother Drenell, "come
back to services at seven this evenin."

The men hurry off the platform to a big table spread
under the beech trees for the preachers and the Free Willer elders. Uncle John takes big steps down the hollow
with Brother High.

"I don't know how it happened," says Brother High to the Baptist elders, "but Brother John got choked on the first bite—just went to coughin and coughed his teeth out and—"

"Lordy," says Aunt Mollie as we run down the hollow to the elders' table.

When we get to the table, Aunt Mollie is nearly out of breath.

"John," she says.

Brother Edgeworth is rollin Uncle John on the ground and every time he turns him over, he pounds him on the back. It doesn't do any good. Uncle John is on the ground by the long table. A crowd is gatherin around him.

"Take him to Brother Litteral's," says Brother High. "You young bucks get hold of him and get him to a good bed."

Erf, Porter, Manley and I get a leg and an arm apiece and Felix holds his head. We go down the hollow to Brother Litteral's with Uncle John. The bed is too short for him and his feet stick over the end of the bed.

"It ain't in my windpipe," says Uncle John. "It's down in my gullet or I could swallow."

Uncle John can barely talk. The day passes and night comes.

"I hate to miss church," says Uncle John.

We stay with Uncle John. The night passes. He isn't any better. He cannot swallow a bite of food. He cannot drink water. Another day passes and another night.

The big Free Willers Association is over. The elders and preachers have prayed for Uncle John and they meet at Brother Litteral's house to pray for Uncle John before they leave. They pray long prayers for Uncle John; then we see the long caravan of wagons move down the hollow. Erf takes Aunt Mollie home with all the children but Felix.

He stays with me and Uncle John. Aunt Mollie has to get back to Ohio to the other children.

The fourth day Uncle John isn't any better. Doctor Hornbuckle talks about bleedin Uncle John. "No use to bleed him," I says. "He's got somethin in his throat."

The fifth day passes. Uncle John is gettin weaker. The sixth day passes, the seventh, eighth, and ninth. We believe Uncle John is goin to kick the bucket. We think we'll haf to take Uncle John home in a wooden overcoat. He hasn't eaten a bite. He hasn't tasted water. He is a pile of skin and bones.

"Don't worry Shan," Uncle John whispers to me. "I ain't goin to die. I'm prayin not to die. It's the Devil temptin me like he did Job. I'll show you that I'll live."

It was encouragin to hear Uncle John say this. If Uncle John said he wasn't goin to die, then Uncle John wouldn't die. He always did what he said he'd do. The tenth day passes and Uncle John can't eat.

"I believe Pap's a gorner," says Felix.

"No he ain't," I says. "He says he won't die and I say he won't."

The eleventh day comes. Uncle John, a long heap of skin and bones, wallows in the bed. He wheezes louder than a horse. A white ball flies from his throat—it is dry and hard. It is a piece of beef.

"Praise the Lord," says Uncle John. "I've whopped the Devil. Bring the water. Have Brother Litteral to kill me a couple of squirrels and make me a couple of gallons of broth." Uncle John sits up now. He eats chicken broth and drinks milk.

"The twelfth day," says Uncle John. "Boys you must take me home today. Get me a rig. Get two fast horses and a surrey."

"I've got the rig," says Brother Litteral. "I've a travelin span of mares and a rubber-tired surrey. The best rig in

these parts. Take my rig over and I'll send my Tarvin
along to bring it back."

"How much do I owe you, Brother Litteral," Uncle
John asks, "for my keeps and the boys' keeps for these
twelve days and all your trouble?"

"Nothin Brother Fonson," says Brother Litteral, "we'll
square this off with a good handshake and a laugh, yon-
side the Pearly Gates."

"Amen," says Uncle John. "Praise the Lord. The Devil
couldn't bait me with beef."

We get in the surrey. I ride beside of Uncle John and
drive the horses. Felix and Tarvin ride in the back seat.

*"His eye is on the sparrow," Uncle John sings, "And
I know He watches me."*

Library of Congress Cataloging in Publication Data

Stuart, Jesse, 1907-
    Men of the mountains.

    Reprint of the 1st ed. published by Dutton,
New York.
    1. Kentucky—Fiction.   I. Title.
PZ3.S9306Men 1979 [PS3537.T92516]   813'.5'2
ISBN 0-8131-0143-3   79-11419